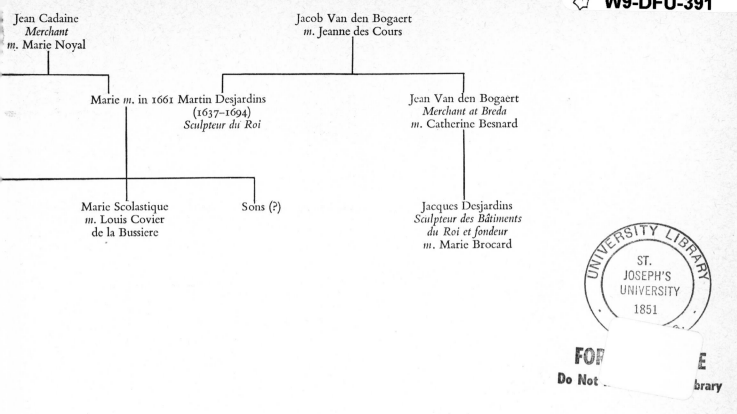

Jean Cadaine
Merchant
m. Marie Noyal

Jacob Van den Bogaert
m. Jeanne des Cours

Marie *m.* in 1661 Martin Desjardins
(1637–1694)
Sculpteur du Roi

Jean Van den Bogaert
Merchant at Breda
m. Catherine Besnard

Marie Scolastique
m. Louis Covier
de la Bussiere

Sons (?)

Jacques Desjardins
Sculpteur des Bâtiments
du Roi et fondeur
m. Marie Brocard

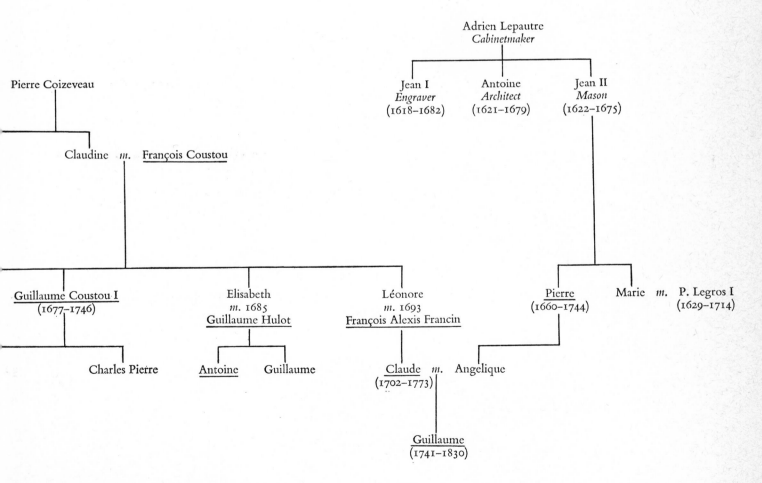

Adrien Lepautre
Cabinetmaker

Pierre Coizeveau

Jean I
Engraver
(1618–1682)

Antoine
Architect
(1621–1679)

Jean II
Mason
(1622–1675)

Claudine   *m.*   François Coustou

Guillaume Coustou I
(1677–1746)

Elisabeth
m. 1685
Guillaume Hulot

Léonore
m. 1693
François Alexis Francin

Pierre
(1660–1744)

Marie   *m.*   P. Legros I
(1629–1714)

Charles Pierre

Antoine   Guillaume

Claude   *m.*   Angelique
(1702–1773)

Guillaume
(1741–1830)

FRENCH SCULPTORS

of the 17th and 18th centuries
The reign of Louis XIV

by

FRANÇOIS SOUCHAL

Vol. 1
A — F

FRANÇOIS SOUCHAL

FRENCH SCULPTORS

of the 17th and 18th centuries

★

The reign of Louis XIV

Illustrated Catalogue

A — F

With the collaboration of
FRANÇOISE DE LA MOUREYRE
HENRIETTE DUMUIS

CASSIRER

Translated from the French by
Elsie and George Hill

©
1977
Wildenstein Foundation

ISBN 0 85181 062 4

Published 1977
Bruno Cassirer Publishers Ltd
31 Portland Road, Oxford
Distributors:
Faber and Faber
3 Queen Square, London WC1
Printers:
Robert MacLehose and Co. Ltd, Glasgow
Blocks:
Gilchrist, London

CONTENTS

FOREWORD

Sculpture is not greatly appreciated in our time. Yet it is one of the great Arts. Socrates, son of a sculptor, even said that it had taught him the basic principles of philosophy.

Sculpture has often been compared with painting. Diderot, always very much to the point, said: "in sculpture there is no in between, either sublime or flat" and his friend and spiritual mentor, the sculptor Falconet, explained that "painting attracts through the variety of colours, attributes, ornaments, backgrounds; sculpture mostly speaks only with one word. And that should be 'sublime' ".

One of the great periods in which sculpture flourished was the 17th century in France. Voltaire was right when he said that "sculpture reached perfection under Louis XIV". That is why, when I conceived the plan of publishing a catalogue of French sculptors (which today does not exist, Lami's work being out of date and un-illustrated) I decided to begin with the 17th century.

Professor François Souchal, the editor, is eminently qualified for this task. He is perhaps the only French art historian with a profound knowledge of and a great love for the sculpture of the 17th and 18th centuries, as he has shown in his beautiful book on the Slodtz and his essays on Girardon. The extensive research work carried out by Professor Souchal and the team working under his direction and the soundness of his knowledge and judgement have my greatest admiration.

DANIEL WILDENSTEIN
Membre de l'Institut de France

INTRODUCTION

This book, the first volume of a series of publications on French sculptors from the Middle Ages to the late 19th century, is published under the auspices, and with the generous help, of the Wildenstein Foundation, which, in accordance with its enlightened policy of supporting the cause of Art and Art History, has taken the greatest interest in this long drawn out enterprise.

May we first of all salute the memory of Georges Wildenstein and recall his great kindness towards the author: he loved French sculpture and had a profound knowledge of it. He handed on to Daniel Wildenstein his deep interest in an art which both considered to have been unjustly neglected by the historians. The idea of this book took shape thanks to Daniel Wildenstein, who entrusted it to the author, while the Wildenstein Foundation took over the entire financial responsibility; without it the realization of the plan would have been impossible. We wish to thank him for his initiative and for his support given in a spirit of helpfulness and understanding.

Here then is the first of three volumes devoted to the reign of Louis XIV, an indication of the wide scope of the undertaking.

Art lovers, scholars as well as enlightened amateurs, have always turned more easily towards painting than to sculpture because of the greater attraction of colour, smaller size and easier mobility. Yet France has been the sculptor's promised land, and at certain periods French sculpture has reached a force of expression and originality that ensure it a leading position in the history of art. Its neglect by modern scholars is unjustified and the author intends through this book to provide the means for an artistic re-appraisal and a far more intensive study.

Stanislas Lami, when he undertook his survey, already had a similar idea, no less comprehensive and no less ambitious. Aware of his mediocre talent as a sculptor, he turned to another project in the services of the art in which he had been trained: a monumental dictionary of sculptors from antiquity to his own time. A somewhat bold undertaking, but suited to his own energetic temperament and the character of the age, which presumed that it could acquire the sum total of all knowledge. From the Middle Ages onwards he confined himself to artists of the 'French School', also a concept characteristic of his period. Even today we are amazed at the extent of the research and documentation displayed in Lami's multi-volume dictionary, which is still highly valuable; indispensable to all those in any way interested in sculpture, it remains the starting-point for all future research in French three-dimensional art. This enormous amount of documentation Lami presented clearly and systematically. In the Foreword to his volume on the sculptors of the time of Louis XIV, he added the following judicious remark: "In order to complete the work which I have undertaken, I am planning to add, as a supplement to each volume, one or two albums with reproductions of extant works of French sculpture by known artists. I shall be glad if in this way I can throw some light on one part, not the least important, of our artistic heritage". Unfortunately, his intention remained unfulfilled and Lami's Dictionary is still without any pictorial evidence.

Since then more than half a century has passed, during which considerable progress has been made in research and discovery; criticism and appraisal have become much more stringent. With all sincere appreciation of our indefatigable predecessor, we cannot overlook his weaknesses and shortcomings, nor the fact that, inevitably, his work has become obsolescent. Furthermore, Art History unillustrated is no longer acceptable. Our first task was therefore to illustrate each work, either by modern photographs if extant, or, where it has disappeared, by drawings, engravings and old photographs, wherever possible. However, simply to add illustrations to Lami's Dictionary would not have been sensible. As he proceeded, the author had to develop his own method. He has thus produced a new work of different character, which he will now try to justify.

The reason for starting the dictionary with the reign of Louis XIV is twofold. First, our collection of documents for this period is much further advanced than for the others; second, we believe that one of the most prodigious periods of Western sculpture was centred round the French court at the time of the Sun-King who attracted and gathered around him a team of renowned artists, often of provincial or even foreign origin. By the vigour of their talent and the high quality of their work, several of these artists held pre-eminent positions; yet it has often been said—unjustly—that, because they adhered to the rules of an academic classicism, their art was lacking in individuality. Many historians have even deemed it superfluous to differentiate clearly between individuals, mentioning only four or five names; often the majority of works has been treated collectively or simply credited to Le Brun as the designer of the various projects.

In fact, however, the art of this period was far from uniform, even though, due to an official policy of 'guidance', certain general trends are discernible. This has led the author to a basic decision, which is not without problems. No sculptor's career coincides exactly with the King's reign. In each case we had to make a choice and always a somewhat arbitrary one. On the whole, we have included those artists, who devoted at least part of their career to works ordered by the Sun-King, and who were actually in the service of the King; yet we have excluded men as important as Michel Anguier, Buyster and Van Opstal; they were commissioned by Louis XIV at the end of their long and fruitful careers, during which, together with Sarrazin, they had become the most celebrated sculptors in Louis XIII's reign. Despite their contributions to the rising glory of the young monarch, they belong to an earlier generation and should logically be listed with François Anguier and Sarrazin, as an artist's career should always be considered in its entirety. Following the same principle, we have included those who worked during the Regency as well as in the last years of Louis XIV. Moulded by the great art of Versailles, their proper place is in this volume. We have also included work done by these artists abroad, as for example by Frémin in Spain and by Legros in Rome. Difficulties of this kind have not been evaded.

Under Louis XIV, sculpture was not confined to work on the royal sites in the capital or its environs. Centres in the provinces remained active for their own local requirements, but clearly the court and the capital attracted the most talented among the artists, even though some of them later returned to their native regions, like Arcis to Toulouse and Dedieu to Provence. We are mainly concerned with those who at any moment of their careers held the title of 'Sculptor to the King'. Regretfully, sculpture in the provinces had to be omitted, owing to the lack of research and documentation in the regional inventories. Important schools existed in Provence, Picardy, Lyon, Nancy, Toulouse and elsewhere. They are well worth studying and a true picture of sculptural art in France requires a supplement, which the author hopes to produce at some future date. This does not modify his conviction that the most significant works, milestones of the evolution, bear the signature of the King's artists. Even Puget, with his highly individual temperament, belongs to this category.

Even the most distinguished of Louis XIV's sculptors practised a great variety of forms and techniques; they accepted humble tasks which might have been left to modest craftsmen considered fit to do ornamental work, but not to carve the figures reserved for the more highly talented. This modesty of even the greatest men explains in part the exceptional quality and unity of their work down to the smallest decorative detail—a perfection rarely attained since. Admittedly our modern conception of the artist as a creative genius and a guardian of the divine flame was not current among the sculptors of the great century.

In evaluating an artist's work, it is essential not to separate the purely ornamental part of his work from his 'great' sculpture. However, we have not included artists such as Dugoulon or Lalande, who practised ornamental work only, or who were essentially marble masons, like Jérôme Derbais, metal-founders like the Kellers, moulders like Langlois, goldsmiths such as Ballin, sculptors in ivory like Guillermin, in wax like Benoit, or the medallists; not out of indifference or disdain, but simply because a limit had to be set to the scope of this survey. Lami's Dictionary is still a valid source of information in these specific fields. Lastly, we have excluded the innumerable unknown chisellers whom Lami mentions by name only, because they appear in some obscure document as 'sculptors', a description which covers a variety of activities. Only those have been included who in our opinion deserve to be called artists and who produced at least one work which has survived.

Our working methods should be sufficiently obvious not to require long explanations.

Listing the artists by name in alphabetical order was the only practicable arrangement. Each catalogue is preceded by a short biography, followed by a bibliography. The main sources of information are given in abridged form for easy reference by the reader. The verification of all sources quoted in earlier works has led to many corrections and clarifications. Entries, presented in chronological order, contain all the details to be expected from a scientific catalogue, the size, material, signature, state of preservation, the date and circumstances in which the work was ordered, its initial price, its subsequent history and lastly its present location. Undated works are relegated to the end. In the case of works which have disappeared reference is made to old reproductions. Last-minute additions and corrections are included in the appendix.

As most entries are accompanied by reproductions, descriptions have been reduced to a minimum, except that, for instance, it was thought desirable to identify the accessories of statues, seeing that sculpture of that period makes such frequent use of allegory.

Detailed discussion about origin, authenticity, attribution and style, especially delicate in the field of sculpture, had to be omitted. Should this book have included copies made at the same time as the original or at a later date, replicas, reductions or moulds? This would have led to dangerous complications. Or should works of doubtful origin have been listed separately? The scope of our work did not allow this. Where several versions exist, only the original has been fully dealt with, the others are mentioned briefly. Even so it was not practicable to give a list of the countless copies and bronze reductions of Louis XIV on horseback or the Marly horses. Some readers may be surprised at the omission of certain well-known works which are exhibited in public collections under a definite label. The answer is that, where the absence of documentary evidence made it impossible to prove our personal opinion, silence seemed preferable.

Since no-one is infallible, such a rule might be unfair, or could well be contradicted by later discoveries; the author also realises that this catalogue is exhaustive in intent only: some private, perhaps even some public collections, may contain works which have slipped through our nets. Such are the hazards of the game and it is our greatest wish that, through new finds and rediscoveries, this tentative inventory may lead to a wider knowledge of both Art and History. Finally, there is no doubt that, in spite of our vigilance, errors, omissions, confusions have found their way into the text. We ask for the reader's indulgence.

For easy reference a number has been allocated to each original work, with subdivisions for different versions and reductions. A detailed index has been added for the convenience of the reader.

We hope we have shown that our work is not just a new edition of Lami's Dictionary, brought up-to-date and illustrated. The author believes that, having carefully weighed up the problems of research and method, (with all due respect to his predecessor) he has produced an entirely new book, the result of many years of intensive work in museums and collections, catalogues and archives. Lengthy sessions at an unexplored source, the Minutier Central des Notaires (the Notary's Record Office), were rewarded by several discoveries and important attributions.

Such a long-drawn-out undertaking could never have been brought to a successful conclusion, had it not been for the work of a dedicated team whose enthusiasm overcame all obstacles and discouragements. The members of this small team worked with a complete unity of purpose and, because of their expert knowledge, proved to be ideal collaborators. No praise is too great for the part played by Mesdames H. Dumuis and F. de la Moureyre, both "Diplômées d'Etudes supérieures d'Histoire de l'art" at the Sorbonne. Mme. Dumuis' task was to investigate the documents, in particular the records of the Notaries, while Mme. de la Moureyre critically evaluated the information obtained, thereby providing the basis for the text. She also undertook the extensive research required to assemble the illustrations. Without their help this book, which is their book, would never have seen the light of day.

The difficulties of publishing are such, that if a work of this kind is not assured of a wide sale it can not be considered a viable proposition. There is no need to enlarge on the importance of English today as an international language. Whatever feelings of regret we may experience for our native language, there is some comfort in the thought that, thanks to the use of English, this important part of our artistic history, of our culture, will become more universally known and appreciated. Has not the English-speaking world always shown the greatest interest and admiration for French sculpture?

It also gives us great satisfaction to see this book in the hands of a most conscientious publisher. The reputation of the Cassirer imprint speaks for itself. This tradition is upheld by the present directors, Mr. George and Mrs. Elsie Hill. Their insistence on an impeccably high standard was for us the best guarantee for the accuracy of the translation and the high quality of the presentation. The book has undoubtedly gained by the friendship which quickly developed as a result of our close personal collaboration.

Help and encouragement have not been lacking on our long journey. It would be impossible to draw up a detailed list. The author expresses his thanks to all those many librarians, museum keepers and curators, historians and record keepers who willingly gave their assistance, with special gratitude to M. Jean Adhémar, Conservateur en chef du Cabinet des Estampes, Bibliothèque Nationale; Madame Bercé, Conservateur des Archives et de la Bibliothèque des Monuments Historiques; M. Raymond Cazelles, Conservateur au Musée Condé, Chantilly; M. Collard, attaché au Minutier Central des Notaires, Archives Nationales; M. Jean-René Gaborit, Conservateur au Département des Sculptures, Musée du Louvre; Mr. Terence Hodgkinson, Director of the Wallace Collection, London; Madame Hoog, Conservateur au Musée National de Versailles; Mademoiselle Jacquiot, Conservateur au Cabinet des Médailles, Bibliothèque Nationale; M. Pierre Lemoine, Conservateur en chef, Musée National de Versailles; Miss Jennifer Montagu of the Warburg Institute, London; Mr. John Physick of the Victoria and Albert Museum, London; M. Racinais, attaché à la Conservation du Palais de Versailles; Miss Olga Raggio, Chairman of the Metropolitan Museum, New York; Mademoiselle Mireille Rambaud, Conservateur Honoraire aux Archives Nationales; Herrn Dr. Theuerkauff, Curator of the Berlin-Dahlem Museum and M. Jaques Thirion, Professor at the Ecole Nationale des Chartes.

FRANÇOIS SOUCHAL

'THE NEW ROME'

Reflections on French Sculpture during the reign of Louis XIV

When trying to evaluate French sculpture during the reign of Louis XIV, one is struck by the predominance of statues ordered to decorate the great parks of the royal residences, especially of Versailles and Marly. During the years between 1660 and 1710 this desire to enliven the gardens with figures, in marble or bronze, led to a constant flow of commissions which allowed an exceptionally large group of artists to flourish—certainly as far as the quality of their work was concerned. Otherwise, although they were fully assured of work, most of these sculptors led a frugal existence and never became wealthy. The great sculptors of Louis XV's reign became very much richer. It is true that Girardon was able to form an important collection of works of art, but this was due to his personal connections and his official position, rather than to his fortune, which was not immense. It is notable that in the later 17th century those who held the title 'Sculptor to the King' worked almost exclusively for Louis XIV and had hardly any time left for other work. The King did not pay his artists well, but he employed them regularly without, however, reserving their services entirely to himself. As a result private clients had either to be satisfied with a small share of the greater sculptors' time, or had to employ minor artists.

It was no secret that Louis XIV's aim was to turn Versailles into a second Rome. We might ask: "Which Rome?" Was it the capital of Antiquity? In view of the King's obsession with a classicist revival which dominated all art at the Court for 20 years, one could well believe it. Or was it the capital of the Popes?—which since the 16th century had become the artistic capital of modern time.

The great plans of the Sun-King remind us of the way in which the triumphant Roman Baroque was established. This was due as much to the effort of replanning which transformed the Eternal City, as to the use of sculpture for its decoration, which led to the gathering around Bernini of large numbers of sculptors of greater or lesser talent, among them Algardi and Duquesnoy, who later became his rivals, if not his antagonists.

The enormous number of statues produced in the studios of Rome in the 17th century, compares with the equally large number done in Paris and Versailles. However, the result is not the same in both countries: on one hand we have an essentially religious sculpture; on the other a profane and mythological art. In both cases, the unceasing activity of a whole generation of sculptors fostered a spirit of competition very favourable to the creation of great sculpture, which thus blossomed both in Rome and at the 17th century French Court.

Of course, a policy of public patronage and an abundance of commissions does not always produce masterpieces: the official art of the Second Empire in France produced mostly mediocre works. The grandiose schemes of the 17th century could only be executed successfully because, by happy coincidence, there appeared at the same moment artists of genius like Bernini in Italy, or a number of richly talented sculptors inspired by a great dream, as in France under the Sun-King.

The religious nature of the Roman High Baroque made it unsuitable as a direct model for French art. This, incidentally, may well have saved French sculpture from servile imitation and, in response to the King's clearly conceived plan, have assured French art of genuine originality. It is true that Bernini, especially at the beginning of his career, devoted himself to worldly and allegorical works which inspired Royal art beyond the frontiers of Italy, but the groups and statues of the Villa Borghese were not really conceived as part of a great monumental programme within a frame of landscape architecture: they were still collectors' pieces. However, this is no longer true of the Neptune in the Villa Montalto and the River Gods of the Piazza Navona. The sculptures which, since before the 16th century, in Florence and elsewhere embellished the great fountains of the public squares and the gardens of the Italian villas are among the greatest inventions of Italy's artistic genius; they opened the way for statuary set firmly in great parks such as the French monarch spread around his enormous palaces like a sumptuous and indispensable frame, inhabited not only by the King and his family, but by a vast entourage in need of wide spaces which were as 'civilised' as the courtiers themselves.

The statues provided individual pleasure to the princely amateurs in the gardens of Italian villas or more widely to the community in public squares where they adorned the fountains,—open-air art, one could call them. In the parks of the French palaces they had an infinitely larger setting.

It all began with the fountain and basin, the water forming a marvellous marriage with marble and bronze. In Versailles, the first great designs, Apollo, Latona, the Parterre d'eau, were all closely linked with the decoration of the basins.

The great blocks of marble with four abduction scenes, envisaged for the Parterre d'eau, were still reminiscent of Roman Baroque and Bernini, but fortunately they were abandoned in favour of much happier solutions, better adapted to the whole framework and closer to the models of antiquity from which the bronze gods of streams and rivers derive their attitudes. Step by step the sculptural decoration was developed not only to suit the basins but also the allees, rond-points, demi-lunes, parterres and bosquets in various forms, from statues larger than life—to keep in scale—to terms and busts on high pedestals. The evocation of antiquity is not more than a pretext. Here is a new art, for which the antique statuary provided only a starting point, a model soon to be surpassed, but to which one had to refer in order to conform with contemporary prejudices. It has hardly ever been pointed out how revolutionary was this use of sculpture in the great parks in the service of a new architectural conception; we have become so used to it that to us it appears entirely natural. The great sculptural programme at Versailles has often been imitated, but it had no precedent except perhaps in Vaux-le-Vicomte, which is known to have served as a kind of testing-ground where the future creators of Versailles, Le Vau, Le Brun, Le Nôtre, Girardon, came together. We do not know with certainty the extent of the programme envisaged for the park at Vaux, because it was still incomplete when work was suddenly stopped in 1661. The first plan for the sculptural decoration of the park at Versailles, in which many members of the Maitrise★ took part, showed much hesitation and uncertainty: in the end it was abandoned. The final scheme developed only gradually, details constantly being perfected or relinquished; large plaster models were used which sometimes remained in position for several months. It was a very elaborate process without pre-conceived ideas, but certainly not without much thought and consultation. It has rightly been said that Louis XIV's genius consisted in his ability to listen to the men he had chosen, usually with good judgement, and to realise when the moment had come to make a decision, based on the best of their opinions. We probably have to consider the King himself as the foremost creator of Versailles and the sculptural decoration of the park.

At that time France was the undisputed leader of European monarchic civilisation in the aesthetic field and its newly created form of sculptural decoration became a model for the rest of Europe. It was a long way from the fountains and bases which enlivened the Italian villas and even from the parterres and terms of Vaux-le-Vicomte to the hierarchy of figures in marble, bronze and gilded lead at Versailles. The splendour of the Palace deserves admiration, although there existed other European palaces of comparable magnitude and richness. But the parterres and bosquets with their statuary were unique—though only for a short time, because, inspired by admiration and fame, imitation very soon followed.

One must remember, that Louis XIV himself considered the parks at Versailles and Marly as his unsurpassable, incomparable work. He was so proud of them that when he wanted to honour distinguished guests, he often acted as cicerone. He cared for them and, throughout his long life, was constantly trying to perfect them, obsessed by the wish—as expressed in his imperious device "Nec pluribus impar"—to leave an imperishable masterpiece behind. His attitude seems almost incoherent. He tried to reconcile at least two basic tenets: on one hand the logical iconographic development of the myth of Apollo in support of a rigorous policy, a manifestation of the excellence of the absolute monarchy; on the other hand the goal of a majestic architectural balance between plants, stone and water, subject to the laws of proportion and perspective as studied and developed by the academies. But these two different aims did not always coincide, especially as among the contemporaries of the Sun-King there were men of very refined taste, perfectly able to distinguish

★ The Maitrise was the old Guild of Artists, against whose tyrannical régime the Academie Royale was founded in 1648.

between works of mediocrity and excellence. In spite of lively competition in so numerous a team of artists, not every member was a master and even masters have moments of weakness. There had to be compromises. Sometimes the programmes so clearly drawn up according to an intellectual scheme, as for instance Le Brun's great plan of 1674, seemed to fall to pieces once everything had been put into place.

The result is an overwhelming impression of harmonious spaciousness, even today when the original vegetation is missing which had been artistically arranged as an ornamental architectural background and support for the sculpture.

A new Rome—yes, if you like, since the creators of Versailles themselves thought so, believing that imperial antiquity had in the same way proudly deployed its figures alongside forums and stadiums, even though the connection may appear to us somewhat remote. The new Rome surpassed the ancient city, surpassed also modern Rome, which, in its own way, intended to resurrect the grandeur of antiquity.

There is no need to repeat here how the king's vast creation fitted into his far-reaching political programme by providing the proud and seductive façade which he needed, and how it even became an instrument of this policy. In the process, French classicism—and this is above all a moral lesson—gained mastery over itself, learning to dominate obscure and evil forces in the search for an equilibrium which did not exclude sensibility. The demonstration is specially dazzling and eloquent at Versailles, where nature offered itself somewhat ungraciously to the great project; in the beginning a despotic domination had to be established which in a way did violence to the existing environment. Standing before the seemingly endless façade which looks out over the park and walking around in the haunting presence of all these marble personages, one can hardly fail to observe, as in the arrogant foreign policy of the Sun-King, some lack of moderation in this gigantic city of marble and bronze, of foliage and living water, composed in the disguise of a myth to the glory of a single human being. And seen in this perspective, Versailles is indeed a masterpiece of the Baroque.

FRANÇOIS SOUCHAL

CATALOGUE

Works no longer extant are shown in italics
Asterisks indicate an illustration

All measurements in centimetres
Height (H) before Length (L)

ABBREVIATIONS

For bibliographical abbreviations see p. 362

acc. to:	according to
acc (on):	on account
accomp:	accompanied
acqu:	acquired
anon:	anonymous
Arch:	Archives
arch:	architect
attrib (to):	attribution, attributed to
Attr:	attributes
av:	average
bât:	bâtiment
bibl:	bibliography, bibliothèque
cat:	catalogue
chât:	château
civ:	civile
comm:	commissioned
compl:	completed
contr:	contract
corresp:	corresponding
dd:	dated
depart:	department
disapp:	disappeared
distr:	distributed, distribution
doc:	document
engr:	engraver, engraving
estim:	estimate, estimated
exec:	executed
exh:	exhibition, exhibited
expo:	exposition
fig:	figure
fr:	français
gall:	gallery

hist:	historique
inscr:	inscribed, inscription
instalm:	instalments
invent. a.d:	inventory after death
l. (livre) s. (sol) d. (denier)	
Mus. des Mon. fr:	Musée des Monuments français
munic:	municipal
not:	notes, noted
not ident.	not identified
or disapp:	or disappeared
opp:	opposite
par:	paroisse, parish
pitt:	pittoresque
pl:	place
pres:	presented
publ:	published
rec:	received
recept. piece:	reception piece for the entry to the Academy
reg. des délib:	registre des déliberations
repl:	replaced
repr:	representing
sc:	sculptor
S. et O:	Seine et Oise, department
s. app:	see appendix
s:	sol
stat:	statue
suppl:	supplied
supp:	supported
symbol:	symbolising
val:	valued, valuation
Vers:	Versailles

ANDRE, Antoine (16?–after 1710)

Sent to Carrara in 1669 by Colbert to select marble for the King, Arch. Nat., O^I 13, fol. 153; O^I 14, fol. 394. Sent again to Carrara in 1688 by Superintendent Seignelay, *Comptes*, III, 91, 355. T-B, I, 1907, p. 444 (Lami). A. was a native of Calais.

1*
Flora Farnese

1676 Statue Marble H:215 Signed: ANTONIVS ANDREAS: CALISSIENSIS SCULPSIT ANNO 1676
Copy of the antique Flora Farnese (Naples, Nat. Mus.). Originally in the parterre of the Orangery in the park at Sceaux, cf. F. de Catheu, 'Le chât. de Sceaux', in *GBA*, 1939^I, p. 299. Trsf. in 1798 to the Tuileries garden; now beside the Bassin Rond. Restored several times since the 18th c., cf. Millin, *Descr. Statues Tuileries*, 1798, p. 72; *Rich. Art. Fr.*, *Mon. civ.*, IV, p. 229; P. Vitry, *Cat. sculpt.*, *jardins du Louvre*, 1931, p. 30.

PARIS. TUILERIES GARDEN

Detail   6

1

2
Two Models of Vases for Versailles

1679–80 Wax
To be cast in bronze. Payment 550 L., *Comptes*, I, 1161, 1289. Not ident. or disapp.

3
Stucco-work for the South Wing, Versailles Palace

1681
Payment 600 L., *Comptes*, II, 10. Destroyed

4
Two Statues for the Façade of the South Wing

1682 Stone H: over 200
Acc. to *Comptes*, II, 137, A. made at least two figures, for which he rec. 600 L. and 310 L., *Comptes*, II, 182. Not identified.

VERSAILLES, PALACE

5
Work on a Cornice, Apartment of the Duc de Vendôme, Versailles Palace

1682
In collab. with Lambert. Payment 200 L., *Comptes*, II, 137. The apartment was on the 2nd floor at the end of the South Wing. Destroyed.

6
Two Double Trophies on the Coping of the South Wing, Versailles Palace

1683 Stone
Payment 1200 L., *Comptes*, II, 310. Engr.* in Blondel, *Arch. Fr.*, IV, liv. 7, pl. 15. Destroyed.

7

7
Two Cockle-shell Basins at the Ile Royale, Versailles Park

1683–4
In collab. with Lambert. Total payment 1038 L., *Comptes*, II, 278, 472. A drawing* in the Cab. Dessins, Louvre no. 34226 shows the former Ile Royale with the basins. Destroyed.

8*
Tiridates, King of Armenia

1684–7   Statue   Marble   H: over 200.
Payment 2500 L., *Comptes*, II, 439, 626, 993, 1172, plus 500 L. "as compensation, in consideration of the fact that he lost an eye through a marble splinter when working on this figure". Copy after an antique (formerly Pal. Farnese, now Nat. Mus., Naples). Also called 'Un Roi Esclave'. The King, arms crossed, wears an elaborate costume with a kind of Phrygian cap. Placed on the surround of the Parterre de Latone on the north side, as a pendant to Lespagnandelle's 'Prisonnier barbare'. *See appendix.*

VERSAILLES, PARK

9
Term

1686
Undertaken for the King in collab. with J. Regnault and J. Moinart, Min. Centr. Arch. Nat., Et. XV, 306, société 27 Aug. 1686. Not ident. or disapp.

10
Marble Basin

1686
In collab. with J. Regnault and J. Moinart for the Colonnade; *ibid.*, and *Comptes*, II, 992, 1182. cf. Cornu no. 17*.

VERSAILLES, PARK

11*
Two Capitals

1688   Marble
Capitals of Ionic corner-pilasters; payment 326 L., *Comptes*, III, 91.

VERSAILLES, GRAND TRIANON

12
Eight Culs-de-Lampe for the Dôme des Invalides

1691–2   Stone
On the bosses in the passages of the chapels in the Dôme des Invalides; in collab. with Carlier (no. 12). Payment 1300 L., *Comptes*, III, 560, 703. Pen drawing* in Bibl. Nat. Est., Hc 14, 2. Destroyed.

13
Work in the Chapel, Versailles

1710   Stone
a. Sculpture on the cornices and flat moulding of the Salon bas, in collab. with numerous sculptors, incl. François (no. 34), Dumont (no. 10) and the younger Tuby, *Comptes*, V, 529.

8

11

b.* Trophy   Bas-relief   Stone   250 × 42
The trophy, on a pier in the chapel, with the figure of
Temperance in a carved cartouche, and appropr.
attribs. Payment 600 L., Mém., Arch. Nat., O^I 1784.

VERSAILLES, PALACE CHAPEL

14
Niobide

On 12 Sept. 1685 A. rec., by order of Louvois, from the
Magasin des Antiques the cast of a statue of one of
Niobe's daughters, to make a copy, Arch. Nat., O^I
1964^3. It is not known what became of this commission.

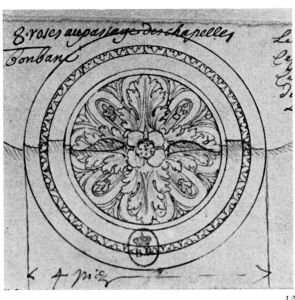

12

13b

85

ARCIS, Marc (1655–1739)

b. 1655 in Cunq, near Mouzens; son of a carpenter, specialist for the sluice-gates of the Languedoc canal. At the age of 10, drawing-lessons with J.-P. Rivalz (1625–1706), then sculpture-lessons with the Augustinian monk, Father Frédeau (1589–1673), and with Gervais Drouet. Work at the Town Hall in Toulouse; in 1678 to Paris as a protégé of Colbert, who found him a place with Girardon. Friendship with the Arles sculptor, Jean Dedieu, Arch. Munic. de Toulouse, DD 296, fol. 541. Became Sculpteur des Bâtiments du Roi. Pres. to the Acad. 6 June, 1682, agréé 29 Aug. 1682, *P-V*, II, 222, 227; made Academician 26 Aug. 1684, *P-V*, II, 276, 281–2. Travelled to Pau in 1688; gave up residence in Paris; settled in Toulouse. After the death of his first wife, Marie Renaud, married Jeanne le Blanc of Toulouse. Established a free school of drawing where the sculptors Lucas, Parant, N. Hardy were trained, as well as two of his sons, one of whom, Jean-Marc Arcis, also made his career at Toulouse. Timid and without ambition as an artist, he died comparatively poor in Toulouse 26 Oct. 1739. cf. Mariette, *ABC*, I, p. 29; Joseph Malliot's Ms., 'Recherche historique sur les monuments de la ville de Toulouse' and his 'Notice biographique sur M. Arcis', written c. 1800, are the principal sources for the *Biogr. Toulousaine ou Dict. hist.*, Toulouse, 1823, ed. La Mothe-Langon, I, p. 19–21 and for A. Fontaine, *Acadέm. d'autrefois*, 1914, p. 230–47; T-B, II, 1908, p. 71 (Lami). Revaluation of A.'s work in R. Mesuret, *Evocation du vieux Toulouse*, 1960.

Two portrait paintings of Arcis, one in Paris, by Bon Boullogne, the other in Toulouse, by his friend Antoine Rivalz, cf. R. Mesuret, 'Antoine Rivalz et les portraits de M. Arcis', in *Rev. des Arts*, 1958, p. 92–4.

1–30
Thirty busts for the Galerie des Illustres

1677–8   Terracotta, painted   H: c. 80
Comm. for the newly-created Gallery in the Capitole (Town Hall), Toulouse. In addition to the bust of Louis XIV, Arcis handed over 30 busts of famous citizens of Toulouse, distinguished in different fields from the beginning of its history. On 2 Dec. 1677, A. rec. 120 L.: i.e. 60 L. for the bust of the King, and 20. L. each for three other busts of famous people in the Great Gallery, finally "200 L. pour diverses journées, paynes et soucis extraordinaires qu'il a employés à la faction et agencement de tous les bustes des hommes illustres", Arch. Municip. de Toulouse, DD 302; Comptes de l'Hôtel de Ville in E. Roschach, *Cat. Mus. de Toulouse*, 1865, p. 323. By the end of 1677 five busts were already in position in oval niches arranged in two rows along the walls of the Gallery (Engr. by Ferat after Dusan, Musée Paul Dupuy*); the Gallery was destroyed in 1892, but the busts were preserved. cf. *Analyse des ouvrages dans l'Hôtel de Ville de Toulouse*, Toulouse, 1770, p. 18–21; A. du Mège, *Descr. du Mus. antique de Toulouse*, 1835; H. Rachou, *Cat. des Coll. au Mus. de Toulouse*, 1912; R. Mesuret, *Evocation du vieux Toulouse*, 1960. Most of the busts have been preserved in the Capitole; some were returned to the restored Gallery. Those exec. in 1677 are:

1   THEODORIC, first King of Toulouse, 419–51.
2   THEODORIC, Count of Toulouse, 425–66.
3*   BERTRAND, Count of Toulouse, 1068–1112.
4   RAYMOND DE SAINT-GILLES, Count of Toulouse, 1088–1105.

1–32

3

12

5   ARNAUD DE FERRIER, Jurist, Ambassador to the Council of Trent, c. 1508–85.

6* CUJAS, Jurist, 1520–90.

7   AUGIER FERRIER, Physician, c. 1513–88.

8   JEAN DE PINS, Bishop of Rieux, Counsellor in the Parliament of Toulouse, d. 1537.

9   ANTOINE TOLOZANY, Superior General of the Canons of St. Augustin, d. 1615.

10 ANTOINE DE PAULO, Grand-master of Malta, c. 1551–1636.

11 GUY DU FAUR DE PIBRAC, Diplomat and Poet, 1529–84.

12* PHILIPPE DE BERTIER, President of Parliament, d. 1618.

13 PIERRE CAZENEUVE, "Editeur du Franc-alleu", 1591–1652.

14 FRANCOIS MAYNARD, Poet, 1582–1646.

15 GUILLAUME MARAN, Lawyer, 1549–1621.

16 GUILLAUME DU CATEL, Historian, 1560–1626.

6

21

22

17 JEAN-ETIENNE DURANTY, President of Parliament of Toulouse, 1534–89.
18 PIERRE DUFFAUR DE SAINT-JORY, President of Parliament of Toulouse, d. 1600.
19 GUILLAUME DE NOGARET, famous judge under Philippe le Bel, c. 1260–1314.
20 BENOIT XII, Pope in Avignon from 1334–42.
21* NICOLAS BACHELIER, Sculptor, 1487–1556.

28

One bust is kept in the Musée des Augustins:

22* ANTONIUS PRIMUS, Senator, Roman General, c. 20–80.

The following have been lost:

23 EMILIUS MAGNUS ARBORIUS, Rhetor, 4th cent. A.D.
24 STATIUS SURCULUS OR URSULUS, c. 60 A.D.
25 VICTORINUS, Rhetor, died c. 425.
26 JEAN NOGARET DE LAVALETTE, Viceroy of Aquitaine in the 16th c.
27 GUILLAUME DE FIEUBET, first President of the Parliament of Toulouse, 1585–1628.
28 PIERRE GOUDELIN, Poet, b. 1580. Engr.* by Baour.
29 EMMANUEL MAGNAN, Mathematician.
30 PIERRE BUNEL, Scholar, 1499–1546.

1–21: TOULOUSE, CAPITOLE
22:   TOULOUSE, MUSEE DES AUGUSTINS
23–30: Not ident. or disapp.

31*
Louis XIV

1677 Bust Terracotta, gilded H: 84
See above, nos. 1–30. Acc. to the biographer Malliot, *op. cit.*, not delivered before 1688. Arch. Munic. Toulouse, DD 204, 63. In a niche at the south end, dominating the gallery. The King wears the cuirass and cloak of the Roman Emperors. Trsf. to the Museum between 1822 and 1835, Cat. 1912, no. 885.

31 TOULOUSE, MUSEE DES AUGUSTINS

34b

32
Eight Coats of Arms of the Capitouls

1677   White Stone
Estim. 31 May 1677, contract 7 June, fee 320 L., Arch. Munic. Toulouse, DD. 302; délib. XXXI, 2 Dec. 1677, fol. 217, DD34, Hôtel de Ville; publ. J. Chalande, 'Hist. Mon. de l'Hôtel de Ville de Toulouse', 2nd part, in *Rev. hist de Toulouse*, 1915–19, p. 209; 1924, p. 192–8. In the Gal. des Illustres opposite the bust of Louis XIV, on either side of the north window. Cartouches with the coats of arms of the Capitouls, hung from parts of arms. Destroyed.

33
Four Vases for the Palace of Versailles

1680   Stone
On the balustrade of the chât., payment 268 L., *Comptes*, I, 1290; replaced by copies. Destroyed.

34
Work on the Petite Ecurie at Versailles

1680
  a. Masks   Stone
  b.★ Children sitting on trophies   Stone
A. rec. 600 L. for the masks, *Comptes*, I, 1290 and, together with Le Conte and L. Magnier, 500 L. for unspecified work at the Petite Ecurie, *Comptes*, I, 1285. Félibien des Avaux, *Versailles* (Table); Piganiol, *Vers.-Marly*, 1764, I, p. 9, attrib. to A. the sculptures on the pediments of the wings of the Petite Ecurie. Very much restored in the 20th c.

VERSAILLES, PETITE ECURIE

35
Work for the King, Unspecified

1680
Payment 1434 L. in 1681, *Comptes*, II, 93.

36
Trophies for the Grande Galerie

1680–1   Bas-reliefs   Bronze, gilded
In collab. with Le Conte, Raon and Coysevox; cf. Coysevox no. 15★. Total payment 3096 L., *Comptes*, I, 1285; II, 93.

VERSAILLES, PALACE

39

41

37
Ornaments in the Salon de la Guerre

1680–82   Stucco
In collab. with Le Conte and Coysevox; cf. Coysevox no. 24*. Total payment 1987 L., *Comptes*, I, 1285; II, 159 & Ms. Malliot, in Fontaine, *op. cit.*

VERSAILLES, PALACE

38
Work on the South Wing, Versailles, *Unspecified*

1681–2
Payment of 1320 L. in several instalm. 1681–2; incl. 500 L., for no. 39, *Comptes*, II, 11, 137, 169.

39*
La Raison d'Etat

1682   Statue   Stone   H: more than 200
One of the 32 statues on the cornice at the attic storey of the South Wing. Payment 500 L., *Comptes*, II, 137. Identified through a drawing in the coll. de Cotte, Bibl. Nat. Est., Fb. 26. Helmeted woman, a sword at her side, her hand on the head of a lion; cf. Souchal, in *GBA*, 1972¹, p. 89.

VERSAILLES, PALACE

40
Work for the Château d'Anet

1682–3
  a. *Trophies above the two fire-places in the Salon*
  b. *Four groups of children with tripods of Apollo*
Contract between Louis-Joseph, Duke of Vendôme, and Marc Arcis, signed before a notary 12 Sept. 1682, fee 1100 L.; publ. M. Jusselin, 'Doc. sur le Chât. d'Anet au 17è s.' in *Bull. de la Soc. archéol. d'Eure et Loir*, 1954, XX, p. 27–74. The payment incl. 400 L. for other undefined work, previously done by A. in the same place.
  c. Consoles in Vernon stone, supports for marble busts
Contract 23 Mar. 1683, fee 30 L. per console, *ibid*. In 1683, during restorations under the architect Desgots, some marble busts from Chenonceaux were placed on the stone consoles between the first storey windows of the façade of the centre courtyard facing the gardens (demolished betw. 1779 and 1810); others are still in position on the great staircase of the left wing.
  d. *Work in the lower Salon of the left wing*
In the contract of 23 Mar. 1683 A. undertook to make for the two sides of the lower Salon two plaster bas-reliefs and lead metopes at the cornice for 32 L. for each sculpture, 14 L. for each metope.
Destroyed.

41*
Saint Mark

1682–4   Oval medallion   Marble   H: 80
Reception piece for the Acad. Full-size model pres. in 1682, *P-V.*, II, 227; marble in 1684, *P-V*, II, 281; Guérin *Descr.*, 1715, p. 76. The Saint, half-figure, his face in profile, writes in a book lying on the head of a lion. Trsf. to the Petits-Augustins in 1792, in 1815 to Notre-Dame de Versailles.

VERSAILLES, NOTRE-DAME

42*
Model for Equestrian Statue of Louis XIV for Toulouse

1685
  a. Louis XIV on horseback
Group   Terracotta   H: 180
The King, dressed as a Roman general, rides his horse at walking pace.
  b. Four bas-reliefs on the socle
Terracotta
On the long sides: Louis XIV on horseback, riding down his enemies, preceded by St. Michael killing the dragon; Louis XIV leading heretics back to religion. On the short sides: the royal French escutcheon and opp. a radiant sun, both supported by putti.
  c. Four chained seated slaves
Four statuettes   Terracotta   H: 23
Intended for the angles of the socle.
One of the three models for the Place d'Armes in front of the Capitole, Toulouse; Town Council decision 28 July 1676. In 1685, the Capitouls called A. to Toulouse;

42

42c

42c

between Aug. and Dec. he made the models, at once accepted by the council for a fee of 1800 L., Arch. de l'Hôtel de Ville, publ. in E. Roschach, *Cat. Mus. Toulouse*, 1865, p. 323. The project was never carried out. The wax models of Louis XIV on horseback and the four slaves were kept during the 18th c. in the Salle du Petit Consistoire of the Capitole in Toulouse. Descr. in *Analyse des Ouvrages dans l'Hôtel de Ville de Toulouse*, Toulouse, 1770. For the history, see *Cat. Mus. Toulouse.*, 1865, p. 323; H. Chalande, 'Hist. mon. de l'Hôtel de Ville', in *Rev. hist. de Toulouse*, 1925, p. 88–9.

TOULOUSE, MUSEE DES AUGUSTINS

43
Angel for the Church of the Sorbonne, Paris

1685–7
An adoring angel, kneeling on the pediment of the

High Altar, symmetrical with that by Van Clève, acc. to Piganiol, *Descr.* 1765, VI, p. 352 and Dezallier, *Paris*, 1752, p. 280; see also Ms. Malliot in Fontaine, *op. cit.*, p. 232. Disappeared during the Revolution. *See app.*

44*
Vase

1687–8   Marble   H: 225
For the Allée Roy. at Versailles, similar to the one by Joly opposite. Payment 1100 L. in two instalments, *Comptes*, II, 1172; III, 91. Type of the Medici vases, with fluting and acanthus leaves at the base of the body. *See appendix.*

VERSAILLES, PARK

44

45
Ionic Capitals

1687–8   Marble
Payment of 769 L. for two rectangular pilaster capitals
and three corner capitals on the outside of the Palais de
Trianon, *Comptes*, II, 1172; III, 91. cf. André no. 11⋆.

VERSAILLES, GRAND TRIANON

46⋆
Term of Flora

1688   Marble   H: over 200
After a small model by Girardon, Arch. Nat., O^I 1472.
Begun in 1688 by A., who supplied the plaster model,
payment 600 L., *Comptes*, III, 91. Finished by Mazière,
who received 1500 L. Placed in the Demi-lune of the
Bassin d'Apollon in 1702, *Comptes*, IV, 963. The
goddess, allegory of Spring, is crowned with flowers
and carries garlands.

VERSAILLES, PARK

47
Monument of Louis XIV for Pau

1688–97
  a. *Pedestrian statue of Louis XIV*   Bronze
  b. *Four bas-reliefs*   Marble
cf. J. Guiffrey, 'Notice sur la place roy. de Pau:
Documents publ. par L. Lacaze sur la statue de Louis
XIV pour la place roy. de Pau par Girardon et M. Arcis',
in *NAAF*, 1879, p. 343–50.
Comm. by the Etats de Béarn for the Place Royale, Pau.
After a wax model by Girardon. Fee 27,000 L. increased
to 30,000. Documents in the Arch. des Basses-Pyrénées,
C 741–5. First contract signed in Paris, 4 Sept. 1688,
2nd contract in Pau, 18 Aug. 1690. Unveiled in June
1697, destroyed 1792; no illustration preserved. The
King was shown "with his sceptre and in the dress of the
King of Peace". Destroyed.

46

48—49

50—51

48–51
Work for the Chapelle Notre-Dame du Mont-Carmel

48* Elias
49* Eliseus
50* Saint Albert, Patriarch of Jerusalem
51* Saint Simon Stock

Before 1691   Four statues   Polychromed terracotta
Av. H: 175
Comm. after 1678 by Gabriel de Vendages de Malapeire, magistrate of Toulouse, who wanted to dedicate a richly ornamented chapel to the Virgin. The statues of the four supposed founders of the Carmelite order were placed on the steps of the retable of the High Altar. Their attitude expresses amazement at the miracle of the Virgin's assumption, represented above the altar. Acc. to the *Biogr. Toulousaine, op. cit.*, the statues were to be executed in marble. The convent was disbanded in 1791, demolished in 1806–8. The statues were saved by du Mège, and preserved in the Mus. des Augustins (cat. 1912, nos 739–42). cf. M. Desazars, 'L'art à Toulouse: Vendages de Malapeire et la chapelle de Notre-Dame du Mont-Carmel' in *Mém. de la Soc. archéol. du Midi de la Fr.*, XV, 1894, p. 123–60.

TOULOUSE, MUSEE DES AUGUSTINS

52
Tomb of Gabriel de Vendages de Malapeire

1702
In the chapel of Mont-Carmel in acc. with Malapeire's wish. The mon. was surmounted by a bust of the deceased by A. with the inscription "Nec intus nec intra". cf. J. Malliot, 'Recherches hist. sur les mon. de Toulouse' (Ms. in Toulouse Library) and *Biogr. Toulousaine, op. cit.*, p. 477. Destroyed when the chapel was demolished.

53
Inscriptions in the Galerie de Peinture at the Capitole

1702
The Galerie de Peinture at the Capitole in Toulouse was decorated, betw. 1684–1723, with large compositions illustr. the history of the town. A. was comm. to incise the titles of these compositions in gold letters on slate tablets, inside carved plaster cartouches. Arch. Munic., délib. XXXV, fol. 138–9, and estim. 26 Sept. 1702, fee 300 L. reduced to 170 L. Arch. Munic., DD, 296, fol. 659. cf. E. Roschach, 'La Gal. de peinture de l'Hôtel de ville de Toulouse' in *Mém. de l'Acad. des Sciences, Inscript. et Belles-Lettres de Toulouse*, 1889, p. 16–38. Destroyed.

54
Jean-Pierre Rivalz, painter and architect (1625–1706)

Before 1706   Bust Terracotta   H: 64
Exh. Salon Acad. Toulouse, 1751, no. 96; then owned by Bruno du Castel, treasurer. Acq. by the Mus. des Augustins, *Cat.* 1865, no. 862; 1912, no. 882. Recently disappeared.

55

55*
Francois de Nupces

1708   Bust   Marble   H: 72 (without socle)
President of Parliament in Toulouse, died in 1703. The bust was part of the tomb erected by his widow in the Church des Récollets, Ste.-Marie-des-Anges. Removed during the Revolution, acc. to du Mège, *Descr. du Mus. des Antiques de Toulouse*, 1835; placed in the Mus. des Augustins, *Cat.*, 1828, no. 460; 1912, no. 883. Attrib. to A. by the author of the *Biogr. Toulousaine, op. cit.*

TOULOUSE, MUSEE DES AUGUSTINS

56–61
WORKS CARRIED OUT FOR JEAN-BAPTISTE COLBERT DE VILLACERF, ARCHBISHOP OF TOULOUSE

Between 1693–1710
cf. J. Lestrade, 'Oeuvres d'art commandées à M. Arcis par Colbert' in *Rev. hist. de Toulouse*, 1925, p. 193–4. Bacot, the Archbishop's superintendent, whose duty it was to deal with A., died before the sculptor had been paid. A. therefore sent a Mém. to the Archbishop listing all the works done for him, asking for instructions. This Mém. is preserved in the Arch. of the Sisters of Mercy of St.-Etienne. Whereabouts of the works themselves unknown. They were:

56
Designs for a Chimney-Piece

For the great hall of the Archbishop's Palace. On the mantelpiece a bust of Louis XIV with trophies of arms and ornaments. Not ident. or disapp.

63

57
Jean-Baptiste Colbert de Villacerf

Bust   Terracotta
A. executed the bust for the apothecary of the Grey
Sisters. Not ident. or disapp.

58
Crucifix

Small model
To be cast in bronze. Not ident. or disapp.

59
Unicorn

Small model
To be executed in stone and placed upon the pilasters at
the entrance to the Archbishop's Château de Balma.
Several of these unicorns appear in an anon. painting of
the Château (London, Apsley House, Wellington Mus.).
Not ident. or disapp.

60 61
Heraclitus and Democritus

Two small busts.
Exh. Salon Acad. Toulouse, 1769, *Livret*, 18, 19; at that
time in the Coll. Balard-Dugalin. Not ident. or disapp.

62
Works in the Chapel of the Pénitents Blancs

1705–14
    a. *Six prophets*
Six terracotta statues in niches in the side walls of the
chapel.

    b. *Two adoring angels*
Two plaster statues of young angels, standing in
niches on either side of the Tribune.
    c. *Eight terracotta bas-reliefs*
Under the niches with the prophets and angels.
    d. *Ornamentation of the niches*
Above each niche a cartouche and garlands; at the
sides, consoles with foliage and underneath a kind of
cul-de-lampe. In the cut corners of the chapel were four
false niches, similarly decorated.
    e. *Cornices*
Wood. The old cornice was enriched by mouldings on
the new pilasters and the piers.
    f. *Glory of angels*
Half relief on the façade of the Tribune. The name of
God was carved in Hebrew characters, surrounded by
rays and clouds with children and cherubim.
    Contract for all these works betw. A. and the officers
of the Brotherhood of the Pénitents Blancs, 7 Apr. 1705,
fee 2000 L, after A.'s design had won a competition.
The work, supposed to be completed in two years, was
not finished until 1714, Arch. Dept. of Haute-Garonne,
E 931, fol. 124. Payment was held over until 1714,
E 931, fol. 120. Summary of the documents publ.
H. Bégouen, 'Les travaux de M. Arcis pour la chapelle
des Pénitents blancs' in *Bull. de la Soc. archéol. du Midi*,
1910–12, p. 326–36.
    g. *The infant Jesus*
Statue, gilded wood. Payment 20 L., 7 July, 1710 for the
altar of the Sisterhood, cf. Adher, 'Notes sur M. Arcis',
meeting 6 Apr. 1909 in *Bull. de la Soc. archéol. du Midi*,
1906–9.
    All works destroyed when the chapel was demolished.

63*
Germain de Lafaille (1616-1711)

1711   Bust   Clay   H: 75, without socle
Capitoul, 1673–4, syndic and famous chronicler. After
his death, the bust was placed in the Gal. des Illustres.
Estim., undated, in Arch. Munic. of Toulouse, DD 302.

TOULOUSE, CAPITOLE

64-72
WORKS FOR MONTAUBAN CATHEDRAL

1715–22
cf. Fontaine, *op. cit.*, p. 240 and M. Huillet d'Istria,
'L'art de François d'Orbay révélé par la cathédrale de
Montauban', in *Bull. du XVIIe s.*, 1966, no. 72, p. 3–79.
Acc. to the *Biogr. Toulousaine, op. cit.*, A. did ten huge
statues for the façade of Montauban Cathedral, built
by F. d'Orbay.

64 65
**Two Seated Figures representing Hope and
Religion**

    a. *Two statues*   Stone
On the pediment. Destroyed.
    b. Two models   Terracotta   H: 21 (Hope)*;
31 (Religion)*
Exh. Salon Acad. Toulouse, 1752, no. 12. Now in the

65b

64b

70

71

72

Mus. des Augustins, cat. 1912, no. 858. Religion, draped in a cloak, holds an open book and a chalice (broken). Hope, her head crowned with flowers, carries an anchor.

TOULOUSE, MUSEE DES AUGUSTINS (64b, 65b only)

66–69

The Four Evangelists
66★ Saint Matthew and the angel
67★ Saint Mark and the lion
68★ Saint Luke and the ox
69★ Saint John and the eagle

a. Four statues   Stone   Over life-size
The statues stood on the entablature of the first order under the pediment. Contract with the building contractor Simon and with A. 1715, Arch. du Tarn & Garonne, C 67⁴⁰; cf. Fontaine, *op. cit.* They deteriorated rapidly because of the poor quality of the stone from the quarry of Les Granges; St. Luke's head has been replaced. Arch. Tarn & Garonne, C 68². The four groups were removed to the vestibule of the Cathedral and replaced with works by Saupique.

MONTAUBAN, CATHEDRAL

b. St. Matthew★ and St. John★
Maquettes   Terracotta   H: 40
Exh. in the Salon Acad. Toulouse, 1752, nos. 4 & 5.

TOULOUSE, MUSEE DES AUGUSTINS

c. *St. Mark*
Maquette   Terracotta
Exh. Salon as above, no. 11. Whereabouts unknown.

70★ 71★
Fathers of the Church, Saint Ambrose and Saint Augustine

Two statues   Stone   H: over life-size
Contract 1715 as for no. 66(a). The four Fathers of the Church, seated, were also to be placed on the entablature of the first order on either side of the Evangelists. They appeared thus in several drawings of the façade, Bibl. Nat. Est., Coll. de Cotte, no. 1765; Stockholm, THC 8123. A collapse in 1722 caused the project to be changed; the two statues already completed were placed inside the cathedral on either side of the choir; the project of statues for SS. Athenasius and Chrysostom was abandoned.

MONTAUBAN, CATHEDRAL

72★ Saint Athenasius

Model   Terracotta   H: 38
Exh. Salon Acad. Toulouse, 1752, no. 9.

TOULOUSE, MUSEE DES AUGUSTINS

66a   66b   67a

68a   69b   69a

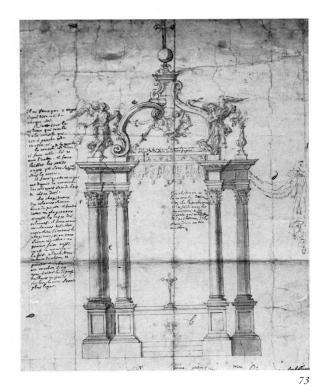

73

73*
Design for the Baldachin in the Cathedral at Tarbes

1717
The drawing combines a plan and elevation with two

variants; the hand-written note reads: "Drawn by the undersigned on this day, 3rd December 1717, M. Arcis". One of the variants has been carefully followed in the Cathedral at Tarbes. A. drew on this design for the baldachin at St.-Sernin in Toulouse (no. 84). Discussed by F. Legrand in a lecture on 'Le dessin de M. Arcis pour le baldaquin de Tarbes', Colloque de l'Art baroque à Lyon, Oct. 1972.

TARBES, ARCHIVES DU GRAND SEMINAIRE

74*
Work for the High Altar of Saint-Sernin, Toulouse

1720–21
a. *Designs for the High Altar:*
Carried out by Galinier and Girard, two stone-masons from Caunes, cf. Mesuret, *op. cit.* p. 472–3. The cross and six torches have disappeared.
b.* The Martyrdom of St. Sernin
Bas-relief Lead Gilded 120 × 247
Signed. M. ARCIS, ANNO MDCCXX
cf. *Biogr. Toulousaine, op. cit.*; Fontaine, *op. cit.*, p. 243 and Mesuret, *ibid.* The High Priest on the steps of the temple orders the bull dragging the Saint to be unleashed; onlookers are fleeing.
c.* Two adoring Angels
Statues Wood Gilded H: 145
cf. Mesuret, *ibid.*; on either side of the altar. See no. 84.

TOULOUSE, ST.-SERNIN

74c¹

74c²

75
Saint Augustine in Ecstasy

1721–2   Bas-relief   Stucco
Above the high altar of the Augustinian Church,
Toulouse. Contract 12 May, 1721 betw. the prior of the
monastery and A., fee 750 L. The receipts show that the
work was finished and paid for a year later. St. Augustine
in bas-relief stood in a great niche supported by angels,
surmounted by a glory and the Trinity (Christ, the
Dove of the Holy Spirit and the Triangle of the Trinity,
surrounded by small angels, clouds and rays). The
contract appeared in the sale of Jules Boilly's autographs,
publ. by H. Jouin in *NAAF*, 1879, p. 146–8. Destroyed
in 1834 during the restoration of the Mus. des Augustins.

76
Eight Coats of Arms of Capitouls

1723   Plaster
Placed above two pictures in the Gal. de Peinture in the
Capitole. Contract 17 Nov. 1723, fee 150 L., Arch.
Munic. Toulouse, DD 296, fol. 537, 539. Destroyed.

77
Jean-Galbert de Campistron (1656–1723)

1723   Bust   Terracotta
Poet and Dramatist. Bust made after his death for the
Gal. des Illustres, acc. to Malliot, Ms. *op. cit.* Not ident. or
disapp.

74

74b

79a

Detail   *79b*

Detail   *79b*

78–79
DECORATION FOR THE OPERA, TOULOUSE

1725
A. was comm. to decorate the old Hall of the Jeu de Paume in rue Montardy, converted under Louis XIV to an Opera House. In spite of a fire in 1748 and use of the hall for other purposes, this decoration remained more or less intact until the hall became a cinema in 1927. cf. P. Mesplé, in *l'Auta*, May, 1966, p. 76–7; Apr. 1971, p. 92–7 (ill.). The subjects were:

78a
Poetry; Orpheus lulling Cerberus to sleep with his lyre; both surrounded by trophies of musical instruments. (On the ceiling).

78b
Orpheus building towns to the sound of his lyre; Orion on the Dolphin's back. (Above the two fireplaces). All these decorations were removed and destroyed in 1927.

79
Apollo and the Muses

a.★ Maquette   Wax   25 × 50
Exh. Salon Acad. Toulouse, 1752, no. 8.

FOIX, MUSEE DE L'ARIEGE

b.★ Bas-relief   Stucco   400 × 910
Under Apollo's foot, signed: MARCUS ARCIS FACIEBAT MDCCXXV
The only part of the decoration to survive; partially visible behind the cinema projectors on what originally was the rear wall of the stage. This was A's most famous work, acc. to Mariette, *ABC*, I, p. 29 and the *Biogr. Toulousaine, op. cit.*: Apollo in the centre, sitting on Mount Parnassus; with him are Pegasus and nine Muses. The Muse Clio is directly inspired by Raphael's fresco of Parnassus in the Vatican. At the end of the 18th c., the sculptor Carcenac added below Apollo a tenth figure, the nymph Hippocrene (signed), where, as the maquette shows, there was originally a door.

TOULOUSE, 24, RUE MONTARDY

Detail   *79b*

Detail   *79b*

80

81

80★   81★
Saint Mark and the Lion
Saint Matthew and the Angel

1727   Two groups   Marble   H: c. 200
In two of the niches of the High Altar of the Cathedral,
replacing earlier works by Mercier. The two other
Evangelists are by A.'s pupil, N. Hardy. cf. Fontaine,
op. cit.; J.-M. Cayla, *Toulouse mon. et pittoresque*, s.d.,
p. 119; Mesuret, *op. cit.*, p. 226.

TOULOUSE, CATHEDRAL ST.–ETIENNE

82
Work at the Church of Saint-Jérôme (Blue Penitents)

a.★   Ten figures of Virtues
Before 1734   Bas-reliefs   Stucco   c. 175 × 200
Acc. to the *Biogr. Toulous.*, placed above the arches of
the tribunes around the nave. The theological Virtues
(Faith, Hope, Charity), the cardinal Virtues (Strength,
Justice, Prudence, Temperance) and the penitential
Virtues (Penitence or Mortification, Good Deeds,
Modesty) are repr. by seated women with children and
appropr. attr.
b.★ Eighteen Ecclesiastical Trophies
Stucco, gilded and polychromed.
Placed between the pilasters around the nave and in the
sanctuary.
c.★   Cherubim in a glory
Stucco
Above the High Altar.

TOULOUSE, CHURCH OF ST.–JEROME

82a

82a

82a

82b

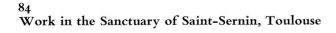

82c

83*
Antoine Rivalz, painter (1667–1735)

1735   Bust   Terracotta   H: 80
Done at the time of the painter's death for the Gal. des
Illustres, to which it was recently returned. A. Rivalz
was the son of Jean-Pierre R. (see no. 54). Acc. to
Chalandes, 'Hist. Mon. de l'Hôtel de Ville, Toulouse',
in *Rev. hist. de Toulouse*, 1915–19, no. 3, p. 209, this
bust is by his friend Arcis.

TOULOUSE, CAPITOLE

84
Work in the Sanctuary of Saint-Sernin, Toulouse

1736–8
The plans and a wooden model for the re-arrangement
of the sanctuary were provided by A., who had already

84b

83

worked on them in 1720 (no. 74), cf. A. Auriol, 'Notes sur l'ameublement et la décor. du sanctuaire de St.-Sernin au XVIIIᵉ s.', in *Rev. hist. de Toulouse*, 1924, p. 161–7.

a. *Model for the Baldachin*

1736   Wood

From this model, P. Michau made in 1736 the baldachin for the main altar above the tomb of St.-Sernin. It consists of six columns, weighed down by two pots à

feu and four standing angels; these columns support the acanthus-decorated volutes. Probably destroyed.

b.★ *Model for the Grilles of the Sanctuary*

Under A.'s supervision, the blacksmith Maurette made the communion grilles and those encl. the Sanctuary, also two doors. Contract 26 June, 1736; cf. Auriol, *loc. cit.* The grilles are extant.

c.★ Decoration for the High Altar

1737–8   Lead and tin

A. made a Dove of the Holy Spirit with rays for the front of the altar (width 575); for the four corners, four cherubim heads; beneath the table, a festooned moulding. Contract: 16 Feb. 1737 between A. and Canon Terraube, fee 400 L., quoted in Auriol, *loc. cit.* Payment after completion of the work in the following year.

TOULOUSE, ST.-SERNIN

85★
Marc Arcis, Self-portrait (see p. 4★)

Bust   Terracotta   H: 70
Exh. Salon Acad. Toulouse, 1751, no. 98. It then belonged to Bruno du Castel, Treasurer. Acq. by the Acad. des Arts de Toulouse in 1751. Mentioned in the Catal. of the Mus. des Augustins, 1828, no. 561; 1865, no. 860; 1912, no. 881. The sculptor appears approx. 50 years old.

TOULOUSE, MUSEE DES AUGUSTINS

Detail   *85*

84c²

84c¹

86*
Louis XIV

At the Salon Acad. Toulouse, 1752, no. 1, a white marble medallion, diam. 67, sculpted by A., was exh. Acc. to the *Biogr. Toulousaine*, *op. cit.*, it had been comm. by the towns of either Rieux or Pau. Mentioned in the Mus. des Augustins, cat. 1828, no. 462; 1865, no. 859; 1912, no. 882, but since disappeared. The Mus. acq. from an antique dealer a fragment of a stone bas-relief, showing a male head: the profile of Louis XIV and A.'s style seem to be recognisable.

TOULOUSE, MUSÉE DES AUGUSTINS

87
Old Man

Bust   Terracotta   H: 40
Mus. des Augustins, cat. 1912, no. 886. Not ident. or disapp.

88
Christ on the Mount of Olives

Acc. to the *Biogr. Toulousaine*, *op. cit.*, in the Convent of the Filles Repenties, i.e. the Convent of la Madeleine, in the rue des Cordeliers, which no longer exists. Destroyed.

89

90

89*
Saint Joseph

Maquette   Terracotta   H: 40
Exh. Salon Acad. Toulouse, 1752, no. 7.

TOULOUSE, MUSEE DES AUGUSTINS

90*
Saint John Costa

Maquette   Terracotta   H: 37
Exh. Salon Acad. Toulouse, 1752, no. 13.

TOULOUSE, MUSEE DES AUGUSTINS

91   92
Zephyr and Diana

   a. *Two statues* (?)
Mentioned by the *Biogr. Toulousaine, op. cit.* Possibly
confused with the models. Not ident. or disapp.
   b.* Two models   Terracotta   H: 36
Exh. Salon Acad. Toulouse, 1752, nos. 6 & 3. Diana
walking with her dog; Zephyr, greatly damaged.

TOULOUSE, MUSEE DES AUGUSTINS (91b, 92b only)

86

91b   92b   93

93*
Flora

Model   Terracotta
Exh. Salon Acad. Toulouse, 1752, no. 10. Seated, her hair dressed with flowers, holding a basket of fruit.

TOULOUSE, MUSEE DES AUGUSTINS

94
Pieta

Bas-relief
Exh. Salon Acad. Toulouse, 1752, no. 16, then in the possession of the lawyer M. Artaud. Not ident. or disapp.

95
Saint Peter

Head   Terracotta
Exh. Salon Acad. Toulouse, 1752, no. 2. Not ident. or disapp.

96
The Holy Family

Bas-relief
Exh. Salon Acad. Toulouse, 1752, no. 14. Not ident. or disapp.

97
Narcissus

Exh. Salon Acad. Toulouse, 1755, no. 113; 1760, no. 68; 1779, no. 127, then in the possession of the Chevalier Rivalz. Not ident. or disapp.

98
Amphitrite

Exh. Salon Acad. Toulouse, 1755, no. 111. Not ident. or disapp.

99
Adoring Angel

Exh. Salon Acad. Toulouse, 1755, no. 112. Not ident. or disapp.

100
Arcis the younger

Bust
A son of A. Exh. Salon Acad. Toulouse, 1755, no. 110. Not ident. or disapp.

101
Saint Madeleine

Exh. Salon Acad. Toulouse, 1760, no. 68. Not ident. or disapp.

102
Portrait of a Woman

Exh. Salon Acad. Toulouse, 1760, no. 68. Not ident. or disapp.

103
Pierre-Paul Riquet, Engineer (1604–80)

Bust
Exh. Salon Acad. Toulouse, 1776, no. 252. Not ident. or disapp.

104
Saint Basine (Sabine ?)

Model
Exh. Salon Acad. Toulouse, 1779, no. 126, then in the possession of the Chevalier Rivalz. Not ident. or disapp.

105
Virgin and Child

Medallion
Exh. Salon Acad. Toulouse, 1786, then in the possession of the merchant M. Fontan. Not ident. or disapp.

2

BAROIS, François (1656–1726)

b. Paris 1656. Son of Louis Barois or Barrois, bourgeois of Paris. In 1682, Second sculpture prize at the Acad., see no. 1; 1st prize to N. Coustou. Between 1683 and 1686, pensionnaire at the Acad. Fr. in Rome with N. Coustou, *Comptes*, II, 378. 5 May 1693, elected to Acad. St.-Luc, cf. J. Guiffrey, *St.-Luc*, p. 175; 30 Oct. 1700, admitted to the Acad., *P-V*, III, p. 303; 24 July 1702, Asst. Prof.; 3 July 1706, Prof, *ibid.*, IV, p. 31; 3 Dec. 1707, gift to his sister Anne, wife of Guillaume-Denis du Choiselle, King's counsellor, secretary and contrôleur général de l'extraordinaire des guerres et cavalerie légère de France, Arch. Nat., Y 280, fol. 136; 1716, ill, *P-V*, IV, 225, 227; 26 Oct. 1720, Asst. Recteur, *ibid.*, IV, 303; 11 Oct. 1726, "François Barois, Recteur of the Acad. roy., aged about 70, who died yesterday in the rue St. Honoré, in this parish, has been buried in the cemetery", reg. St.-Roch, publ. Herluison, p. 21. T-B, II, 1908, p. 534 (Lami).

I
Cain building the Town of Enoch

1682
Second sculpture prize, Acad., *P-V*, II, p. 200, 219, 229; *AAF*, V, 1857, p. 278. Whereabouts unknown.

3

4

2*
Venus Callipygos

1683–5 Statue Marble H: 175
Copied by B. during his stay at the Acad. Fr., Rome after an antique from the Coll. Farnese (now Mus. Nat., Naples). Cast made for the Acad. Fr.; Errard asked B. to "change the position of the right arm"; he also had to "re-shape a leg and the spine, which had been left rather indistinct", *Corr. Dir. Acad. Fr. Rome*, II, p. 17, letter 9 May 1694. In 1686, B. rec. 220 L., "in view of the satisfaction of H.M.", *Comptes*, II, 956. The statue was sent to France, placed at first at the Théâtre d'eau at Versailles, then in 1695 in the park at Marly, Arch. Nat., O^I 1460^{126}, on a sculpted plinth (drawing in Stockholm, THC 7150). At the beginning of the 18th c., Thierry added a drapery, cf. Fontenai, II, p. 627. Trsf. to the Tuileries in the 18th c., cf. Millin, *Descr. Stat. Tuileries*, 1798, p. 101.

PARIS, LOUVRE

3* **4***
Vertumnus and Pomona

1686–96 Terms Marble H: 280
After models by Girardon, Arch. Nat., O^I 1472. First account in 1686, *Comptes*, II, 995; final payment in 1696, 9950 L., incl. two terms and the large vase for the Allée roy.; the terms were "made and placed in the garden of the Pal. of Versailles", *ibid.*, IV, 55. The invent. of 1722 describes them as near the "grand bassin du fer à cheval at the end of the grande allée of the Tuileries"; Vertumnus, "in one hand a mask, holds with the other the drapery on his head", Pomona "holds a basket of flowers and fruit", Arch Nat., O^I 1969^A, p. 204. Pomona personifies Spring; Vertumnus, Autumn. The other two seasons were represented by a term of Ceres, or Summer, by Dumont (no. 25) and G. Coustou (no. 64); and a term of Winter by Raon.

PARIS, TUILERIES GARDEN

7a

5*
Vase

1687–96   Marble   H: 240
Payments in 1687 and 1688, *Comptes*, II, 1172; IV, 11;
final payment, cf. *supra*. Part of the grand ensemble for
the Allée roy.; average payment 1800 L. for each vase.
Decor. with cornucopias; the similar vase on the south
side opp. is by Rayol. Engr.: Thomassin no. 213. *S. app.*

VERSAILLES, PARK

6
Two Capitals

1687–8   Marble
Payment 280 L., *Comptes*, III, 91. Two Ionic pilaster
capitals on the exterior of the Grand Trianon. cf.
André no. 11*.

VERSAILLES, GRAND TRIANON

5

7c

9

10e

10d

7
Ornaments at the Grand Trianon

1687–8   Stone and wood
In collab. with Mazeline and Jouvenet
   a.* For cornices at Versailles and Trianon, payments
6700 L., *Comptes*, II, 1115 and 9200 L. in 1688, *ibid.*, III,
35.

VERSAILLES, GRAND TRIANON

   b. *For architraves in the King's apartments*
At Trianon-sous-bois, payment 1000 L., *ibid.*, III, 35.
Destroyed.
   c. *Eight stone groups of two children*
In collab. with Jouvenet and Cornu. Surmounting the
Trianon peristyle, six groups faced the garden, two the
Cour d'honneur. cf. Cornu no. 19. B., who carved
four with Jouvenet, rec. 1040 L., *ibid.*, III, 248. Engr.
by Mariette, Bibl. Nat. Est., Va 448f*. Destroyed.

8
Capitals in the Vestibule of the former Chapel at Versailles

1688–9   Stone
First payment 2000 L. in 1688, *Comptes*, III, 55; final
payment 2550 L. in 1689, *ibid.*, III, 260. Destroyed.

10a

10b

9
Four Couronnements de Frontons for the Royal Pavilion, Marly

1688–9   Stone
In collab. with Mazeline and Jouvenet. First payment in 1688, 5500 L., *Comptes*, III, 167; balance (total 8136 L.) paid the following year, *ibid.*, III, 336. Extant drawings and engr. show that these ornam. were scrolls, vases, garlands and winged cupids (Watercolour Arch. Nat., O^I 1472, p. 4)*. Destroyed.

10f

10*
Ornaments on the Dôme des Invalides

1690–9   Stone
   a.* Metopes on the ground-floor exterior, 1690. Of 40 finely carved bas-reliefs of military trophies, B. did 20, *Comptes*, IV, 422; Bibl. Nat. Ms. fr. n.a. 22936; Félibien des Avaux, *Invalides*, p. 20–22: Descr. without attrib.
   b.* Angels sitting on either side of a vase. 1690. Outside, above the bays on the 2nd storey; Félibien des Avaux, *ibid.*, p. 295. In collab. with Mazière, Granier and Joly, B. made four of the twelve, *ibid.*; for the two series he rec. 1340 L.
   c. In 1691, B. rec. 85 L. "for the models in clay and wax and the plaster moulds." Details unknown.
   d*. 1692–3. Several small angels in bas-relief supporting the frames of the paintings in the cupola of the chapel of Saint-Jérôme in the Dôme; Félibien des Avaux, *ibid.*, p. 295. First payment 2200 L. to B., Le Conte, Granier and Mazière, who shared the work. Final payment in 1699, *Comptes*, III, 703, 845; IV, 873.
   e.* Heads of cherubims, above the windows inside the four chapels. "16 dessus de vitraux" as described in *Comptes*, III, 846; IV, 331, 469. B. was the sole artist, and rec. 75 L. for each, 1200 L. in all; Félibien des Avaux, *ibid.*, p. 295. Probably exec. in 1693.

PARIS, DOME DES INVALIDES

   f. *Model for a group of Patriarchs*
1699   Full-size model   Plaster
One of four two-figure groups intended to be exec. in St.-Leu stone and placed outside, at the four corners of the Massif Carré on the second storey. Comm. in 1699, Arch. Nat., O^I 1665, 35–7; each group to be carved by two sculptors in collab; B. with Van Clève; Flamen (no. 39) with Poultier; Mazeline with Hurtrelle; S. Slodtz with N. Coustou (no. 18). The models were probably put in place, but never exec. in stone. Appears in an engr.* of the façade by Hérisset and Chevotet in Pérau, p. 87, pl. 21 (detail). Bibl. Nat. Est., Hd 135d, pet. in fol. cf. Félibien des Avaux, *ibid.*, p. 30–34 (descr. without attrib.). Destroyed.

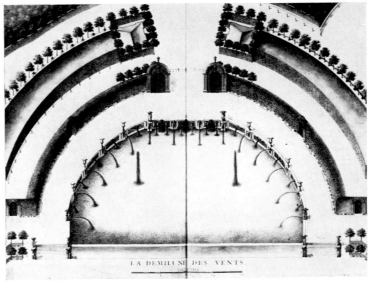

11–12

11
Vase for the Demi-lune des Vents, Marly

1696–8   Marble   H: 130
One of 12 vases comm. by Hardouin-Mansart for the balustrade of the semi-circular bassin into which flowed La Rivière at Marly; six different models had been submitted by Coysevox (no. 62) and N. Coustou (no. 17), Dedieu (no. 37) and Raon, S. Slodtz and Joly, Flamen (no. 37) and Mazière, Barois and Van Clève, Tuby and G. Hulot; inspired by the Medici vase, decor. with vegetable and geometrical motifs; descr. Arch. Nat., O^I 2773⁵. B.'s vase was similar to that by Van Clève. Payment to B. 850 L. in two instalm., 1697–8, *Comptes*, IV, 189, 336. Watercolour drawing of the Demi-lune des Vents in Arch. Nat., O^I 1470, p. 12★. Whereabouts unknown.

12
Head of Winds

1697   Lead
The water gushed into the bassin of the Demi-lune des Vents out of heads of winds on the retaining wall. B. made two, for which he rec. 200 L. in 1697, *Comptes*, IV, 189. Arch. Nat., O^I 2773⁵. The other sculptors, who made two heads of winds and two masks each, were Dedieu (no. 38), Vigier, S. Slodtz, Raon, Granier, and P. Legros I; Mazeline did the great centre-piece of two sea-horses; Van Clève and Flamen (no. 36) together made two gryphons. Destroyed.

13

13*
Cleopatra Dying

1700   Statuette   Marble   48 × 100
B. was made Academician on 30 Oct. 1700 on presentation of the small statuette of Cleopatra, *P-V*, III, p. 303.
First in the Louvre in the room reserved for the Acad.,
cf. Guérin, *Descr.*, p. 62, then in the Museum. The Queen
of Egypt semi-recumbent on her funeral couch; in her
right hand, the asp which bites into her breast. Her
head is turned backwards with an expression of despair.

PARIS, LOUVRE

15
Pieta

1704   Bas-relief   Marble
Exh. at the Salon 1704, *Livret*, p. 38. The Virgin at the
foot of the cross, her dead son on her knees. Not ident.
or disapp.

16
Two Nymphs

1706   Lead and tin
B. had been comm., together with Bertrand (no. 13),

14²   14¹   17

14
Saint Gregory

1702   Statue   Plaster   H: over life-size
The four round chapels of the Dôme des Invalides were
consecrated to the Fathers of the Church. Twelve
statues were envisaged for the niches in these chapels;
Girardon had supplied all the designs, if not the models;
they presented a real unity of style, but owing to the
bad state of finance they remained as large plaster
models. Apparently this work was undertaken after
1700, but the first payment to B., for the St. Gregory,
was made only in 1705, *Comptes*, IV, 1177 and the
final payment of 700 L. in 1709, *ibid.*, V, 349; cf.
Félibien des Avaux, *Invalides*, p. 295; Granet, p. 110;
Pérau, p. 77. Execution in marble began only under
Louis XV by another team of artists, who preferred to
produce individual works. The plasters were stored and
finally destroyed. J.-B. Lemoyne then made a new
St. Gregory in marble, cf. Dreyfus, 'Les stat. du Dôme
des Inval. au XVIIIe s.', in *BSHAF*, 1908. An engr.* by
Cochin of B's work is in the *Descriptions* by Granet and
in Pérau, pl. 64. Pen drawing* in Coll. de Cotte, Bibl.
Nat. Est., Hc 14, 2. Destroyed.

to carve a group of two nymphs on rocks for the
Bassin des Perlées (des Sénateurs) in the park at Marly.
First payment in 1706, *Comptes*, V, 41, balance in 1711,
ibid., V, 537, total 2000 L. Destroyed.

17*
Faith

1707   Statue   Tonnerre stone   H: c. 300
One of the four Christian Virtues on the balustrade
bordering the roof of the Lady-chapel. First payment in
1707, *Comptes*, V, 123, balance in 1711, *ibid.*, V, 526,
total 1050 L. cf. Mém., Arch. Nat., O¹ 1784. Faith,
draped in a veil, gazes at a cross in her right hand, the
left presses a large open book against her thigh.

VERSAILLES PALACE, CHAPEL

18*
Pomona

1706-9   Statue   Marble   H: 146
In Sept. 1706, B., Le Lorrain, Frémin (no. 14), Thierry,
P. Bertrand (no. 14), and S. Slodtz were commissioned to

181

182

execute six statues for the Cascade Rustique (or Champêtre) in the Bosquets de Louvecienne at Marly, in alternation with vases. For Pomona, B. received a first payment in 1706, *Comptes*, V, 41 and afterwards others, *ibid.*, V, 72, 240; final payment in 1709, total 2900 L. *ibid*, V, 340. "Posed on her left leg, crowned with flowers, the right hand resting on the trunk of a tree supporting her, holding in her left hand, which lacks a finger, a scrap of drapery which hides the lower part of her figure; beside the supporting leg a basket of fruit, on the plinth a pruning-knife", Invent. of 1722, Arch. Nat., O^I 1969^A, p. 159–60. Trsf. to Paris during the Revolution, Pomona stands today with Bertrand's 'l'Air' (no. 14★). A water-colour drawing of the Cascade Rustique is in Arch. Nat., O^I 1471, p. 25–6★.

PARIS, GARDEN OF THE MINISTRY OF FOREIGN AFFAIRS

19
Saint Louis

1707   Wax model   H: 40
In his mém. for 'Faith', B. claims 150 L. for a "model of St. Louis in wax, fifteen pouces high, finished with care, which had been cancelled", Arch. Nat., O^I 1784. Destroyed.

BERTIN, Claude (?-1705)

b. Paris, son of a sculptor who died c. 1671; brother and first teacher of the painter Nicolas. Louvois writes that he has "esteem" for Bertin, "who works well here and is a good craftsman", *Corr. Dir. Acad. Fr. Rome*, I, p. 178. Married Agnès Belu; in 1717 their daughter Marguerite married Jacques Loubradou de la Penière, Chef de fruiterie to the King, Bibl. Nat., Fich. Laborde, 4485. Lived in Versailles, where he died in 1705. Had the title 'Sculptor in ordinary to the King', but was never a member of the Acad. From 1685 to his death, he rec. a standing fee for "maintaining and cleaning the statues and vases at Versailles", *Comptes*, passim. In add. to these fixed appointments, he rec., acc. to the *Comptes*, numerous sums for restoration of the decorative sculpture, vases, terms and statues at Versailles, usually in the park, and in the parks at Marly, Trianon and Meudon. He had a team of restorers under him, fitted draperies and vine-leaves to nude statues and arranged transport and repositioning of displaced works. T-B, III, 1909, p. 497 (Lami).

I
Children Seated

1682   Two Groups   Marble   25 × 75
Seen by Cronström in 1697 in B.'s studio, together with other sculptures by B. (cf. nos. 12–25), *Tessin–Cronström Corresp.*, 30 July–3 Aug. 1697, p. 176. Pen and wash drawings of all these sculptures are in the Kunst-bibliothek, Berlin: these are probably Bertin's original drawings. Another set is in the Coll. Tessin in Stockholm, Nat. Mus.: these are perhaps Cronström's own drawings. Drawings of the two groups of children in

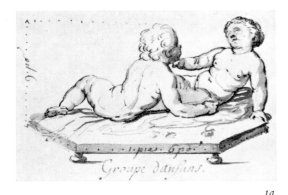

Groupe d'anfans.

1a

Groupe d'anfans.

1b

the Kunstbibliothek, Berlin, Hdz. 2710, 2713; in Stockholm, THC 3834*/5.* One of the two groups was at the sale Lespinasse d'Arlet, Paris, 11 July, 1803, cat. no. 6: "A group of two pretty children sitting on the ground, caressing each other. This work, full of natural grace in the attitude and the character of the children, represents one of B.'s good sculptures from 1682". Whereabouts unknown.

2
Several Ornaments at the Colonnade

1686   Marble
"to B. as payment for workmen and works of sculpture done by himself at the Colonnade and for repairs to vases in the little park, 5586 L. 14 s.", *Comptes*, II, 891.

VERSAILLES, PARK

3*
Four Frogs and Six Lizards at the Bassin de Latone

1687–91   Lead
Payment 937 L. 13 s. in 1687 and 1691, *Comptes*, II, 1116; III, 526.

VERSAILLES, PARK

4
Cornices

1688   Stucco?
"cornices for four rooms in Trianon-sous-bois", *Comptes*, III, 38, payment 1,500 L. Destroyed.

3¹

**5
Several Vases**

1687–1705   Marble   H: 125

Acc. to the *Comptes*, B. made at least 18 marble vases for Versailles. He rec. payment from 1687 onwards "as reimbursement for working days of craftsmen sculptors on vases for the King", *Comptes*, II, 1116. Other payments the following year, *ibid*., III, 37, 249, 355. In 1691, total payment of 19892 L. 6 s. "for the expense of 14 white marble vases . . . that he had delivered and placed in various parts of the garden at Versailles", *ibid*., III, 513, 543. Another block of marble for two vases is mentioned in 1696, *ibid*., IV, 20; in 1711 payment to his widow for two vases "placed in the gardens of Versailles and Trianon", *ibid*., V, 534. Perhaps there were even more; the 14 vases paid for in 1691 may not have included those comm. in 1687. The descriptions are our only help in locating some of these vases.

a. Vase with eagles' heads on a bas-relief repr. Numa Pompilius confiding the care of the sacred fire to the Vestal Virgins. Piganiol, *Vers.-Marly*, 1707, p. 243–4; Soulié, III, p. 498. Model for the bas-relief by P. Legros I. *Comptes*, II, 1116.

VERSAILLES, PARTERRE DU MIDI

b.⋆ Vase with eagles' heads and a bas-relief repr. a sacrifice to Bacchus. Model for the bas-relief by P. Legros I. *Comptes*, II, 1116; Piganiol, *ibid*.

VERSAILLES, PARTERRE DU MIDI

c/d.⋆ Two vases with garlands supp. by satyrs. *Comptes*, *ibid*.; Piganiol, *ibid*.

VERSAILLES, PARTERRE DU MIDI

e/f.⋆ Two vases with trophies of arms and dolphins In the centre an escutcheon with the arms of France, effaced during the Revolution. Piganiol, *ibid*.; Soulié, III, p. 499.

VERSAILLES, PARTERRE DU MIDI

g/h.⋆ Two vases with vine-branches supp. by young fauns
Piganiol, *ibid*., p. 181; Soulié, III, p. 503.

VERSAILLES, PARTERRE DU NORD

3²

5b

5c/d

5g/h

5e/f

5m

i/j. *Two vases with festoons of vines and small terms as handles*
Piganiol, *ibid.*, 1701, p. 308; 1724, p. 226. Formerly in the Salle du Conseil, Versailles Park, then in the Salle des Marronniers at Trianon. Not ident. or disapp.

k/l. *Two vases with festoons of holly, olive branches etc., with small harpies as handles*
Piganiol, *ibid.*, 1701. Formerly in the Salle du Conseil, Versailles Park, then in the Salle des Marronniers at Trianon. Not ident. or disapp.

m. *Four Vases*
Marble   H: 123
A pen drawing in the Kunstbibliothek, Berlin, Hdz. 2718*, has the following mss. note: "Two vases on the balustrade of the Orangerie after (Hardouin-)Mansart's design. Carried out in marble by Bertin; there are two similar ones in Meudon". These four vases, two in Versailles and two in Meudon, did not remain in their original position. Piganiol, *Vers.-Marly*, 1701, p. 385, mentions two in the park at Marly close to the Fontaine d'Agripine. The Invent. of 1707, Arch. Nat., O^I 1976^A, p. 723–4, shows all four in the same place. Decor. with a vine-branch and two billy-goat heads. Whereabouts unknown.

n. *Eight Vases*[?]
Piganiol, *ibid.*, 1701, p. 376. Formerly in the park at Marly, in the Parterre de la Demi-lune. Whereabouts unknown.

o. *Eight Vases*[?]
Piganiol, *ibid.*, 1701, p. 379. Formerly in the parterre opposite the King's Pavilion at Marly. Whereabouts unknown.

6
Consoles

1689   Plaster models[?]
"For three consoles made as models for a Cabinet des Glaces for the King, and several other works of sculpture", 133 L. 105 s., *Comptes*, III, 397. Not ident. or disapp.

7
Cornices

1691   Stucco[?]
"For his works of sculpture in the cornice of the Grand Cabinet in the ground floor apartment of the Surintendance at Versailles", 280 L. in all, *Comptes*, III, 536, 690. The surintendance is at 6 rue de l'Indépendance Américaine. Destroyed.

8
Seven Vases

1692   Saint-Leu stone
On the balustrade of the Grand Trianon. Payment 350 L., *Comptes*, III, 679. Destroyed.

9
Cornices in Monseigneur's apartment at Versailles Palace

1693–5   Stucco
In the Grand Cabinet, payment 229 L. in 1693, *Comptes*, III, 825; in the Bedchamber, payment 126 L. in 1695, *ibid.*, III, 1105. Destroyed.

10   11
Aristaeus and Eurydice

1694   Statues   Marble   H: c. 130
The two statues were placed in the garden at Marly in Spring 1694. Payment 3344 L., *Comptes*, III, 950. At first in the Bosquet de Louveciennes near the Amphithéâtre, they were separated ca. 1702, cf. Piganiol, *Vers.-Marly*, 1701, p. 387–8; 1707, p. 381. Eurydice was moved to the Bosquet de Marly near the Pièce des Sénateurs; Aristaeus to Trianon, near the Jardin des Marronniers. Both disappeared during the Revolution. The invent. of the King's sculptures, Arch. Nat., O^I 1976^A, p. 347–8, descr. Aristaeus thus:
"Aristaeus has an antique crown on his head and is clad in a military tunic ornamented with scales and mantling, with a cloak over his shoulders which falls down his back; his right arm is half-lifted, the hand open; in the left, which is held back, he carries flowers and has a sword at his side . . . The small finger of the right hand, the right heel and the end of his sword are broken and have been restored", and Eurydice, p. 326–7: "her hair is knotted behind her head and falls over her right

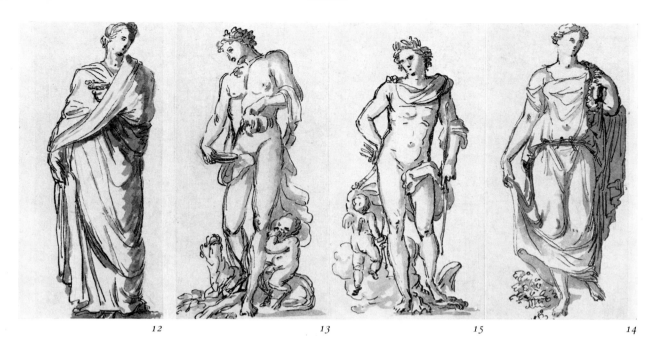

12   13   15   14

shoulder. Her drapery, fastened at the tip of her left shoulder passes to the right like a sash; she lifts the right arm over her head and in the hand of her half-lifted left arm she holds flowers; she has an armlet above her left elbow and a serpent, of which she is afraid, is clinging to her foot . . . the two arms have been restored and a finger of the right hand is broken." Whereabouts unknown. *See appendix.*

12
Vestal Virgin

Before 1697   Statuette   Marble   H: c. 91
Seen by D. Cronström in B.'s studio at Versailles with other of his works, cf. *Tessin–Cronström Corresp.*, 30 July/3 Aug. 1697, cf. Bertin no. 1. Drawings in Berlin Kunstbibl., Hdz. 2702*; Stockholm, Nat. Mus., THC 3827. Whereabouts unknown.

13
Bacchus

Before 1697   Statuette   Marble   H: c. 91
cf. *supra.* Drawings: Berlin, Hdz. 2703*; Stockholm, THC 3828. Whereabouts unknown.

14
Flora

Before 1697   Statuette   Marble   H: c.91
cf. *supra.* Drawings: Berlin, Hdz. 2705*; Stockholm, THC 3825. Whereabouts unknown.

15
Apollo

Before 1697   H: c. 91
cf. *supra.* Drawings: Berlin, Hdz. 2704*; Stockholm, THC 3826. Whereabouts unknown.

16
The Nile

Before 1697   Statuette   Marble   L: 75
cf. *supra.* Drawings: Berlin, Hdz. 2707*; Stockholm, THC 3829. After an antique. Whereabouts unknown.

17
The Tiber

Before 1697   Statuette   Marble   L: 75
cf. *supra.* Drawings: of the she-wolf and the children in Berlin, Hdz. 2708; of the whole group, Stockholm, THC 3831*. After an antique. Whereabouts unknown.

16, 18

17

18
The Seine

Before 1697 Statuette Marble L: 75
cf. *supra*. Drawings: Berlin, Hdz. 2706*; Stockholm,
THC 3830. Whereabouts unknown.

19
Venus and Cupid

Before 1697 Group Marble H: 54
cf. *supra*. Drawings: Berlin, Hdz. 2708*; Stockholm,
THC 3832. Whereabouts unknown.

20
Diana

Before 1697 Group Marble H: 43
cf. *supra*. Drawings: Berlin, Hdz. 2709*; Stockholm,
THC 3833. Whereabouts unknown.

21
Popea

Before 1697 Bust Marble H: 62
cf. *supra*. Drawings: Berlin, Hdz. 2715; Stockholm,
THC 3836*. Whereabouts unknown.

22
Berenice

Before 1697 Bust Marble H: 62
cf. *supra*. Drawings: Berlin, Hdz. 2710; Stockholm,
THC 3837*. Whereabouts unknown.

23
Dido

Before 1697 Bust Marble H: 62
cf. *supra*. Drawings: Berlin, Hdz. 2710 (called Cleopatra); Stockholm, THC 3838*. Whereabouts unknown.

24
Cleopatra

Before 1697 Bust Marble H: 62
cf. *supra*. Drawings: Berlin, Hdz. 2711; Stockholm,
THC 3839*. Whereabouts unknown.

25
Zenobia

Before 1697 Bust Marble H: 81
cf. *supra*. Drawings: Berlin, Hdz. 2711; Stockholm,
THC 3840*. Whereabouts unknown.

25

20

Detail   19

21   22   23   24

26
Work at the Château de Meudon

1698
Acc. to *Comptes*, IV, 407, B. rec. 113 L. for
   a. *Stucco work at the cornice of the Cabinet du Roi in the Appartement du Dauphin.*
   b. *Alterations in the Gallery.*
   c. *Ornaments in the Cabinet and the Salon.*
cf. P. Biver, *Hist. Chât. Meudon*, 1923, p. 157.
Destroyed.

27
Roses and Modillions

1704   Stone
Mém. for 50 modillions, and 50 roses between the modillions, on the outside cornice, in collab. with Lambert. In all 1050 L., Arch. Nat., O¹ 1784; *Comptes*, IV, 1048.

VERSAILLES, PALACE CHAPEL

28
Four Consoles

1704   Hard stone
For the benches of the Galerie d'eau, *Comptes*, IV, 1048.

VERSAILLES, PARK

29
Flammes de Vases

1704   Stone
For the balustrades, *Comptes*, IV, 1157.

VERSAILLES, PALACE

30*
Minerva as a Child

1704–5   Statue   Marble   H: below life-size
Comm. at the same time as two vases; placed in the
Jardin des Marronniers at Trianon; payment to his
widow after B.'s death, 5500 L. incl. the two vases,
Comptes, V, 15, 534; Piganiol, *Vers.-Marly*, 1764, II,
p. 248. In the Bosquet de l'Etoile during the 19th c. Put
into store.

VERSAILLES

33

31
Bust of Louis XIV

Bronze Medallion
Sale Mme. Merle, 2 Dec. 1889, no. 185; anon. sale, 24–7
Aug. 1892, no. 116; "round medallion in bronze
showing in bas-relief on one side the bust of Louis XIV
and on the other the cipher of the King surmounted by
the crown of France, work signed 'Bertin' in full and
carrying his stamp." Whereabouts unknown.

32
Venus de Medici

On 4 Dec. 1683 B. rec. from the Magasin des Antiques,
by order of Louvois, a plaster cast of the Venus of
Medici in order to make a copy for Meudon, Arch.
Nat., O^I 1963^3. It is not known what happened to this
commission.

33
Bust of a Child Crowned with Vine-leaves

Drawing in the series at the Kunstbliothek, Berlin,
Hdz 2712*. Whereabouts unknown.

34
Seated Child

On the same sheet as no. 33. The child holds an indeter-
minate object. Whereabouts unknown.

35
Man Standing

Drawing in the Kunstbibliothek, Berlin, Hdz. 2716*.
Arms folded across the chest, wearing a kind of armour
and a long cloak. Whereabouts unknown.

36
Head of a Philosopher

Drawing in the Kunstbibliothek, Berlin, Hdz. 2714*.
Bas-relief on an oval medallion. Whereabouts unknown.

30

34

35

36

BERTRAND, David (?-1697)

Rec. into the Acad. St.-Luc, 9 Feb. 1657. cf. J. Guiffrey, *St.-Luc*. Husband of Judith Meusnier, father of sculptor Philippe Bertrand, cf. below. The marriage contract of his son dated 21 June 1699, Min. Centr. Arch. Nat., Et. IX, 541, shows that David was by then dead, that his widow, sister of the sculptor Henri and the mason Jean Meusnier, and aunt of the architect Jean Meusnier, lived in exile "for religious reasons", and that David had lived in the rue Michel-Le-Comte, with the title of 'Sculptor to the King'. Therefore, it must be he who is mentioned in Brice, 1684, I, p. 133 as a sculptor appreciated for his plaster bas-reliefs on chimney-pieces, to whom payments are recorded in the *Comptes* of 1673–4. In a letter of 15/5 Nov. 1697 Cronström notes that he has just died, very much in debt, cf. *Tessin–Cronström Corresp.*, p. 182. T-B, III, 1909, p. 513-4 (R.). *For biography and no. 1 see appendix.*

2
Work for the Château of Saint-Germain-en-Laye

1673–4
Payment 91 L. and 289 L. for unspecified works of sculpture, *Comptes*, I, 693, 753. Not ident. or disapp.

3
Work for the Château de Clagny

1674–6
Payment 2,600 L., and 877 L. for work in marble, *Comptes*, I, 773, 845; and 42 L., *ibid.*, I, 845 for a marble fireplace. Destroyed.

4
Designs for Seven Mantelpieces

Pen and wash
Stockholm, Coll. Tessin–Harleman–Cronstedt. Probably acq. by Cronström after B.'s death, cf. Biography. A fairly homogeneous ensemble, dateable to the period 1680–90, certainly before 1690, when Hardouin-Mansart introduced the large mirrors. Acc. to the designs, the mantelpieces were to be 350–400 high. It is not known whether they were carried out.

a. THC 1326★, signed by B.: "dessein de bertrand Sculpteur". "Dans le Cabinet de Meudon dit le Cabinet aux Miroirs". Inside the frame: "Sculpture ou Peinture". The Chât. de Meudon belonged from 1679–91 to the Marquis de Louvois, who redecorated it. The Cabinet of Mirrors was at the north end of the East Wing.

b. THC 1328★; "fait par bertrand Sculpteur". Bust may represent the Marquis de Louvois. On the shield and buckler, a gorgon and a seated river-god, symbol of war and of peace and prosperity; in the medallion, an almost effaced cypher under a coronet.

c. THC 1327★; signed "Bertrand"; above the fire-place: "Glace", two small angels with a laurel crown, a plumed helmet, a shield with three crowns. On the frame, on top and both sides, three stars (from the Louvois coat-of-arms?).

4a   4b   4c

4d   4f   4g

4e

BERTRAND, Philippe (1663-1724)

b. Paris 1663; son of David Bertrand and Judith Meusnier. Went to Montpellier in 1694; married his first cousin, Marie Meusnier, on 21.6.1694 with papal dispensation, Min. Centr. Arch. Nat., Et. IX, 541. 30 Jan. 1700, agréé by the Acad.; 26 Nov. 1701, made Academician; 29 May 1717, Asst. Prof.; 26 Oct., Prof., *P-V*, III, p. 286, 328; IV, 247, 303; 1721, ill, *ibid*, IV, p. 321; died 30 Jan. 1724, aged 60, rue de Sève; death cert. publ. E. Piot, *Etat Civil d'art. fr.*, extr. regist. par., 1873, p. 12; Actes Notariés de l'Et. I, 267, 293-4, 298, 403, de l'Et. VIII, 897 and de l'Et. IX, 600, 624, publ. M. Rambaud, II, 1971, p. 408-11, 498-9, 1038; the Invent. a.d. of 13 Mar. 1724, Et. IX, 624, records two minor sons, of whom one, Thomas, a sculptor, was rec. into the Acad. St.-Luc, 13 July 1735. cf. Fontenai, 1776, I, p. 192; Herluison, 1873, p. 33; A. de Champeaux, *Dict. des Fondeurs*, 1886, p. 116-7.; T-B, III, 1909, p. 516-7 (Lami).

d. THC 1332*; "dessein de Bertrand Sculpteur". In the medallion: "un chiffre ou une glace", and a nearly effaced drawing of a cypher under a coronet (of the marquis ?).

e. THC 1324*; "dessein de bertrand Sculpteur". In the frame: drawing for a bas-relief of a seated, armed Minerva; under her feet, a lion; two putti, a shield with a gorgon head: a fitting motif for the War Minister.

f. THC 1331*; "dessein de bertrand Sculpte."; in the frame: "pour mettre une glace ou une frise de sculpteur". "Table de marbre ou de bois ainsy que le chambranle". In the big frame: "Achille ou Ullisse".

g. THC 2142*; "dessein de bertrand Sculpteur"; in the oval frame: design for a painting of "les quatre saisons de l'année".

STOCKHOLM, COLL. TESSIN–HARLEMAN–CRONSTED

1
Democritus and Heraclitus

1692   Two Statuettes   Terracotta   Signed & dated
Sale E. Marcelin, 19 Nov. 1888, no. 243. Perhaps the same as the "two terracotta statuettes, signed Bertrand 1692" sold for 79 L. at the sale Fr. Fêtis, 18-20 Apr. 1887, no. 423. Whereabouts unknown.

2
Works at the Arc de Triomphe du Peyrou

a.★ **The Triumph of the Catholic Faith**
b.★ **The Construction of the Canal des Deux Mers**
c.★ **The Capture of Mons and Namur**
d.★ **The Victories over England and the Empire**
1694   Four medallions   Bas-relief   Stone
For the triumphal arch, Place du Peyrou, Montpellier, constr. 1691-3 by d'Aviler after d'Orbay's designs. Placed in the arches over the false side doors, cf. A. Fliche, *Les villes d'art célèbres*, Montpellier, 1935; 'Le Peyrou', *Congrès Archéol.*, 1950, Montpellier, pp. 38-44.

On the side towards the Place du Peyrou, Military Triumphs. Left, Triumph over England and the Empire: Louis XIV as Hercules, crowned by Victory, crushes underfoot a dead warrior; the imperial eagle tries to escape. Right, the surrender of Mons and Namur: France triumphant, seated, laurel-crowned and holding a shield with a sun-face, receives the keys of the conquered towns, offered by a slave; a lion lies on the ground. On the town-side, the Triumph of Religion and an allegory of the construction of the Canal du Languedoc, showing the joining of the two Seas; cf. Mariette, *ABC*, I, p. 130; L. de la Roque, *Biogr. Montpell.*, 1887, pp. 102-4.

Wax models exh. Salon, 1704, *Livret*, p. 24.

MONTPELLIER, ARC DE TRIOMPHE DU PEYROU

5-9 see appendix

2a

2b

2c

2d

Ph. Bertrand

3a

8

3*
The Rape of Helen

1700–1   Bronze Group   H: 64.8
Comm. 30 Jan. 1700; sketch approved 27 Feb. *P-V*,
III, p. 287; full-size model, made under direction of
Boulongne the Elder and Van Clève, approved 7 Sept.
1700, *ibid.*, III, p. 300, 302. The bronze, pres. on 26 Nov.
1701, earned him the title 'Academician' and a gratuity
of 100 L., *ibid.*, III, p. 328. Exh. Salon 1704, no. 26; exh.
Acad., cf. *Descr. Acad.*, 1715, p. 4; 1781, p. 133; then in
the Museum, Arch. Nat., F[17] 1267. In 1803 in St.-Cloud,
Arch. Louvre S 12; Arch. Nat., O[2] 751, no. 125. Since
the Second Empire, in the Chât. de Fontainebleau, cf.
J. P. Samoyault, 'Les remplois de sculptures au Palais de
St.-Cloud', in *BSHAF*, 1971, p. 153–91. Engr. by
L. Desplaces after design by Natoire. Descr. by Guérin, in
Descr. Acad., 1715, p. 4. "Paris carries Helen in his arms;
the complaisance with which she looks at him suggests
that the rape was not against her will. A sailor in his boat
tries to cast off from the port where he awaited them".
Another version in the Hermitage, Leningrad.* The
work inspired the bronze group 'Rhea Sylvia abducted
by Mars' in the Louvre (some modifications).

3b

PALACE OF FONTAINEBLEAU, MUSEUM

5

6

4
Models for the Feet of Clocks

1701
In collab. with S. Slodtz. Payment 200 L., *Comptes*, III, 735; cf. F. Souchal, *Les Slodtz*, p. 596. Destroyed.

5
Tomb of Joseph Le Clerc de Lesseville

1702   Marble   154 × 97
Lenoir, in 1793, attrib. to Bertrand "a large bas-relief in white marble repr. Immortality, holding in one hand the medallion of a magistrate; beside him a sphere; on the other side a putto holding the medallion of his wife". From the convent of the Grands Augustins; stored at the Petits Augustins, cf. Courajod, *Lenoir*, II, p. 269; A. Lenoir, 'Cat du Dépôt des Petits Augustins', in *Arch. Mus. Mon. fr.*, II, p. 191; Millin, *Antiq. Nat.*, II, p. 28–9 mentions the tomb of J. Le Clerc de Lesseville as in the Convent of the Grands Augustins since 1702. It was attached to a wall, with a bas-relief like that descr. by Lenoir, in an architectural frame of black marble. J. Le Clerc de Lesseville died on 7 Sept. 1700; the tomb was erected by his widow, Marie Guyot, on 7 July 1702; engr.★ by Ransonnette, in Millin, *ibid.*, p. 1, IV, fig. 2. Destroyed.

6
Saint Satyrus

c. 1702   Statue   Plaster   Over life-size
For a round chapel at the Dôme des Invalides. Remained in plaster, like the other 11 statues planned for the niches. First payment in 1705, *Comptes*, III, 1177; final payment of 700 L. in 1709, *ibid.*, V, 349; cf. Félibien des Avaux, *Invalides*, p. 295; Granet, p. 111; Pérau p. 80. Repl. by a marble statue of the same subject by J.-J. Caffieri, cf. C. Dreyfus, 'Les Statues du Dôme des Inval. au 18ᵉˢ.' in *BSHAF*, 1908. The plaster model was put into store, then destroyed. Engr. by Cochin★, in Pérau and in Granet, pl. 78. Sketch in the Coll. de Cotte, Bibl. Nat. Est., Hc 14, 2. Destroyed.

7
Prometheus

1703   Group   Bronze   Signed & dated
Salon 1704, *Livret*, p. 27. One cast in the Royal Coll., England; another in the Art Trade.★

8
The Rape of Psyche

Before 1704   Group   Bronze
Salon 1704, *Livret*, p. 26. One cast in the Royal Coll., England★; another, without the caduceus, in the Hermitage, Leningrad. *See p. 51.*

7

9
Lucretia

Before 1704   Statue
Salon 1704, *Livret*, p. 22. Not ident. or disapp.

10
Portrait of Marie Meusnier, the artist's wife

Before 1704   Bust
Salon 1704, *Livret*, p.24. Not ident. or disapp.

11
Portrait of Jaques-Philippe Ferrand, miniaturist,
painter in enamel, 1655–1732

Before 1704   Bust
Salon 1704, *Livret*, p. 24. Not ident. or disapp.

12²

12
*Work on the Small Baldachins for the Bains
d' Apollon in the Bosquet du Marais, Versailles*

1705   Lead
The Small Baldachins protected the two groups of Sun-

12³

12¹

horses of the Bains d'Apollon. B. and a large team of sculptors, incl. Ph. Magnier, Vigier, Frémin (no. 13), Le Lorrain, Herpin, Chauveau (no. 27), S. Slodtz, Nourrisson, Tuby the younger, Raon, Robert, Varin, Fournier and Bercher, rec. for this decorative work 16,300 L. in 1711, *Comptes*, V, 538. The group of 'Apollon servi par les Nymphes' was placed between the Sun-horses, under a larger baldachin decor. by another team, cf. Bourdy no. 6. A drawing* by Martin in the Coll. de Cotte, Bibl. Nat. Est., Va 78 f, 4, repr. the Bosquet du Marais. A maquette* of one of the three baldachins in Versailles Mus., a drawing* in Stockholm, CC 2985.

13
Nymphs and Rocks

1706   Group   Lead
B. and Barois (no. 16) worked together on a group in lead and tin "two nymphs and rocks" for the Bassin des Perlées (des Sénateurs) in the park at Marly; total payment 2000 L. in two instalm., 1706 and 1711, *Comptes*, V, 41, 537. Destroyed.

14*
Air

1706–9   Statue   Marble   H: 146
One of six statues for the Cascade Champêtre (or Rustique), at Marly. cf. Barois no. 18*. B. rec. for 'Air', 2900 L. paid in several instalm. between 1706–09, *Comptes*, V, 41, 72, 240, 365, 510. Dispersed during the Revolution; saved by Lenoir, cf. Courajod, *Lenoir*, III, p. 321. Today the statue stands beside Barois' 'Pomona'. A young woman, almost nude; in her left hand a light drapery which the wind flaps round her hips; with the tips of her feet, she seems to skim the clouds which carry her, ready to fly away, her glance lost in the distance; her eagle gazes at her. The salamander which she held in her right hand has disappeared.

PARIS, GARDEN OF THE MINISTRY OF FOREIGN AFFAIRS

15
Portrait of Mabillon

Before 1707   Bust
This bust is the best-known of the many portrait engravings of the famous Benedictine (1632–1707). Profile on a medallion, designed and engr. by C-L. Simonneau after a carving by Bertrand*, Bibl. Nat. Est., N2; cf. Heinecke, *Dict. des artistes*, II, 1788. Whereabouts unknown.

14

16*
Heads of Cherubim

1707   Hard stone, gilded
B. did two of the ten cherubim heads on the keystones of the high windows of the chapel at Versailles; the

15

54

16

others were by P. Lepautre, G. Coustou (no. 20), Frémin (no. 16), Le Lorrain, Raon. Total payment 700 L., *Comptes*, V, 124. All the cherubim after the same model: the chubby head of a child framed by its wings.

VERSAILLES PALACE, CHAPEL

17
Group of Children

1707   Lead
In collab. with Frémin (no. 15), Le Lorrain, Raon, G. Coustou I (nos. 14/15★) and Lepautre; after models by Lepautre and Coustou. Payment 3,500 L., *Comptes*, V, 124. One of two groups at the ends of the ridge of the chapel roof.

VERSAILLES PALACE, CHAPEL

18a

18
a.★ Father of the Church

1707   Medallion   Bas-relief   Hard stone, gilded
Diam: 62
B. and the sculptors Chabry, G. Coustou (no. 19), Frémin (no. 17a), Le Lorrain and P. Lepautre were entrusted with the six medallions repr. Fathers of the Church: busts in three-quarter or full profile, inside the chapel, on the bottom frieze of the west wall and round the semidome of the apse, against a mosaic of fleurs-de-lis. For each medallion, exec. in 1707, payment of 150 L. in 1709 and 1710, *Comptes*, V, 321, 531, and Mém., Arch. Nat., O^I 1784.

VERSAILLES PALACE, CHAPEL

18b

b.★ Ecclesiastical Trophies
1707   Bas-relief   Hard stone, gilded   62 × 57
The 28 bas-reliefs on the same frieze and at the springing of the ribs of the vaulting, were carved by nine sculptors: B., Chabry, G. Coustou I (no. 18), Defer (no. 5), Frémin (no. 17b), Le Lorrain, P. Lepautre, Raon and Tuby the younger; they repr. the accessories for the celebration of mass, each individually different. Estim. 3,360 L., Mém., Arch. Nat., O^I 1784. Payment in 1711 for each trophy 120 L., *Comptes*, V, 124, 531.

VERSAILLES PALACE, CHAPEL

19

19*
Secrecy and Patience

1707–8   Bas-relief   Bonbanc stone   L: 194
Twenty-six figures of Virtues above the 13 windows of the Tribune were carved by B., Le Lorrain, Poirier, Lapierre, Frémin (no. 18), S. Slodtz, Thierry, Mazière, J.-L. Lemoyne, Lepautre, Poultier, G. Coustou (nos. 21, 22). The two by B. are on the south side over the third window from the entrance. Each is repr. by a sitting woman in a long tunic with traditional attribs. 'Secrecy'

has a seal, not the lamb descr. in the Mém., which was reserved for 'Humility' by Lapierre; 'Patience' carries a yoke on her shoulder. The whole work was estim. at 1,600 L., Mém., Arch. Nat., O^I 1784, and *Comptes*, V, 213, 319.

VERSAILLES PALACE, CHAPEL

20
Model for a Soleil of the Holy Sacrament

1707–8   H: 167
Contract of 14 Oct. 1707, B.'s fee 500 L., Min. Centr. Arch. Nat., Et. CV, 1083. After a design by de Cotte; exec. in silver gilt by Ballin le fils. Offering of Canon de la Porte. On the high altar in the choir of Notre-

20

21

Bertrand 22 (*Frémin 19*)

Dame, Paris. Engr: d'Argenson*, Bibl. Nat. Est., Va 254b. Repr. in a picture by Jouvenet: 'La Messe du chanoine de la Porte' in the Louvre. Many old *Descriptions*. An angel supported the monstrance with the Book of the Apocalypse and the Divine Lamb, surrounded by the Ancients; the celestial host in a glory of rays and cherubim heads. cf. Lefèvre, *Eglises de P.*, 1759, p. 285; Thiery, 1787, II, p. 113–4; P. Mantz, 'Hist. de l'Orfèvrerie fr., III, 18th c.', in *GBA*, 1861², p. 115. Destroyed.

21
Work for the Royal Tribune

1709
   a.* Culs-de-lampe
At the Royal Tribune two semicircular projections indicate the places for the King and Queen. For the ornamentation of the attached culs-de-lampe a number of tentative designs were submitted. B. suppl. two wax models 40×65; one of them repr. "the arms of the King supported by two angels sitting on clouds and a child holding palm and laurel branches"; the other was "a cartouche supported by three children holding palms and laurels with clouds"; Mém., Arch. Nat., O^I 1784. Payment 100 L., but B.'s design was rejected. Another model by Frémin (no. 24) was also unsuccessful. At last, in 1709, de Cotte decided in favour of "a rose on the ceiling" in hard limestone, diam. 97, the boss 21 high. The one on the right jointly by B. and Dumont (no. 1).
   b. Moulding
The same two sculptors were comm. to carve in limestone the pulvinated course "on the circular face of the above-mentioned tribune" consisting of "beads with palm leaves", and cyma recta and reversa. Estim. and payment for the total, 925 L. 10 s., Mém., Arch. Nat., O^I 1784 and *Comptes*, V, 530.

Bertrand 23 VERSAILLES PALACE, CHAPEL (*Frémin 19*)

282

22*
Allegory of Christ before Herod

1709   Bas-relief   Bonbanc stone   195 × 270
In the spandrel of the arcade supporting the Royal
Tribune, as a pendant to Frémin nos. 19, 20. One of 16
allegorical bas-reliefs evoking the Passion of Christ.
The others were done by: N. Coustou (nos. 55–6),
G. Coustou (no. 27), F. Dumont (no. 4), Cornu (no. 30),
Le Lorrain, Thierry, Frémin (no. 19), Poultier, Poirier,

P. Lepautre, Lapierre, L. Magnier, J.–L. Lemoyne,
Mazière. Descr. by B. in his Mém.: "an angel rising up
on clouds holding in one hand the robe of Our Lord,
accomp. by a child and a glory of three cherubim with
clouds". Estim. at 1200 L., Mém., Arch. Nat., O^I 1784,
paid in 1710 and 1711, *Comptes*, V, 319, 413, 530.

VERSAILLES PALACE, CHAPEL

23*
Trophy, related to the Appearance of Christ before Herod

1709   Bas-relief   Bonbanc stone   248 × 71
On the pillar underneath the great allegorical bas-relief
(no. 22). In most cases, the same sculptor was asked to do
a bas-relief of trophies corresp. to the scene above. Two
small nude angels, flying in the clouds, support the
cartouche illustrating the scene, attached to a long
ribbon with accessories of royal power: crown, palm,
sword, lance and the cap of the Prince of Princes; cf.
descr. in Mém., Arch. Nat., O^I 1784. Payment 750 L.,
Comptes, V, 319, 413, 530, 541.

VERSAILLES PALACE, CHAPEL

24
Model for Organ-case, Versailles Palace, Chapel

1709   Clay
B.'s Mém., Arch. Nat., O^I 1784, details his work, estim.
at 165 L. as: a bas-relief of King David playing the harp,
on the lid of the keyboard; two figures of victory
emerging from volutes, each sounding a trumpet and
supporting the arms of the King; the cornices of three
turrets; three groups of two infant musicians above
them; groups of cherubim heads and a rose for the culs-
de-lampe of the same turrets; lastly two cherubim heads
in full relief between the turrets. The execution in wood

281

in 1710 by Belan, Taupin, Dugoulon, Goupil and La Lande, largely followed this arrangement, but with five turrets, not three; the group of children above and the cherubim heads between the turrets were not retained. There were large palm-trees at the corners of the organ-case and trophies of music in bas-relief. Destroyed.

25
Model for Pulpit, Versailles Palace, Chapel

1709   Wax
In August 1709, B. made for the pulpit a small wax model, changed several times. Payment 100 L., Mém., Arch. Nat., O^I 1784. The sculptors Lapierre and Vassé were also asked to submit models. Destroyed.

26
Model for Archepiscopal Throne at Notre-Dame, Paris

1710–11   Wax
B. rec. for this work, 112 L. 1 s., incl. cutting some marble, *Comptes*, V, 510. Not ident. or disapp.

27
Work in the Vestibule, Versailles Palace, Chapel

1712   Stone
The *Comptes*, V, 590, record works of stone sculpture by B., Frémin and Offement "in the new vestibule near the chapel". Payment 588 L., not mentioned in the *Mém.* of the sculptors.

VERSAILLES PALACE, CHAPEL

28
Justice and Fortitude

1712–13   Bas-relief   Lead
In fulfilment of a Vow made by Louis XIII, when he hoped for the birth of a son, a grand programme for the re-decoration of the choir at Notre-Dame was entrusted in 1699 to de Cotte. It was taken up again between 1708–14 and comprised: 1.) marble sculptures: a Pietà by N. Coustou (no. 61), with Louis XIII by G. Coustou (no. 38) and Louis XIV by Coysevox (no. 98) kneeling in front of the Virgin, offering their kingdom; 2.) a new high altar with bronze ornaments and two kneeling angels by Cayot (no. 7a) and Vassé; 3.) six great bronze angels with the instruments of the Passion, by Flamen (no. 61), Hurtrelle, Poirier, Van Clève and Magnier; 4.) a glory in gilded lead at the back of the sanctuary by the brothers Coustou (N. Coustou no. 66); 5.) above the six arcades, 12 figures of Virtues in gilded lead and cherubim at the keystones by Poultier, Frémin (no. 28), P. Lepautre, J.-L. Lemoyne, P. Bertrand and Thierry; also ecclesiastical trophies in bas-relief on the pillars.

B. executed the two Virtues of Justice and Fortitude and rec., like each of the other sculptors, 300 L. for the cardboard model in 1712 and 150 L. for casting them in lead in 1713, *Comptes*, V, 610, 695. The works, mentioned in all the *Descr.* of Paris in the 18th c., were melted down during the Revolution, except the marble

sculptures and the six bronze angels. Engrs. of the choir of Notre-Dame by Delamonce and Blondel in Mariette, *Arch. Fr.*, pl. 1/2★. Destroyed.

29★
Zephyr and Flora

1713–26   Group   Marble   H: 232
In 1713, B. and Frémin (see no. 29) jointly rec. a comm. for a group for the Trianon gardens, *Comptes*, V, 695; for some years, only a full-size plaster model was in position; cf. Bibl. Nat. Est., Va 424, gr. fol., plan of the park of Trianon. In 1721, Frémin departed for Spain, B. fell ill; the sculptor Bousseau was comm. to complete the group which was only two-thirds finished, with two marble blocks of Flora and the child still incomplete, cf. Invent a.d., 14 March 1724, Et. IX, 624. After B.'s death, the group, estim. at 12,200 L., was sent to the Salle des Antiques in the Louvre, Arch. Nat., O^I 2220 and O^I 2226, accounts for 1720 and 1726. In 1769 the King offered it to Marigny for the park at Ménars, Arch. Nat., O^I 1251, Etat des grâces et dons, given by the King to the Marquis de Marigny, 26 Feb. 1769. Arch. Nat., Comité d'instr. publ., DXXXVIII, note by Pajou; and *Notice des stat. et bustes de marbre dans les jardins du chât. de Ménars prov. de la succ. de M. de Marigny*, 1788, no. 6, with engr. of the work. It remained on the terrace until 1881, when the property of the then owner, the Prince de Bauffremont, was seized and the statues sold by auction. Baron A. de Rothschild acq. the

29

31

group for 92,000 f. with the marble plinth added by the M. de Maginy, cf. E. Plantet, *La coll. de statues du M. de Marigny*, 1885, p. 114, 116, 130, 147–8; *NAAF*, VIII, 1892, 3rd ser., p. 123; Furcy-Raynaud, p. 301; F. Lesueur, *Ménars*, 1913, p. 97–9. The group shows Zephyr as a winged youth, flying towards the goddess Flora to crown her with flowers.

PRIVATE COLLECTION

30
Glory of Cherubim

1714 Gilded metal
In 1714, B. rec. 200 L., "for two angels made in lead for the choir of the church of Notre-Dame", *Comptes*, V, 787. This probably refers to one of the glories of cherubim above the trophies on the pillars; all these ornaments, "figures and trophies", were made in "gilded metal", see no. 28★. Destroyed.

31★
Allegorical Group

1714 Bronze, black patina H: 47 Signed
On 25 Aug. 1714, Abbé Juilhard du Jarry rec. from the Acad. Fr. a poetry prize at a special competition organised by a private donor. The subject was the transformation then taking place in the choir of Notre-Dame, Paris, in acc. with the vow of Louis XIII. The prize-winner was awarded a bronze group by B., commemorating the event. It repr. Fame flying above Religion, Piety and an angel, each of the three holding medallions with portraits of Louis XIII and Louis XIV; J.-G. Mann, *Wallace Coll., Cat. Sculpture*,

1931, p. 67–68. In the Arcambale sale, 22 Feb. 1776, Cat. no. 214; sold for 251 f.

LONDON, WALLACE COLLECTION

32
Christ

1714–15 Statue Lead Over life-size
During the reconstruction of la Samaritaine, the pump-house at the Pont Neuf, B. and Frémin (no. 30) were comm. to replace the old lead group by Etienne Blanchard (nos. 2 and 3) on the façade. Christ seated on the well-side, talking to the standing Samaritan woman. In 1714–15, 15,278 L. were paid to the sculptors for the figures of Christ by B. and the Samaritan woman by Frémin (no. 30), *Comptes*, V, 786, 874; Piganiol, *Descr.*, 1765, II, p. 52; F. Boucher, *Le Pont-Neuf*, 1925, I, p. 124–53. Numerous 18th c. engr. of the pump-house; drawing of the principal group in Stockholm, THC 261★; a maquette★ from the end of the 18th c. in Mus. Carnavalet. Destroyed, together with the pump-house, in 1813.

33 34 35 36
Spring Summer Autumn Winter

Four Busts Marble H: 80
In the Beaujon sale, 25 Apr. 1787, cat. no. 163. These busts, "forte nature", carried attribs. characterising the seasons. "Believed to be by Philippe Bertrand". Bought by Donjeux for 975 L. Perhaps re-sold after his death,

32¹

sale 29 Apr. 1793, no. 498 or 499. Whereabouts un-known.

37
Vulcan Seated

Group   Terracotta
Julienne sale, 20 Mar. 1767, no. 1296, descr. in cat. as "Vulcan seated, forging a helmet at the request of Venus, who stands behind him with a cupid holding a sword". Whereabouts unknown.

38
The Massacre of the Innocents

Group   Terracotta
Sold with no. 37 at the Julienne sale. A group of "five figures repr. the massacre of the innocents". Like the 'Seated Vulcan' it was placed on a pedestal done in marquetry of scales with gilded bronze attachments. Whereabouts unknown.

SCULPTURE FOUND IN B.'S STUDIO AFTER HIS DEATH, not previously listed

Invent. a.d. 14 March 1724, Min. Centr. Arch. Nat., Et. IX, 624.

Acis and Galatea

Marble
Val. at 300 L. Not ident. or disapp.

32²

THE BLANCHARDS Etienne: (1632–93); Jacques (1634–89)

Etienne b. 7 Oct. 1632, son of Jean, sculptor. God-mother: the wife of Simon Lerambert, Sculptor to the King. His brother Jacques b. 26 Sept. 1634. Godfather: Jacques Sarrazin, godmother: the wife of Simon Guillain. Bibl. Nat. Fich. Laborde 3439, 5426. Etienne married Marie Berthault in 1661; died 22 Nov. 1693. Jacques married Toussainte Morel in 1662; died 22 Oct. 1689, leaving a son, André, a painter. cf. Herluison, p. 37–8; Jal, p. 224; Piot, *Etat civil de quelques art. fr.*, 1873 p. 13. In the *Comptes*, the Christian name is not always given. T-B, IV, 1910, p. 92–3 (Lami).

I
Decoration of Bassins at Chantilly

1664–7
At the five bassins designed by Desgots for the terrace at Chantilly, Jean and Etienne B. carved shells, lion's muzzles and various figures as ornaments, mentioned in Dom Loppin's letters, 4 & 24 Apr. 1664, 13 Nov. 1667, cf. G. Mâcon, *Arts dans la maison Condé*, 1903, p. 22. Destroyed.

2   3
Christ and the Samaritan Woman

1665–6   Statues   Lead
Payment of 1,200 L. to Etienne B. for replacing statues attrib. to Germain Pilon on the façade of la Samaritaine, the pump-house at the Pont Neuf in Paris, *Comptes*, I, 75, 132; Brice, 1684, p. 298; F. Boucher, *Le Pont Neuf*, Paris, 1925, p. 133. The group was later replaced by one made by P. Bertrand and Frémin (see Bertrand no. 32★). Destroyed.

4
Thirteen Busts

1670   Marble
In 1670, the *Comptes*, I, 474, show a payment of 2413 L. 10 s. to "Des Essarts, Moussy, B. and others for marble busts supplied to the King", then 3500 L. to B. alone, without Christian name, "for thirteen white marble busts sold to the King and delivered to his store", *ibid.*, I, 480. Moussy was a moulder, Desessarts a sculptor; the first busts may not have been marble. Not ident. or disapp.

5★
Several Animals for the Labyrinth at Versailles

1672–5   Lead and tin
    a. Twelve small dolphins. 1672. Payment 480 L., *Comptes*, I, 624.
    b. Several animals and birds. 1673–4. Payment 2920 L., *ibid.*, I, 618, 696; *NAAF*, 1876, p. 53; for the Fountain of the Peacock and Magpie and the Bassin of the Monkey. cf. A. Marie, *Naissance de Vers.*, I, p. 126–7.

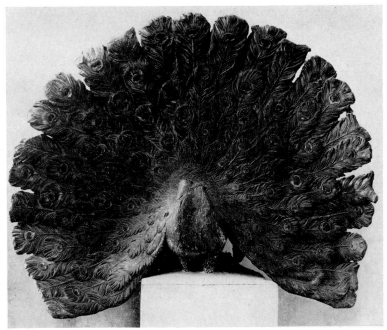

5b¹

5a

5b²

8

Most of these have disappeared; among the remains of animals from the Labyrinthe, three have been attrib. to the Blanchards: the peacock spreading its tail★ and two dolphins★. Engr.★ of 'La Fable du Paon et de la Pie' by S. Leclerc.

VERSAILLES, MUSEUM

c. *Several small birds and animals*. 1675. Payment 193 L., *ibid.*, I, 876, for the 'machine de la Fable d'Esope'. The *Comptes* refer to "the Blanchards". cf. Félibien des Avaux, *Versailles*, p. 230; P. de Nolhac, *La Création de Vers.*, 1901, p. 142; J. Wilhelm, 'Le Labyrinthe de Vers.', in *B. Mus. Fr.*, 1936, p. 44–63. Destroyed.

6
Work at the Château de Clagny

1675
Payment 512 L., *Comptes*, I, 846; II, 160. Destroyed.

7
Models for the Fontaine de l'Encelade, Versailles

1676
In collab. with Mazeline, payment 312 L., *Comptes*, I, 902. The existing groups for the fountain (in lead) are by Marsy. Destroyed.

8
Ornaments for Two Lanterns above the Roof at Versailles

1679   Lead
In collab. with Mazeline and Houzeau, payment 2200 L., *Comptes*, I, 1157. Drawing★ of the roof and the lanterns of the pavilions in the forecourt in Arch. Nat., O¹ 1768. Destroyed.

9★
Cornice and Ornaments

For the Salons at the end of the Great Gallery and the Grand Salon of the Queen's Apartment.

1679   Stucco
In collab. with Mazeline and Houzeau. Payment 2500 L., *Comptes*, I, 1157.

VERSAILLES, PALACE

9

10^{I}

10
Work at the Bosquet of the Arc de Triomphe

1678–80   Lead, tin and marble
In collab. with Mazeline and Houzeau, payment
53,337 L. 13 s., *Comptes*, I, 1157, 1283 "for the fountain
at the Arc de Triomphe and work on the Pyramids".
Contract with the three sculptors for the fountains
of Victory and Glory, Arch. Nat., O^{I} 1790. cf. P. de
Nolhac, *La Création de Vers.*, p. 168 and *Hist. du Chât. de
Vers.*, 1911, p. 40. Drawing of the Bosquet de l'Arc de
Triomphe in the Cab. Dessins, Louvre, no. 9799★.
The Fontaine de la Gloire was engr.★ by Thomassin,

pl. 131. Several sanguine drawings★ for the ornaments
on the Fontaine de l'Arc de Triomphe and on the
Obelisk in Bibl. Nat., Va 78 f, 4. Destroyed.

11
Moulds of Groups of Children and other figures for the Bassins of Venus and Thetis

1685   Plaster
Two bassins at the Parterre d'eau, at that time dedicated
to the Triumphs of Venus and Thetis. 'Blanchard'
(no first name) rec. 1100 L., *Comptes*, II, 628. Destroyed.

10^3 *Thomassin* 10^2 10^3

1

BOURDERELLE, or BOURDEREL, David (1651-1706)

b. Eu 11 Nov. 1651; son of Michel B., and Catherine Anguier, sister of François, Michel and Guillaume Anguier. In 1686 he inherited the house and studio of François and Michel Anguier in the rue Neuve Saint-Honoré. Married on 10 July 1687 Antoinette Fromentel, daughter of a wood-corder (mouleur de bois), Min. Centr. Arch. Nat., Et. XXXV, 347. Agréé by the Acad. 28 Aug. 1683; made member 31 Dec. 1688, *P-V*, II, p. 251, 386. Died 8 Feb. 1706, Herluison, p. 53, leaving four young children. Invent. a.d. 3 Mar. 1706, Min. Centr. Arch. Nat., Et. X, 278. Valuation by C. Van Clève of the sculpture in his studio (mostly by the brothers Anguier). T-B, IV, 1910, p. 455 (Lami).

1*
Saint Matthew

1688
    a. Oval medallion   Marble   65 × 50
Recept. piece for the Acad., pres. 31 Dec. 1688, *P-V*, II, p. 786. Exh. in the Acad., Guérin, *Descr.*, p. 45. The saint, writing the gospel, looks at an angel behind him who holds an inkpot and seems to be dictating to him.

VERSAILLES, CHURCH OF NOTRE-DAME

    b. *Two clay maquettes*
Submitted by the sculptor to the Acad. 8 Nov. 1687, *P-V*, II, p. 365. Whereabouts unknown.

2
Metopes on the Dôme des Invalides

1690–1   Bas-reliefs   Stone
Acc. to Félibien des Avaux, *Invalides*, p. 296, B. did "half of the metopes on the main façade of the Invalides". Perhaps this is the "stone sculpture at the church of the Invalides" for which he rec. 250 L. in 1691, *Comptes*, III, 557. cf. Barois no. 10a*.

PARIS, DOME DES INVALIDES

3

3*
Angels holding Liturgical Implements

1698–9   Bas-relief   Stone   140 × 230
Payment 450 L., *Comptes*, II, 701; IV, 472. Arch. Nat., O¹ 1665, 36, 37. One of the twelve groups above the niches in the circular side-chapels; the others were by Granier, Poirier, Prou, Renard, Rousselet and S. Slodtz. cf. Félibien des Avaux, *Invalides*, p. 296.

PARIS, DOME DES INVALIDES

BOURDY or BOURDICT, Pierre (16?–after 1711)

b. probably in Lyon. His sister Claude was the second wife of Coysevox. B. went to Paris, perhaps following his brother-in-law. 21 Oct. 1684, 3rd Acad. sculpture prize, *P-V*, II, p. 288; 3 Sept. 1685, 2nd prize, see no. 1. 8 Jan. 1686 arrives in Rome as pensionnaire of the Acad. Roy., together with Doisy and Z. Adam, cf. *Corr. Dir. Acad. Fr. Rome*, IV, p. 418 and H. Lapauze, *Hist. de l'Acad.*, I, p. 94–116; on 25 Apr. 1690, left Rome for Paris. Active on royal work sites until 1711. In March 1693 he was in Germany, Arch. Nat., O¹ 2773, 1. T-B, IV, 1910, p. 459–60 (Lami). From 1700–06 B. worked in Lorraine for Duke Léopold. By brevet dd. 1.1.1700 appointed 'First Architect and Director of Sculpture'; in 1702, 'First Prof. at Acad. of Painting and Sculpt.'. In 1700 designed and organised the Funeral Service in Nancy of Duke Charles V, of whom in 1702 he made 2 marble busts, since disapp. Prov. many drawings for the internal decor. of Lunéville Palace.

I
The Building of Noah's Ark

1685
2nd Acad. Sculpture prize, *P-V*, II, p. 306. Not ident. or disapp.

2*
The Tiber

1687–9   Group   Marble   163 × 317
Signed P. BOURDICT
Copy of an antique found in Rome. In 1715, shortly before his death, Louis XIV had B.'s copy installed in the gardens at Marly, *Corr. Dir. Acad. Fr. Rome*, IV, p. 418. Under the Regency, trsf. from Marly to the Tuileries gardens, as a pendant to the 'Nile' by Lorenzo Ottone, copied at the same time. "Holding in one hand an oar, in the other a cornucopia filled with a variety of fruit, he leans on a she-wolf which is suckling Romulus and Remus." Invent. 1722, Arch. Nat., O¹ 1969 A, p. 202–3. cf. *Rich. Art. Fr., Mon. civ.*, IV, p. 214. (The antique original went to the Louvre under Napoleon.)

PARIS, TUILERIES GARDENS

3
Virtue

1691   Statue   Lead
Payment 452 L., in 1691, *Comptes*, IV, 560; one of the four figures on the lantern of the Dôme des Invalides; the three others were by N. Coustou (no. 9), Flamen (no. 26), and Granier. cf. Félibien des Avaux, *Invalides*, p. 59 (*Descr.* without attrib.). The lantern and the Virtues are shown in an anon. engr. of the façade of the Dôme (detail*), Bibl. Nat. Est., Va 271, 3. Melted down in 1793.

2

TION DU PO | *RTAIL ET DI*
se de l'hostel | *Royal des J*

3

Comptes, V, 347. cf. Félibien des Avaux, *Invalides*, p. 296; Granet, p. 109; Pérau, p. 82. Three panels, on each side of the double door, decorated with medallion monograms of St. Louis, winged angels' heads and the arms of France; the latter were re-carved after the Revolution. cf. *Rich. Art Fr., Mon. Relig.*, III, p. 233.

PARIS, DOME DES INVALIDES

4*
Sculpture on the Door of the Dôme des Invalides

1706   Wood, stone, lead and marble
In collab. with Louis-Armand Collignon, Monthéan, Nourrisson and J. Rousseau. Total payment 17,365 L.,

5
Sculpture at the Entrance to the Hôtel Soubise

1705   Stone
  a. *Hercules crushing Cacus, Minerva crushing Gorgon*
Two groups, St.-Leu stone   H: c. 260
  b. *Children and lions supporting an escutcheon*
St.-Leu stone
  c. *Two trophies in bas-relief*
  d. *Eight capitals*
  e. *Eight free-standing trophies*
  f. Head of Abundance in a shield*. Keystone of the portal.
  g. *Console in a shield.* Keystone of the portal. All in collab. with G. Coustou I (no. 9*). Estim. and contract 14 July and 21 Nov. 1705, Min. Centr. Arch. Nat., Et. XCIX. Engr. of the entrance portal of the Hôtel by Delamair*. Total payment 3300 L., cf. *Descriptions* by Piganiol, Brice, etc. Destroyed except for the head of Abundance (5f), still at the Hôtel Soubise, Paris. Acc. to the contract, the models were by Coysevox (*see appendix after no. 85*).

4

5

5f

6
Great Baldachin for the Bains d' Apollon

1705–7   Lead and tin
In collab. with G. Coustou I (no. 8), J.-L. Lemoyne, Granier, Thierry, Mazière, Rousseau, Monthéan, Armand, Dugoullon, J. Desjardins and Langlois. Designed to shelter the group "Apollon servi par les nymphes" in the Bosquet du Marais, *Comptes*, V, 538.

See also P. Bertrand no. 12★. Lost during the re-arrangements by H. Robert.

7★
Saint Barnabus

1707–8   Statue   Stone   H: 300
On the outside balustrade of the chapel, Mém., Arch. Nat., O^I 1784. Payment 500 L., *Comptes*, V, 123.

VERSAILLES PALACE, CHAPEL

7

9

8

8*
Two Child Angels

1708 Bas-relief Stone 320×345
"Sitting on clouds, holding a mitre, attribute of St. Augustine", Mém., Arch. Nat., O^I 1784. Payment 800 L., *Comptes*, V, 213. Heavily restored at the beginning of the 20th c.

VERSAILLES PALACE, CHAPEL

9
Work in the Chapel, Versailles

1708–9 Bas-reliefs Stone
Mém., Arch. Nat., O^I 1784. Payment 1660 L., *Comptes*, V, 319, 526, plus 400 L., shared with Martin and Mazeline, *ibid.*, V, 319. In the last vault of the side aisle:
a.* "Grande rose en forme de cul de lampe . . . ornée de feuilles de refentes et feuille d'eau et graine renfermée d'une bordure d'architecture et accompagné de grands ornemens fort riches composé de platte-bandes et roulleaux dont naissent des feuilles de refente et les bandes renfermans plusieurs fleurons et se termine en saustoir avec des roulleaux d'où sortent plusieurs fleurons, feuilles de refentes et feuilles d'olive". Diam.: c. 100.
b. "un cordon qui renforme led. cul de four ou calotte . . . ornemens . . . composez de feuilles de refentes en tournant des Baguettes, au dessus dud. cordon est un tallon en doucine orné d'un rez de coeur de feuille refendue".

VERSAILLES PALACE, CHAPEL

BUIRETTE, Jacques (1631–1699)

b. Paris 1631, baptised 2 Mar. at St.-Jean-en-Grève; son of Claude Buirette, joiner, and Anne Tuby (app. not

Detail

related to the sculptor Tuby, born at Rome during the same period). His teacher was his godfather, Sarrazin. In c. 1660 the sculptor Martin Desjardins worked under B.'s direction, esp. on the decorative work for the great staircase of the Hôtel Salé, rue de Thorigny, *Mém. inéd.*, I, p. 387. Agréé by the Acad. 27 Aug. 1661; made Academician 2 June 1663, *P-V*, I, p. 184, 228; became blind towards the end of his life; found refuge at the Hospice des Quinze-Vingts, where he rec. from the King a yearly bounty of 150 L., *Comptes*, IV, 128, 274, 417; died 3 Mar. 1699; buried 4 Mar. in the church of the Hospice, cf. Jal, p. 292–3; Herluison, p. 60; Mariette, *ABC*, I, p. 205; Lépicié, obit. in *AAF.*, III, 1853–5, p. 72; Florent le Comte, *Cabinet*, III, p. 142; T-B, V, 1911, p. 212 (Lami); M. Digard, *J. Sarrazin*, 1934, p. 258. Antoine Benoît painted B.'s portrait for his reception into the Acad.; now in the Mus. at Versailles*.

I
Saint John and the Virgin

Before 1660   Two statues   (Wood?)
The old *Descr.* of Paris attrib. to B. the two figures of the Virgin and St. John on either side of a wooden crucifix by Sarrazin, above the door of the choir of the Church of St.-Gervais in Paris, which therefore must have been made before Sarrazin's death in 1660. "These are masterpieces" wrote Piganiol, *Descr.*, 1765, p. 133. Disappeared during the Revolution.

2*
Union of Painting and Sculpture

1661–3   Bas-relief   Marble   78 × 76
Reception piece for the Acad. roy., *P-V*, I, pp. 179, 184, 228, cf. Guérin and Dezallier, *Descr. Acad.*, p. 41, 191. Two young women with allegorical attribs. A copy, in an oval medallion, is in a Private Coll.

PARIS, LOUVRE

3*
Tomb of Louis-Emmanuel de Valois, Duc d'Angoulême

1661–3   White and black marble and bronze   440 × 390
L.-E. de Valois (1596–1651), grandson of King Charles IX and Marie Touchet, was successively Bishop of Agde, Colonel-General of the Light Cavalry of France and Governor of Provence. His widow, Henriette de La Guiche, commissioned B. by contract 19 Dec. 1661, Min. Centr. Arch. Nat., Et. XXVI, 101; the monument was placed in the church of the Convent of the Minimes de La Guiche (Saône et Loire), acc. to the wish of the deceased. The tomb, attrib. by local tradition to a Genoese sculptor, was mutilated during the Revolution; publ. L. Lex, 'Le mausolée de Louis de Valois' in *RSBAD*, 1894, p. 950–6 (without identifying the artist). Acc. to the contract, the monument consisted of Ionic columns supporting an entablature and a tympanum. The base of the monument was covered by a lion's skin in bronze surrounding the engraved epitaph; on top of the

2

3

3

sarcophagus reclined the effigy of the deceased in ducal armour and coat, wearing the orders of St.-Michael and of the St.-Esprit; at his feet, a kneeling putto in tears, leaning on a helmet. On the tympanum, the Duke's coat of arms with cavalry trophies. Extant today only three slightly chipped pieces. During the Restoration in a niche in the Chapel of the Convent, now the Parish Church. cf. F. Souchal, 'Mon. funér. du duc d'Angoulême et d'Hardouin-Mansart' in *BSHAF*, 1972, p. 155–9.

LA GUICHE (SAÔNE-ET-LOIRE), PARISH CHURCH

4
Trophies and Bas-reliefs for the Porte Saint-Antoine

1672–3
Payment 1450 L., Arch. Nat., KK 492 fol. 61. The old *Descr.* of Paris do not mention B.'s participation. Engr. of the Porte St.-Antoine by Simonneau le fils★. Destroyed.

3

4

5★
Work on the Fontaine de la Renommée, Versailles

1678–9   Plaster, lead and tin
  a. *Maquette of one of the Cabinets de la Renommée*
B. rec. 780 L. in 1677, *Comptes*, I, 959, 962.
    b. Lead and tin ornaments in one of the pavilions,

most of them, damaged; in the Mus., Versailles★.
  c. *Models of the bronze trophies* between the pilasters of the pavilions; coats of arms repr. the four continents. Estim. by B., Lespingola and the founder Ladoyreau: Arch. Nat., O¹ 1790. Nos. 5b & c in collab. with Lespingola, total payment 21,450 L., *Comptes*, I, 1050, 1151, 1284. Several drawings★ for a.) b.) c.) in Bibl. Nat. Est., Va 78 f, 5. Destroyed, except for three recently acquired bronze fragments★ in the Mus., Versailles.

6★
Democracy

1681–3   Statue   Stone   H: more than 200
One of the statues on the south wing, Versailles. B. certainly made another one: not identified. Payments: 1681, 300 L., *Comptes*, II, 11; 1682, 300 L. *ibid.*, II, 137; 1683, 460 L., "for another stone figure repr. Democracy and two masks", *ibid.*, II, 310. Le Brun's sketch in the Louvre, Cab. des dessins, Guiffrey-Marcel, *Invent.* no. 6016★; on the back in old handwriting: 'Burette'. At the same time B. made other unspecified sculptures in the south wing, again in collab. with Lespingola; in 1681, they rec. 800 L., "for their works", *Comptes*, II, 11. cf. F. Souchal, 'Versailles', in *GBA*, 1972¹, p. 90.

VERSAILLES, PALACE

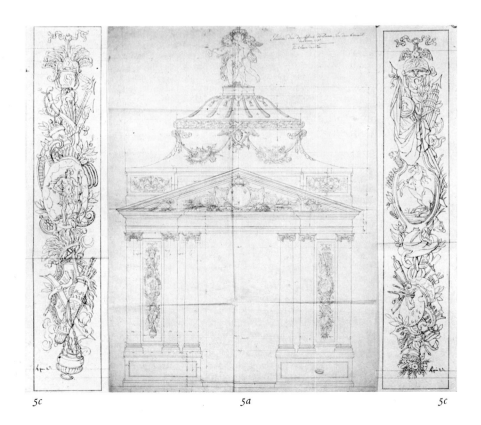

5c   5a   5c

5b

5b

5b

5c

5c

7
Two Masks

1681–3   Stone
For the keystones of the windows in the south wing.
Payment, cf. *supra*.

VERSAILLES, PALACE

8
Several Trophies of Arms

1682–93   Models   Clay
In collab. with Lespingola
    a.★ for the Salon de la Guerre, payment 1600 L.,
Comptes, II, 139, 277. Ladoyreau made the bronzes in
1683, *ibid.*, II, 279.
    b. for the Grande Galerie. Six large models repr.
"des trophées et chuttes d'armes", payment 3300 L. in
1693, *Comptes*, III, 869. Cast and positioned in 1702.

VERSAILLES, PALACE

5c

62

61

9
Work in the Apartment of the Prince de Vermandois

1682
In collab. with Lespingola. Payment 2366 L., *Comptes*, II, 172. The prince, legitimatised son of the King and Louise de la Vallière, occupied an attic apartment in the south wing at Versailles; he died in 1683. Destroyed.

10*
Amazon

1685–93 Statue Marble H: over 200
After an antique; original in the Mus. of the Capitol, Rome. B. worked from a cast. First account in 1685, *Comptes*, II, 623. Total payment in 1693, 8800 L. incl. a marble vase, cf. *ibid.*, III, 807. The Amazon was placed in the Allée Roy. She holds her bow with both hands, not with one, as in the antique model.

VERSAILLES, PARK

11*
Vase

1685–93 Marble H: over 200
After a model by Hardouin-Mansart, Arch. Nat., O^I 2772. Decorated with vine branches; the handles are women's heads crowned with ivy. In the parterre of the Orangery, opposite the Pièce d'eau des Suisses. Raon made a similar one. Payment at the same time as the Amazon, cf. *supra*.

VERSAILLES, PARK

for 9–11 see appendix.

8

10

14

11

12
Vase for the Gardens of the Grand Trianon

1687   Marble
B. rec. 400 L. in 1687 "for a marble vase for Trianon",
Comptes, II, 1173. Not ident. or disapp.

13
Two Capitals

1687   Marble
One Ionic capital for a column, the other for a pilaster;
payment 440 L., *Comptes*, II, 1173; III, 92. cf. André
no. 11★.

VERSAILLES, GRAND TRIANON

14★
Group of Children

1687   Model   Clay and wax   H: 142
In collab. with Lespingola. Cast in bronze by Aubry for
the Bassins of the Parterre d'eau. Three children
standing on dolphins. Payment 1000 L., *Comptes*, II,
1173; III, 92.

VERSAILLES, PARK

16

15

18

17

15
Work for the Funeral Service of the Grand Condé

1687   Plaster and cardboard
Ornamentation for the triumphal arch erected at the
door of the choir for the funeral service of the Prince
de Condé at Notre-Dame in Feb. 1687; B. made two
figures on pedestals between two columns, one more
than 200 high repr. Memory, seated on trophies,
writing on a shield; also nine trophies to be put above
the cornice. Payment 1100 L., contract 4 Feb. 1687,
Min. Centr. Arch. Nat., Et. XCII, 152. Engr.★ of the
funeral service of the Prince de Condé by Dolivar.
Destroyed.

16
The Wrestlers

Two small groups in bronze after antique works. *Gal.
Girardon*, pl. 4, no. 14, engr.★ by Charpentier. Not
ident. or disapp.

17
The Nile

Small bronze, after an antique. *Gal. Girardon*, pl. 1,
no. 22, engr.★ by Charpentier. Not ident. or disapp.

18
Laocoon

Small bronze after the antique. *Gal. Girardon*, pl. 2,
no. 38, engr.★ by Charpentier. Not ident. or disapp.

19
Hercules driving out Vice

Bas-relief   Plaster
Claimed for the King of Sweden by Tessin in his letter
to Cronström, 17 May 1693, cf. *Tessin–Cronström
Corresp.*, p. 19, incl. also a plaster cast of B.'s bas-relief
'La Peinture et la Sculpture'. Not ident. or disapp.

CARLIER, Martin (16?-after 1700)

b. Piennes (Somme). To Rome in 1675 as pensionnaire of the Acad. Fr. The director Errard reported unfavourably on him, *Corr. Dir. Acad. Fr. Rome*, I, p. 63. Playing in the Forum he had his sword stolen, *ibid.*, p. 70; sent down by the Acad., then reinstated, *ibid.*, p. 77. Returned to France in 1680. Witness to the marriage of Lespingola in 1697 (his signature is preserved); at the time he lived in the Rue St.-Vincent, parish of St.-Roch; cf. Herluison, p. 250. Not mentioned in the *Comptes* after 1700. René Carlier, pupil of de Cotte and First Architect to King Philippe V of Spain from 1710–22, was probably his son and François-Antoine Carlier, Architect to Ferdinand VI, his grandson. T-B, V, 1911, p. 607 (H. Vollmer).

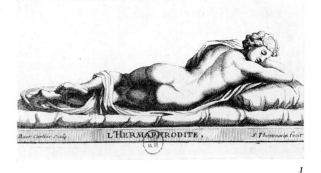

1

I
Hermaphrodite

1679–80   Statue   Marble
Copied at Rome from the antique in the Coll. Borghese; sent to France, *Corr. Dir. Acad. Fr. Rome*, I, p. 130; engr by Thomassin*, pl. 41. Must soon have disappeared from Versailles, as it is not mentioned in the old *Descr.* of Paris. Not ident. or disapp.

2
Ganymede

1679–80   Model for a Statue
Modelled by C. after an antique, executed by Joly; Joly's marble was sent from Rome to the Bosquet de l'Etoile, Versailles, where it still stands; *Corr. Dir. Acad. Fr. Rome*, I, p. 133. Probably destroyed.

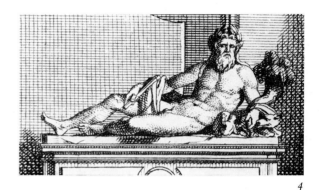

4

3*
Vases, Shells and Masks

1682   Metal   H. of Vase: 150
C. made eight vases, six shells and eight masks for the balustrade of the 'Bassin sous le Dragon', the future 'Bassin de Neptune', *Comptes*, II, 140, 278; III, 948, 1004.

VERSAILLES, PARK

5

4
The Tiber

Small bronze
Copied at Rome after an antique. cf. *Gal. Girardon*, pl. 6, no. 11, engr. by R. Charpentier*. Not ident. or disapp.

5
The Nile

Small bronze
Copied at Rome after an antique. cf. *Gal. Girardon*, pl. 6, no. 13, engr. by R. Charpentier*. Not ident. or disapp.

6
Two Groups at Marly

1683–4   Stucco
On the façade of the pavilions.
Payment 900 L., *Comptes*, II, 367, 522. Destroyed.

7*
Urania

1684   Statue   Marble   H: over 200
Copied from an antique in Rome. The muse of Astronomy, "holding in one hand a telescope, and in the other a paper scroll with the signs of the Zodiac", Piganiol, *Vers.-Marly*, 1764 II, p. 85. C. rec. 2300 L., *Comptes*, II, 440, 625, 992; the balance incl. other works, *ibid.*, III, 948. Engr. by Thomassin, pl. 51. Stands at the Bassin de Latone. *See appendix.*

VERSAILLES, PARK

3

3

7

8b

12a

8
Venus de Medici

1685–6
    a. *Marble statue*
After an antique. In the park at Versailles, acc. to *Comptes*, III, 968, 1004. Payment in 1694, incl. other works. Whereabouts unknown.
    b. *Wax Model*
After the antique. cf. *Gal. Girardon*, pl. 3, no. 5; engr. by R. Charpentier★ as a pendant to Meleager (no. 14). Not ident. or disapp. *See appendix.*

9

9★
La Paix des Grecs

1685–8   Group   Marble   H: c. 200
After an antique in the Villa Ludovisi, Rome. This group of two people holding hands, one dressed in a toga, the other almost nude, has been interpreted as repr. the two emperors, Marcus Aurelius and his brother Lucius Verus, curiously entitled 'The Peace of the Greeks and Romans'. Others see it as Papirius and his mother, referring to an episode recounted by Gellius extolling the young man's discretion. Later the group was called 'Orestis and Electra' (Winckelmann). The copy was begun in collab. with Monnier. Payments 1700 L. in 1685; 800 L. in 1686; 900 L. to C. alone in 1688; *Comptes*, II, 626, 993; III, 93. Final payment incl. other works in 1694, *ibid.*, III, 948. First in the Salle de Bal; today in the Demi-Lune in front of the Tapis-Vert. Drawings in Stockholm, THC 3723, 5132; engr. by Thomassin, no. 56. Piganiol, *Vers-Marly*, 1764, II, p. 151–2; Soulié, III, p. 510. *See appendix.*

VERSAILLES, PARK

10
Two Supporting Feet for a Basin

1685   Marble
C. made two feet for a basin at the Colonnade begun by Monnier; payment 800 L., *Comptes*, II, 992, 1174. cf. Cornu no. 17★.

VERSAILLES, PARK

11
Four Capitals

1687–8
For the Grand Trianon "two square Ionic pilaster capitals and two Ionic corner capitals"; payment 746 L., *Comptes*, II, 1174; III, 93. cf. André no. 11★.

VERSAILLES, GRAND TRIANON

14   15   16   17

12
Work at the Dôme des Invalides

1691–9   Stone
  a★. Sculpture above the two great windows of the upper order of the south façade (trophies and piles of arms); payment 480 L., *Comptes*, III, 423.
  b. Models for *Eight hanging keystones* in the aisles of the chapels under the ceiling, in collab. with André (no. 12). Payment 720 L., *Comptes*, III, 560, 703, 843. Destroyed.
  c. Two vaults in the aisles of the chapels; payment 1200 L., *Comptes*, III, 703, 846; IV, 472; Félibien des Avaux, *Invalides*, p. 297. Drawing in Bibl. Nat. Est., Hc 14, 2★.

PARIS, DOME DES INVALIDES

13
Work at the Château de Meudon

1699–1700
  a. *Stucco cornice for the salon of the Dauphin's Apartment*
In collab. with Lespingola, payment 1080 L., *Comptes*, IV, 545, 676; cf. P. Biver, *Hist. du Chât. de Meudon*, Paris, 1923, p. 154. Destroyed.
  b. *"Modèles de bronze des cheminées et réparage des cires"*
In collab. with Lespingola, payment 375 L., *Comptes*, IV, 479, cf. P. Biver, *op. cit.*, p. 152. Destroyed.

14
Meleager

Wax model after an antique, cf. *Gal. Girardon*, pl. 3, no. 5, engr. by R. Charpentier★. Whereabouts unknown.

15
Cupid Riding a Centaur

Wax model after an antique, cf. *Gal. Girardon*, pl. 3, no. 11. engr. by R. Charpentier★. Whereabouts unknown.

16
Borghese Faun

Wax model after an antique, cf. *Gal. Girardon*, pl. 1, no. 8, engr. by R. Charpentier★. Whereabouts unknown.

17
David

Wax model, holding the head of Goliath. cf. *Gal. Girardon*, pl. 1, no. 42., engr. by R. Charpentier★. Whereabouts unknown.

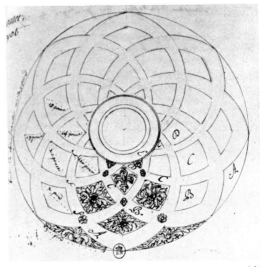

12c

CAYOT or CAILLOT, Claude-Augustin (1677–1722)

b. Paris 1667, son of Nicolas, carver and sculptor in wood, Fich. Laborde 12063; acc. to Fontenai, *Dict.*, I, p. 341 he studied painting with Jouvenet, then sculpture with Le Hongre; 29 Dec. 1691, Third sculpture prize, *P-V*, II, p. 78; 3 Sept. 1695, first prize for a bas-relief (see no. 1); 1 Sept. 1696, another first prize (second prize went to G. Coustou), for a bas-relief (see no. 2). He was not a pensionnaire at the Acad. Fr. in Rome, as incorrectly stated by Fontenai, Lami and others. Acc. to Fontenai, for 14 years collaborator of Van Clève who was present at his marriage to Anne Hamelin on 13 Aug. 1714 as a friend and witness, Fich. Laborde 12063. Presented himself to the Acad. 26 Jan. 1709; agréé 26 July, 1710; made Academician 31 Dec. 1711, *P-V*, IV, p. 76, 108, 137; took the oath before the Director Van Clève; Asst. Prof. 26 Oct. 1720, *ibid.*, IV, p. 304. In 1719, submitted estim. for the sculpture in the chapel of St.-Denis at the entry of the choir of Notre-Dame in Paris, but the contract went to Monthéan and Offement, Bibl. Nat. Est., Hd 135a, pet. in fol. (papiers de Cotte).

Lived in the rue Fromenteau in 1691, Fich. Laborde 10148; rue St.-Thomas du Louvre in 1701, *ibid.*, 10147; in the rue du Roule at the time of his death, 6 Apr. 1722. He was then a widower with the rank of 'Sculpteur Ordinaire du Roi' and of 'Entrepreneur dans

3c

les Bâtiments du Roi', Jal, p. 336; Herluison, p. 68. Buried at St.-Germain l'Auxerrois. Left two daughters, Anne-Geneviève and Marthe, Arch. Nat., Y 352 fol. 233. T-B, VI, 1912, p. 242–3.

3a

5b³

1
Jacob and Rachel

1695   Bas-relief
First Acad. prize, subject: Shepherds pointing out
Rachel, Laban's daughter, to Jacob; *P-V*, III, p. 162.
Not ident. or disapp.

2
Joseph and Pharaoh

1696   Bas-relief
First Acad. prize, subject: Joseph interpreting Pharaoh's
dreams; *P-V*, III, p. 196; *AAF*, v (1857–8), p. 282.
Not ident. or disapp.

3*
Cupid and Psyche

1706
  a.* Group   Marble   H: 84   Signed & dated
Two nude children embracing, seated on a rock; Cupid
with little wings, Psyche with a ribbon in her hair.
J. G. Mann, *Cat. Wallace Coll.*, *Sculpture*, London 1931,
p. 7.

LONDON, WALLACE COLLECTION

b. Group   Terracotta
A terracotta version of this group is in the Mus.
Granet, Aix-en-Provence (the wings broken); Donation
Bourguignon.

AIX-EN-PROVENCE, MUSEE GRANET

  c.* Another version is in the Art Trade.

4
Two Vases

1706–7   Bronze
For the staircase in the Chât. Neuf de Meudon, Mém.
1st Sept. 1710, signed by C., for 120 L., Arch. Nat., O^I
1523, p. 39. Not ident. or disapp.

5*
Sculpture in the Chapel, Versailles

1709–10
  a. *Four plaster models for bas-reliefs*
On the small altars. The models made by C. for the altars
of St. Charles, St. Adélaïde, St. Victoire and St. Anne,
were put in position in 1710, Arch. Nat., O^I 1784, état
de 1734. The bronzes were cast in the reign of Louis XV

5d^1 5d^2 5e   5d^3 5b^1

5*b*²

from other models. cf. L. Deshairs, 'Les bas-reliefs des petit autels de la chapelle de Vers.', in *RAAM*, 1906, p. 217. Incl. in the total paid to C., Vassé, Thierry and J. Desjardins "for the bronzes cast for the altar of the Virgin and the five small altars in the aisles of the chapel: 28847 L., 5 s.", *Comptes*, V, 317, 412, 413. Destroyed.

b.★ Ornaments for the Lady Chapel and the Five Altars on the Side Aisles
1709–10   Bronze
Acc. to the *Comptes* quoted above, the same artists made bronzes, mainly young angels sitting or kneeling in pairs on the altars; impossible to distinguish the work of individual artists; all the figures were cast by J. Desjardins.

VERSAILLES PALACE, CHAPEL

c. Ornaments for Two Niches
1709   Stone
In collab. with F.-A. Vassé: "à Cayot et Vassé, sur les ornements à deux arrières voussures des niches du bout des bas-côtéz", 500 L., *Comptes*, V, 320.

VERSAILLES PALACE, CHAPEL

d. Three Trophies
1709   Bas-reliefs   Limestone
On the second pillar on the right, C. carved three trophies, after his own design and models.

I★ Martyrdom of St. James the Greater. 248 × 48
A shrine in the form of a tomb under the medallion 'portrait' of St. James; payment 700 L., Mém., Arch. Nat., O^I 1784. Pen, wash and watercolour drawing in Stockholm, THC 1008, wrongly attrib. to Charpentier.
II★ The Gospel
248 × 48
An open book on a pulpit in the form of a lectern, payment 650 L., *ibid.* Drawing in Stockholm, THC 1007.
III★ The Baptism of Christ
248 × 44
St. John baptising Christ, repr. in an oval medallion in the centre of the trophy; payment 600 L., *ibid.* Drawing in Stockholm, THC 1004.

VERSAILLES PALACE, CHAPEL

e.★ Head of a cherubim
Stone
At the bottom of the spiral staircase leading up to the Royal Tribune, on the south side; in collab. with Vassé. Payment 300 L., Arch. Nat., O^I 1784. The cherubim at the north staircase was by Voiriot and Monthéan.

VERSAILLES PALACE, CHAPEL

6a

6b

cf. Guérin, *Descr.*, p. 61. Dido stabbing herself on the funeral-pyre heaped with the gifts of Aeneas.

PARIS, LOUVRE

b.★ A smaller version in bronze with some variations, H: 51, in the Hermitage, Leningrad.

7
Sculpture on the High Altar of Notre-Dame, Paris

1713–15   Gilded bronze
cf. Bertrand no. 28. C. and Vassé together carved ornamental sculpture for the high altar and for the 'Autel des Féries' after designs by de Cotte; cast by J. Desjardins. Total payment 29900 L. between 1713 and 1721, *Comptes*, V, 694, 696, 787–8, 875. Arch. Nat., O¹ 2219, 2221. Drawing★ of the High Altar and angels in Coll. de Cotte, Bibl. Nat. Est., Va 254b Fol.
   a. *Two Angels in Adoration*
On either side of the high altar, on bronze scrolls.

6
The Death of Dido

1711   Statuette   Marble   H: 89
   a.★ Reception piece for the Acad. Sketch pres. 25 Jan. 1710; marble, 31 Dec. 1711, *P-V*, IV, p. 93, 137;

7

Models by C. acc. to the old *Descr.* of Paris (e.g. Piganiol, 1765, I, p. 324). Installed 1720; fee 7400 L. incl. in the total. Melted down during the Revolution.

   b. *Ornaments on the Steps of the High Altar*
Bas-reliefs between the angels; in the centre, an oval cartouche with the monogram of the Virgin; symbolic trophies on either side. Generally ascribed to F.-A. Vassé in the old *Descr.* of Paris. Melted down during the Revolution.

   c. *Ornaments for the 'Autel des Féries'*
Bas-reliefs on the base of the Pietà, scattered fleurs-de-lis and, underneath, consoles, cherubim, festoons and a scroll, cf. M.C.P.G., *Descr. Hist. des curiosités de l'église de P.*, Paris, 1763, p. 66–7. Destroyed.

8
A Nymph of Diana

1718   Statue   Marble   H: 160
On the subject of Companions, or Nymphs, of Diana in general, cf. Furcy-Raynaud, *Invent.*, p. 386–93; L. Réau, 'Les Compagnes de Diane', in *GBA*, 1932[I], p. 136–54. Estim. in 1718, 5200 L., reduced to 3600 L.; delivered in the same year to the King's store; Arch. Nat., O[I] 1921[A] and O[I] 2218. Acc. to the Invent. of 1723, *ibid.*, O[I] 1969[A]: "in the act of walking, holding in her left hand the leash of a greyhound running beside her, in her right hand the bow, on her back the quiver; supported by pieces of rock". At that time in the Garden of the Infanta in the Tuileries; confirmed in 1776 by Fontenai, I, p. 342. Confused with a 'Nymph' by G. Coustou (no. 79) in L. Réau's article, *loc. cit.*, p. 153. Disappeared during the Revolution.

9
A Nymph of Diana

Model   Terracotta and plaster
Bibliogr: see no. 8. Payment 740 L. to C. for models of a Nymph "to be executed in marble during 1722", Arch. Nat., O[I] 2222. C.'s death in 1722 ended the project. Not ident. or disapp.

CHARPENTIER, René (1680-1723)

b. Cuillé (Mayenne), 1680. Son of Jaques Ch., Contrôleur au Bureau de Champagne. Rec. in 1698 from the Acad. a 2nd small prize, then a 1st great prize, *P-V*, III, 227, 232, 241, 246, but did not go to Rome. Pupil of Girardon, under whom, acc. to Mariette, *ABC*, I, p. 361, and Dezallier, *Vie*, p. 234, he worked in 1705 on the model for the tomb of St.-Landry. Worked in Berlin together with the architect Jean de Bodt, cf. F. Nicolai, *Descr. de Berlin et Potsdam*, Berlin, 1769. Returned to France; presented to the Acad. in 1707; made Academician 27 May, 1713, *P-V*, IV, 51, 166. Worked for the King from 1710 onwards in collab. with Monthéan (Invent. a.d.). Married Marianne Leschevin, 19 Apr. 1711, Min. Centr. Arch. Nat., Et. X, 299, cf. Rambaud, *Doc.*, II, p. 415. Lived in the Grande Rue du Fbg. St.-Honoré until his death on 11 May 1723, Arch. Nat., Y 15320. Invent. a.d. 5 July, 1723, Min. Centr. Arch. Nat., Et CXVII, 331. Left three minor children, Marie-Anne, René, and Jeanne. cf. *Mercure de Fr.*, Sept. 1723, p. 549; Moreri, *Grand. Dict. Hist.*, 1759, II, p. 535; Dezallier, *Vie*, p. 234; Mariette, *ABC*, I, p. 361; Bellier de la Chavignerie; Herluison, 'Scellés et invent. d'art.', in *NAAF*, 1883, p. 240. T-B, VI, 1912, p. 410 (Hans Vollmer). C. made trophies for Huquier and engraved a number of plates collected in a volume called *Galerie de Girardon* with various views of his master's famous gallery at the Louvre and reproductions of the celebrated sculptures it contained, Bibl. Nat. Est., Aa 56 (pl. VI, detail*). His 'Mise au Tombeau'* is in the Cabinet des Dessins in the Louvre, Guiffrey-Marcel, *Invent.*, no. 2246. He himself engraved at least two plates: *Jésus expirant sur la croix** and *Le corps du Christ descendu par les disciples** (R. Charpentier in. et fec. 1708), Bibl. Nat. Est., Aa 3, gr. fol.

1

3a   3b

1*
Decorative Sculpture on the Portal of Fortuna,
Potsdam, Stadtschloss

1701   Stone
Design by the architect Jean de Bodt, cf. W. Boeck,
'Les sculpteurs fr. à la cour de Frédéric I de Prusse',
in *GBA*, 1933², p. 104–16. Destroyed, probably in 1945.

2
The Death of Adonis

1707   Model   Plaster
Presented to the Acad. for approval, 29 Oct. 1707,
P-V, IV, 1. C. was then asked to do a bust of L'Antin
(Antinous), *ibid.*, IV, 66, but then was released from this
task; the 'Death of Adonis' was changed to 'Death of
Meleager', cf. no. 9. Not ident. or disapp.

3
Two Trophies

1708–9   Bas-reliefs   Stone   248 × 43
On a pillar in the chapel at Versailles, C. carved:
   a.* Prudence, in the centre in a cartouche, helmeted,
holding a mirror. Payment 600 L., Arch. Nat., O¹ 1784.
Pen, wash and watercolour drawing in Stockholm,
THC 1009.
On the pilaster opposite:
   b.* Religion treading underfoot Heresy, holding in
one hand a cross, in the other the Holy Book; attributes
on either side. Payment 500 L., *ibid.*

VERSAILLES PALACE, CHAPEL

4*
Sixteen Credence-tables

1710   Marble
For the altars of the Chapel in Versailles. In collab. with
Monthéan, Voiriot and Loysel, payment 745 L.,
Comptes, V, 873.

VERSAILLES PALACE, CHAPEL

4

5

5*
Fourteen Trophies of Arms

1710 Stone 130 × 162
In the Salon Bas leading to the Chapel, above the four great arcades of the walls. In collab. with Voiriot, Monthéan, Gaillard and Noël; payment 180 L. each, *Comptes*, V, 529, 590. Mém., Arch. Nat., O^I 1784.

VERSAILLES, PALACE

6
Work for the Choir of Notre-Dame

1711–14
  a. *Sculpture* Stone
In collab. with Monthéan and Voiriot. Payment 900 L., *Comptes*, V, 511.
  b. *Ornaments above the side doors* Lead
In collab. with Monthéan. Payments 850 L., *Comptes*, V, 610, 696, 788.

  c. *Design for the pilasters of the stalls*
Acc. to Montjoie, *Curiosités de Notre-Dame de P.*, 1753, p. 27. Destroyed.

7
Work on the Grande Cornice of the Tuileries

1713 Stone
In collab. with Monthéan, payment 60 L., *Comptes*, V, 696. Destroyed.

8
Arms of Louis XIV

1713 Lead and tin
For the convent of the 'Filles de l'Ave Maria'. In collab. with Monthéan, payment 190 L., *Comptes*, V, 696. Destroyed.

9

9*
The Death of Meleager

1713 Statuette Marble 52 × 96
Reception piece for the Acad. 27 May 1713, *P-V*, IV,
166. Meleager clutches his bowels "déchirées par des
douleurs mortelles, à mesure que le tison fatal, d'où
dépendait le cours de sa vie, se consumoit". Beside him
the head of the wild Calydonian boar, cf. Guérin,
Descr. p. 62–3. See no. 2.

PARIS, LOUVRE

10
Trophies on the staircase, Hôtel de Toulouse,
Paris

1714–15
In collab. with Monthéan and Offement, under de
Cotte's direction. Great trophies between Ionic pilasters
repr. Hunting and Fishing, cf. Dezallier, *Paris*, 1752,
p. 121; Piganiol, *Descr.*, 1765, III, p. 258; Hurtaut &
Magny, III, 1779, p. 272; Thiery, 1787, I, p. 305; engr.
after Charpentier by Péquégnot★, Bibl. Nat. Est., Hd
150c, in 4°, pl. 346, probably repr. one of these trophies;
engr. of a cross-section of the staircase in Mariette, *Arch.
Fr.*, pl. 449★. Destroyed.

11
Work in the Apartments, Luxembourg Palace

1717–19 Wood and plaster
In collab. with Monthéan, Rousseau, Offement,
Bergéa. Payment: 680 L. in 1717; 193 L. in 1718;
2478 L. in 1719, Arch. Nat., O^I 2217, p. 137, 138; O^I
2219, p. 284. Not ident. or disapp.

10^I

12
Work at the Hôtel du Maine, Paris

1719
In 1719, C., together with Monthéan and Rousseau,
rec. payments for sculpture on the garden façade of the
Hôtel du Maine, rue de Bourbon; docum. in Catheu,
see *infra*. Reprod. in Blondel, *Arch. fr.*, I, ch. XXV,
p. 276★. The two pediments show: one, an allegory of
Spring, Flora with cupids★, the other a River Goddess★.
Partly removed to the former Hôtel Pontalba, built
in 1840 at 43 rue du Fbg. St.-Honoré, later the Hôtel
Rothschild, cf. F. de Catheu, 'La décor. des hôtels du
Maine au Fbg. St.-Germain', in *BSHAF*, 1945–6,
p. 100 sq. Attr. of River Goddess to C. doubtful.

PARIS, US. EMBASSY (Hôtel Rothschild)

10^2

12^I

12^3

13
Work in the Louvre

1717–22   Plaster
In collab. with Monthéan, Bergéa, Rousseau and Offement.
   a. *Four Fireplaces in the Pavillon de Flore*, 1717
Payment 2588 L., Arch. Nat., O^I 2216, p. 252.
   b. *New Accommodation for the Infanta*, 1722
Payment 1348 L., Arch. Nat., O^I 2222.
   c. *Non-identified work at the Louvre*
Payment 500 L., 1721, Arch. Nat., O^I 2222; 1800 L., 1723, Arch. Nat., O^I 2223.
Not ident. or disapp.

14
Work in the Chapel of Saint-Denis, Notre-Dame, Paris

1719–22   Marble, lead, wood
In collab. with Monthéan and Offement. Estim. 9 Dec. 1719 for 13,680 L. accepted by the Archbishop of Paris 16 Dec.; Bibl. Nat. Est., Hd 135 a, pet. in fol. (Coll. de Cotte). Mém of the alterations to the altar of St.-Denis, reduced by de Cotte on 4 May 1722 to 1940 L.; *ibid.*
   Specification: six capitals, the cresting of the altar, two groups of children, two vases, eighteen medallions, two cartels, four ornaments on the panels, a large frame, bronze ornaments in the entablature, two consoles, two bronze candelabra with three sconces, two angle consoles for the front of the altar, two credence-tables, some pedestal ornaments. Alterations because of a change of design: a niche for a statue of St. Denis by N. Coustou (no. 72) instead of a picture. Destroyed.

15
Work at the Château de la Muette

1720   Lead and plaster
Payment 1474 L., Arch. Nat., O^I 2220, p. 307. Destroyed.

12^4

16
Work in the Church of Saint-Roch, Paris

1720–23   Stone
   a. *Altar in the choir* in the form of a tomb. Destroyed.
   b. *Rose above the sanctuary*, "which he finished only fourteen hours before his death", cf. Moreri, *op. cit.* (Biogr.). Destroyed.
   c. *Decorative sculpture in the nave*: Recumbent angels in the spandrels. Disapp. during the Revolution.

12^2

16d¹   *16d²*

d. Decorative sculpture in the choir. "M. d'Antin
and M. de Coste . . . laid down that Charpentier's designs
for the carved decoration of the choir should be
followed", Moreri, *op. cit.* Completed accordingly,
but after C.'s death, cf. Dezallier, *Paris*, 1752, p. 108.
Only two bas-reliefs, 'Faith'★ and 'Charity'★ (200 ×
200), are preserved in the spandrels of the open arcade
at the back of the choir, cf. *Mercure de Fr.*, Sept. 1723,
p. 549; J. Cousin, 'Les Mon. de sculpture de l'Eglise
St.-Roch' in *Rev. Univ. des Arts*, 1859, p. 126; J. Bayet,
in *Les Rich. d'art de Paris, Mon. relig.*, p. 76.

PARIS, CHURCH OF SAINT-ROCH

17
Carvings in the Hôtel des Mousquetaires Gris

1721   Plaster?
Formerly Rue du Bac. Payment 1046 L., Arch. Nat., O¹
2220, p. 297–310. Destroyed.

18
Tomb of Comte Fortunat Rangoni

1723   Bronze
On entering the chapel of the Virgin, in St.-Roch, on
the right. A weeping Virtue leans on base of a column,
cf. Piganiol, *Descr.*, 1742, VI, p. 329; Dezallier, *Paris*,
1752, p. 109; Thiery, I, p. 163. Pen and wash drawing in
the Mus. Carnavalet★, cf. F. Boucher, 'Mon, fun. disparus
d'Eglises de Paris', in *NAAF*, XXII, 1959, p. 201.
Destroyed.

SCULPTURES FOUND IN C.'S APARTMENT
AFTER HIS DEATH, not previously listed.

Invent. a.d., 5 July 1723, Min. Centr. Arch. Nat., Et.
CXVII, 331:
*Two plaster models; one wooden model of a tabernacle; four
plaster statues; one wooden vase; two plaster statues; one
plaster figure of Christ on a wooden cross; several plaster
and terracotta figures; 50 lead medallions; 137 copper discs.*
Not ident. or disapp.

18

2¹

CHAUVEAU, René (1663-1722)

b. Paris. 1st Apr. 1663, son of François, famous engraver; his elder brother, Evrard, was a well-known painter. René was a pupil of Girardon, then of Philippe Caffieri in the Gobelins factory in Paris. Married 7 Feb. 1690 Catherine Cucci, daughter of Domenico, 'Ebeniste et fondeur' to the King, thus becoming the brother-in-law of the sculptor S. Slodtz, who was married to Catherine's sister. After a dispute with his father-in-law, although given accommodation in the Louvre, he accepted a proposal by Cronström, envoy of the Swedish King and in 1693 went to Stockholm as 'First Sculptor to the King' with an emolument of 1500 L. After submitting his presentation piece, he was accepted in absentia by the Acad. St.-Luc on 4 May 1693 as painter, sculptor, engraver and illuminator; Arch. Nat., Y 9322; Guiffrey, *St.-Luc*. Remained in Stockholm until the end of 1700, spent several weeks in Berlin before returning to France, where he worked mostly in the provinces. In 1705, lived in Paris, rue des Postes. Died 7 July 1722, rue du Petit Pont, Paris, debilitated by his own hypochondria and ruined, it seems, by the financier Law. Invent. a.d. 14 Sept. 1722, Min. Centr. Arch. Nat., Et. XVII, 626. Had at least nine children, several of them born in Sweden. His son René-Bonaventure, b. 1693, was his pupil and faithful assistant. Much information in the family memoir by the engraver Papillon, husband of C.'s youngest daughter, Charlotte-Magdeleine-Thérèse: *Vie de François Chauveau et de ses deux fils, Evrard et René*, publ. 1854; cf. Fontenai, I, p. 364; T-B, VI, 1912, p. 439–40 (Vollmer); monograph, in Swedish, by Ragnar Josephson, *René Chauveau, En Fransk Barock-Skulptöri det Karolinska Sverige*, Stockholm, 1929, mainly about his Swedish work, but generally important.

I
Work at the Château de Sceaux

1683–90
During alterations after Colbert's death, the Marquis de Seignelay comm. C. and other sculptors to decorate the interior of the château:
    a. *Cornices and panelling* in the Cabinet de la Chine and the Cabinet doré. Destroyed.
    b.* Stone cornices and masks inside the Orangerie.

DOMAINE DE SCEAUX

2
Carvings in the King's Chamber, Grand Trianon

1687–91   Wood
In collab. with La Lande, *Comptes*, III, 526, 679. Payment 1239 L., Arch. Nat., O¹ 1665, cf. H. Magnien, 'Le Trianon de marbre pendant le règne de Louis XIV', in *Rev. Hist. Vers.*, 1908, p. 12. Tinted drawing, Arch. Nat., O¹ 1884*; handwritten notes: 1) at the bottom: "Lalande et Chauveau, la chambre du Roy au prix de la salle"; 2) on the back: "La face de la cheminée et l'oposée de la pièce proche le Cabinet des Glaces".

VERSAILLES, GRAND TRIANON

1b

2²

4b

3
Carved and Gilded Frames

1689   Wood
For paintings by Van der Meulen at the Château de Marly, payment 666 L., *Comptes*, III, 288. Destroyed.

4
Work at the Dôme des Invalides

1680–93
   a. Cornices (roses, modillions and ornaments) in a chapel at the entrance.
1690   Stone
In collab. with Goupil, under the direction of Jouvenet, who made the models. Work in the other chapel by Legrand and Briquet. The four sculptors rec. together 1850 L. of the 1944 L. demanded, Arch. Nat., O^I 1665, d^r 37; *Comptes*, III, 558, 846.
   b.* Forty capitals, eight large consoles, four pilasters
1690   Stone
In collab. with the Jouvenets and Dedieu (nos. 31/32), payment 4008 L., *Comptes*, III, 422, Arch. Nat., O^I 1665, d^r 89.
   c. Frames (roses and panelling borders) in the chapels
Stone
In collab. with Jouvenet, Varin, Langlois, Monier, Dedieu (no. 34), Maubeuge, Massou, Lange and Rousseau. Payment 2200 L., *Comptes*, III, 844, Arch. Nat., O^I 1665, d^r 96.

PARIS, DOME DES INVALIDES

5
Work in the Apartment of the Grand Dauphin, Versailles

1690–2
   a. *Pedestal for a large clock*
Wood
"In the room of Monseigneur, incl. the design and model", payment 60 L., *Comptes*, III, 397. Not ident. or disapp.

   b. *Several consoles*
Wood
"For the rooms of Monseigneur, notably the Cabinet des Bijoux (22 consoles) and the Cabinet doré (two large consoles)", total payment 780 L., *Comptes*, III, 526, 679. Not ident. or disapp.

6
Twenty-six Culs-de-Lampe for Versailles

1693   Wood
Above the pilasters of the panelling in the ante-room of the Salon Ovale of the King's small apartment; in collab. with Briquet, Taupin, Legrand, Belan, Goupil, La Lande, Hulot and Armand. Payment 520 L., *Comptes*, III, 825. Destroyed.

7
Mouldings in the Hôtel de Seignelay

1693   Gilded bronze
In 1692–4, Catherine-Thérèse Goyon de Matignon, widow of Jean-Baptiste Colbert de Seignelay, made alterations to her hôtel, rue de Vivienne, Paris: new fireplaces in coloured marble were installed by Lisque in her reception room and her private room, as the old ones protruded too much and were no longer in fashion. The bronze mouldings for these fireplaces were designed and fitted by C., at a cost of 81 L. 7 s., *Mém.*, Arch. Nat., T 1123^{28A}. C.'s drawing*, sent by Cronström to Tessin in Stockholm, with a note "dans la chambre de Mme. de Seignelay", is in Stockholm, THC 2148*, cf. *Corresp. Tessin–Cronström*, p. 26, 60. The Hôtel was later used by the Regent as stables. Destr.

7

93

10a

11

10b

12

10b

12

8
Decoration for the Catafalque of Queen Ulrika-Eleonor of Sweden

For the obsequies in the Riddarholm Church at Stockholm in 1693; design by Tessin; engr. by Lepautre★, cf. Papillon, *op. cit.* Destroyed.

9
Reliefs in the Royal Chapel, Stockholm

1693
The subject of one of these was 'The Circumcision', cf. Böhiger, *Etudes concernant le chât. de Stockholm*, I, 20. Destroyed in the fire at the Palace in 1697.

10
Decoration of the Gallery Charles XI

1694–9
  a.★ Apotheosis of Charles XI and of Ulrika-Eleonor
Two High-reliefs   Stucco
On either side of the gallery above the doors; the busts of the King and Queen surrounded by allegorical figures and attributes; cf. Josephson, *op. cit.*
  b.★ Figures of Virtues
High-reliefs   Stucco
Above the cornice on the south side, with the collab. of the stuccoer, Pietro Pagani. Seated women with attributes and cupids repr. Justice, Religion, Generosity, Truth etc.

STOCKHOLM, ROYAL PALACE

94

8

14

Tombs of Count Bengt Oxenstierna and of his two wives

c. 1697   Plaster, painted bronze
Attrib. to C. by Josephson, *op. cit.*; design by Tessin.
  a.⋆ Tomb of the Count
'History' seated on a sarcophagus, writes in a book on the back of 'Time', a crouching old man. Above, 'Fame' with a medallion of the deceased. The tomb appeared on a medal struck in 1697.

UPSALA, CATHEDRAL

  b. *Tomb of the Count's two wives*
'Love' and 'Fidelity', also seated on a sarcophagus, holding a medallion of the deceased. Above, 'Fame' with three trumpets. Destroyed by fire in 1702. Engr.⋆ by Fr. Arnvidi after design by Johannes Peringskiöld in *Monumenta Ullerakerensia*, Holmia, 1719, p. 105.

11⋆
Decoration of the Ceiling in the Salon de Psyché

1694–9   Reliefs   Stucco
Figures and scrolls; bearded men in pairs, seated, in the corners, a small flying cupid between them.

STOCKHOLM, ROYAL PALACE

12
Decoration of the Bedroom of Gustav III

1694–9   Reliefs   Stucco
With Pietro Pagani. Eight seated female figures repr. the Liberal Arts⋆; in medallions four Vices: Egoism, Envy, Ignorance, Calumny.

STOCKHOLM, ROYAL PALACE

13
Decoration of the Salons of Don Quixote and of Svea

1694–9   Stucco
With Pietro Pagani; cornice and scrolls.

STOCKHOLM, ROYAL PALACE

14a

14b

15*
Charles XII

1698   Bas-relief   Plaster, painted bronze   Signed &
dated
The King, wearing a crown, framed by palms and
winged figures; the royal insignia on a kind of altar,
decorated with a frieze. Probably to commemmorate the
coronation in the Royal Palace.

LJUNG, PALACE

16*
Figures of Fame

1699   Stone
On the north façade of the Royal Palace; two figures
of Fame, lying on the curved central pediment, sounding
trumpets. cf. Josephson, *op. cit.*

STOCKHOLM, ROYAL PALACE

17*
Apollo and Minerva

c. 1699.   High Reliefs   Plaster   Life-size
Attrib. with great probability to C., by Josephson,
op. cit.; also the carved decoration of the hôtel designed
and built by Tessin at Slottsbaetten. The two divinities,
with their attributes, in niches in the vestibule.

STOCKHOLM, HÔTEL TESSIN

16

18*
The Four Seasons

c. 1699   Four bas-reliefs   Plaster
Rectangular sopra-portes in the vestibule. Attrib. to
C., cf. *supra*. The Seasons are repr. by the traditional
deities, surrounded by cupids.

STOCKHOLM, HÔTEL TESSIN

19*
Tomb of the Painter David Klöcker Ehrenstrahl

c. 1699   Bas-relief   Plaster, painted bronze
Attrib. to C. by Josephson, *op. cit*. The deceased in an
oval medallion; on either side two weeping children;
a large drapery as background. Below, an epitaph. The
court painter died in 1698.

STOCKHOLM, STORKYRKAN

15

17¹

17²

18¹

18²

18³

18⁴

20
Mythological Bas-reliefs

On the Great Staircase and in the Parade Room
1699–1700   Bas-reliefs   Plaster, Lead or Bronze
Most of C.'s mythological scenes are preserved, either
in the original plaster, or in lead or bronze casts made
after the artist's departure. Titles and order, acc. to the
accounts:

a.★ Apollo in love with Daphne.
b.★ Pentheus torn to pieces by his mother and her
   sisters.
c.★ Juno turning Ino's companions into birds and stones.
d.★ Apollo meeting Cupid after killing Python.
e.   Ajax and Ulysses quarrelling about the arms of
   Achilles.
f.★ Polyxenes sacrificed on the tomb of Achilles.
g.★ Paris killing Achilles.
h.★ Echo amusing Juno with a long discourse.
i.★ Perseus about to sever Medusa's head.
j.★ Jupiter crushing the giants.
k.★ The flood with Deucalion, Pyrrhus and Helen.
l.★ Perseus and Andromeda. Two versions with slight
   variations.
m.★ Achilles, in female clothing, unmasked by Ulysses.
   Two versions: the plaster one is larger with an
   extra figure on the right.

STOCKHOLM, ROYAL PALACE

19

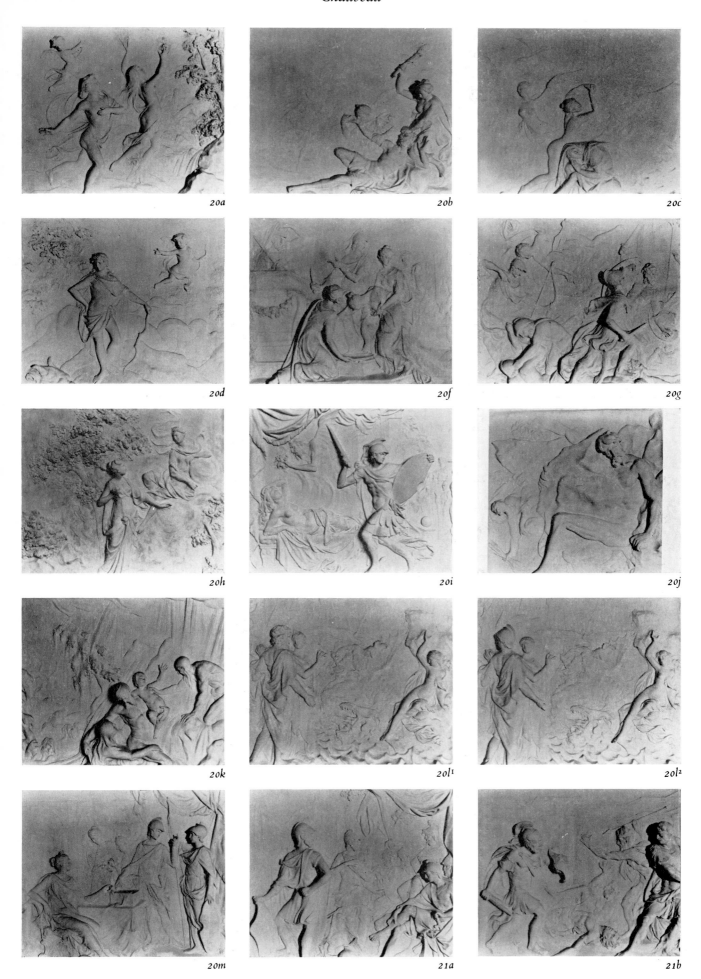

20a   20b   20c

20d   20f   20g

20h   20i   20j

20k   20l¹   20l²

20m   21a   21b

20m²

21
Bas-reliefs in the Great Gallery

    a.* Scipio's Leniency.
    b.* Emperor Augustus closing the Temple of Janus.
Dimensions and treatment suggest that these two reliefs belong to the same series as no. 20, although their subjects are historical, not mythological. Now in the Great Gallery.

STOCKHOLM, ROYAL PALACE

22
Carvings on a Cabinet

1700
During his stay in Berlin, at the request of the Elector, C. made in six weeks a cabinet for Schloss Schönhausen, near Berlin. Payment, acc. to Papillon, *op. cit.*, 3000 L. Not ident. or disapp.

23
Work at the Château de Gaillon

After 1701
Acc. to Papillon, *op. cit.*, C. was employed after his return by Colbert, Archbishop of Rouen; he had already worked at the château before his journey to Sweden. Not ident. or disapp.

24
Maquette

1704–5
The architect Tessin submitted to Louis XIV a project for joining the Louvre and the Tuileries; C. worked on the maquette. cf. Josephson, *Un architecte suédois à la cour de Louis XIV, Nicodème Tessin*, Paris, 1930, p. 53. Not ident. or disapp.

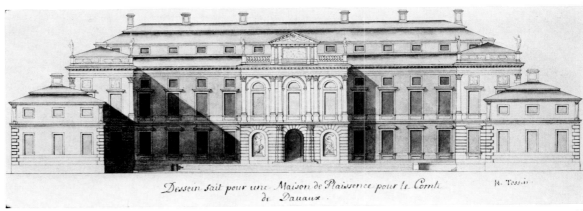

Dessein fait pour une Maison de Plaissence pour le Comte de Danaux.

N. Tessin

25

31

25
Three carved pediments, Château de Roissy-en-France

1704–5   Stone
Acc. to Papillon, *op. cit.*, C. carved decor. for the Chât. de Roissy, built after Tessin's plans for the Comte d'Avaux, former ambassador to Sweden. Two of these pediments showed Love, Sacred and Profane; the third, at the end of the Orangerie, symbol. the merits of the Comte. Pen and wash drawing in Stockholm, THC 2401*. Destroyed. *See appendix.*

26
Work for Monsieur Panyot (*Procureur at the Chambre des Comptes at Rouen*)

Before 1705
Fee 450 L. Invent. a.d. of Catherine Cucci (C.'s wife), 19 Dec. 1705, Min. Centr. Arch. Nat., Et. LIII, 133. Unidentifiable. cf. no. 35.

27
Work on the two small Baldachins in the Bosquet des Bains d'Apollon Versailles

1705   Lead
In collab. with several sculptors, total payment 1802 L., *Comptes*, V, 538. cf. Bertrand no. 12*. Destroyed.

28
Saint Etienne and *Sainte Genevive*

1705–6   Statues
Acc. to Papillon, *op. cit.*, these stood on the High Altar of the church of St.-Etienne-du-Mont. Not mentioned in the old *Descr.* of Paris. Not ident. or disapp.

29
Plan and Designs for the Chapel of Saint-Luc

1705–6
Acc. to Papillon, *op. cit.*, C. designed the redecoration of the old church of St.-Symphorien in the Cité, given to the Acad. St.-Luc. He is also supposed to have made the Glory. Not confirmed by the old *Descr.* of Paris. Not ident. or disapp.

30
Two Frames

1709   Gilded bronze
Papillon, *op. cit.*, states that the King comm. C. to make a frame enclosing four small round paintings of the four Seasons. C. depicted the Seasons and the Sun, emblem of the King, on the frame, which was reproduced when copies were made of the pictures. Payment 250 L., *Comptes*, V, 340. Not ident. or disapp.

31*
Work on the Altar of the Holy Sacrament in the Chapel, Versailles

1709–10   Plaster and bronze
In collab. with P. Lepautre and Offement, C. modelled in plaster a glory, two young angels in adoration on consoles decorated with cherubim heads, two cherubim heads on the two upper corners of the altar-piece, two falls of leaves, two consoles under the corners of the frame, two children carrying candelabra above clouds, the tabernacle with angels, a radiating sun and consoles, the decoration of the altar, a crown of thorns and rushes, consoles and cherubim heads, palm-branches, and a bas-relief of the three Maries at Christ's tomb. All the ornaments except the bas-relief were cast in bronze. Arch. Nat., O¹ 1784; for the payment, cf. no. 32. Only partly preserved.

VERSAILLES PALACE, CHAPEL

32¹

32*
Work on the Altar of Saint-Theresa in the Chapel, Versailles

1709–10   Plaster and bronze
In collab. with P. Lepautre and Offement, C. modelled in plaster the cross above the altar, two children in adoration in the round, cherubim heads, crowns of flowers, branches of lilies, rosettes of acanthus leaves, a bas-relief "repr. the death of St. Theresa, composed of nine figures and a glory of cherubim". The same

32²

artists carved ornaments in stone for the altar, the monogram of St. Theresa, a glory of three cherubim heads. All these were cast in bronze, except the bas-relief which was replaced thirty years later by a work of Vinache. Arch. Nat., O^I 1784. Total payment for nos. 31–2: 36,058 L., *Comptes*, V, 305, 317, 413, 532.

VERSAILLES PALACE, CHAPEL

33
Work at the Château d'Harcourt

1709–18
Acc. to Papillon, *op. cit.*, C. worked for several years for the Maréchal d'Harcourt (died 1718) on the carved decoration for the Chât. at Thury-Harcourt (Calvados), destroyed in 1944. cf. Soulange-Bodin, *Les chât. de Normandie*, Paris, 1928, I, p. 46–58. Destroyed.

34
Tomb of the Marquis de Beuvron

1709–18
Acc. to Papillon, *op. cit.*, the Maréchal d'Harcourt comm. from C. a tomb for his father, at La Meilleraye, near Rouen. Destroyed.

35
Work at Ecouis (Eure)

1709–18 (?)
Acc. to Papillon, *op. cit.*, C. did several sculptures at Ecouis "at Madame Paviot's, [mis-spelt by Papillon, read Panyot; cf. no. 26], widow of the Attorney General at the High Court of Rouen". Not ident. or disapp.

38a, b

36
Work at the Château de Frascati

1709–17   Stone and stucco
For his residence Frascati or Frescati, near Metz, the Bishop of Metz, Mgr. de Coislin, comm. C. to do decorative carvings in the interior and the chapel as well as on the statues in the park. Letters in the Coll. de Cotte contain accounts of the artist amounting to c. 11000 L., later reduced. Bibl. Nat. Est., Hd 135 a, pet. in fol. (702); cf. also Papillon, *op. cit.* and Bibl. Doucet, Fich. Laborde. Frascati was demolished at the end of the 18th c. *See appendix.*

37
Work at the Château de Saverne

c. 1710   Stucco
Acc. to Papillon, *op. cit.*, C. worked in the great salon at Saverne for the Cardinal de Rohan, who, after a fire in 1709, undertook extensive rebuilding in 1710. Another fire caused heavy damage in 1779. Destroyed.

38
Decoration on the Altar, Chapel of the Château d'Harcourt

1714
   a.* Annunciation   Bas-relief   Stone
   b.* Adoration of the shepherds   Bas-relief   Stone
Traditionally attrib. to C., cf. Duc d'Harcourt, 'La chapelle du chât. d'Harcourt', in *Art de Basse Normandie*, no. 43. Set in a border of red Languedoc marble; one relief decorated the retable, the other the front of the altar. They survived the fire of 12 Aug. 1944.

CHATEAU D'HARCOURT, CHAPEL

39
Designs for the Château de Sablé

c. 1720
Acc. to Papillon, *op. cit.*, C. was introduced by the Maréchal d'Harcourt to the Marquis de Torcy, who comm. from him the decorative carvings for his château, built by Desgots. C. died before he could begin the work.

SCULPTURES FOUND IN C.'S STUDIO AFTER HIS DEATH, not previously listed.

Invent. a.d. 1 Sept. 1722, Min. Centr. Arch. Nat., Et. XVII, 626.

Amphytrite on the Waters
Group   Bronze
With cupid and triton. Valued at 150 L.

Two Sphinxes
Bronze
Ibid. Valued at 150 L.

Four Figures
Group   Bronze
Ibid. Valued at 119 L.

CLERION, Jean-Jacques (1637-1714)

b. Aix-en-Provence 16 Apr. 1637; studied under Antoine Bobean, sculptor of Aix, went to Paris in 1661, cf. J. Boyer, 'Une oeuvre inédite de J.-J. Clérion', in *Rev. des Arts*, 1953, p. 210, note 3. Lapauze, I, p. 24 mentions that, during classes at the Acad. in 1663, he behaved badly and insulted Girardon. In 1666 pensionnaire of the Acad. Fr. in Rome, *Comptes*, I, 106. In 1673, still in Rome, cf. A. Castan, 'Les premières installations de l'Acad. Fr. à Rome', in *RSBAD*, 1889, p. 83. Married before 1681 Geneviève Boullongne, sister of the painters Bon and Louis B., herself a painter and member of the Acad. Their children died in 1684 and 1689, cf. Herluison, p. 80. Stayed several times in Marseilles and Aix, in 1688, from 1697–1700, in 1702, 1703, 1708 and 1711, cf. J. Boyer, *loc. cit.* Presented himself to the Acad. in 1676; agréé 5 Apr. 1687; made Academician 24 Sept. 1689, *P-V*, II, p. 73, 349; III, p. 16. Deeds of joint ownership (between husband and wife) in 1698, Arch. Nat., Y 270, fol. 490–1. His wife died at Aix on 7 Aug. 1708. He died in Paris, in the parish of St.-Paul, 28 Apr. 1714, *P-V*, IV, p. 181; cf. Jal, p. 388, T-B, VII, 1912, p. 91 (H. Vollmer). *See appendix.*

1

1★
Venus de Medici

1666–73   Statue   Marble   H: 165
Signed: I. CLERION FEC.
Copy made in Rome, *Corr. Dir. Acad. Fr. Rome*, I,
p. 130; sent to France, placed in the vestibule of the
Appartement des Bains in Versailles, cf. Piganiol,
Vers.-Marly, 1701, p. 17; removed in 1724, *ibid.*, 1730,
p. 18; given by the King to the Marquis de Marigny in
1769, for his Château de Ménars, cf. Plantet, *Coll. Stat.
Marq. de Marigny*, 1885; sold by auction in 1881 to the
purchaser of the Château, M. Vatel. Several fingers
broken. In the Art Trade.

2
Young Bacchus

1666–73   Statue   Marble   H: c. 134
Carved by C. during his stay at the Acad. in Rome, cf.

1

A. Castan, *op. cit.*, p. 108; in the Trianon gardens,
above the Salle des Marronniers, cf. Piganiol, *Vers.-
Marly*, 1707, p. 382. Not ident. or disapp.

3
Louis XIV

c. 1763   Bust   Marble
Acc. to the Invent. a.d. of 1673, cf. A. Castan, *op. cit.*,
p. 109, C. was then still working on the bust. Not ident.
or disapp.

4
History of the King

1674–8   Medals
C. rec. separately, or together with Hérard and Loyr,
payments for medals repr. the history of the King,
Comptes, I, 803, 874, 928, 1089; cf. N. Rondot, *Les
Médailleurs en France*, 1904, p. 313. Not ident. or disapp.

5
Hyacinthe Serroni, Archbishop of Albi

1678   Medal
cf. Blanchet et Dieudonné, *Man. numismatique*, III,
1930, p. 178 and A. Michel, Hist. de l'art, VII, 1925,
p. 399–400. Not ident. or disapp.

6
Two Models for Vases

1680   Wax
To be cast in metal; perhaps intended for the future

6

Bassin de Neptune in the park at Versailles, cf. no. 12. Payment 550 L., *Comptes*, I, 1285. A pen and wash drawing in Stockholm, THC 5140⋆, with the hand-written note, "Vasses par Clérion" shows a vase similar to the two vases at the Bassin de Neptune, but with some variations. It seems, therefore, that the model was modified. Another drawing for the same vase is at Berlin, Kunstbibliothek, Hdz. 2298, without the sculptor's name. cf. no. 12. Not ident. or disapp.

7
Trophy and Children

1680 Stucco
One of the trophies on the cornice of the Grande Galerie, payment 400 L., *Comptes*, I, 1286, 1290; II, 14.

VERSAILLES, PALACE

8
Work on the South Wing, Versailles

1681–4
  a.⋆ Clio Statue Stone H: c. 200
On the façade of the South Wing; payment 500 L., *Comptes*, II, 11

VERSAILLES, PALACE

  b. *Unspecified work*
Payment 650 L., *Comptes*, II, 473, not ident. or disapp.

9
Cornice, Apartment of the Duc de Vendôme, Versailles

1682 Stucco
Payment 1000 L., *Comptes*, II, 137. Not ident. or disapp.

10
Decoration on a Balcony at Versailles

1682 Stone
Above the passageway alongside the Parterre de l'Amour, at the South Wing, cf. *Comptes*, II, 197, (300 L.) and 473. Not ident. or disapp.

11
Two Masks for Versailles

1682 Stone
On the key-stones of the doors and windows of the chapel on the petit parc side (i.e. the old chapel). Payment 510 L. at the same time as for no. 10, *Comptes*, II, 473. Not ident. or disapp.

12
Two Vases, Two Masks and Two Shells for the Bassin de Neptune, Versailles

1682–3 Metal
C. made two of the 22 vases surrounding the Bassin 'sous le Dragon', the future Bassin de Neptune; also two masks and two shells for the same setting; cf. Piganiol, *Vers.-Marly*, 1701, p. 182. Perhaps these are the two vases with lobsters as handles and masks, which still stand at the ends of the parapet, cf. no. 6⋆. First payment 1400 L., *Comptes*, II, 140, 278; final payment not until 1685 incl. other work, *ibid.*, III, 1083. cf. Carlier no. 3⋆.

VERSAILLES, PARK

8

13
Model for a Group for the Bassin de Neptune, Versailles

1684   Plaster
In collab. with Lespingola. Payment 350 L., *Comptes*, II, 473. Not ident. or disapp.

14
Hercules

1684   Statue   Stone
"Placed in the niche beside the porte des bains below the passage from the courtyard of the palace [of Versailles] to the grotto". Payment 200 L., *Comptes*, II, 473. Engr. by Thomassin★, *Vers.*, pl. 117. Not ident. or disapp.

15★
Venus Callipygos

1684–6   Statue   Marble   H: more than 200
Copy after an antique in the Mus. Nat., Naples. 2500 L. on account, *Comptes*, II, 439, 625, 991; final payment in 1685 incl. other works, *ibid.*, III, 1083. On the ramp of the Parterre de Latone, cf. Piganiol, *Vers.-Marly*, 1701, p. 226–227. Drawing at Stockholm, THC 3743. *S. app.*

VERSAILLES, PARK

14

15   17   18

20

16
Work on the Grand Commun

1685   Stone
Payment 200 L. for "work on the pediment", *Comptes*, II, 654; the final payment in 1695 mentions "work of sculpture in stone at the Grand Commun", *ibid.*, III, 1083. Probably on the west façade above the main entrance; altered at the end of the 18th c.

VERSAILLES, GRAND COMMUN

17*   18*
Jupiter and Juno

1686–7   Terms   Marble   H: 270
The term of Jupiter after a model by Mignard, Arch. Nat., O¹ 2772. Payment on account 2700 L., *Comptes*, II, 991, 1174; III, 93; final payment incl. other works in 1695, *ibid.*, III, 1083. Placed side by side in the Demi-lune between the Allée Roy. and the Bassin d'Apollon, on the north side, cf. Piganiol, *Vers.-Marly*, 1701, p. 208. *See appendix.*

VERSAILLES, PARK

19
Two Capitals

1687–8   Marble
Ionic pilaster capitals on the façade, payment 280 L., *Comptes*, II, 1174; III, 93. cf. André no. 11*.

VERSAILLES, GRAND TRIANON

20*
Saint James the Less

1687–9   Oval medallion   Marble   87 × 66
Reception piece for the Acad., cf. Biogr.; model presented in 1687, *ibid.* The Saint, in right profile, "reading a parchment" held in the left hand, his right hand on "a kind of club indicating the instrument with which he was killed", cf. Dezallier, *Descr. Acad.*, p. 132.

PARIS, LOUVRE

21
Model for Equestrian Statue of Louis XIV

1688
Presented to the aldermen (échevins) of Marseilles, but never realised, *AAF*, Doc. inédits, VI, 1858–60, p. 88–91; cf. L. Lagrange, 'Pierre Puget', in *GBA*, 1866¹, p. 350; E. Parrocel, 'Doc. et autogr. rel. à des Travaux exéc. à Marseille par Puget et Clérion', in *RSBAD*, 1893, p. 228–36; A. Lapauze, I, p. 25. Not ident. or disapp.

22
Cartouche with Two Children

1688   Stone   200 × 100   Signed: J.C.
Above the entrance door of the Domaine Court de Payen, 87 rue Sainte, Marseilles, cf. E. Parrocel, 'Une oeuvre de J. Clérion', in *NAAF*, 1887, p. 177–9. Restored in the 19th c., plaster casts were made; the maquette was still extant in 1887. Everything has disappeared.

23
Two Busts

In the Church of St.-Jean, Aix-en-Provence before the Revolution, cf. E. Parrocel, *Annales de la Peinture*, Marseilles, 1852, p. 388. Not ident. or disapp.

24
Father François de la Chaise

1699   Medal   Lead   Signed
cf. Blanchet et Dieudonné, *Man. numismatique*, 1930, III, p. 166. On the reverse, a high priest raises the veil of the Holy of Holies.

AIX-EN-PROVENCE, MUSEE GRANET

25

25*
Virgin and Child

1704   Silvered wood   H: 140
Maquette for a silver statue for the Church of the Grands Carmes, Aix-en-Provence, payment 120 L., cf. J. Boyer, 'Une oeuvre de J-J. Clérion', in *Rev. des Arts*, 1953, p. 209–12. The Virgin, standing, holds the smiling infant Jesus, who stretches out his arms; the sceptre in her right hand has disappeared.

AIX-EN-PROVENCE, CATHEDRAL

26
Coat of Arms

1711   Stone
Above the portal of the Hôtel de François de Boniface-Leydet, Conseiller au Parlement de Provence. Payment 40 L., cf. J. Boyer, *op. cit.* Formerly at Aix-en-Provence, 10, cours Mirabeau. Destroyed.

27
Portrait of Bachet de Méziriac, Academician

Oval Medallion   Bronze
Exh.: *Les artistes français en Italie de Poussin à Renoir*, Paris, 1934, Mus. des Arts Décoratifs, no. 755. The signed medallion is inscribed: 'Principibus placuisse viris non ultima laus est'. Whereabouts unknown.

COLLIGNON or COLIGNON, Gaspard or Jean (?-1702)

Probably from Lorraine. Active in Paris from 1673 until his death in 1702. In 1673 and 1677 he lived in the rue d'Orléans, Faubourg St.-Marcel (as stated in the contracts for nos. 1 & 5 below). Acc. to Piganiol, *Descr.*, 1765, V, p. 324, his character was 'singularly bizarre and intractable'. T-B, VII, 1912, p. 227–8 (H. Vollmer).

1*   2*
Apollo and Diana

1673   Two Statues   St.-Leu stone   H: c. 210
Comm. by Maximilien Titon du Tillet for 440 L., contract 21 Dec. 1673, Min. Centr. Arch. Nat., Et. CV, 853 (notified by M. L.-H. Collard). Probably identical with two statues of Apollo and Diana (companion pieces), which we believe can be attrib. to Collignon. In the Art Trade.

3*
Tomb of Julienne le Bé, mother of the painter Le Brun

Between 1668–90   Marble, stucco and plaster
Designed by Le Brun for his mother, who died in 1668. The deceased is emerging from her tomb at the Resurrection; an angel sounds the trumpet of the Last Judgement. Two children in stucco beside an urn (now disappeared). Owing to a mistake by Dezallier, some authors attrib. the figure of the mother to Tuby. In fact the whole monument was by C., cf. M. Dumolin, 'Le tombeau de la mère de Le Brun', in *BSHAF*, 1929, p. 179. Engr. by P. Choffard* in Dezallier, *Paris*, 1778, p. 249. *See appendix.*

PARIS, SAINT-NICOLAS-DU-CHARDONNET

3

3

4
Charles Le Brun

1676   Bust   Marble
Listed by Missirini, *Mem. per serv. alla storia della R. Acc. S. Luca*, Rome, 1823, p. 135. The bust was then apparently in the Coll. Acad. St.-Luc, Rome. Not ident. or disapp.

5*
Victory

1677–8   Bas-relief   Marble   H: c. 200
Upper part of the tomb of the Marquis de Vaubrun; the rest by Coysevox (see no. 9*). Contract: 1st May 1677, notaries Mouffle and Ogier. C. to do "a white marble figure repr. Victory, one hand holding a crown directly over the head of the figure . . . the other hand holding a trophy with the palm of glory, the aforesaid figure to be about five and a half pieds high in proportion to the other figures, in add. the said Collignon to make the black marble background of the said tomb, up to the ceiling of the cornice of the chapel . . .". Fee 3200 L.; to be completed in 18 months, but acc. to the epitaph, erected in 1704. cf. Sainte-Beuve, 'Le tomb. du marq. de Vaubrun', in *GBA*, 1928[I], p. 153–62.

CHATEAU DE SERRANT (Maine-et-Loire)

Detail   2

1

5

63

6*
Music

1682   Statue   Stone   H: over 200
For the façade of the South Wing, Versailles. Payment 550 L., *Comptes*, II, 137. Identified by Le Brun's drawing in the Coll. Cronstedt, Stockholm, no. 1547* (notified by J. Montagu). 'Music' holds a harp. The statue on the façade is a copy*; the original, in two parts, is in the store*.

VERSAILLES, MUSEUM

7
Two Trophies for the South Wing

1682   Bas-reliefs   Stone
On the window arches of the 1st floor. Payment 520 L., *Comptes*, II, 137, 169. cf. Flamen 11b*.

VERSAILLES, PALACE

8
Four Large Trophies for the South Wing, Versailles

1682–3   Stone
On the balustrade of the South Wing. In collab. with Granier, payment 1400 L., *Comptes*, II, 137, 301. Destroyed.

9
Vases, Basins, Masks, Shells

1682–3   Metal
For the Bassin 'sous le Dragon', later the Bassin de Neptune. Payment 1200 L., *Comptes*, II, 140, 278. cf. Carlier no. 3*.

VERSAILLES, PARK

64

62

10
Groups for the Bassin de Vénus, Versailles

1685 Models
"Four moulding and casting in bronze", payment 200 L., *Comptes*, II, 628. See also Drouilly no. 20*.

11
Group of Children for the Petit Parc, Versailles

1685 Model
Payment on account 200 L., *Comptes*, II, 628; yet C. refunded 400 L. "received in 1686 on account for models of a group of children for the Allée d'eau, on which he had not worked", *ibid.*, II, 875. Not ident. or disapp. *See appendix.*

12*
Jean–Baptiste Lulli

Before 1687 Bust Bronze
Part of the tomb of the composer at Notre-Dame-des-Victoires. Wrongly ascr. to Cotton or Coysevox. Attrib. by Sainte-Beuve to C., based, convincingly, on the caption of an engraving by Saint-Aubin, cf. 'Le Tomb. Lulli' in *GBA*, 1926², p. 198; Keller-Dorian, *Coysevox*, I, p. 59. A cast is in the Mus., Versailles. See Cotton no. 4*.

PARIS, NOTRE–DAME DES VICTOIRES

13
Models for the King's Throne

1687
Payment 1420 L., 6 Apr. "for work done on various sketches and models for the King's throne" at Versailles, *Comptes*, II, 1172. Not ident. or disapp.

14
Work at the Hôtel de Titon du Tillet

Acc. to Brice, 1717, II, p. 123, C. executed "life-size figures in the niches, repr. the four seasons as well as the bas-reliefs painted bronze above them". Not ident. or disapp.

15
See appendix.

6¹

12

4

CORNU, Jean (1650-1710)

b. Paris 1650. Apprenticed at Dieppe to a sculptor in ivory, cf. Mariette, *ABC*, II, p. 11. 27 May 1673, 2nd prize at the Acad. (see no. 1). 6 Apr. 1675, sent to Rome, *ibid.*, II, p. 47, where he stayed until 1679. In 1676, joined with Le Comte and Flamen in the revolt against Errard, Director of the Acad., *Corr. Dir. Acad. Fr. Rome*, I, p. 63. In June 1679, supervised at Le Havre the unloading of crates with works from Italy bought by Louis XIV, *ibid.*, I, p. 83, 84, 103. 5 July 1681, received into the Acad., *P-V*, I, p. 370. 6 March 1688, married Françoise-Louise Perronet, daughter of Jean Perronet, Contrôleur général at the Town Hall. Children: Louise, b. 1689, who became a nun at Lisieux; Dominique, b. 1690; Jean-François, b. 1691; Gabriel, who became a painter, b. 1693; cf. Mariette, *ABC*, II, p. 11; Jeanne-Thérèse, b. 1694; Jean-Baptiste, b. 1709; cf. Jal, p. 430; Fich. Laborde, Bibl. Nat. 12071, 13522-8. 14 July 1704, Asst. Prof.; 30 Dec. 1706, Prof., *P-V*, III, p. 398; IV, p. 36. Lived then in a small house in the Place du Vieux Louvre. Died at Lisieux during a journey on 21 Aug. 1710, *ibid.*, IV, p. 112; Invent. a.d., 13 Oct. 1710, Min. Centr. Arch. Nat., Et. XV, 424. His widow died in 1715; Invent. a.d., 20 May 1715, Min. Centr. Arch. Nat., XV, 468; Jal, p. 430; Bellier de La Chavignerie, I, p. 291; Ph. de Chennevières, *Notes d'un compilateur sur les sculpteurs en ivoire*, Amiens, 1857, p. 11; T-B, VII, 1912, p. 445 (E. Vial).

1
The Crossing of the Rhine

1673   Bas-relief
2nd prize at the Acad., Louis Le Comte received the 1st prize, Anselme Flamen, the 3rd, *P-V*, II, p. 7, 45. Not ident. or disapp.

2
The Rape of the Sabines

Between 1675-9   Bas-relief   Terracotta
Made during C.'s stay in Rome. Incl. in the Invent. of the sculptors of the Acad. left by Errard to La Teulière, 6 Dec. 1684, *Corr. Dir. Acad. Fr. Rome*, I, p. 133. Not ident. or disapp.

3
River and Enslaved Queen

Between 1675-9   Model   Terracotta
Part of the maquette for a monument designed by Errard to the glory of Louis XIV, executed by the pupils of the French Acad. in Rome. Mentioned in the Invent. of 1684, cf. *supra* (descr. each sculptor's share). The figure of the King at the top of a pyramid surrounded by four slaves, two rivers, two streams and two enslaved queens. Apparently not carried out in marble. Not ident. or disapp.

4
The Wrestlers

Between 1675-79   Group   Marble
"The wrestlers of Florence, copied in marble by Cornu". Acc. to the Invent. of 6 Dec. 1684, the group was sent to France, *Corr. Dir. Acad. Fr. Rome*, I, p. 129. Engr. by Thomassin (no. 55)*, so it must have been at some time in the park at Versailles. Fight between two naked athletes, one being beaten to the ground. (Not to be confused with 'The Wrestlers' by P. Magnier, copied betw. 1684-7 from the same model, in the Appartements Verts at Marly.) Whereabouts unknown.

5
Crucifix

Between 1675-9   Terracotta, painted gold
Invent. 6 Dec. 1684, *Corr. Dir. Acad. Fr. Rome*, I, p. 129. Not ident. or disapp.

6
Anatomical Study

Between 1675-79   Bas-relief   Terracotta
Invent. 6 Dec. 1684, *Corr. Dir. Acad. Fr. Rome*, I, p. 153; after design by Errard. Not ident. or disapp.

7*
The Roman Charity

1681   Bas-relief   Marble   75 × 75
Reception piece for the Acad. roy., *P-V*, II, p. 192.

10

Exh. at the Acad. during the 18th c.; Guérin described it as: "a woman who, in order to prolong his life, gives her milk to her father, condemned to starve to death in prison; and a small child, apparently not pleased at being deprived", cf. Guérin, *Descr. Acad.*, 1715, and Dezallier, *Descr. Acad.*, 1781, p. 60, 135. Rediscovered in 1866 in the 2nd courtyard of the Ecole des Beaux-Arts, cf. E. Müntz, *Guide Ecole des Beaux-Arts*, 1889, p. 62. Threatened by corrosion, now inside the school, cf. C. Saunier, 'Vandalisme officiel', in *Les Arts*, Sept. 1907.

PARIS, ECOLE DES BEAUX-ARTS

8
Work in the South Wing, Versailles

a. *Undefined work, 1681–2*
Part of the decoration, stucco for the interior, stone for the exterior. C. rec. 300 L., 7 Dec. 1681; 1800 L. in 1682, *Comptes*, II, 11, 134.
b. Two statues
1682   Stone   H. more than 200
Total payment 700 L. for "two figures in stone for the great wing", *Comptes*, II, 182, each statue val. 350 L. C.'s part in the 32 statues on the 2nd floor is not exactly definable.

VERSAILLES, PALACE

9 a b c
Two Vases   Two Shells   Two Masks

1682–4   Metal Vases   H: c. 150
Of the 22 lead vases, shells and masks on the retaining wall of the Bassin de Neptune (formerly 'sous le Dragon'), two of each are by C., *Comptes*, II, 139, 278; III, 945, 1003. The vases are all different. C.'s work is not definable. cf. Carlier 3★.

VERSAILLES, PARK

d. *Plaster model*
In 1684, C. rec. a total payment of 600 L., *Comptes*, II, 477 for the model of a group intended for the new decoration of the retaining wall of the Bassin. Repr. the Triumphs of Neptune and Amphitrite; several sculptors shared the work, which was never completed owing to lack of money. Whereabouts unknown.

10★
Africa

1682   Statue   Marble   H: over 200
Begun by Sibrayque, who rec. 3400 L. towards it. So Sibrayque must have made considerable progress before he died. Completed by C., payment incl. other works, *Comptes*, III, 945, 1003. 'Africa' is a negress, her head covered "with the skin of an elephant's head whose tusk she holds at the tip. A crouching lion licks her left foot", cf. Piganiol, *Vers.-Marly*, 1701, p. 192.

VERSAILLES, PARK

7

11
Venus

1683   Group   Stucco
Comm. for the façade of one of the twelve small pavilions at Marly; payment 1000 L. in two instalm., 1683–4, *Comptes*, II, 367, 522. Destroyed.

12
Two Vases

1683   Marble
  a.★ Vase of the Sacrifice to Diana   H: 150
  b.★ Vase of the Bacchanal   H: 190
Eight large white marble vases surr. the Parterre of the Bassin de Latone, decor. with friezes in bas-relief. Six are copies of the famous antique vases at the Villa Borghese and the Villa Medici; Piganiol, *Vers.-Marly*, 1701, p. 162, and other guide books, wrongly attrib. all six to C., while the accounts for 1683 mention a total payment of 4000 L. to C. for only "two large white marble vases placed next to Latona", *Comptes*, II, 319. Confirmed by a descr. of Versailles, which ascribes the two centre vases to C., the four others to Hurtrelle, Laviron and Le Conte, cf. Mme. Jourdain 'Remarques hist. sur les figures, termes et vases qui ornent le parc de Versailles', Bibl. Arsenal, Ms. 2546, 3 Jan. 1695.

VERSAILLES, PARK

13★
Two Vases

1684   Marble   H: 184
In 1684, C. rec. 2200 L. for "two models of vases and two vases done by him in marble to be placed in the petit parc", *Comptes*, II, 438. Both are still in their

13

original positions in the Parterre Nord next to the terrace wall (mentioned by Mme. Jourdain, *op. cit.*, Piganiol and other historians). Their bodies are decorated with oak leaves in flat relief. Drawing in Stockholm, THC 2127.

VERSAILLES, PARK

12a

12b

14
Models for two Groups of Children

1684   Plaster
In 1684, C. rec. 660 L. "for two groups of children in plaster for the Allée du Dragon", *Comptes*, II, 438. Probably rejected; C.'s name does not appear among the artists of the 22 groups of children later cast in bronze. Not identified.

15
Work in the Gallery, Château de Clagny

1684–6   Stone
From 1684–6 C. rec., the considerable sum of 35,666 L. 11s. 3d. These years correspond to the final phase of the carved decoration of Clagny, *Comptes*, II, 438, 654, 1132. Acc. to Brice, *Descr.*, 1706, p. 111, all stucco ornaments in the gallery were by C. The gallery measured 67 × 8.125 m.; the relief groups on the cornices repr. the Olympian deities, the elements, the seasons and the continents. In the great central salon eight slaves, apparently supporting the vault; at the four corners, nymphs carrying baskets of flowers and fruit. Descr. in *Mercure Galant*, Nov. 1686, pp. 86–98. Destroyed.

16*
Hercules Farnese

1684–8   Statue   Marble   H: over 300
Copy after the antique, a cast of which was at the Acad. roy., cf. Guérin, *Descr. Acad.*, 1715, p. 50. Payments, incl. other works, were spread over 1684–94; the completed statue was put in the Jardin du Roi in 1688, *Comptes*, II, 438, 1174, 1183; III, 85, 93, 945, 1003. The hero leans wearily on his club, holding behind his back the golden apples from the Garden of the Hesperides. Pendant to Raon's 'Flora Farnese.'

VERSAILLES, PARK

16

17*
Work at the Colonnade, Versailles

  a.*   Three masks   1685–6   Marble
  b.*   Pedestal for a basin   1686   Marble
C. had been comm. to produce three statues for the arcades: two Satyrs and one Bacchante, Arch. des Bât. civ., cf. Nolhac, 'Les Marbres de Vers.', in *GBA*, 1911[2], p. 267. The project was not carried out; the statues were replaced by 29 marble basins, their pedestals carved after a model by Raon. C. made one of them; payment 400 L., *Comptes*, II, 992, 1174.

    The keystones of the arcades were decorated with masks, three of them carved by C. Payment 450 L. in 1685 and 1686, *Comptes*, II, 625, 992. Engr.* of the whole Colonnade by Rigaud.

VERSAILLES, PARK

17

17a

18* (*cont.*)

Originals restored:

1–12:	p. 117
14–20:	p. 118
21–24, 27-32:	p. 119

Originals removed to store:

13¹, 25¹, 26¹: p. 118

Copies:

13², 25², 26²: p. 118, 119

19
Four Groups of Children

1688   Trossy Stone
Eight groups of two children were comm. from Jouvenet, Barois and C. for the peristyle of the Trianon; cf. Barois no. 7*. Estim. 260 L. for each group. C. did four of them and rec. 1040 L., *Comptes*, II, 35; Bibl. Nat. Est., Va 448 f, gr. fol., p. 40. Destroyed.

18*
Thirty-two Statues

1687–8   Stone
In collab. with Rayol. Acc. to Brice, *Descr.*, 1706, p. 111, the whole north wing of the Palace of Versailles 'is embellished with his [C.'s] sculptures. All the twelve large figures on the new wing at the same side as well as those on the wing of the Salle des Ballets are by his hand''. The very considerable sum of 22,000 L. rec. in 1687 and 1688 by C. and Rayol, for "ornaments" and "works of sculpture" on this façade, *Comptes*, II, 1132; III, 55, was surely connected with this big project of 32 statues, for which no other sculptor's name appears anywhere. The statues illustrate, from right to left, the Sciences and the Arts, the Seasons, the four genres of Poetry and the Muses. Many of them have been restored, some even replaced by copies in the 19th c.; fragments of the originals are preserved*, cf. F. Souchal, 'Versailles' in *GBA*, 1972¹, p. 65–112.

VERSAILLES, PALACE

20

20
Nine Large Cassolettes and Consoles

1688–9   Stone   195 × 162
Of the numerous stone vases and baskets on the roof of Trianon (except the Trianon-sous-Bois), C., Dufour and François (no. 10) made the great Cassolettes at the corners, each estim. at 200 L. C. rec. 1800 L. in 1688–9, *Comptes*, III, 35, 248. The drawing* is among de Cotte's papers, Bibl. Nat. Est., Va 78 g, 2. No. 1462. Destroyed.

17b

1

2

3

4

5

6

7

8

9

10

11

12

13¹   26¹   45¹

13²   14   15   16

17   18   19   20

21   22   23   24

25²   26²   27   28

29   30   31   32

22¹

21
Work at the Dôme des Invalides

1687–91

a. *Work at the Great Arcade*   1687

C. rec. 500 L. "for works of sculpture done by him at the corners and on the great arcade separating the two Eglises des Invalides", i.e. l'Eglise du Dôme and l'Eglise des Soldats, *Comptes*, II, 1174. Probably ornamental work: cornices or capitals. Destroyed.

b. *Six apostles*   Stone

The drum supporting the cupola was rhythmically accentuated by sixteen statues repr. the twelve apostles,

St. Paul, St. Barnabus, St. John the Baptist and a prophet. cf. the anon. engr. of the façade, Bibl. Nat. Est., Va 271, 3, cf. Coysevox nos. 54b and c★. Six of the sixteen statues, each estim. at 350 L., were comm. from C.; payment in 1690–91, *Comptes*, III, 422, 557, and Bibl. Nat., Ms. fr. n.a. 22936. cf. Félibien des Avaux, *Invalides*, p. 298, who attribs. only four to C. The others were executed by Rayol, Poultier, Magnier, Van Clève, Raon and Hurtrelle. Destroyed.

c. *Models of transverse arches*   1691

C. and Noël Jouvenet rec. 192 L. 14s. "for works of sculpture on plaster models of Arcs Doubleaux in the interior of the above mentioned chapel", *Comptes*, III, 553. Destroyed.

22★
Work for the High Altar at Narbonne

1694   Bronze

On the occasion of his installation as Archbishop of Narbonne in 1694, Cardinal de Bonzy donated the High Altar to the Cathedral. C. designed it and produced in his Paris studio most of the bronze ornaments (cf. Brice, *Descr.*, 1706, p. 111) which the local foreman Laucel assembled and erected together with marbles from Italy. The design of this great altar with its baldachin, greatly admired ever since it was erected, was inspired by the altar in the Dôme des Invalides. Partly dismantled during the Revolution, it was re-assembled by Viollet-le-Duc, but has lost the original baldachin, the bronze bases of its columns, the urns and vases, the coat of arms of the cardinal supported by two child angels, the tabernacle, the retable and a great bas-relief of the Last Supper. Still extant are the two cherubim on volutes and the corner ornaments of the altar table, the glory in beaten copper, the ornamented entablature with two large incense-bearing angels, two damaged small angels, bronze cherubim, modillions and the six bronze capitals of the columns supporting the baldachin, cf. J. Yche, 'Le maître-autel de St.-Just', in *Bull. Soc. archéol. de Narbonne*, 1910, XI, pp. 281–8.

NARBONNE, CATHEDRAL OF SAINT-JUST

22²

22³

23
Decoration at the Château de Saint-Cloud

c. 1697

A pencil sketch★ with the note "Veu du Salon de Mignard desiné du dedans la Galerie de St.-Cloud desiné par Cornu" seems to indicate that C. made the stucco ornaments for the vault and walls in this gallery. Bibl. Nat. Est., Va 92 b, 3. Destroyed.

24
Small Bronzes after Antique Works

   a. *The Farnese bull*
   b. *The Laocoon*
   c. *Unspecified works*

Brice, *Descr.*, 1698, p. 81, saw in C.'s studio "small bronzes after the most beautiful antiques". In the Invents. a.d. of C. and his wife, Min. Centr. Et. XV, 432 and 468 is noted "the Farnese bull, with several figures all in bronze, mounted on an ebony pedestal decorated with representations of birds in small picture frames", "the Laocoon with his two sons and several serpents, also all in bronze mounted on a pedestal of darkened wood", "finally, divers bronze figures, not finished, nor repaired". Not ident. or disapp.

25
Pendulum Clocks and Clock-cases

Before 1698

Acc. to Brice, *Descr.*, 1706, p. 111, C. had made "clock cases embellished with bronze figures of great beauty". In c. 1700, C. presented to the Superintendent Hardouin-Mansart a pendulum clock enclosed in a case repr. the Temple of Janus, closed, to symbolise Peace. It was embellished with a statuette of the King treading underfoot his defeated, chained enemies; the King was accompanied by the figures of Justice, Might, History, Fame, Glory, Abundance and Valour crushing Discord, all in bronze. On the dial, in a cartouche, the triumph of the King over Heresy was recalled by an inscription giving the number of heretics converted by Louis XIV. Letter in Arch. Nat., O¹ 1907ᴬ, 5. In C.'s Invent. a.d. are in fact mentioned "two clock cases, each with a dial and many gilded ornaments and bronze figures, mounted on a marquetry box", and "two small clocks, each with two bronze figures". Not ident. or disapp.

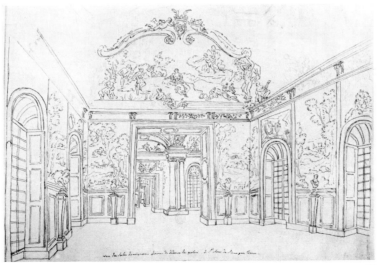

23

30¹ *31¹*

26
Work on the Façade of the Vieux Château de Meudon

1699–1700   Stone
Mazeline and C. together carved the pediment of the new avant-corps and military trophies in bas-relief at the first floor, for which they rec. 1760 L. in 1699 and 1700, *Comptes*, IV, 545, 677. The vieux château was demolished in 1803, cf. P. Biver, *Hist. du chât. de Meudon*, Paris, 1923. Destroyed.

27
Two Vases

Before 1701   Marble   244 × 70
Piganiol mentions two vases by C. in the Amphithéâtre de Mercure in the Bosquet de Marly, on either side of an antique statue of Mercury, cf. *Vers.-Marly*, 1701, p. 387, et seq. The inventory of 1722 says: "the body is decorated on one side with a sunflower, accompanied by two palms and on the other face with the same flower and an olive branch. The bulge is decorated with fluting and bands." Arch. Nat., O¹ 1969ᴬ. Whereabouts unknown.

28
Venus Handing Arms to Aeneas

Before 1704   Group
Salon of 1704, *Livret*, p. 26. Not ident. or disapp.

29
Aeneas and Anchises

Before 1704   Group   Gilded bronze
Salon of 1704. The *Livret*, p. 26, notes that in the group of Aeneas carrying his father Anchises "there are also Creusa and Ascanius". This must, therefore, be the work mentioned in the sculptor's Invent. a.d. as paired with 'The Rape of the Sabines', Min. Centr. Arch. Nat., Et. XV, 424. Not ident. or disapp.

30²/31²

30*
Allegory of Saint Peter Penitent

1709 Bas-relief Bonbanc stone 195 × 389
In the spandrels between the arches of the royal chapel at Versailles; the episodes of the Passion of Christ are depicted allegorically by angels. C. carved the scene of St. Peter penitent after his denial of Christ. In a detailed memoir C. himself descr. his bas-relief as: "an angel repr. St. Peter penitent; he is seated on clouds, at his feet the cock, which makes him think of what the Lord has predicted; above his head several heads of cherubim, signifying that God has forgiven his sin; at his side a young angel bearing a tiara and the key indicating the position which God had granted him as Head of the Church", Arch. Nat., O¹ 1784, Mém. of Cornu with a sketch*. Estim. at 900 L., paid between 1708 and 1713, *ibid.*, and *Comptes*, V, 216, 321, 530. At the third arcade of the south wall. cf. Ph. Bertrand no. 22.

VERSAILLES PALACE, CHAPEL

31*
Ecclesiastical Trophies

1709 Bas-relief Limestone 248 × 86
C. was also comm. to execute on the pillar supporting the arcade a bas-relief of trophies connected with the scene above. It repr. "the mystical symbol of Jesus Christ; one sees the phoenix which kills itself in order to nourish its children, seated on a cross intertwined with olive branches and adorned with several penants or ensigns in which are shown the portraits of the first martyrs such as St. Peter, St. Paul and several others; underneath one sees the tiara and the keys; then one sees St. Peter's throne very richly ornamented; in its centre the mystical book of the New Testament; underneath, a lamp, fumes rising from it, repr. the prayer, sacrifice and homage which we should render to God in His Holy Temple; at the side palms signifying the peace which God grants to our souls if we follow His Holy Will", Arch. Nat., O¹ 1784, Mém. with sketch* by C. who received for this work 500 L. paid in 1711; *Comptes*, V, 530. cf. Bertrand no. 23.

VERSAILLES PALACE, CHAPEL

32
Mars Seated

1710 Statue Marble
On 12th Dec., 1710, the sculptor Jacques Martin gave C.'s widow an undertaking "to complete the white marble figure commenced by her late husband repr. Mars seated" for a consideration of 200 L., Min. Centr. Arch. Nat., Et. XV, 468. Not ident. or disapp.

33
Work at Sceaux

a. *Sculpture in the park*
C. rec. 450 L. for unspecified work of sculpture; F. de Catheu, 'Le Décor du Chât. de Sceaux', in *GBA*, 1939², p. 301. Not ident. or disapp.
b. *Furniture*
C. rec. 615 L. "for a piece of furniture enriched with embroidery in silver and white satin," *ibid.* Not ident. or disapp.

WORK FOUND IN C.'s STUDIO AFTER HIS DEATH, not previously listed.

Invents a.d. of C. and of his wife, 13 Oct., 1710 and 20 May, 1715, Min. Centr. Arch. Nat., Et. XV, 424, 468. Not ident. or disapp.

Various Vases
"Two large sculpted vases in white marble" and "two medium-sized bronze vases, each mounted on a white marble base". Brice also noted some vases in the studio, *Descr.*, 1698, p. 81.

Apollo and Diana
Two busts Marble

The Rape of the Sabines
Group Gilded bronze
Group of three figures. Not in the Invent. a.d. of C.'s wife.

River and Naiad
Two figures Bronze
Not in the Invent. a.d. of C.'s wife.

COTTON, Pierre (not Michel, as he is wrongly called)

Pupil of the brothers Anguier. 2nd prize at the Acad. in 1675 (see no. 1). Member of the Acad. St.-Luc as sculpteur peintre, 12 Oct. 1678, having submitted a reception piece, Arch. Nat., Y 9320 and Guiffrey, *St.-Luc*. Lived in the rue Royale, parish of St.-Roch. cf. Sainte-Beuve, 'Le tombeau de Lully', in *GBA*, 1926², p. 199. Married Madeleine Molin; two children, Michel, born c. 1678 and Joseph. In 1701, he lived in the rue des Moineaux, parish of St.-Roch, Min. Centr. Arch. Nat., Et. XIII, 140, donation of 20 Feb., 1701. T-B, VII, 1912, p. 564.

1
The Fall of Adam

1675
2nd sculpture prize at the Acad., *AAF*, V, p. 277; *P-V*, II, p. 56. Not ident. or disapp.

3

2
Work on the Bassin 'Sous le Dragon', Versailles

1683   Models
For this Bassin, the future Bassin de Neptune, C. collab. with Legeret and Caffieri on vases, cuvettes, masks and shells. Payment 400 L., *Comptes*, II, 278. cf. Carlier no. 3*. Not ident. or disapp.

3
Work for the Funeral Service of the Grand Condé

1687   Cardboard
Together with Hardy and Regnaut, C. produced decor. for the choir of Notre-Dame, Paris, for the funeral of the Grand Condé in Feb. 1687: skeletons holding torches 'à l'antique', skulls with bats' wings,

trophies, shields, helmets, medals, Roman eagles, scrolls. Contract for 2550 L. signed 1 Feb. 1687, Min. Centr. Arch. Nat., Et. XCII, 152. After designs by Berain. Engr. by Dolivar*. Destroyed.

4*
Tomb of Lulli

1688   Marble
Estim. 3500 L. Specification publ. by Sainte-Beuve, *op. cit.* (p. 199): Two marble figures, H: 160, repr. 'Poetry' and 'Music'*; two small children, marble, H: c. 60, on either side of the bronze bust of the composer (by Collignon, no. 12*); a curtain lifted up by a skeleton (both stucco). The monument was in the Mus. des Mon. fr., no. 202; after the Revolution,

*4*¹   *4*³

Detail   *4*

returned to Notre-Dame-des-Victoires, former Convent of the Reformed Order of Augustins, but without the stucco parts, and to a different place; cf. Piganiol, *Descr.*, 1765, III, p. 90; Guilhermy, *Inscript. de la Fr.*, 1873, I, p. 418; *Rich. Art Fr., Mon. Rel.*, II, p. 227. Drawing in Coll. Gaignières, Bibl. Nat. Est., 4712★.

PARIS, NOTRE-DAME-DES-VICTOIRES

                                                          5

5

Tomb of André Le Nôtre and his wife, Marie Langlois

After 1700   Marble
Le Nôtre died in 1700, his wife in 1707. The tomb was formerly in the chapel of St.-André in the Church of St.-Roch. Above the sarconphagus Religion seated, an open book on her right knee, holding the epitaph. Above her, an escutcheon with the arms of the Le Nôtre family. Under the sarcophagus, a bust of the deceased. Acc. to Dezallier, *Paris*, 1778, p. 125, the tomb was executed by Cotton, the bust by Coysevox (see no. 76★), as confirmed by all the old *Descriptions*. Destroyed during the Revolution, except for the bust. Two drawings with slight variants in the Coll. Gaignières, Bibl. Nat. Est., 4492★, 4631. Destroyed.

6
See appendix.

COUDRAY, François (1678-1727)

b. 1678 at Villacerf, near Troyes in Champagne; cf. Dezallier, *Vie.*, II, p. 241. Son of François Coudray, concierge of the Marquis de Villacerf. Worked in 1697 in the Coysevox studio, *Comptes*, V, 342. In Jan. 1698 apprenticed at the Gobelins, *ibid.*; 20 Dec. 1698 received 2nd Petit Prix of the Acad. from Coypel; 23 Mar. 1699 another 2nd Petit Prix from Hardouin-Mansart, *P-V*, III, 246, 290. 3 Apr. 1700 selected to compete for the Grand Prix, *ibid.*, III, 293. Married Marie Larue on 7 Feb. 1706, and lived in the rue Mouffetard, Paris, Min. Centr. Arch. Nat., Et. XVII, 499. Agréé by the Acad. 5 Jan. 1709; made Academician 20 Apr. 1712, *P-V*, IV, 77, 145. In 1714 birth of son, Pierre (who later worked as a sculptor in Dresden until his death in 1770, cf. G.-O. Müller, *Vergessene Künstler*, Dresden, 1895). 15 July 1715 royal permission to move to Dresden, cf. *NAAF*, 1878, p. 11; 3 Aug. 1715 departure to Dresden, *P-V*, IV, 206. Established in Dresden in the service of Augustus the Strong from 1716 until his death. Comm. in 1716 to submit the model for an equestrian statue of Augustus. When unsuccessful after several attempts, he relinquished the comm. in favour of Vinache, cf. S. Asche, *B. Permoser*, Frankfurt, 1966, p. 267-9, 374-5. Died 9 Apr. 1727, *P-V*, V, 24. cf. Jal, p. 435; L. Dussieux, *Les art. fr. à l'étranger*, 1852, p. 39; G. Servières, 'Les art. fr. á la cour de Saxe', in *GBA*, 1911², 121-35; T-B, VII, 1912, p. 569 (E. Sigismund).

1

1*
Models for the Chapel, Versailles

1710
  a. *Wax models* for door and window furniture
  b. *Wax models* for a console
C. was comm. to model in wax various pieces of door and window furniture for the royal chapel in Versailles. Lock-plates, latches, door knobs, bolts, tringles etc. were covered with cartouches of the King's arms supported by cherubs, suns, cherubim heads, royal attributes such as the King's cypher, his judge's staff and sceptre, the collars of the orders of the St. Esprit and of St. Michael, allegories of Europe and Asia for the windows of the Salon haut and a host of plant and geometrical ornaments.
C. also furnished the model of the console which was to carry the 'unconsecrated wafer', resting on the head of a cherubim. In the long detailed mém. about these models the total of 2455 L. was reduced to 885 L., Arch. Nat., O[I] 1784; payment in two instalm., 1710–11, *Comptes*, V, 414, 531. The gilded bronze locks★, cast after C.'s wax models by the founders Lochon & J. Desjardins, are still extant.

2
Saint Sebastian

  a.★ 1712 Statuette Marble H: 89
Reception piece for the Acad., *P-V*, IV, 145. The Roman centurion, tied naked to a tree trunk, his head drooping, the left arm hanging down, is about to die. C. was given 100 L. by the Acad. for the pedestal, *ibid*. Exh. in the Acad, during the 18th c., cf. Guérin, *Descr.*, 1715; Dezallier, *Descr.*, 1781, p. 51, 135. In the Petit Trianon during the Restoration; since 1854 in the Louvre, cf. Fontaine, 1910, p. 162.

PARIS, LOUVRE

  b.★ Statuette Bronze H: 89
After the Louvre model.

WASHINGTON D.C., NATIONAL GALLERY

3*
Prince Friedrich August of Saxony

1715 Bust Marble H: 67.5
Made by C. in Paris in 1715, sent to Dresden; as a result, C. was called to the service of the father, Augustus the Strong. The Prince, smiling faintly, his bewigged head in three-quarter profile, is wearing a cuirass.

DRESDEN, ALBERTINUM

4
Elector Augustus the Strong

  a.★ 1720 Oval medallion Marble Signed & dated
Half length portrait, left profile, wearing wig and cuirass.

LEIPZIG, STADTBIBLIOTHEK

2a

2b

4a

b.★ c. 1725   Oval medallion   Stucco
Unsigned variant of no. 4a. The stucco medallion is
encased in the architectural decoration of a chimney-
breast in the dining hall in Schloss Moritzburg.
C.'s name is mentioned in 1725 in connection with
unspecified work in Moritzburg, cf. Dresden, Landhauptarchiv loc. 354, acta Chatoullensachen, 1718–22,
quoted and attrib. to C. in Asche, *op. cit.* (Biogr.).

SCHLOSS MORITZBURG

5★
Christopher von Manteuffel

c. 1725   Oval medallion   Marble
Formal analogies between this medallion and nos. 3 and
4 have led Asche, *op. cit.*, to attrib. no. 5 to C. All three
show a similar half-length portrait in right profile of a
gentleman in wig and cuirass.

GAUTZSCH, near LEIPZIG, MARTIN LUTHER CHURCH

4b

3

5

6–7

6* 7*
Bacchants and Young Satyrs

c. 1725   Two groups   Stone
Two nude Bacchants, each giving a drink to an infant satyr; both groups were in the Stadt Pavilion of the Zwinger, opposite each other, before being trsf. to the Nympheum. After considerable restoration, both groups were put back in the high niches of the Stadt Pavilion. cf. Asche, *op. cit.* (ill. 306), who attribs. both groups to C.

DRESDEN, ZWINGER, STADT PAVILION

8
Group of Children

c. 1718 or 1725   Stone
Carved, together with other groups of children, for the balustrade of the Zwinger. Asche, *op. cit.* (ill. 310), suggests C. as the artist. A boy offering flowers to a girl, who turns away. Sold together with several other sculptures from the Zwinger in 1891; Dresden, Art Trade, 1927; Zwinger Bauhütte, 1960; now in the French Pavilion.

DRESDEN, ZWINGER, FRENCH PAVILION

9
Two Terms

c. 1727   Marble
In collab. with Thomae. Acc. to the Dresden archives, a payment of 1300 Thaler was made to the sculptors for two marble terms in the Dutch Pavilion. Landhauptarchiv, Dresden, 1730, quoted by Asche, *op. cit.*, who assumes that both works were destroyed when the Dutch Pavilion was transformed into a Japanese one.

10
Sphinxes

1727   Length of plinth: 175
Acc. to a report by Count Wakkerbarth to Augustus the Strong, dated 8 Jan. 1727, C. was comm. to supply for the terrace of Schloss Gross-Sedlitz near Heidenau, sculptures of dolphins, sphinxes and a group of Neptune and Amphitrite; Landhauptarchiv, Dresden, loc. 713, vol. CXCVIII, quoted by Asche, *op. cit.* C. had started only on the sphinxes when he died on 9 April 1727. Completed by Kirchner; extant, but in bad condition.

GROSS–SEDLITZ

11
Zephyr and Flora

Between 1715–27   Group   Marble
One of the many groups, antique and modern, Italian and French, with which from 1715 onwards Augustus the Strong decorated his 'Grossen Garten' in Dresden. Destroyed during the siege of Dresden in 1760; we know the group only through Lindemann's engr.* of 1735 in Leplat, *Recueil des marbres antiques dans la Gal. du roi de Pologne à Dresde*, 1773, pl. 217*. Both figures are semi-nude; Zephyr is shown as a winged child picking a flower from Flora's garland. Destroyed.

12 13 14 15
Spring, Summer, Autumn, Winter

Between 1715–27   Four terms   Marble
Done by C. for the same Grossen Garten; known only through Lindemann's two engr. in Leplat (see no. 11), pl. 215–6*. Each figure with its traditional attribs.: Spring, or Flora, holding flowers; Summer, or Ceres, a sheaf of grain; Autumn, or Bacchus, crushing a bunch of grapes; Winter, an old man, shivering and crossing his arms. Disappeared.

11

12	*13*	*14*	*15*

succession, 9 Aug. 1746, are missing. cf. Rambaud, II, p. 419–20, acte de l'étude VI, liasse 671.

C.'s portrait was painted by Delyen in 1725 as reception piece for the Acad. (now in the Mus., Versailles★); in front, a small bronze version of 'The Rhône' (no. 40 b). Engr. after this portrait by N. de Larmessin, 1730.

I
Joseph interpreting Pharaoh's Dreams

1696   Bas-relief
2nd sculpture prize, Acad., *P-V*, III, 195. Not ident. or disapp.

COUSTOU, Guillaume (1677-1746)

b. Lyons 29 Nov. 1677, son of François, wood-carver, reg. Parr. St.-Nizier, Lyons; pupil of his elder brother Nicolas and of his uncle Coysevox. 2nd sculpture prize, in 1696, see no. 1; 1st sculpture prize in 1697, see no. 2. From 1697–1700, in Rome where he worked with the French sculptor Pierre Legros II. In 1704, received into the Acad.; in 1706, Asst. Prof., *P-V*, III, 361, 404; IV, 31. Married Geneviève-Julie Morel in 1710 (Fich. Laborde Bibl. Nat., no. 14134); 15 children incl. the sculptor Guillaume II, cf. Jal, p. 443–4. In 1715, made Prof., in 1726, Asst. Recteur, *P-V*, IV, 217; V, 16. Gravely ill in 1729; Recteur in 1733, *P-V*, V, 64–5, 112. Died in Paris, 22 Feb. 1746, cf. Herluison, p. 92; Abbé Gougenot, *Vie de Coustou le jeune*, Paris, 1903; Dezallier, *Vie*, II, p. 302; Mariette, *ABC*, II, p. 21–2; Cochin, *Mém. inédits*, p. 39, 68–69; Fontenai, II, p. 433–4; T-B, VII, 1912, p. 601–2 (M. Audin); M. Audin & E. Vial, *Dict. des artistes, Lyonnais*, Paris, 1918; E.-F.-S. Dilke, 'les Coustou', in *GBA*, 1901[2]; J. Coolidge, 'Two Portrait Busts attr. to G. C. the Elder', in *Essays in Honour of W. Friedländer*, New York, 1965. Actes notariés concerning G. C., Min. Centr. Arch. Nat., Et. XCV, liasses 56, 64, 65, 67, 68, 69, 85 (1710, 1719, 1720); Et. LXXXIII, liasses 339–48, 351, 356, 360, 362, 365–7, 372–3, 377, 380, 383–4, 387 (1731–45), especially the Invent. a.d. of Geneviève Morel, 13 Oct. 1734. In Et. LVI: C.'s Invent. a.d., 28 Feb. 1746 and partage de

(*see no. 40b*)   *G. Coustou*

2

Joseph's Brothers held by Pharaoh on Suspicion of Spying

1697   Bas-relief
1st sculpture prize, Acad., *P-V*, III, 218. Not ident. or disapp.

3 4

Faun carrying a Kid.   Fluteplayer

Between 1698–1700   Two statues   Marble
Copies of antiques; after Gougenot. Bought by Frederick the Great for the park at Sans-Souci. Not ident. or disapp.

5

Adoring Angel

1702   Lead
C. was comm. to do one of the angels for the Altar of the Virgin, Dôme des Invalides, Arch. Nat., O^I 1665, 54; the other was by Poirier. The altar of St. Thérèse opposite was also flanked by two adoring angels, by J.-L. Lemoyne and Lapierre. The plaster model was made in 1702, acc. to Félibien des Avaux, *Invalides*, pp. 287, 299. cf. Granet, p. 108; Pérau, p. 75; engr.★ by Lucas in Pérau, pl. 46. Destroyed after Pigalle had carved angels in marble in 1748.

6

Work on the Baldachin of the High Altar, Dôme des Invalides

1702   Bronze
In collab. with Van Clève. Decorative work: angels, vine-branches, ears of corn, palm branches, fleurons etc. The plaster model was made in 1702, acc. to Félibien des Avaux, *Invalides*, p. 287, 299; cf. also Pérau, p. 84; engr.★ by Chevotet and Lucas in Pérau, pl. 26. In 1709, C., together with other sculptors, rec. 20,307 L., incl. payment for work on the baldachin, *Comptes*, V, 347. Destroyed during the Revolution.

6

7b^I

5

7a

10

7
Hercules on the Funeral Pyre

1704
   a.⋆ Statuette   Marble   H: 74
Reception piece for the Acad. roy., 25 Oct. 1704, *P-V*,
III, 361, 404–5. In the salle des Assemblées of the Acad.
Hercules, on the funeral pyre, frantically trying to tear
off the fatal tunic of Nessus.

PARIS, LOUVRE

   b¹.⋆ Terracotta version   H: 53
Some variations from the marble. *See appendix.*

ROUEN, MUSEE DES BEAUX–ARTS

   c. Bronze versions
One in the Coupry-Dupré sale, 21 Feb. 1811, no. 46, is
perhaps the one now in

KASSEL-WILHELMSHÖHE, LÖWENBURG (H: 28)

8
*Work on the Grand Baldachin of the Bains
d'Apollon*

1705–7   Gilded lead
C. was one of a team of sculptors comm. to create in
the Bosquet du Marais the great baldachin for the group
'Apollon servi par les Nymphes', *Comptes*, V, 538. cf.
Bourdy no. 6. Destroyed.

9
**Sculpture decorating the Entrance Portal, Hôtel
de Soubise, Paris**

1705
   a. *Hercules crushing Cacus; Minerva crushing Gorgon*
Two groups   St.-Leu stone   H: c. 260
   b. *Children and lions supporting a shield*
St.-Leu stone
     c. *Two trophies*   Bas-relief
     d. *Eight capitals*
     e. *Eight trophies*, in the round
     f. Head of Abundance in a cartouche, Keystone
     g. *Console in a cartel*, Keystone

All in collab. with Bourdy (see no. 5⋆). Contract and
specif. 14 July and 21 Nov. 1705, Arch. Nat. Min.
Centr., Et. XCIX. Total payment 3300 L. Destroyed,
except no. 5 f.

10⋆
Work on the Cornice of the King's Chamber

1706   Stucco
In collab. with Van Clève, Magnier, Poirier, Lapierre
and J.-L. Lemoyne. Payment 920 L., *Comptes*, V, 494;
cf. Fiske Kimball, 'Transform. des Appart. de Trianon',
in *GBA*, 1938¹, p. 86.

VERSAILLES, GRAND TRIANON

11⋆ 12⋆
Faith and Religion

1707   Two statues   Tonnerre stone   H: 292
Mém. de Coustou, Arch. Nat., O¹ 1784. Payment
2600 L., *Comptes*, V, 124. Above the pediment of the
garden façade of the chapel at Versailles.

VERSAILLES PALACE, CHAPEL

11–15

**13★
Cherubim in Clouds**

1707   Bas-relief   St.-Leu stone   162 × 267
Mém. in Arch. Nat., O^I 1784. Payment 350 L.; for the keystone of the window in the west façade of the chapel below 'Faith' and 'Religion' (nos. 11, 12).

VERSAILLES PALACE, CHAPEL

**14   15★
Two Groups of Children**

1707   Lead, formerly gilded   H: 210
Placed at either end of the ridge of the Chapel roof. Model and execution by G. C. and P. Lepautre for 8000 L. On one of the two groups Raon, Frémin (no. 15) and Bertrand (no. 17) participated. *Comptes*, V, 124, 318, 412; Mém., Arch. Nat., O^I 1784.

VERSAILLES PALACE, CHAPEL

**16★   17★
Saint Jerome and Saint Augustine**

1708   Two statues   Tonnerre stone   H: 286
Mém., Arch. Nat., O^I 1784. Payment 2000 L., *Comptes*, V, 123. On the cornice outside the upper storey on the south side of the chapel.

VERSAILLES PALACE, CHAPEL

16   *17*

**18
Ecclesiastical Trophies**

1707   Bas-relief   Hard stone, gilded   62 × 57
cf. P. Bertrand no. 18b★; *Comptes*, V, 124, 530–1.

VERSAILLES PALACE, CHAPEL

**19
Father of the Church**

1707   Medallion   Bas-relief   Hard stone, gilded
Diam: 62
One of six medallions; cf. P. Bertrand no. 18a★. Payment 150 L., *Comptes*, V, 321, 531.

VERSAILLES PALACE, CHAPEL

**20
Two Cherubim Heads**

1707   Hard stone, gilded
On the keystones of the high windows of the chapel; total payment for 12 keystones, in collab. with five other sculptors, 700 L., *Comptes*, V, 124. cf. Bertrand no. 16★.

VERSAILLES PALACE, CHAPEL

**21★   22★
Hope and Faith**

1707–8   Two Bas-reliefs   Bonbanc stone   L: 194
cf. Bertrand no. 19. Above a window of the North Tribune in the chapel, in the first bay. Mém., Arch. Nat., O^I 1784. Payment 1700 L., *Comptes*, V, 213.

VERSAILLES PALACE, CHAPEL

**23–26
WORK ON THE ROYAL TRIBUNE**

Carved decoration: on the North wall by G.C.; on the South wall by Poirier.

**23
A Door Frame, a Cornice, two Consoles and a Border**

1708   Stone
Payment 166 L., 86 L., 120 L., 125 L. respectively. Detailed Mém., Arch. Nat., O^I 1784.

VERSAILLES PALACE, CHAPEL

**24★   25★
Heads of Cherubim in Clouds**

1708   Two Half-reliefs   Stone   L: 121 and 265
Payment 450 L., Arch. Nat., O^I 1784.

VERSAILLES PALACE, CHAPEL

21–22

25

26*
The Boy Jesus among the Teachers in the Temple

1708   Bas-relief   Bonbanc stone   283 × 240
Payment 2800 L., Arch. Nat., O^I 1784; *Comptes*, V, 213, 414.

VERSAILLES PALACE, CHAPEL

24

26

27

31

27–31
SCULPTURE IN THE NAVE OF THE CHAPEL

28

27*
Allegory of The Last Supper

1708–9   Bas-relief   Bonbanc stone   194 × 148
One of the sixteen scenes evoking the Passion of Christ
in the spandrels of the choir arcades at ground level. cf.
Bertrand no. 22. Payment 1490 L., Arch. Nat., O^I 1784,
Comptes, V, 318. An angel taking the bread beside the
chalice from a large paten held by a cherub.

VERSAILLES PALACE, CHAPEL

28*
The Institution of the Blessed Sacrament

1708–9   Bas-relief   Bonbanc stone   248 × 130
Payment 800 L., Arch. Nat., O^I 1784. Below The Last
Supper (no. 27), on the inner face of the pillar. Three
cherubim with a palm branch, a ciborium, a paten and a
monstrance. cf. Bertrand no. 23.

VERSAILLES PALACE, CHAPEL

29   30
Cherubim in Clouds

1709–10   Two Bas-reliefs   Stone   130 × 56
On the keystones of the two arcades of the nave behind
the High Altar. Estim. 450 L. for both. Mém., Arch.
Nat., O^I 1784; *Comptes*, V, 213.

VERSAILLES PALACE, CHAPEL

31*
Angel in Adoration and Cherubim

1709–10   Bas-relief   Painted & gilded stone   H: 162
Payment 850 L. On the right-hand pillar behind the
High Altar. Mém., Arch. Nat., O^I 1784. The one on
the left-hand pillar by P. Lepautre.

VERSAILLES PALACE, CHAPEL

33

34

32–34
WORK IN THE SALON HAUT OF THE CHAPEL, SOUTH WALL

G.C. was responsible for the south wall, Poirier for the north wall, Poultier for the west wall, Lapierre for the east wall. G.C. rec. a total payment of 19,657 L., *Comptes*, V, 412.

32
Sculpted Ornaments

1709–10
  a. Stone sculpture on the door frames
Payment 1406 L., Arch. Nat., O^I 1784; *Comptes*, V, 412.
  b.★ Stone sculpture decorating the niche.
Ornaments on the cornice and uprights, a shell in the

cul de four and a cartouche of the King's arms above the archivolt. Payment 1100 L., *ibid.*
  c.★ Trophy of Europe
Bas-relief Stone 65 × 56
On the pedestal supporting Bousseau's statue of 'Magnanimity'. Payment 250 L., *ibid.*

VERSAILLES PALACE, CHAPEL

33★ 34★
Meditation and the Desire for God
Divine Love and Wisdom

1709–10 Half-reliefs Stone Each figure L: 178
The four Virtues, grouped in pairs, reclining on the arches above the doors. Payment 2560 L., Arch. Nat., O^I 1784; *Comptes*, V, 412.

VERSAILLES PALACE, CHAPEL

35
Diana

1710 Statue Marble H: 210
Payment 4300 L., *Comptes*, V, 432, 510, after the 'Diana of Ephesus'. In the park at Marly, in the Bosquet de Diane, counterpart to the Bosquet de Bacchus (see no. 37). Invent. of 1722, Arch. Nat., O^I 1969^A. Wrongly described by Gougenot as comm. for Versailles. Shown in a water-colour drawing★, Arch. Nat., O^I 1472, p. 11. Not ident. or disapp.

32c

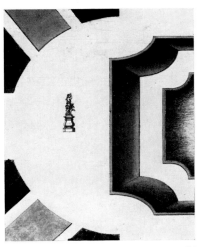

32b¹   *32b²*   *35*

36¹

36²

Payment 4200 L., *Comptes*, V, 511, 611. One of the four 'Coureurs'; pursuing Atalanta (by P. Lepautre). On an island in the Bassin des Carpes at Marly; during the Revolution trsf. to the garden of the Tuileries, cf. Millin, *Descr. des Tuileries*, 1798, p. 82-3; Philipon la Madeleine, *Le Guide . . . aux Tuileries*, an VI, p. 107; *Rich. Art. Fr., IV, Paris, Mon. civ.*, 1913, p. 222-3. Drawing* in Coll. de Cotte, Bibl. Nat. Est., Fb 26. cf. N. Coustou no. 60.

PARIS, LOUVRE

36*
Hippomenes

1711 Statue Marble H: 134
Signed: G. COUSTOU FECIT 1712

38

37
Bacchus

1712 Statue Marble H: 162
After an antique; payment 4300 L., *Comptes*, V, 511, 695. In the Bosquet de Bacchus at Marly, counterpart to the Bosquet de Diane (see no. 35); in 1717 in the Théâtre d'Eau at Versailles, cf. Piganiol, *Vers.-Marly*, 1717, I, p. 170. Not ident. or disapp.

38*
Louis XIII

1712–15 Statue Marble H: 175
For the monument repr. the Vow of Louis XIII. cf. Bertrand no. 28*. Model in 1712, *Comptes*, V, 695. Payment 8100 L., *Comptes*, V, 694, 786, 873; Arch. Nat., O^I 1790 and 1921^A. In the choir of Notre-Dame, *NAAF*, 1873, p. 356 as a pendant to Louis XIV by Coysevox (no. 98) on either side of N. Coustou's Pieta (no. 61). The King, kneeling, offers his sceptre and crown to the Virgin. During the Revolution in the Mus. des Mon. Fr., no. 327.

PARIS, NOTRE-DAME

39*
Daphne

1713–14 Statue Marble H: 133
Signed: G COUSTOU FECIT
One of the 'Coureurs', pursued by Apollo. See no. 36 and N. Coustou, no. 60. Payment 4300 L., *Comptes*, V, 694, 785. On an island in the Bassin des Carpes at Marly; during the Revolution trsf. to the Tuileries Gardens. Drawing * Bibl. Nat. Est. Va 351, IV Fol.

PARIS, LOUVRE

39^1

40
The Rhône

1714–20
a.* Bronze group L: 324
See 'The Saône' by N. Coustou (no. 64).

LYONS, PLACE BELLECOUR

b. Several smaller bronze replicas, especially in the former Coll. Doucet (Lyons, Mus. Arts Décoratifs), and at Stockholm, Royal Palace *. See also C.'s portrait p. 129.

41
Trophies

1715 Bas-relief Bronze 180 × 160
In collab. with his brother Nicolas for the monument in Lyons, cf. N. Coustou no. 65. Destroyed.

39^2

40b

40a

42*
Nymph of Diana

1717 Statue Marble H: 178
For the bibl., see Cayot no. 8. Payment 3600 L., Arch.
Nat., O^I 2227. Original position unknown. Drawing in
the Coll. de Cotte, Bibl. Nat. Est., Fb 26. Lost; rediscovered in a private coll. by L. Réau, *GBA*, 1932^I,
p. 150. The nymph, holding a trumpet in her right hand,
lifts her left to her ear, listening. Given to the Mus. in
Jerusalem by Baron Edmond de Rothschild in 1969.

JERUSALEM, MUSEUM

43 44
River and *Nymph*

c. 1719 Two statues Stone
Two seated figures for the façade of the ancient
Château d'eau of the Palais-Royal, Paris. Attrib. to
G.C. by all the authors of the *Descriptions*. The sum of
300 L. rec. by the sculptor in 1719 is, however, too small
for a work of such importance, Arch. Nat., O^I 2219.
The façade and sculptures of the Château d'eau are
shown in an engr.* by de La Planche and Marque in
J.-F. Blondel, *Arch. Fr.*, III, liv. V, no. IX, p. 17. De-
stroyed.

45*
Tomb of Maréchal d'Estrées and his wife

c. 1720 Relief Marble 142 × 92
Attrib. to G.C. by Gougenot, *Eloge*, p. 12; cf. Brière,
'Deux oeuvres de G. Coustou', in *BSHAF*, 1922, 2^e
fasc., p. 362–5. Originally in the Church of the Couvent
des Bons Hommes at Passy. Engr.* by Ransonnette in
Millin, *Antiq. Nat.*, II, chap. XII, pl. 4.

VERSAILLES, MUSEUM

42

43–44

46

45²

46
Monument of the Heart of Louis XIV

c. 1720   Silver, copper and silver-gilt
Payment 64,107 L., Arch. Nat., O^I 2228. Formerly in
the Eglise de la Maison Professe des Jésuites (to-day
St.-Paul-St.-Louis), a pendant to the Monument of the
Heart of Louis XIII by Sarrazin; it showed two silver
angels holding the heart of the King. During the
Revolution trsf. to the Mus. des Mon. fr.; destroyed
during the Empire. cf. G. Montaillier, 'Les Anges
de St.-P.-St.-L.', in *La Cité*, Jan. 1918, no. 65, p. 150–4.

Drawing* in Bibl. Nat. Est., Coll. Gaignières, no. 4740.
Destroyed.

47*
Marc-René de Voyer de Paulmy, Marquis d'Argenson

c. 1721   Bust   Marble   H: 89
Part of the tomb of St.-Nicolas du Chardonnet. In the
Salle des Antiques at the Louvre during the Revolution,
then Mus. des Mon. fr., no. 390; attrib. to G. Coustou.

VERSAILLES, MUSEUM

45¹

47

48*
Saint François-Xavier

1722 Statue Marble H: c. 200
cf. Piganiol, *Descr.*, 1765, VI, p. 358; Brice, 1742, III, p. 433. Formerly in the Noviciat des Jésuites, rue du Pot de Fer.

PARIS, CHURCH OF SAINT-GERMAIN-DES-PRES

49
Saint Ignace

1722 Statue Marble H: c. 200
Pendant to St. François-Xavier (no. 48). Both sold by Lenoir, with other statues, to a dealer in exchange for architectural fragments from the demolition of Anet. In 1802, the Church of St.-Germain-des-Prés reclaimed both, but recovered only St. François-Xavier, cf. J. Vanuxem, 'Le chât. d'Anet', in *XVIIe siècle*, 1957, p. 392–406. Disappeared.

51¹

51²

48

50

52

50
Louis XV between Truth and Justice

1722   Group   Plaster model
Part of the new decor. comm. by Cardinal Dubois for
the Great Chamber of Parliament at the Palais de
Justice, for the Proclamation of the majority of Louis
XV on 22 Feb. 1723. C. supplied the model for a marble
group above the fireplace. Sketch by St.-Aubin on the
margin of Piganiol's *Descr.*, 1765, II, p. 8–9 (preserved
in the Petit-Palais, Paris). Appears in the engraving* of
the ceremony, Bibl. Nat. Est., Coll. Hennin no. 7993,
p. 3. Destroyed.

51
Sculptures for the Bridge at Blois

1724   Stone   Signed & dated
Facing upstream: an obelisk surmounted by a globe and
a cross, decor. with a cartouche supported by tritons,
a shield, plant and allegorical motifs; facing down-
stream: a simple cartouche; cf. F. de Dartein. *Etude sur
les ponts*, 1907, with engr.* of the sculptures.

BLOIS (Loir-et-Cher)
See appendix.

52
Sculptures for the Palais-Bourbon

c. 1724–30   Stone
For the street portal, C. carved on the façade a bas-relief
of two angels carrying the arms of the Princesse de
Bourbon; on the pedestals flanking it, seated statues of
Minerva and Abundance; on the pediment of the main
façade, a bas-relief of the Earth crowned by Zephyr;
above, the chariot of the Sun. On the balustrade,
numerous groups of children repr. the Zodiac, the
Seasons, the Elements, cf. Piganiol, *Descr.*, 1742, VII,
p. 163–8; Blondel, *Arch. Fr.* I, p. 265–7, with an engr.*
of the façade, pl. 4. Destroyed.

53*
Louis XV as a Boy

c. 1725   Bust   Marble   H: 71
Sent to Rome for the Acad. de France by d'Antin,
Corr. Dir. Acad. Fr. Rome, VIII, p. 242; Fontenai,
I, p. 434; Coolidge, *op. cit.* (Biogr.).

ROME, VILLA MEDICI

53

54²

54*
Tomb of Cardinal Dubois

c. 1725   Statue   Marble   H: 150
Remains of a tomb in the Church of St.-Honoré;
trsf. during the Revolution to the Mus. Mon. Fr., *Arch.*,
III, p. 303. Engr.* in the Bibl. Nat. Est., Va 233,
agrees with the old *Descriptions*. The prelate is kneeling,
his hands clasped.

PARIS, CHURCH OF SAINT-ROCH

54¹

57

56
Cartouches and Trophies for the Pedestal of the Equestrian Statue of Louis XIV, Place Louis-le-Grand

1727–30
Contract and estim. 9 Dec. 1727, Arch. Nat., Q^I 1140, with drawings* by Beausire. Payment 65,000 L. The decorative motifs were allegories of the glory of the King. Melted down during the Revolution, cf. *Mém. de la Société de l'Hist. de P.*, XV, 1888. Destroyed.

57*
Samuel Bernard

c. 1727   Bust   Marble   H: 98
cf. Gougenot, *op. cit.* (Biogr.). In the family of the Comtes de Coubert until the middle of the 20th c.

NEW YORK, METROPOLITAN MUSEUM

55*
Marie Leczinska as Juno

1726–31   Statue   Marble   H: 195
Signed: G. COUSTOU F.A^{no} 1731
Comm. in 1725 as pendant to Louis XV as Jupiter by N. Coustou (no. 74). Payment 6000 L., Arch. Nat., O^I 2231. In the Château de Petit-Bourg until 1746, then in the park at Versailles.

PARIS, LOUVRE

Small replicas, terracotta and bronze, in the art trade.

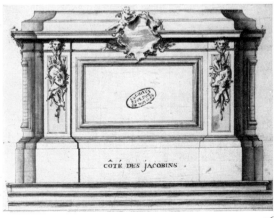

56

55

58b

58a

58
Louis Phélypeaux, Comte de Pontchartrain

1727
a.★ Bust   Marble   H: 82
Signed: GUILLAUME COUSTOU FECIT 1727
From the store of the Petits Augustins, wrongly
entitled 'd'Aguesseau'; cf. G. Brière, 'Deux oeuvres de
G. Coustou', in *BSHAF*, 1922, 2ᵉ fasc., p. 364.

LIMOGES, MUSEE MUNICIPAL

b.★ Bronze Version   H (without socle): 68
Signed: GUILL. COUSTOU F. 1727
Formerly coll. Marquise d'Avrincourt.

PRIVATE COLLECTION

59★
Fountain of the Bridge of Juvisy-sur-Orge

1728   Over life-size
One of two fountains on the bridge; Time, a nude,
winged old man, accomp. by a putto, displays a
portrait of Louis XV and crushes Discord. The other
fountain consists of a globe surmounted by a royal
crown, presented by two children. The old *Descriptions*
attrib. one of these fountains to G.C.; cf. Piganiol,
Descr., 1765, IX, p. 259; Dezallier, *Environs de P.*, 1755,
p. 201; Millin, *Antiq. Nat.*, II, chap. XVI; Dartein, *op.
cit.* (no. 51). Removed to store in 1972.

JUVISY–SUR–ORGE

59

Detail 61

60*
Equestrian Monument of Louis XV

1730   Wax model   H: c. 50
Project for the Place Royale, Bordeaux; not carried out. cf. P. Courteault, 'Place Roy. de Bordeaux', in *AAF.*, XII, 1922.

PRIVATE COLLECTION

61
The Ocean and the Mediterranean

1730–36   Group   Marble   520 × 600
Model passed in 1729, payment 5300 L., Arch. Nat., O^I 2229–30. Final payment 55,000 L., *ibid.*, O^I 1481 and 2239. On the lower part of the former Rivière at Marly. Damaged during the Revolution despite Lenoir's attempt to protect it, cf. Furcy-Raynaud, p. 88–94. The Ocean was evoked by an old man, the Mediterranean by a young woman, reclining on either side of an urn. The group is shown in an engr.* by Rigaud in *Maisons Royales*, p. 98 (detail). Destroyed.

62
Sculptures for the Bridge at Compiègne

1730–33
Pyramid and coats of arms, cf. Piganiol, *Descr.*, 1765, IX, p. 154. Shown in a medal* struck by Duvivier in 1730, Bibl. Nat. Cab. Médailles, 68A 17068. Destroyed during the first world war.

63
Louis XV

1732   Bust   Gilded bronze
For the Consulate in Lyons, acc. to Audin and Vial, *op. cit.* (Biogr.); Arch. Comm. de Lyon, BB 296. Payment 1500 L. Not ident. or disapp.

62

60

64*
Ceres or Summer

1733–5   Term   Marble   H: 300
After a model by F. Dumont (no. 25), to complete the
series of Terms at the Bassin Octogone in the Tuileries,
carved in 1686–96 by Raon and Barois (nos. 3 & 4).
Payment to C. 5500 L., Arch. Nat., O^I 2235 and O^I
1969^A (Invent. of 1722, annotated in 1746).

PARIS, TUILERIES GARDEN

65–70
SCULPTURE AT THE PORTAL OF THE HOTEL
DES INVALIDES

65   66*   67*
Louis XIV on Horseback, **surrounded by Justice
and Prudence**

1733–4   Bas-relief   Stone
Mém., Arch. de la Guerre, Carton 36, quoted by
C. Dreyfus, 'Le bas-relief de G. Coustou', in *BSHAF*,
1908, p. 30; a more detailed mém.: carton 17, liasse
B, pièce 13. Of the total estim. of the façade (26,300 L.),
C. rec. 18,000 L. in all. He asked 12,000 L. for the King
and the two Virtues*. The statue of the King, destroyed
during the Revolution, was redone by Cartellier in
1815. Engr.* by Cochin in Pérau, pl. 3.

PARIS, HOTEL DES INVALIDES

65–67

68b

64

69b

67

66

68b

69a

70

147

73

68 69
Mars and Minerva

1733–34
    a.★ Two statues   Stone   H: 380
Mém., Arch. de la Guerre, cf. above. C. asked 1000 L. for the models and 8000 L. for execution in stone. Replaced by copies in 1967. Removed to store.

PARIS, HOTEL DES INVALIDES

    b.★ Terracotta models

PRIVATE COLLECTION

70★
Head of Hercules

1733–34   Marble
On the keystone of the arch above the portal; Mém., Arch. de la Guerre, cf. above. C. asked for 3500 L., plus 100 L. for the model.

PARIS, HOTEL DES INVALIDES

71
Nine Portrait Medallions

1734   Bas-reliefs   Marble
Contract 3 Feb. 1734, Arch. Nat., K 1058, fol 133; H² 2020. Payment 5000 L. Portraits of the masters of the merchant guilds in the courtyard of the old Hôtel de Ville, Paris, cf. Le Roux de Lincy, *L'Hôtel de Ville de P.*, 1844, p. 12, 23, 84–5; L. Lambeau, *L'Hôtel de Ville de P.*, 1920. Destroyed.

72
Drapery for the Bust of Scipio Africanus

1735   Marble
Payment 1500 L., Arch. Nat., O^I 1088, O^I 2276. cf. Piganiol, *Vers.-Marly*, 1738, p. 265; Furcy-Raynaud, p. 86. Not ident. or disapp.

73★
Michel-Etienne Turgot

1735   Bust   Marble   H: 94
Signed & dated: G. COUSTOU F. 1735
Presented to Turgot by the City of Paris, see inscription on the pedestal.

PRIVATE COLLECTION

74★
Cardinal Armand-Gaston de Rohan

c. 1735   Bust   Marble
cf. Fontenai, *Dict.*, and Cochin, *Mém. inéd.*, p. 92–3. At first in the salon of the Hôtel de Soubise, Paris, then trsf. to Saverne and, during the Revolution, to the Château of Sychrow in Bohemia belonging to the Rohan family. Engr.★ in Boffrand, *Livre d'arch.*, 1742. cf. B. Lossky, in *Bull. d'Inform. du Haut-Commiss. de la Rép. fr. en Autriche*, no. 20, Jan.–Feb., 1947, p. 149–58. Whereabouts unknown. *Engr.★ see appendix.*

75
Restoration of an Apollo

c. 1738
Payment 554 L., Arch. Nat., O^I 2238.

74

76a

77a

76b

77b

76–77

76 77
Horses restrained by Grooms

1739–45
   a.* Two groups   Marble   H: c. 350
Both signed: G. COUSTOU 1745
At the Abreuvoir at Marly, replacing the equestrian
statues of Mercury and Fame by Coysevox (nos. 77–8),
which had been criticised. Payment 90,000 L., Arch.
Nat., O^I 2246; cf. G. Pélissier, 'Les Chevaux de Marly',
dans *Soc. hist. et archéol. des VIIIe et XVIIe arr. de Paris*,
1915–16, p. 195–216; Furcy-Raynaud, p. 94–104. G.
Coustou II shared in the work and the installation at
the horse-pond at Marly. Engr.* of the Abreuvoir by
Rigaud. Trsf. to Paris in 1794.

PARIS, PLACE DE LA CONCORDE

   b. Many smaller bronze versions, one in the Wallace
Coll.*, London.

78
Marble Icicles for a Grotto

1740
Payment 2100 L., Arch. Nat., O^I 1486, p. 10, O^I 2240.
In the Bassin at the lower part of the former Rivière at
Marly. Destroyed.

81

79*
Nymph of Diana

1742–4   Statue   Marble   H: 192
Begun in 1699 by G. Hulot, C.'s brother-in-law;
Comptes, IV, 479, 619. C. completed the statue; rec.
4600 L., Arch. Nat., O^I 2244. Wrongly attrib. to
Cayot by L. Réau, in *GBA*, 1932^I, p. 136–54. For
bibl. see Cayot no. 8.

PRIVATE COLLECTION

UNDATED WORKS

80
Frisoton

Statue   Marble
Shown in a plan of the park at Petit-Bourg, in Mariette,
Arch. Fr., 1727, II, pl. 320. Therefore prior to 1727.
Not ident. or disapp.

81*
Augustus the Strong of Saxony

Bust   Marble   H: 63   Signed: G. COUSTOU F.
cf. Audin & Vial, *op. cit.* (biogr.), III, p. 223; P. Vitry,
'Expo. XVIIIe s. à Berlin', in *GBA*, 1910, p. 357.

79

DRESDEN, NATIONAL GALLERIE

82

83a

82
Nicolas Coustou

a.★ Bust   Terracotta   H: 59
Given to the Mus. des Mon. fr. by C.'s grandson,
Arch. Mus. des Mon. Fr., I, p. 139; II, 414; III, 295.

PARIS, LOUVRE

b. Marble version   H: 59
Perhaps a studio work.

LIVERPOOL, WALKER ART GALLERY

83
Father Darérès de La Tour

a.★ Bust   Marble   H: 73 (incl. base of 12)
cf. G. Brière, 'Deux oeuvres de G. Coustou', in *BSHAF*,
1922, p. 362–9.

TOURNON, LYCEE

b.★ Terracotta head   H: 39

PARIS, LOUVRE

84
Lectern

Copper
In the form of an eagle, acc. to Dezallier, *Vie.*, p. 309.
Formerly in the Church of St.-Honoré. Not ident. or
disapp.

85
Two Statues

Tonnerre stone
In the chapel at the house of Michel Velut de la
Crosnière, rue de l'Arbre-Sec, Paris, on either side of
the altar; Invent. a.d., 24 Jan. 1735, Min. Centr. Arch.
Nat., Et. XVII, 690. Subjects not specified.

83b

Detail

COUSTOU, Nicolas (1658-1733)

b. Lyons. Father, François, wood-carver. Mother Claudine Coysevox, sister of Antoine. Baptised 9 Jan. 1658, cf. Jal, p. 443–5. Went to Paris in 1676 to live with his uncle, Coysevox, as his pupil. First sculpture prize in 1682 (see no. 2). Pensionnaire of the King at Rome from 1683–6, *Corr. Dir. Acad. Fr. Rome*, I, pp. 119–20, 122–3, 134. Agréé by the Acad. in 1687, *P-V*, II, 349, 351, 357, 362, 370; III, 4, 121. In 1690 married Suzanne Houasse, daughter of the painter René-Antoine Houasse, cf. Jal and Bibl. Nat. Fich. Laborde, no. 14140. Made Academician in 1693; Asst. Prof., 1695, *P-V*, III, 104, 121, 168. In 1700, succeeded to Girardon's studio, *Corr. Dir.*, III, 57. In 1702 made Prof.; 1715, Asst. Recteur; 1720, Recteur, *P-V*, III, 346; IV, 211, 303; 1733, Chancellor, *ibid.*, V, 112. Died 1 May 1733 in Paris at the Galeries du Louvre where he had lived for 30 years; buried at St.-Germain l'Auxerrois. Testament 26 Apr. 1733 and Invent. a.d. 4 May 1733, Min. Centr. Arch. Nat., Et. LXXXIII, 346–7. His brother Guillaume also had a brilliant career as a sculptor. One sister, Elisabeth, married in 1685 the sculptor Guillaume Hulot, the other, Léonore, in 1693, the sculptor Francin. cf. Cousin de Contamine, *Eloge hist. de M. Coustou l'aîné.*, Paris, 1937; Dezallier, *Vie.*, 1787, II, p. 276 ff; Mariette, *ABC*, II, p. 22; Jal, p. 443–4; Herluison, p. 91–2; E.-F.-S. Dilke, 'Les Coustou, les chevaux de Marly et le tombeau du Dauphin', in *GBA.*, 1901[1], p. 514 and [2]203–14; T.-B, VII, 1912, p. 603–4 (M. Audin); M. Audin and E. Vial, *Dict. des artistes*, *Lyonnais*, Paris, 1918; M. Rambaud, I, pp. 244, 697–8; II, pp. 43, 294, 420–1.

Contemporary portraits of N. Coustou: 1.) painting attr. to N. de Largillière, in a private collection, showing him in his studio, surrounded by blocks of marble and maquettes, working on the goup of "Autumn" (no. 63); exh. *N. de Largillière*, 1928, Paris, Gall. Cailleux. 2.) painting, three-quarter length, his hand on the head of "The Seine" (no. 22). 3.) painting by J. Legros, 1722, as reception piece for the Acad., now in the Mus., Versailles★; three-quarter length, his hand on the head of "The Saône" (no. 64). Engravings after this portrait by Ch. Dupuis, 1723, and by Oubrier. 4.) sanguine drawing from c. 1728 showing him from the back, Bibl. Nat. Est. rés Ne 80. From this a lithograph★ (p. 359) was made by Legrip, Bibl. Nat. Est., Na 54a, pet. fol. 5.) Terracotta bust by G. Coustou (no. 82), now in the Louvre.

1
Saint Etienne (Saint Stephen)

Before 1676   Statue   Wood
"Praying on his knees for the people who stoned him to death." Formerly at Lyons, acc. to Abbé Lambert, *Hist. lit. du règne de Louis XIV*, 1751, IV, p. 318. Not ident. or disapp.

2
Cain Building the Town of Enoch

1682   Bas-relief
First Acad. Sculpture Prize. cf. Guiffrey, *Liste des pensionnaires; P-V*, II, 229. Not ident. or disapp.

3

3
The Borghese Gladiator

1683
  a.* Statuette   Terracotta   H: 58
Signed: N. COUSTOU, OCTOBRE 1683
Copied at Rome from the antique. Given to the Louvre in 1874 by the Vte. de Fredy, a descendant of the sculptor.

PARIS, LOUVRE

  b. Bronze versions from different periods in private colls. (M. sale, 21 Dec. 1778, no. 20; Lambert du Parail sale, 27 Mar. 1787, no. 240 and others).

4
Hercules Commodus

1683–6
  a.* Statue   Marble   H: over 200
Copied in Rome from the antique in the Vatican. The sculptor has replaced the child Hylas by the golden apples of the Hesperides and changed the position of the rocks, the lion's skin and the face of Hercules, cf. Cousin de Contamine, *op. cit.* (biogr.); *Corr. Dir. Acad. Fr. Rome*, I, 47.

VERSAILLES, PARTERRE DE LATONE

  b.* Maquette   Terracotta   H: 43
Holback sale, 16 Mar. 1789, no. 85; then Coll. Fredy.

SAINT-ETIENNE, MUSÉE D'ART ET D'INDUSTRIE

4b

5
Bacchus

1687 (?)   Statue   Stone
Acc. to Dezallier, *Vie*, II, p. 287, formerly in the garden of the Doyenné at Lyons. Not ident. or disapp.

6
Saint Anne teaching the Virgin to read

1687 (?)   Group   Gilded wood
Formerly on the altar of the north transept of the Church St.-Nizier at Lyons; made by Coustou on his return from Italy acc. to *Hist. de Lyon*, Lyons, 1761, p. III; Dezallier, *Vie.*, p. 287. Not ident. or disapp.

7
Work at the Grand Trianon

1687–8
  a. Four Ionic capitals on the façade   Marble
Payment 748 L., *Comptes*, II, 1174; III, 93. cf. André no. 11*.

VERSAILLES, GRAND TRIANON

  b. *Models of Composite capitals for the Galerie*
In collab. with Joly. Payment 300 L., *Comptes*, III, 97. cf. Coysevox no. 50*. Whereabouts unknown.

4a

7c

7d

c.★ Trophies on the façade   Bas-reliefs   Stone
In collab. with Joly. Payment 11,465 L., *Comptes*, III, 35.

VERSAILLES, GRAND TRIANON

d. *23 Stone Paniers and Flower Baskets*
On the balustrade of the roof. In collab. with Joly, payment 2530 L., *Comptes*, III, 35. Jouvenet and Herpin executed the other baskets after the same model. Drawing★ Bibl. Nat. Est., Coll. de Cotte, Va 363, II, Fol. and *NAAF*, 1875, IV, p. 68. Whereabouts unknown.

e. *Fifteen Stone Baskets with Lead Flowers*
On the walls at the entrance to the Trianon; in collab. with Joly. Payment 3750 L., *Comptes*, III, 35, 248. Series completed by the sculptor Legrand. Whereabouts unknown.

8
Work on the Model for the Façade of the Dôme des Invalides

1690–1
Payment 252 L., *Comptes*, IV, 554, Arch. Nat., O^I 1665, 89. Not ident. or disapp.

9
Virtue

1691   Statue   Lead
One of four statues above the lantern of the Dôme des Invalides; cf. Bourdy no. 3★. cf. Félibien des Avaux, *Invalides*, p. 298–9 and Pérau, p. 90. Payment 448 L., *Comptes*, III, 558. Melted down in 1793. Destroyed.

10★
Four Groups of Prophets and Two Groups of Angel Musicians, for the Dôme des Invalides

1691–9   Six bas-reliefs   Stone   260 × 370
Sixteen groups of two figures in the four round chapels of the Dôme above the cornice, facing the four cardinal directions. Eight groups of prophets are in the Chapels of St.-Jérôme and St.-Augustin, eight groups of angel musicians in the Chapels of St.-Grégoire and St.-Ambroise. *Comptes* and documents in the archives attrib. six groups to N.C., three of them begun by Joly, three groups to Flamen (no. 30), three to Raon, two to Poultier, two to Martin, *Comptes*, III, 556, 558–9, 702–3, 844–6; IV, 330, 470–2, 611–2; Arch. Nat., O^I 1665, 35–7, 47, 54, 86–7; Bibl. Nat. Est., Hc 14, 2. Payment for each group 400 L. N.C. confirmed having done four groups of prophets and two groups of angels, Etat des mémoires, publ. *NAAF*, III, 138; *Comptes*, III, 558, 702, 845; IV, 471, 611. Engrs. of all these groups by Cochin in Pérau, pl. 68/9, 80/1, 93/4, 106/7. As the attribs. are partly contradictory (Félibien des Avaux, *Invalides*, p. 298–9; Dezallier, Paris, 1752, p. 370–1; Pérau, p. 77–81; Hébert, I, p. 230–1) we accept with some reservations those of Félibien, who was a contemporary, except for the collaboration of Hardy and Dedieu, which is not documented. The following attribs. appear reasonable:

a. Chapel St.-Jérôme, (1) east: group of prophets by Flamen (Félibien); (2) north, (3) south, (4) west: groups by N. Coustou (*Comptes*; Félibien).

b. Chapel St.-Augustin, (1) south and (2) east: group by Flamen; (3) west: group by Martin; (4) north: group by N. Coustou.

c. Chapel St.-Grégoire, (1) west and (2) east: groups by N. Coustou: angels with lutes, one angel with flute (acc. to Félibien, who erroneously places them in the Chapel St.-Ambroise). The groups north and south by Poultier (*Comptes*, Félibien, Pérau, Hébert).

d. Chapel St.-Ambroise: the east, west and south groups must be by Raon, *Comptes*; Félibien attribs. the north group, and angel playing the organ, to Martin.

PARIS, DOME DES INVALIDES

II
Work on the Vaults in the Church of the Dôme des Invalides

1692–9
a. In the Chapel of St.-Grégoire, 1692–6
Acc. to Arch. Nat., O^I 1665, 32, 69; Félibien des Avaux, *Invalides*, p. 299 and *Comptes*, III, 704, 845; IV, 473, the sculptors N.C., Poirier, Hardy and Poultier were responsible for the sculptural decor. of the four panels in the vault: (1)★ 8 angels holding festoons and supporting the paintings; (2) the picture frames; (3) a shell with "feuilles de refend" above the pictures; (4) a buckler with palms and laurels on the "tables d'attente". Total payment to the four sculptors, 2200 L.

PARIS, CHURCH OF THE DOME DES INVALIDES

b. *Angel holding the Book of the Gospels*
1693–9   Bas-relief   Stone
Payment 1000 L., *Comptes*, III, 845; IV, 471. Integrated with the first scheme of decor: the interior of the cupola of the Invalides was to be divided into 12 panels, each with a large angel, sculpted by N. Coustou,

$10a^2$

$10a^3$

$10a^4$

$10b$

$10c^1$

$10c^2$

11a

12²

Renard, de Melo, Van Clève, P. Legros I, S. Slodtz and Granier, Mazière and Lapierre, Flamen (no. 34), Hurtrelle, Le Conte, Dedieu (no. 35), and Lespingola with S. Slodtz and Granier. N.C. also completed the angel holding Noah's Ark, left unfinished by Le Conte at his death; payment 150 L. in 1700, *Comptes*, IV, 611. Arch. Nat., O¹ 1665, 36, 38. Drawing of a similar angel, Bibl. Nat. Est., Hc 14, 2. Destroyed.

12*
Allegory of the Recovery of the King

1693   Bas-relief   Marble   90 × 75
Recept. piece for the Acad., *P-V*, III, 121; Guérin, *Descr. Acad.*, no. 24. Drawing* by Charles Le Brun (Albertina 47717), who had decided on the subject (Inform. Jennifer Montagu). Apollo, as God of Medicine, his foot on a dragon, protects with his cloak the bust of the King against evil spirits in a dark cloud, which signify illness; a reclining female figure repr. France gazes at Apollo in gratitude.

PARIS, LOUVRE

13
Tomb of the Maréchal de Créqui

c. 1695   Marble and bronze
Formerly at the Jacobins in the rue St.-Honoré. In collab. with Coysevox (no. 58*) and Joly; design by Le Brun. N.C. did a marble statue repr. Valour (disappeared) and a bronze bas-relief repr. a Battle (plaster cast* in the Ecole des Beaux-Arts, Paris); cf. Dezallier, *Vie*, p. 276; Thiery, I, p. 151; Lambert, *op. cit.* (no. 1); Millin, *Antiq. Nat.*, I, no. 1, p. 4–5, incl. engr.* by Vangorp and Aubry; *Arch. du Mus. des Mon. Fr.*, III, p. 323. Destroyed.

13²

12¹

13¹

14a

14
Julius Caesar

1696–1713
   a.* Statue   Marble   H: 240   Signed: NICOLAUS
COUSTOU, LUGD. FECIT MDCCXXII
Comm. for Versailles, payment 5780 L., *Comptes*, IV,
478, 678; V, 695. Placed in 1722 in the garden of the
Tuileries, Arch. Nat., O¹ 1969 B. Caesar as victorious
general, laurel-crowned, holding a baton. Preparatory
drawing in Coll. de Cotte, Bibl. Nat. Est., Fb 26.

PARIS, LOUVRE

   b.* Model   Terracotta   H: 60
Signed: COUSTOU INV. ET FECIT 1696
Formerly in the Cab. Lalive de Jully (*Almanach des B-A*,
1762); Montal sale, 8 Jan. 1828, no. 295; Lehman sale,
4 June 1925, no. 39. Exh.: Gal. Cailleux, 1934, no. 116.

PARIS, MUSÉE DES ARTS DECORATIFS

   c. Small copies in bronze, many versions

HAMBURG, MUSEUM FÜR KUNST UND GEWERBE
ENGLAND, ROYAL COLLECTION

15* 16*
Saint Joseph and Saint Augustine

1696   Two statues   Stone   H: c. 210
Comm. by the religious order Visitandines at Moulins,
acc. to Cousin de Contamine, *op. cit.* (biogr.) and
Lambert, *op. cit.* (no. 1), p. 318.

MOULINS (ALLIER), CHAPELLE DU LYCÉE

17
Vase for the Demi-Lune des Vents, Marly

1697–8   Marble   H: 130
cf. Barois no. 11*; descr. in Arch. Nat., O¹ 2773⁵. Payment 850 L., *Comptes*, IV, 188, 336, 340. Whereabouts
unknown.

18
Patriarch for the Dôme des Invalides

1698   Full-size Model   Plaster
cf. Barois no. 10 f.* C.'s statue was to be grouped with
that by S. Slodtz. The models were probably put in
place, but never exec. in stone. cf. engr. in Pérau,
p. 87, pl. 21; Bibl. Nat. Est., Hd 135d, pet. fol., pièce
1698. Destroyed.

19
Six Vases and Baskets for the Avenue, Marly

1699   Stone
For the pilasters of the entrance gates; "en manière de
cuvette et de forme ovalle". Series completed by
Jouvenet with six identical vases. Payment 810 L.,
Arch. Nat., O¹ 1473, p. 12–13; *Comptes*, IV, 517. Pen
drawing of the gates of the Avenue in Bibl. Nat. Est.,
Va 78a, 4. Not ident. or disapp.

14b

15

16

20

Interior Work in the Pavillon Royal, Marly

1699–1700

a. *In the octagonal Grand Salon*

Picture frames, trophies with shields, flags, plumed helmets, piles of arms, nude cupids holding up garlands ending in scrolls and crowned by a female head in a shell; in collab. with Hurtrelle and Van Clève, cf. Piganiol, *Vers.-Marly*, 1701, p. 366–7; Dezallier, *Environs de P.*, 1755, p. 136; a water-colour drawing*

in Arch. Nat., O^I 1472, p. 5, shows a cross-section of the Pavillon Royal with the Octagonal Salon and the vestibules. Destroyed.

b. *Eight stone frames*   Circumf.: 1300; thickness: 25 Frames for Van der Meulen's paintings in the four vestibules in the Pavillon Royal, Marly. Contract Arch. Nat., O^I 1465, 355. N.C. and Jouvenet rec. 462 L. for the two frames in the entrance vestibule, *Comptes*, IV, 516; they also rec., incl. Flamen (no. 40), 1452 L. for the six other frames, *Comptes*, IV, 518. Disappeared in 1758 during alterations by Gabriel.

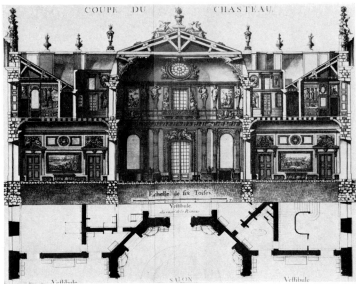

20

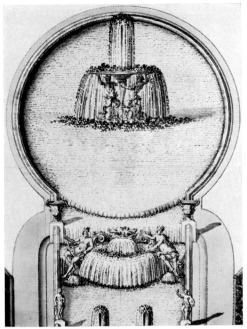

21a

21
River

1699–1701
a. *Wax model*
Intended for the summit of the Cascade Rustique at Marly together with a Naiad by J.-L. Lemoyne. Payment 137 L. in 1701, *Comptes*, IV, 882. The plaster model must have been put in position, cf. Piganiol, *Vers.-Marly*, 1701, p. 411–12. Appears in a water-colour, Bibl. Nat. Est., Va 448 d, gr. fol.* Removed in 1707, Arch. Nat., O^I 1465, 409. Destroyed.
b.* Stone statue   75 × 105
Signed: N. COUSTOU 1701

YALE UNIVERSITY ART GALLERY, USA

21b

22*
The Seine and the Marne

1699–1712   Group   Marble   244 × 270
Signed: NICOLAS COUSTOU LUGD. FECIT 1712
The model was made in 1699, cf. Cousin de Contamine *op. cit.* (biogr.); Arch. Nat., O^I 1465, p. 344; O^I 1474. Payment 16,299 L., *Comptes*, IV, 1072; V, 40, 143, 609. First at the Bassin des Nappes, Marly, *Comptes*, V, 873 as a pendant to 'The Loire and the Loiret' by Van Clève. Removed in 1723 to the Tuileries, Arch. Nat., O^I 1969A. The Seine, a seated old man; the Marne, a re-cumbent woman with two putti. *See appendix*.

PARIS, TUILERIES GARDEN

23
Bacchus

1700   Statue   Tonnerre stone
Payment 600 L. in 1700, Arch. Chat. de Chantilly, Reg. des Comptes, fol. 191. Formerly in the park at Chantilly. Not ident. or disapp.

24
The Prince de Condé

1700   Standing statue   St.-Leu stone   H: 210
Payment 250 L. in 1700, Arch. Chât. de Chantilly, Reg. des Comptes, fol. 192. Formerly in the park at Chantilly at the Bassin du Grand Jet, cf. Dezallier, *Environs de P.*, 1762, p. 386; Mérigot, *Prom. des Jardins de Chantilly*, 1791, p. 48. Whereabouts unknown.

25
Louis XIV

c. 1700   Medallion   Stone   Diam: 100
One of the 12 kings on the base of the cupola of the Dôme des Invalides. An earlier design, not accepted, suggested 12 bas-reliefs with subjects from the history of France. C. would have been comm. to carve: "St. Gontran, King of Orléans and Burgundy, prostrate before a crucifix on a carreau, or emptying vases full of gold and silver coins as alms", Arch. Nat., O^I 1665, fol. 42. Estim. for each medallion 500 L., but C. rec. only 400 L., in two instalm., *Comptes*, IV, 611; Arch. Seine, 6 AZ, 974, pièce no. 3, for the medallion and an adjoining mosaic fragment. cf. Félibien des Avaux, *Invalides*, p. 298–9; Granet, p. 108; Pérau, p. 84, with engr.* by Cochin, pl. 44. Destroyed during the Revolution; replaced with a copy by Cartellier (19th c.), *Rich. Art. Fr.*, *Mon. Rel.*, III, p. 238.

26
Restoration of Laocoon

1701
C. rec. 125 L. for restoring Tuby's copy of the antique statue, then in the Jardin des Marronniers at Trianon, *Comptes*, IV, 709.

VERSAILLES, PARK

22

27ˇ
France and Two Allegorical Figures of Fame

1701   Half-relief   Stucco
Comm. from C. and Lespingola for the decoration of
the King's new bedchamber under the direction of
Hardouin-Mansart, Arch. Nat., O¹ 1869, fol. 72.
Payment to the two artists, 3600 L., *Comptes*, IV, 709;
V, 493 and Piganiol, *Vers.-Marly*, 1707, p. 125. Between
the two reclining allegorical figures holding trumpets,
in the spandrels, France triumphant as a young woman,
seated, her elbow resting on a shield, holding a sceptre
and olive-branch, under a curtain supported by two
putti. Two watercolour drawings of the King's bedchamber with its carved decor. in Stockholm, CC 174
and 513.

VERSAILLES, PALACE

25

28–32
WORK ON THE OPEN STAIRCASES, PAVILLON
ROYAL, MARLY

In collab. with Lespingola and Hardy, total payment
32,400 L., *Comptes*, IV, 965, 1073. Piganiol, *Vers.-
Marly*, 1713, p. 247; Dezallier, *Environs de P.*, 1755,
p. 146, mention only Coustou, who must have done the
models, cf. Cousin de Contamine, *op. cit.* (biogr.).
See Rigaud's engr.* of the Pavillon Royal in Rigaud,
Maisons Royales, p. 98. Destroyed.

28
Eight Sphinxes and Eight Groups of Children

Groups   Gilded lead   Sphinxes 48 × 151
Children, H: 134
On pedestals on the terrace surrounding the Pavillon
Royal, the children in the corners, the sphinxes at the
four axes. Not saved by Lenoir, cf. *Arch. du Mus. des
Mon. Fr.*, I, p. 58. Destroyed.

29 30
Diana and Endymion
Mercury Sending Argus to Sleep

1701   Models for groups
Acc. to Cousin de Contamine, *op. cit.* (biogr.),
C. modelled these groups, to stand on either side of the
staircase descending from the terrace of the Pavillon
Royal towards the Gerbes. The project was abandoned
in favour of the Shepherds and Shepherdesses. Destroyed.

27¹

27²

27³

31 32
Shepherds and Shepherdesses

1702–4   Two groups in gilded lead   227 × 390
Appear in a water-colour★ of the Appartements Verts,
Arch. Nat., O¹ 1472, p. 25–6. Destroyed.

31

28–32

32

33

33*
Angel carrying the Arms of France

1701–6 Bas-relief Stone 240 × 310
Payment 1500 L., *Comptes*, IV, 727; V, 34; Arch. Nat.,
O^I 1665, 54. On one of the four piers supporting the
drum of the cupola, in the tympanum over the entrance
leading to the Chapel of St.-Ambroise. The figure is
accomp. by two winged putti, one supporting the arms
of France; the other, the crown. cf. Félibien des Avaux,
Invalides, p. 298–9; Granet, p. 108; Pérau, p. 83, incl.
engr. by Cochin, pl. 42. The three other angels are by
Coysevox (no. 75), Flamen (no. 47) and Van Clève.

PARIS, DOME DES INVALIDES

34*
Saint Louis

1701–6 Statue Marble H: 350
After a model by Girardon; payment 14,200 L.,
Comptes, IV, 727, 846, 1066; V, 34. Placed in 1706 as a
pendant to 'Charlemagne' by Coysevox (no. 60);
Félibien des Avaux, *Invalides*, p. 298–9; Granet, p. 108;
removed in 1799 to the Mus. des Mon. fr.; returned to
the Church in 1809, *Arch. du Mus. des Mon. Fr.*, II,
p. 399; III, p. 232.

PARIS, DOME DES INVALIDES (Façade)

34

35

38
Vertumnus and Pomona

1702–4   Group   Plaster model
For the Grand Jet at Marly, to replace a group by
S. Slodtz; part of a project which incl. Bacchus and
Ariadne by Van Clève (replacing a group by Prou);
Apollo and Daphne by Poultier; Zephyr and Flora by
Poirier. Payment 600 L., Arch. Nat., O^I 1465; *Comptes*,
IV, 1072. The Bassin of the Grand Jet and the sculpted
groups are visible in an anon. engr.★ 'chez Crepy',
Bibl. Nat. Est., Va 78a, 5. Destroyed.

35★   36★
Child with Two Doves   58 × 76
Child with Dove   57 × 72

1701   Two Groups   Stone
Signed: NICOLAUS COUSTOU FECIT 1701 (*Doubtful*.)

PRIVATE COLLECTION

37
Tritons

1702   Group   Gilded lead
Holding up a bowl in the centre of a circular basin
feeding the Cascade rustique at Marly, cf. Cousin de
Contamine *op. cit.* (biogr.); Piganiol, *Vers.-Marly*, 1707,
p. 411; Dezallier, *Environs de P.*, 1755, p. 244. Appears
in two water-colours, Bibl. Nat. Est., Va 448 d, gr.
fol., and Arch. Nat., O^I 1471, p. 26. cf. no. 21a★.
Destroyed.

36

40

38

39*
Vase

1702–5   Marble   H: 156
One of four vases by N.C., Mazeline, Flamen (no. 48)
and Poirier (after a model by Mazeline) for the staircase
leading to the Bassin des Nappes at Marly. Payment
2500 L., *Comptes*, IV, 734, 852, 963, 1184; V, 451,
452, 538; Mém. publ. in *AAF*, III, 1853–5, p. 140;
descr. in the invent. of Massou, Arch. Nat., O^I 1969 A.

PARIS, TUILERIES GARDEN

40
Work for the Terrace, Château de Chantilly

1703   Tonnere stone
  a. *Two lions*
  b.* *Four sphinxes*
Contract 29 Aug. 1703 for 1200 L., Arch. Chât. de

39

Chantilly, Reg. des Comptes, 1703, fol. 452; 1708,
fol. 447; G. Mâcon, *Les Arts. dans la Maison des Condé*,
p. 52–3. The lions were destroyed at the end of the
19th c., the sphinxes have been restored.

CHATEAU DE CHANTILLY, TERRACE

41
Two Groups of Children

1703   Stone
Payment 600 L., Arch. Chât. de Chantilly, Reg. des
Comptes, 1703, fol. 452; cf. Mâcon, *ibid.* Formerly in
the park at Chantilly. Not ident. or disapp.

42
Diana

1703   Tonnerre stone
For Chantilly; payment 600 L., *ibid.* Not ident. or
disapp.

43
Decoration for the Pièce des Vents, Marly

1703   Gilded lead
  a. *Two Tritons carrying fishes*   H: c. 200
  b. *Shells, Heads of monsters and winds*
Three teams of sculptors rec. payment for the six
groups of tritons, shells and masks which decor. the new
Bassin at the lower part of the Rivière at Marly. N.C.,
Lespingola, and Hardy rec. 8500 L., *Comptes*, IV, 965
(see Dedieu no. 42 and Flamen no. 50). cf. Cousin de
Contamine, *op. cit.* (biogr.); Dezallier, *Environs de P.*,
1755, p. 138–45. The Pièce des Vents disapp. during the
Revolution, but in 1800 a similar group of Tritons was
listed as stored at the Mus. des Mon. fr., *Arch. du Mus.
des Mon. fr.*, II, 454–6. Water-colour in Arch. Nat., O^I
1472, p. 10.*

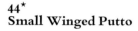

46

45

44

44*
Small Winged Putto

1703   Statue   Marble   H: 90   Signed on the base:
N. COUSTOU 1703
The little cupid, with butterfly wings, stands on a base
in the shape of clouds from which emerge the heads of
two more putti. He holds a torch and a vase against his
shoulder.   (*Doubtful.*)

PRIVATE COLLECTION

45*   46*
Meleager Killing a Stag
Meleager Killing a Boar

1703–6   Two groups   Marble   H: 210
Payment 18,000 L., *Comptes*, IV, 1072, 1127; V, 140, 143,
448. On the parapet around the former Demi-lune des
Vents, Arch. Nat., O¹ 1907, 5, fol. 8. Removed by
Lenoir to the Mus. des Mon. Fr., *Arch. du Mus. Mon. Fr.*,
I, p. 184–6, 193–4, 196, 200–1, 204, 208, 211, 228–9. In
1801, no. 45 was sent to Brest, *ibid.*, p. 230; *Cat. Mus.
Brest*, 1895, no. 9; while No. 46 went to the park of
St.-Cloud. They were brought together again at
Versailles in 1938 and, a few years ago, after restoration,
returned approx. to their original location.

MARLY, PARK

47
Mask and Shell

1704   Model
For decor. of the Bassin des Carpes, Marly; payment
57 L., *Comptes*, IV, 1101. Destroyed.

45

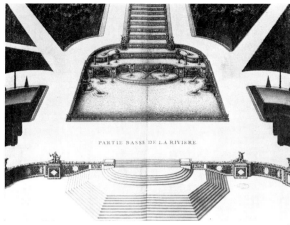

43, 45, 46

48*
Crucifix

1704   Bronze   H: c. 100
Exh. Salon 1704; *Livret*, p. 12.

PRIVATE COLLECTION

49*
Edouard Colbert de Villacerf

c. 1705   Bas-relief in oval marble medallion   78 × 62
Originally on the Villacerf tomb at the Convent of the
Minimes; cf. Marquet de Vasselot, 'Deux oeuvres
incon. de N. Coustou et d'A. Coysevox', in *R. Hist.
Vers.*, 1899, p. 248–53; *NAAF*, 1890, p. 100.

VERSAILLES, MUSEUM

48

50*
Wild Boar

c. 1706   Terracotta
Formerly Coll. Vicomte de Fredy, descendant of the
Coustou family. Whereabouts unknown.

50

49

51*
Restoration of Two Dogs

1708   Stone
Copy of earlier work by Thierry; fee c. 400 L. each,
Arch. chât. de Chantilly, Reg. des Comptes.

CHATEAU DE CHANTILLY, PARK

52*   53*   54*
Adonis
Nymph with Quiver
Nymph with Dove

1708–10   Three Groups   Marble
Adonis, H: 176;   Nymphs, H: 180
Signed: NICOLAUS COUSTOU LUGD. FECIT 1710
Total payment 21,700 L., *Comptes*, V, 240, 339, 431.
First in the Appartements Verts at Marly as pendants to a
'Pan with Flute' between Flora and Hamadryad by
Coysevox (nos. 88–90). In 1721 trsf. to the Tuileries;
since 1970 in the Louvre. The groups form a 'Return
from the Chase'; Adonis is accomp. by his dog; the two
nymphs by a cupid. Several bronze versions of Adonis
in private collections.

PARIS, LOUVRE

55*   56*
Allegories of the Washing of the Disciples' Feet
and of The Resurrection

1709–10   Bas-reliefs   Stone   194 × 89
The first and last of 16 scenes, evoking the Passion of
Christ; cf. Bertrand no. 22. Arch. Nat., O^I 1784.
Payment 1600 L., *Comptes*, V, 318, 414. 'The Washing
of the Feet' repr. by an angel holding a towel, his other
hand on the edge of a large basin; 'The Resurrection'
by an angel indicating the empty tomb and pointing
to the sky.

VERSAILLES PALACE, CHAPEL

53

57*   58*
Subjects from the Old Testament

1709–10   Two bas-reliefs   Stone   232 × 189

51

53

52

54

cf. P. Bertrand no. 23. Payment 1000 L. each, Arch. Nat., O^I 1784 and *Comptes*, V, 318, 414. Cherubs on the right carry the Ark of the Covenant, the Table of the Bread of Oblation, the Altar of the Sacred Fire, the Laver with two sacred vases and the Censer; on the left, the Tables of the Law, the seven-branched candelabra, the Veil and a large vase. Placed on either side of the sanctuary, below the preceding bas-reliefs, on the inner face of the pillars.

VERSAILLES PALACE, CHAPEL

59
Two Angels

1709–10   Models   Clay and plaster
Intended for the Palace chapel, but "n'ont point servy".
Payment 200 L., Arch. Nat., O^I 1784. Destroyed.

60*
Apollo Running

1711–14   Statue   Marble   H: 155
Signed: COUSTOU FECIT ANNO 1714
One of the four 'Coureurs': Apollo pursues Daphne (by G. Coustou, no. 39); symmetrically arranged with Hippomenes (by G. Coustou, no. 36) pursuing Atalanta (by P. Lepautre). Model accepted in 1711, cast in plaster;

54

55

56

Comptes, V, 510. Payment for the statue 4500 L., *ibid.*, V, 695, 786. Formerly in the middle of one of the four Bassins des Carpes at Marly. Watercolour drawings★ in Arch. Nat., O^I 1472, p. 15, 18, 19, 22 show the four bassins with the 'Coureurs'. After the Revolution, in the Tuileries.

PARIS, LOUVRE

61
Pieta

1712–28
 a.★ Group Marble 230 × 280
cf. P. Bertrand no. 28★. The wax and plaster models were

made in 1712, *Comptes*, V, 695, payment 2275 L. Payment for the marble 27,000 L., Arch. Nat., O^I 1790 and 1921^A and 2226; *Mercure*, June 1725, p. 1397. Placed in the choir of Notre-Dame for the Vow of Louis XIII; at the Petits Augustins in 1790, *Arch. Mus. Mon. Fr.*, II, p. 120, 191; returned to Notre-Dame in 1802, *ibid.*, II, p. 60–3. cf. G. Coustou no. 38 and Coysevox no. 98.

PARIS, NOTRE-DAME

 b.★ Model for the bust of the Virgin Terracotta

PRIVATE COLLECTION

58

57

60²

60¹

61b

61a

64b

Detail   *63*

62 63
Spring and Autumn

c. 1712   Two Groups   Stone
By C., acc. to Dezallier, *Paris*, 1752, p. 112; Hébert,
1766, I, p. 238. On the garden façade of the Hôtel de
Noailles, rue St.-Honoré, Paris. They appear in an
engr. in Blondel, *Arch. Fr.* III, liv. V; 'Autumn' also in
C.'s portrait, attrib. to Largillière★. Whereabouts
unknown.

64★
The Saône

1714–20
a. Group   Bronze   L: 324
Ornament on the pedestal of the Equestrian Statue of
Louis XIV by M. Desjardins (no. 47), together with
'The Rhône' by G. Coustou (no. 40) and two reliefs of
trophies; plans by de Cotte, Bibl. Nat. Est., Va 69,
6. Contract 7 Dec. 1714, agreed fee 20,000 L. for
'The Saône' and 49,000 L. in all for the work by the
brothers Coustou, Min. Centr. Arch. Nat., Et. XLI,
355. Paid in several instalm., Arch. Mun. de Lyon,
BB 277, 282, 285.

LYONS, PLACE BELLECOUR

b. Several smaller versions in bronze, especially one,
with variations, in Stockholm Palace.

64a

68

65
Trophies

1717–20   Bas-reliefs   Bronze   80 × 60
Repr. attribs. of Mars and Minerva. In collab. with his brother Guillaume (no. 41), at the same time as the groups of 'The Saône' and 'The Rhône', cf. no. 64. Destroyed during the Revolution.

66
Glory in Notre Dame de Paris

1714   Gilded lead
cf. P. Bertrand no. 28*. In collab. with his brother Guillaume, payment 7670 L., Arch. Nat., O^I 1790, O^I

1921^A and *Comptes*, V, 695; at the back of the choir of Notre-Dame, Paris. Appears in old engrs. of the choir, cf. Mariette, *Arch. Fr.*; MCPG, *Descr. hist. des curios. de l'égl. de P.*, 1763, p. 111–30. Destroyed.

67*
The Crossing of the Rhine

1715–38   Bas-relief   Marble   378 × 296
Comm. in 1715 for the Salon de la Guerre at Versailles, Arch. Nat., O^I 1921^B. Only half-finished at C.'s death, Invent. a.d. 4 May 1733, Min. Centr. Arch. Nat., Et. LXXXIII, 347. Completed by his brother Guillaume. Payment 28,000 L., Arch Nat., O^I 2226, 2237–44. Louis XIV, in antique armour, stands in the centre; behind him Victory, about to crown him with laurel. A recumbent old man person. the Rhine. In the background the army crossing the river. Remained in the sculptor's studio. In 1775 to the Salle des Antiques, then to the Mus. des Mon. fr.; in 1824 to the Invalides, cf. Furcy-Raynaud, p. 79–83. Finally in the Salon bas of the chapel at Versailles; the oval form was modified into a rectangle for adaptation to a new frame. cf. Rambaud, I, p. 697–8.

VERSAILLES, PALACE

68*
Jean-Baptiste Colbert

c. 1715   Bust   Marble   H: 70
Wrongly attrib. to Coysevox. Presented to the Acad. in 1716, *P-V*, IV, p. 184. Was in the Mus. des Mon. fr., *Arch. Mus. Mon. Fr.*, t. II, p. 312–3, 398. Sent to Versailles in 1836. cf. Keller-D., II, p. 106–8.

VERSAILLES, MUSEUM

67

69

70

69*
Tomb of François-Louis de Bourbon, Prince de Conti (1664–1709)

c. 1715   Bas-relief   Marble   H: 151
Carved in 1715, acc. to Cousin de Contamine, *op. cit.* (biogr.) for the Church of St.-André-des-Arts, cf. Millin, *Antiq. Nat.*, I, p. 5. Taken into the Mus. des Mon. fr., cf. A. Lenoir, *Descr. des Mon. de sculpture réunis au Mus. des Mon. Fr.*, Paris, 1799, no. 206; trsf. to Versailles. A female figure repr. Strength holds a portrait medallion of the deceased.

VERSAILLES, MUSEUM

70*
Tomb of Cardinal de Forbin-Janson

1716–38   Marble   H: c. 300
Specification and contract 31 July 1715 for 7600 L.; contract 1st May 1716, Min. Centr. Arch. Nat., Et. XCII, 385; publ. Rambaud, I, p. 697–8. C. was supposed to complete the mausoleum in two years from 1 June 1716; after his death, it was finished by Guillaume C., *Mercure*, June 1733, p. 1196. In the choir of the Cathedral in Beauvais; dismantled during the Revolution, placed into the side-aisle after restoration in 1804, cf. V. Leblond, *Cath. de Beauvais*, Paris, 1926, p. 84–6.

BEAUVAIS CATHEDRAL

71*
The Maréchal de Villars

1719–33   Statue   Marble   H: c. 250
Comm. by the Maréchal de Villars on 28 Mar. 1719 for 6000 L., of which C. rec. only 4000, the last payment on 20 June 1729; Invent. a.d. 4 May 1733, Min. Centr. Arch. Nat., Et. LXXXIII, 347. Intended for the Hôtel de Villars in Paris, acc. to Dezallier, *Vie.*, II, p. 283. Completed by Guillaume C. in 1733, *Mercure*, June 1733, p. 1196. The Maréchal dressed as Imperator, at his feet trophies, military and of the arts and literature.

AIX-EN-PROVENCE, HOTEL DE VILLE

72*
Saint Denis

1721–2   Statue   Marble   H: 210
Comm. by Cardinal de Noailles, contract 18 Apr. 1721, Coll. de Cotte, Bibl. Nat. Est., Hd 135 a, pet. fol. cf.

71   *72*   *74*

G. Brière, 'Marché N. Coustou pour St. Denis à N.D.', in *Corr. hist. et arch.*, Apr. 1899, p. 117–18, for 6000 L. In the north chapel at the entry to the choir. The saint is bare-headed, draped in a large cloak, in a gesture of benediction. The right hand has been re-made.

PARIS, NOTRE-DAME

73
Mercury, with the Attributes of Commerce

c. 1726 Bas-relief Stone 280 × 920
Traditionally attrib. to N.C., cf. C. Lecarpentier, *Itin. de Rouen*, 1816. On the façade of the Hôtel des Douanes at Rouen, built 1723–8. Mercury sits on a rock in the centre; on the right, a porter, two small putti and a dog; on the left, a cock, a putto writing in an account-book and accessories. Cast* in the Mus. des Mon. fr., Paris. Dismantled after bombardment in 1944 and stored.

74*
Louis XV as Jupiter

1726–31 Statue Marble H: 200
Signed: N. COUSTOU FECIT 1731
Comm. by the Duc d'Antin with the statue of Marie Leczinska as Juno by G. Coustou (no. 55) as pendant. Payment 6000 L., Arch. Nat., O^I 2231. First in the Chât. du Surintendant at Petit-Bourg; from 1736 in the Bosquet du Dauphin at Versailles; cf. Piganiol, *Vers.-Marly*, 1738, II, p. 190. Since 1830 in the Louvre, cf. Furcy-Raynaud, p. 82–3.

PARIS, LOUVRE

UNDATED WORKS

75
Abbé Bignon

Bust
Acc. to Cousin de Contamine, *op. cit.* (biogr.); and Dezallier, *Vie.*, II, p. 287. Formerly in the Acad. Not ident or disapp.

76 77
Neptune and Thetis

Two Busts Marble
cf. Hébert, 1768, I, p. 36. Formerly in the Cabinet of Blondel de Gagny. Not ident. or disapp.

78 79
Man and Woman

Two Bas-reliefs in medallions
cf. Hébert, 1768, I, p. 36. Formerly in the Cabinet of Blondel de Gagny. Not ident. or disapp.

80 81
Flora and Bacchus

Statues Stone
Acc. to Cousin de Contamine, *op. cit.* (biogr.) at one time in a private garden at St.-Maur, near Paris. Not ident. or disapp.

82
Diana

Statue Stone
cf. Dezallier, *Environs de P.*, 1779, p. 234 and *Vie.*, I, p. 287, formerly in the château de Villegenis. Not ident. or disapp.

83
Crucifix

Marble   H:65
Acc. to Cousin de Contamine, *op. cit.* (biogr.) comm.
by M. Sanssier, auditor of the Chambre des Comptes.
Not ident. or disapp.

86
Christ Ascending to Heaven

Bronze on a square bronze plinth   H:56
Sale of 15 Dec. 1777, no. 139. Acc. to Cousin de
Contamine, *op. cit.* (biogr.), a terracotta version was
in the possession of G. Coustou.

84

84
Saint John the Baptist

a.* Statuette   Terracotta   H:55
Dressed in an animal skin, holding a staff in the shape of
a cross.

COLL. OF A DIRECT DESCENDANT OF G. COUSTOU

b. *Version in bronze*
Gevigny sale, 1 Dec. 1779, no. 1026. Whereabouts
unknown.

85
Virgin Carrying the Child Jesus

Bronze, mounted on a base of dark pear-wood.
Cressent sale, 15 Jan. 1749, no. 5. Not ident. or disapp.

COYSEVOX, Antoine (1640-1720)

b. Lyons 29 Sept. 1640. Son of Pierre, a joiner, native of
the Franche-Comté, and of Isabelle Morel, from
Lyons. Moved to Paris in 1657; worked under Lerambert and other sculptors, at the same time trained at the
Acad., *P-V*, I, 237, 240, 244–5. In 1666 married
Marguerite Quillerier, niece of Lerambert, who died
the following year. From Nov. 1666 had the title of
Sculpteur du Roi. From 1667–71 at Saverne, Alsace in
the service of Cardinal François-Egon de Furstemberg,
Prince-Bishop of Strasbourg, who comm. him to carry
out the decor. of his new palace; there C. also began to
produce sculptures under his own name. Returned to
Paris in 1671, then to Lyons in 1675–6, where he was
made Asst. Prof. at the Acad. on 11 April 1676; and
Prof. in 1677 in order to establish an Academic School
at Lyons and to teach, *P-V*, II, 78, 98, 100. At the end of
1679, married Claude Bourdy from Lyons, sister of the
sculptor Pierre, with whom he had 11 children; three
of them served in the army of the King of Spain and the
Regiment of Navarre, Min. Centr. Arch. Nat., Et
LXXXIII, Actes in 346, 348, 367. From 1678 C. settled
in Paris; made Prof. by the Acad. in order to teach,
P-V, II, 138–9. In 1684, lived in the Gobelins, *Comptes*,
II, 502 and had a studio in Versailles. Made Asst.
Recteur, 29 Apr. 1690; Recteur, 25 Sept. 1694, *P-V*,
III, 36, 149. On 17 Apr. 1698 given an apartment at the
Galeries du Louvre, *AAF*, I, 250. In 1702, Louis XIV
granted him the unusually high pension of 4000 L.,
Comptes, IV, 1021. On 24 July 1702, elected Director of
the Acad.; re-elected unanimously in 1704, *P-V*, III,
346, 398. In 1709, rented a house in the rue du Chantre,
near the Louvre, where he lived for the rest of his life,
Comptes, V, 208. Ill in 1715–16, *P-V*, IV, 207, 209, but
continued to work until his death on 10 Oct. 1720.
Bibliography:
  Older sources: Fermel'huis, *Eloge funèbre*, 1721;
anon. biogr. in *Mém. inédits*, II, p. 33–9; Dezallier, *Vie.*,
p. 234–46; principal modern sources: Jal, p. 451;
Herluison, p. 94; T.-B, VIII, 1913, p. 31–32 (M. Audin);
G. Keller-Dorian, *Antoine Coysevox, Cat. raisonné de
son oeuvre*, Paris, 1920; Luc Benoist, *Coysevox*, Paris,
1930.

106b

4a

Contemporary portraits of Coysevox: 1.) painting by Rigaud, now in a private coll. Engr. by Jean Audran after this portrait, 1708. 2.) painting attrib. to Rigaud, now in the Mus., Dijon. 3.) painting by Gilles Allou, now in the Mus., Versailles. On the back, 'Fame', see no. 77.

1
Frieze and Other Decorative Sculptures at the Louvre

1667   Stucco ?
Payment 155 L., *Comptes*, I, 244; Keller-D., I, p. 3. Not ident. or disapp.

2
Decoration at the Bishop's Palace, Saverne

1667–71   Stucco and stone
Acc. to Fermel'huis, *Eloge*, p. 5–6, this incl. the cornice in the Great Salon, Apollo and the Muses on the ceiling, trophies and terms inside and in the gardens, Keller-D., I, p. 4–5. Destroyed.

4b

3
Neuville de Villeroy, *Archbishop of Lyons (1606–98)*

Before 1675   Two bronze busts and twelve plaster busts
Payment 2100 L., Arch. Mun. Lyon BB 231, fol. 143 vo.; cf. Keller-D., I, p. 5–6. Disappeared.

4
Virgin and Child

1676 ?
  a.★ Group   Marble   H: 190
Acc. to Expilly, IV, p. 282; Keller-D., I, p. 6–7.

LYONS, CHURCH OF SAINT-NIZIER

  b.★ Maquette   Terracotta   H: 50

LYONS, HOSPICE DE LA CHARITE

5a

5
Charles Le Brun

1676–79
  a.★ Bust   Terracotta   H: 65
Probably the model submitted by C. to the Acad. in 1676. Keller-D., I, p. 9.

LONDON, WALLACE COLLECTION

  b.★ Bust   Marble   H: 65   Signed: A. COYSEVOX FECIT 1679 PAR ORDRE DE L'ACADEMIE
Recept. piece for the Acad., *P-V,* II, p. 142; Keller-D., I, p. 16–17.

PARIS, LOUVRE

There exist a number of models and casts of this bust.

6
Jean-Baptiste Colbert

1677
  a.★ Bust   Marble   H: 70
Presented by the Acad. Roy. to Colbert, *P-V,* II, p. 105–6. The original is still in the Minister's family. cf. Keller-D., I, p. 11–12, 57–8; P. Vitry, 'Le chât. de Lignières', in *Congrès archéol.,* 1931, p. 601–3.

CHATEAU DE LIGNIERES (Cher)

Old replicas, with some variants:

  b.★ PARIS, LOUVRE

  c. LYONS, MUSEUM

5b

6a

7b

b.★ Terracotta H: 68·5 (incl. socle 14); signed
A. COYSEVOX. 1681. With some variants.

PRIVATE COLLECTION

7
The Grand Condé

Busts
a. Bronze 58 × 72 Signed on the slab:
COYZEVOX SCP. 1677. (An analysis of the metal shows
that the bust is more recent.)
The Prince wears armour decorated with two griffins,
each putting a paw on a fleur-de-lis, and a cloak draped
à l'antique. Formerly Coll. Gérard de Berny, Amiens.
Exh: *Louis XIV, Faste et Décors*, Paris, 1960 (no. 705).

PARIS, COLLECTION M. MAURICE HAMBURGER

c.★ Bronze H: 59
Comm. by the nephew of the Grand Condé, Francois
Louis de Bourbon, prince de Conty, at the time of his
uncle's death, for his Hôtel de Conty in Paris. Fee 1600
L., paid 21 Sept. Trsf. 1688 to the Ministère des Finances,
rue Neuve-des-Petits-Champs, during the Revolution in
the Chât. de St.-Cloud, now in the Louvre. *NAAF*,
1877, 403–4 and L. Courajod, in *Chronique des Arts*, 1877,
84.

PARIS, LOUVRE

6b

7c

8b

8a

8c

d. Other bronze replicas, provenience and authenticity not established. Two of them signed: A. COYSEVOX 1686, in Washington, National Gallery (Coll. Widener) and Brussels, Private Coll. Another one in a private Coll., Exh.: *Trésors du Grand Siècle*, 1957, Chât. de Nyon. cf. E. de Callatay, "Un buste en bronze du Grand Condé par Coysevox", in *BSHAF*, 1960, p. 196–9.

8
Michel le Tellier

c. 1677
Acc. to Fermel'huis, *Eloge*, p. 34, C. did four busts of the Chancellor; three are known, all of the same type with some variations:

a.★ Bust Marble H: 79 (incl. 16 for the socle) × 64
Bequeathed by the Chancellor's son to the Génovéfains, cf. Keller-D., I, p. 9–10.

PARIS, LIBRARY OF SAINTE-GENEVIEVE

b.★ *Bust* Bronze H: 80
From the Abbey of St. Germain-des-Prés, cf. Keller-D., I, p. 42–3. Was in the Louvre, but disappeared in a shipwreck some time ago. Some casts exist.

c.★ Bust Marble H: 70
The main variation is a lace collarette replacing the clerical bands on the two previous versions. Exh: *Chefs-d'oeuvre des coll. part.*, Mus. Carnavalet, 1950, p. 62, no. 169 with photo.

NEW YORK, METROPOLITAN MUSEUM

d. *Bust* Plaster
Formerly exh. in the Acad. cf. Fontaine, p. 213. The original plaster (?). Whereabouts unknown.

9★
Tomb of Nicolas Bautru, Marquis de Vaubrun and his Wife

1677–8 Marble and gilded lead
In collab. with Collignon (no. 5). Contract dated 1 May 1677 for 11,840 L., publ. M. Ste.-Beuve, 'Le tomb. du M. de Vaubrun à Serrant', in *GBA*, 1928[I], p. 153. Preliminary sketches by Le Brun for the main group preserved in Amsterdam, Rijksmuseum, A.420★ and Frankfurt, Städelsches Kunstinstitut 1156★; for the bas-relief in the Louvre, Cab. Dessins, Guiffrey-Marcel, *Invent.*, 6268★ (inform. Jennifer Montagu). C. did the base, the armorial bearings, the bas-relief of gilded

9²

9³

metal repr. the battle of Altenheim (where the Marquis was killed), the marble figures of the couple, the Marquis lying, his wife kneeling. Collignon carved the great angel sounding the trumpet; Desjardins (no. 35) the bases and capitals of the Corinthian columns. The inscription shows the monument was not erected until 1704, cf. Keller-D., I, p. 21–2.

CHATEAU DE SERRANT, CHAPEL (Maine-et-Loire)

9¹

9⁴

9¹

10

10
River

1678   Group   Stone   Length: c. 400
Acc. to Fermel'huis, *Eloge*, p. 30 and Dezallier, *Environs de P.*, 1762, p. 25 this group decorated the great Cascade in the Chât. de Sceaux built in 1678 by Colbert. The figure of the River was accomp. by a child. Keller-D., I, p. 14. Drawing★ of the Cascade de Sceaux by Pérelle, Cab. Dessins, Louvre, Guiffrey-Marcel, *Invent.*, 34235. Whereabouts unknown.

11★
Apollo

1679   Statue   Stone   H: 245
Apollo with a lyre in his left hand, a bow in his right. On

the cornice of the attic storey of the garden façade, cf. Keller-D., I, p. 15. Payment on account 300 L., *Comptes*, I, 1156. cf. F. Souchal, 'Versailles', p. 76.

VERSAILLES, PALACE

12★
Louis XIV

1678–81   Bust   Marble   H: 93
Signed: A. COYZEVOX F. LVD.XIIII. 1681
Part of the decor. of the Escalier des Ambassadeurs, which was destroyed in 1750. For payments see no. 13. The King in a corselet with lambrequins and a cloak, cf. Keller-D., I, p. 26. Now in the Salon de l'Oeil-de-Boeuf. cf. Félibien des Avaux, *Versailles*, Table.

VERSAILLES, PALACE

11

12

13¹   13²   13³

13
Decoration on the Grand Escalier (Escalier des Ambassadeurs), Versailles

1678–82   Bronze and gilded lead
In collab. with Tuby. Trophies and festoons in four great niches; in one of these, the bust of the King with helmets and arms on either side (see no. 12); opp., the arms of France and Navarre in the centre of the cartouche. The two other trophies, also pendants, showed the arms of Minerva and Hercules. Engr.* by Surugue. Total payment to the two sculptors 4090 L., *Comptes*, I, 1049, 1156, 1166; II, 11. Disappeared in 1750.

14
Decoration of the Four Pavilions in the forecourt at Versailles

1678–82   Stone, wood and lead
Eight trophies in stone, and various wood and lead ornaments, for which C. rec. two large payments:

12,893 L. and 13,000 L., *Comptes*, I, 1285; II, 20, 57, 168. The trophies appear in a pen and wash drawing, Arch. Nat., O¹ 1768, cf. Blanchard no. 8*. Disappeared during the alterations carried out by Gabriel and later in the 19th c.

15*
Decoration at the Grande Galerie, Versailles

1679–82   Stucco and metal
Decorative sculpture in the Great Gallery, executed after Le Brun's designs by some of the best sculptors of the time, among whom, to judge by the payments he rec., C. must have had an important place. Exact attribution impossible. Partially in collab. with Tuby: 4400 L. for the stucco trophies on the cornice, compr. 24 groups of two children sitting on either side of an escutcheon, *Comptes*, I, 1156, 1285; partially in collab. with Le Conte and Arcis (no. 36): 600 L., *Comptes*, I, 1285. Payment to C. alone for a metal trophy: 850 L., *Comptes*, II, 14, 181. cf. Keller-D., I, p. 20–1, 28–9.

VERSAILLES, PALACE

15

16

17

18

16*
Louis XIV

1679   Bust   Marble   H: 70
Payment 6300 L., together with another bust of the King, and the bust of the Dauphin (no. 17), *Comptes*, I, 1111, 1228; II, 178; cf. Keller-D., I, p. 18.

VERSAILLES, PALACE

17*
The Grand Dauphin

1679   Bust   Marble   H: 65
See no. 16; cf. Keller-D., I, p. 19.

VERSAILLES, PALACE

18*
Consoles

1680   Stone
Payment 1571 L. "for the consoles on the façade of the courtyard of the palace", *Comptes*, I, 1285.

VERSAILLES, PALACE

19
Restoration of Terms in the Petit Parc

1680
Payment 800 L., *Comptes*, I, 1285; cf. Keller-D., I, p. 20.

VERSAILLES, PETIT PARC

20*   21*
Might and Justice

1680   Two statues   Stone   H: c. 200
Seated on the balustrade of the façade above the Cour de Marbre. 'Might', dressed in tunic and cuirass, with the base of a column in her left hand; she formerly held an oak branch on her knee; her right foot rests on a broken column. 'Justice' holds a short sword in her left hand, a balance in her right; her right foot rests on a

20

21

conch shell, from which spills out a heap of chains. Most of the old *Descriptions* attrib. these two statues to C.; there is in fact a payment of 500 L. 'for a group of figures', *Comptes*, I, 1285. cf. Keller-D., I, p. 21–2; Félibien des Avaux, *Versailles*, Table (where he wrongly attribs. to C., 'Wealth').

VERSAILLES, PALACE

22*
Abundance

1680–81   Group   Stone   Over life-size
On one of the great pedestals in the shape of sentry-boxes originally flanking the entrance to the Cour de Marbre; after the Revolution at the entrance to the forecourt of the Palace, placed symmetrically with Tuby's 'Peace'. Abundance "alleviating the suffering caused by famine" is repr. by a woman with a crown of leaves and cornucopias; at her side, a putto, behind her a second one crushing an old woman, symbol of sterility, cf. Keller-D., I, p. 23–4; Félibien des Avaux, *Versailles*, Table. Payment 2332 L., *Comptes*, II, 16, 165. Engr. by Thomassin, p. 71.

VERSAILLES, PALACE

23*
Decoration of the Escalier des Princes

1681–2   Stone, plaster and stucco
In collab. with Ph. Caffiéri, Légeret, Prou and Tuby. On the wall: trophies and seven bas-reliefs of children (still extant, but restored); on the ceiling: ornaments (completely changed during the reign of Louis Philippe).

Payment 3212 L., *Comptes*, II, 11, 136, 172. The same artists did the decoration for the Great Salon (destroyed) next to the staircase, for 1816 L., *Comptes*, II, 178; cf. Keller-D., I, p. 29–30.

VERSAILLES, PALACE

22

23

24
Decoration of the Salon de la Guerre

1681–3   Stucco, metal and bronze
The wording in the *Comptes* does not specify C.'s share
in this collective work, where he played the principal
part, aided by lesser artists, like Le Conte, Arcis
(no. 37), Prou; only Tuby was his equal. Payments,
also collective, of more than 12,000 L., *Comptes*, I, 1285;
II, 14, 138, 139, 314. C.'s dominance is generally
recognised in the designs of the bronze and marble
doors and overdoors with heads and attribs. of the
Four Seasons★; cf. Keller-D., I, p. 30–1.

VERSAILLES, PALACE

25
**Decorative Work on the North Wall of the Salon
de la Guerre**

c. 1681–3
a.★ Triumph of Louis XIV
Oval bas–relief   Stucco   H: 392
The great bas-relief in the Salon de la Guerre is prob-
lematic. Although a work of considerable importance,
there is no mention in the *Comptes* except a payment of
600 L. to C. in 1683, but only for the bronze bas-relief
intended for the false chimney underneath the great
carved oval, *Comptes*, II. 277. Yet the whole work
seems to be C.'s, acc. to Fermel'huis, *Eloge*, and the
author of *Mém. inéd.*, II, p. 33, C.'s contemporary.
Being of such high quality it was hardly intended to
remain in stucco. The unexplained payment of 1350 L.
to C. for a new plaster model in 1715, cannot refer to
this work, already described in 1703 by Félibien des
Avaux, *Versailles*, p. 149–50, as Louis XIV in an oval
frame, in Roman dress, caracolling on his horse which
steps over defeated enemies (wrongly attrib. to Desjardins, *ibid.*, Table).

24

25a, c

b. Slaves and Figures of Fame
Bas-reliefs   Stucco
In the spandrels formed by the oval of the relief. Below, two chained slaves; above, two genies sounding trumpets.
    c.★ History writing on a Shield
Bas-relief   Stucco   Rectangular   L: 190
As indicated by the payment of 600 L., *Comptes*, II, 277, this relief, decorating the false chimney-piece under the great oval frame, was planned in bronze. Yet the extant relief put into that place is in stucco, while the bronze relief was sent to the royal store where in 1707 it appears in the Arch. Nat., Invent. des Bronzes de la Couronne, O¹ 1976ᴬ, p. 971; it has now disappeared. Both versions of the same size and, presumably, composition, showed on the left a winged woman, seated, writing history on a shield held by a child; on the right, another child places a helmet on a coat of mail. A sketch (pencil and wash) in Stockholm, DD 31, is attrib. to Le Brun.

VERSAILLES, PALACE

26
Sopraporte in the Cabinet des Bijoux, Versailles

1682   Bas-relief   Lead and tin
Payment 700 L., *Comptes*, II, 181, 197. cf. Keller-D., I, p. 32. Destroyed. *See appendix.*

27
Two Vases

1682–3   Metal
Payment 1600 L., *Comptes*, II, 140, 278, "for the surround of the pièce d'eau sous le Dragon", i.e. the future Bassin de Neptune. Keller-D., I, p. 32. C. participated with several other sculptors in this project of 22 vases. Attrib. to individual artists is impossible. cf. Carlier no. 3★.

VERSAILLES, PARK

28
Work on the South Wing, Versailles

1682   Stone (?)
Payment 520 L., *Comptes*, II, 235; identification of individual work impossible. C. probably did one or two stone statues for the façade. Keller-D. I, p. 33. Not ident. or disapp.

29
Work in the Bosquet de l'Arc de Triomphe, Versailles

1682–3
Piganiol, *Vers.-Marly*, 1701, p. 320–5 and later editions; Dezallier, *Environs de P.*, 1752, p. 122; Bibl. Nat. Cab. Est., Fb 27, fol. 62 and Bibl. Versailles, Ms. 22. They all attrib. to C. work on two of the fountains of the Arc de Triomphe: on the statues of the 'Fontaine de la France Triomphante' in collab. with Tuby and Prou; and on the 'Fontaine de la Gloire'. The *Comptes* for the Arc de Triomphe do not quote C.'s name, but there is, in 1694, a payment to him of 16,607 L., part of a total payment of 39,247 L., the sum "to which amounts the work which he has done and erected in the gardens of Versailles from 1682 to the present", *Comptes*, III, 952, 1007. The *Mém. inéd.*, II, p. 34 confirm that C. has made "a slave bound to trophies", which seems to correspond either to the statue of Spain or to that of the Empire, accompanying La France Triomphante. Certainly Le Brun designed the fountain, Tuby did the models and most of the execution. With caution, one can attribute to C.:
    a.★ The Group of The Empire (lead), traditionally given to him. The nude figure sits on a great eagle, next to trophies of arms. The eagle turns its head (originally gushing water). H: 144.

VERSAILLES, PARK

b. *The Statue of Glory*, after sketches by Le Brun, one of which (sanguine*) is in the Bibl. Nat. Est., Va 78 f, 4, the other (pencil) at Stockholm, CC 9. Glory, on a globe, holds a laurel crown and a pyramid "parce qu'elle s'élève de même" (Fb 27). The ornaments were by Mazeline and Houzeau. The whole fountain was demolished at the beginning of the 19th c. Engr. by Thomassin. Destroyed.

30*
Queen Marie-Thérèse

1683 Bust Marble H: c. 65 Signed & dated
cf. Y. Bottineau, *L'Art de cour dans l'Espagne de Philippe V*, 1960, p. 239. Originally at Meudon as a pendant to the bust of the Grand Dauphin (see no. 31), cf. 'Invent. des marbres et bronzes à Meudon', Arch. Nat., O¹ 1966³ in P. Biver, *Hist. de Meudon*, p. 436. Both mounted on octagonal pedestals. The two busts, trsf. at least a century ago to Aranjuez, stand in niches on the grand staircase.

SPAIN, PALACE OF ARANJUEZ

29b

29a

30

31

32

34

31*
The Grand Dauphin

1683 Bust Marble H: c. 65 Signed & dated
See no. 30.

SPAIN, PALACE OF ARANJUEZ

32*
The Grand Dauphin

1683 Bas-relief Marble 66 × 33 Signed & dated
The head of the Dauphin, aged 22, in profile in a medallion with a frame of gilded wood decorated with fleurs-de-lis. Noted in an invent. of the royal coll. in the 18th c., Arch. Nat., O^I 1977 B, p. 130; Keller-D., II, p. 95. At one time in the Art market: Gall. Bachstitz, The Hague. Whereabouts unknown.

33*
Nymph with a Shell

1683–5 Statue Marble 115 × 190
Copy after an antique. Payments incl. with those for other works, *Comptes*, II, 335, 437, 620, 735, 987. At first on the surround of the Bassin de Latone at Versailles; trsf. to the Louvre in 1891. Keller-D., I, p. 35–7. Drawing in Stockholm, THC 3761.

PARIS, LOUVRE

33

35

35*
Vase de la Guerre

1684–5   Marble   H: 250
On the terrace in front of the Parterre d'eau on the north side of the Palace, symmetrical with Tuby's 'Vase de la Paix' on the south side. Its body is decorated with a bas-relief repr. the war against the Turks in Hungary, in aid of the Emperor, and the conquest of Spain; cf. Keller–D., I, p. 39–40. One side shows France with sword and shield on which an eagle is perched, pursuing the fleeing Turks. On the other side Spain, repr. by a female figure with a submissive lion, acknowledges the superiority of France (Arch. Nat., O^I 1975^A, p. 735). Payment together with other works, *Comptes*, II, 620, 987, 989.

VERSAILLES PALACE, TERRACE

36
Two Capitals in the Salle des Gardes du Roi, Versailles

1684–6
Paid for together with nos. 33, 34, 35, *Comptes*, II, 437, 620, 987; Keller–D., I, p. 44. Destroyed.

34
Venus de Medici

1683–5   Statue   Marble
Copy after an antique. Payment together with no. 33 and other works, *Comptes*, II, 335, 437, 620, 987. Always attrib. to C., but in fact the statue was carved in C.'s studio, under his supervision, by the sculptor Joly, Arch. Nat., O^I 1907^A, 11. Acc. to an invent. of 1707, Arch. Nat., O^I 1976 A, p. 364, at Marly. Engr.★ by Thomassin, p. 39. cf. Keller–D., I, p. 40–2. Whereabouts unknown.

37
Venus Crouching

1684–6
   a.★ Statue   Marble   H: 183
Signed: A. COYZEVOX. 1686
Copy after an antique. In the Parterre Nord at Versailles. Replaced by the bronze (37b) and trsf. to the Louvre in 1873; Keller–D., I, p. 51–2. Payment 2500 L., *Comptes*, II, 620, 987. Drawing in Stockholm, THC 3758.

PARIS, LOUVRE

Detail   *35*

Detail   *35*

37b

38b

b.★ Statue Bronze
Cast by the Kellers after C.'s statue (37a). In the park at Marly; trsf. to the Tuileries after the Revolution; since 1871, in place of no. 37a at Versailles.

VERSAILLES, PALACE PARK

38
Decoration on the Colonnade, Versailles

1685–7 Bas-relief Marble
a. Three masks on the keystones of the arches. Payment 450 L., *Comptes*, II, 620, 987.

b.★ Seven bas-reliefs repr. genies and cupids
By several sculptors; C.'s work is not identifiable. Payment 2800 L., *Comptes*, II, 987, 1174; Keller-D., I, p. 52–3. cf. Cornu no. 17★.

VERSAILLES PALACE, PARK

39

39*
The Garonne

1685–6
Group   Bronze   122 × 250
Signed & dated: A. COYZEVOX F. 1686
Eight groups around the two bassins of the Parterre d'eau symbol. the streams and rivers of France, by C., Regnaudin, Le Hongre, Tuby; and eight groups repr. the water nymphs by Raon, L. Magnier, P. Legros I and Le Hongre. C. rec. 2800 L. for models of the Garonne and the Dordogne, from which bronzes were cast by the Kellers in 1688, *Comptes*, II, 620–1, 987. The Garonne as a bearded god, crowned with ears of corn, flowers and vines; leaning on an urn he holds a rudder. At his side a child with a cornucopia over-flowing with flowers and grapes. cf. Keller-D., I, p. 45–6. Drawing in Stockholm, THC 3761, 5135.

VERSAILLES PALACE, PARK

37a

40*
The Dordogne

1685–6   Bronze   122 × 250   Signed: F. A. COYSEVOX. See no. 39. The river as a reclining woman, at her side a small child and a cornucopia with fruit and melons. cf. Keller-D., I, p. 46–7.

VERSAILLES PALACE, PARK

40

41³

Detail

41¹

41²

41¹

41
Tomb of Colbert

1685–7   Marble
In collab. with Tuby. Payment 17,000 L. acc. to the
contract, cf. Keller-D., I, p. 53–6. C. did the figure of the
Minister,★ kneeling and praying, and of Fidelity★ (on
the left), who holds a key and a seal and is accompanied
by a dog. Both statues are signed. Formerly behind the
choir in St.-Eustache; when returned to the Church
from the Mus. des Mon. fr. it was put into a radiating
chapel, cf. Catheu, 'Le tomb. de Colbert', in *Bull. Soc.
Hist. Paris, Ile de France*, 1937, p. 136–8. Drawings in
Stockholm, THC 4760 and Bibl. Nat. Est., Coll.
Gaignières no. 4839★.

PARIS, CHURCH OF ST.-EUSTACHE

42★
Castor and Pollux

1685–1712   Group   Marble   H: 235
Signed: A. COYZEVOX. 1712
Both laurel-crowned. Castor holding a kind of medallion with a laurel branch; Pollux, a torch in each hand,
lifting one and extinguishing the other on the pedestal.
A small statue beside him repr. the Earth; behind, a
tree trunk. Originally in the Gall. des antiques; then in
the crescent-shaped opening of the Allée roy. at
Versailles in 1712, the date engr. by the artist on the
stone, cf. Keller-D., II, p. 69–70. Payment 2600 L., in
1685–7, *Comptes*, II, 620, 1174; III, 93. Drawing in Coll.
de Cotte, Bibl. Nat. Est., Fb26.

VERSAILLES PALACE, PARK

42

43

43*
Louis XIV

1686   Bust   Marble   89 × 80
Acq. in 1686 by the Etats de Bourgogne for 2200 L.,
Arch. Côte d'or, C³; Keller-D., I, p. 49–50.

DIJON, MUSEUM

Busts of Louis XIV of a type similar to the one in
Dijon exist in several copies with variants, the King's

face more or less aged compared with the version of
1686. For instance,
   a.* Narbonne, Museum   H: 78
Without cravat. Wrongly attrib. to Puget. Probably
work from C.'s studio.
   b.* Coll. Polignac   Signed
Face heavier and older; restored; the signature is
suspect. Probably studio work; cf. Keller-D., I, p. 51.
   c. Wallace Collection   H: 74
Invent. S21. Probably a modern copy of the bust in the
Coll. Polignac.

43a

43b

45

44
Works of Restoration

1686
On 25 Dec. C. rec. 306 L., "for having restored six children in marble as ordered by S.A.S.", Arch. Chât. Chantilly, Reg. des Comptes, fol. 97, art. 112.

45*
The Grand Condé

1686   Bas-relief in medallion form   Gilded bronze
Diam: 38 × 34   Signed: A. COYZEVOX F. LUD. DVX.
BORBONIUS PRINCEPS. CONDAEUS. 1686
For the funeral services of the Grand Condé in 1686, cf. Keller-D., I, p. 50. The Prince in profile, wearing a laurel wreath.

CHANTILLY, MUSEE CONDE

Another copy in ungilded bronze, formerly Coll. Decourcelle, in a private collection.

46*
The Grand Condé

1686–8   Bust   Terracotta   H: 59 (without socle)
Obvious resemblance with the bas-relief no. 45; the terracotta may therefore also date from 1686. Provenance unknown. cf. Keller-D., I, p. 13–14. The Prince in a cuirass and cloak with heavy folds knotted on his right shoulder.

CHANTILLY, MUSEE CONDE

46

197

47

48

48

49
Equestrian Statue of Louis XIV in Rennes

1686–93   Bronze and marble

a. *Equestrian statue*   H: 486
Contract 9 June 1686 for 90,000 L. Erected in 1726 in the Place royale in Rennes. Destroyed during the Revolution. Engr.★ by Thomassin.

b & c.★ Two bas-reliefs   Bronze   233 × 145
Presentation to the King of C.'s project by the deputies of the Etats de Bretagne in the presence of the ambassadors from Siam. France, triumphant over the seas, as a female figure, seated on a throne, drawn by tritons. C. presented in 1692 an estim. for 45,000 L., reduced by Hardouin-Mansart to 30,000 L., for these two bas-reliefs on the pedestal of the statue; they alone are still extant, cf. Keller-D., I, p. 76–89.

RENNES (Ille-et-Vilaine), MUSEUM

47★
The Grand Condé

1687–90   Statue   Marble   H: 212
Comm. in 1687 for Chantilly for 3000 L., cf. Keller-D., I, p. 70. Decapitated during the Revolution. The head replaced during the Restoration by an approx. replica by Deseine. The Roman costume makes it likely that the statue stems from the same model as the bronze bust in the Louvre, see no. 7.

CHANTILLY, PARK

48
Work for the Hôtel François le Juge, rue du Grand Chantier, Paris

1687   Stone
Acc. to Brice, 1698, I, p. 266 and later eds.; Piganiol etc., C. made several bas-reliefs on the courtyard and garden façades. On 22 May 1897, the former Hôtel Le Juge, later Hôtel d'Anglade, was demolished; the sculptures attrib. to C. were sold by auction, illustr. *Cat.* of the sale, annot. copy in the Bibl. Nat., Cab. Est.★; the two pediments, the masks and consoles were bought by Stettiner for 3180 frs. Whereabouts unknown.

49a

49b

49c

50¹

50²

51a

50
Capitals

1687–88   Marble
Like most of his colleagues, C. carved capitals for the Grand Trianon, one for a single column*, three for square pilasters, a corner Ionic capital and a great Composite capital*. cf. André no. 11*. Total payment 1885 L., *Comptes*, II, 1174; III, 93; cf. Keller-D., I, p. 59.

VERSAILLES, GRAND TRIANON

51
Monument to Louis XIV in Paris

1687–89
    a.* Statue   Bronze   H: c. 250
Comm. in 1687 by the city magistrates of Paris for the Town Hall, cf. Keller-D., I, p. 63–8. The King as Triumphator, his right hand extended, palm forward, his left arm leaning on a helmet and lictor's fasces. He wears a Roman cuirass with lambrequins under a big cloak; a pile of arms at his feet. Several copies, reduced size; cf. A. Girodie, 'Les Titons amateurs', in *BSHAF*, 1928, p. 62.

PARIS, MUSEE CARNAVALET

    b & c.* The King's Charity, repr. by a winged figure distributing bread. Religion triumphant and the guardian angel of France striking down Heresy by lightning.
Two bas-reliefs   Bronze   67.5 × 61.5
Ornaments on the pedestal of a. above. Engr. by Lepautre.

PARIS, MUSEE CARNAVALET

51b

51c

Detail 52a

Detail 52b

Detail 52c

52

52★
Tomb of Cardinal Mazarin

1689–93   Marble and bronze
In collab. with Le Hongre and Tuby; contract in 1689, fee 40,000 L. Design by Hardouin-Mansart. Erected in 1693, dismantled during the Revolution, re-erected in Versailles, then trsf. to the Louvre; finally returned to the original site, but with several decorative parts missing. Drawing in Stockholm THC 4761. C. did:
   a.★ The Cardinal kneeling
Statue   Marble   H: 160   Signed: A. COYZEVOX F. 1692
Behind him a small genie carrying fasces, the Roman symbol of authority.
   b.★ Prudence
Statue   Bronze   H: 160   Signed: A. COYZEVOX F. 1692
The figure, sitting on the left of the pedestal, holds an oar in her right hand, in her left a mirror with serpents entwined around her arm; her foot rests on a globe.
   c.★ Fidelity
Statue   Bronze   H: 140   Signed: A. COYZEVOX F. 1692
Sitting on the right of the statue, the figure holds in one hand a crown, in the other an escutcheon with the royal arms; at her feet, a dog.
   The statue in the middle, 'Peace', is attrib. to Tuby; it is not known which part of the work was done by Le Hongre, who died in 1690. With caution attributable to him are the two marble statues framing the armorial bearings of the Cardinal above the tomb (Religion and Charity). cf. Keller-D., II, p. 5–13; P. Pradel, 'Le tomb. de Mazarin' in *Art de Fr.*, 1964, p. 299.

PARIS, CHAPELLE DE L'INSTITUT

53
Louis XIV

1690   Bust   Marble   Signed: A. COYZEVOX F. 1690
In antique dress, a cuirass draped with a cloak, leaving free the lambrequins on the upper arms. cf. Keller-D., I, p. 69.

PRIVATE COLLECTION

54
Sculptures on the Façade, Dôme des Invalides

1690–1   Stone
Total payment 2400 L., *Comptes*, III, 422, 554.
   a. The French coat of arms in the pediment, flanked by palm branches and the insignia of several orders; cf. Félibien des Avaux, *Invalides*, p. 297. The sculptures appear in an anon. engr.★ of the façade (detail), Bibl. Nat. Est., Va 271, 3. Erased during the Revolution.
   b. *Charity with a child at the breast, another child holding a torch.* cf. Félibien des Avaux, *ibid*. Destroyed.
   c. *Faith, with a child, holding a chalice*
Two figures reclining on the sloping sides of the pediment. cf. Félibien des Avaux, *ibid*. Destroyed.
   d.★ Might, a lion's skin over her head, holding a shield.
   e.★ Justice, holding a 'Hand of Justice' and a pair of scales (now missing).
   f.★ Prudence, a mirror in her right hand, a serpent entwined round her left arm.
   g.★ Temperance, pouring the contents of a phial into a goblet.
   These four statues, each 340 high, stand against the cornice of the first order. *See appendix.*

PARIS, DOME DES INVALIDES

55★
Tomb of Charles Le Brun and his wife

c. 1692   Marble
Attrib. to C. by all the old *Descr.* of Paris. The painter's bust stands in front of a pyramid, while two Virtues,

55²

54a, b, c

54d   54e   54f   54g

55¹

Painting and Piety, sit on the base on either side of an inscription in a circular frame. Two small mourning genii disappeared during the Revolution, cf. Keller-D., I, p. 73–5. Engr.* in Dezallier, *Paris*, 1778, p. 250.

PARIS, CHURCH OF SAINT-NICOLAS-DU-CHARDONNET

56*
Mazarin

c. 1693   Bust   Marble
This work, which Lenoir is supposed to have received from the Gall. des Antiques in the Louvre, is attrib. to C. because of its similarity to the tomb (no. 52a). No documentary proof that it is by C. Perhaps executed in Lerambert's studio, cf. Keller-D., II, p. 14–16.

PARIS, BIBLIOTHEQUE MAZARINE

56

57
Decorative Sculpture on the vault of the Chapelle Saint-Augustin, Dôme des Invalides

1693–6   Stone or stucco
In collab. with Tuby, Joly and de Melo. Payment 2200 L., *Comptes*, III, 843; IV, 331, 471. Arch. Nat., O^I 1665$^{32, 69}$. Frames for the four paintings in the vault; each with a shell above and at the lower part, two putti holding garlands*; cf. Keller-D., II, p. 21–2.

PARIS, DOME DES INVALIDES

58
Tomb of François de Blanchefort de Créqui, Maréchal de France

1695   Marble and bronze
In collab. with N. Coustou (no. 13*) and Joly; design by Le Brun. Originally in the Church of the Jacobins, rue St.-Honoré; dismantled during the Revolution, the figures of the Virtues and all other decorative elements have disappeared except the main figure of the deceased which, originally half-length with hands clasped, was reduced to a bust*, 60 × 53. It is generally agreed that this remaining part of the tomb is by C., cf. Keller-D., II, p. 18–20.

PARIS, CHURCH OF SAINT-ROCH

59*
Tomb of François d'Argouges

c. 1695   Marble   H: 145
First President of the Parliament of Bretagne and Conseiller d'Etat; died 16 Aug. 1695, buried in the Church of St.-Paul, Paris. His bust, in front view, carved in bas-relief on a medallion held by 'Justice'. Acc. to *Mém. inéd.*, II, p. 37; Brice, 1752, II, p. 317; Piganiol, *Paris*, 1765, IV, p. 171; Dezallier, *Paris*, 1778, p. 206; Thiery, I, p. 694, it was designed and executed by C., but the inferior quality seems quite unworthy of him; probably a studio work. During the Revolution, trsf. to the store of the Petits Augustins, *Arch. Mus. Mon. Fr.*, III, p. 210. In 1834, sent to Versailles, Arch. du Louvre; cf. Keller-D., I, p. 75–6. Drawing by St.-Aubin in his copy of Piganiol, *Paris*, 1742, IV, p. 24 (Mus. du Petit-Palais, Paris).

57   VERSAILLES, MUSEUM

58

60*
Charlemagne

1695–1706   Statue   Marble   H: 350
Signed: A. COYZEVOX 1706
Payment 8300 L., *Comptes*, IV, 64, 727, 846, 956, 1066;
V, 34, 947. Keller-D., II, p. 43–4. Félibien des Avaux,
Invalides, p. 297. At the portal of the Dôme, pendant to
St. Louis by N. Coustou (no. 34). The Emperor wears
a crown, a sword in his right hand; his left rests on a
globe.

PARIS, DOME DES INVALIDES

60

59

61

Tomb of Madeleine Blondeau, widow of Michel d'Aligre

1697   Marble and bronze
Acc. to *Mém. inéd.*, II, 37, C. made the "tomb of Mme. d'Aligre" in the Church of the Hôpital de la Miséri-corde, Ste.-Pélagie, Fbg. St.-Marceau, Paris. Thiery, II, p. 169 says that this was the mausoleum of "Madeleine Blondeau, widow of Michel d'Aligre, seigneur de Boislandry, son and grandson of two Chancellors of France of this name. The lady was one of the benefactors of this institution". Born in 1639, died 11 July 1696. Her tomb was "erected in her honour by Messrs. d'Aligre, her sons" (Estienne and Gilles), cf. Thiery, *ibid.* First mentioned in Brice, 1698, II, p. 25 as C.'s work in Ste.-Pélagie, but, mistaking the identity of the deceased, descr. as the tomb of La Chancelière d'Aligre. Repeated in later editions, also by Dezallier, *Paris*, 1778, p. 261–2, and all modern historians. From the edition of 1725, II, p. 380 onwards, Brice calls it the tomb of the Chancellor d'Aligre, an error repeated by Hurtaut & Magny, IV, p. 4. But the tomb of the Chancellor d'Aligre, who died in 1670, is the work of L. Magnier at St.-Germain L'Auxerrois, while the Chancelière d'Aligre, Elizabeth Luillier, his third wife (1608–8 Feb. 1685), was buried in the Church of the Hôpital des Enfants Trouvés, Fbg. St.-Antoine. Thiery, *ibid.*, descr. the tomb of Madeleine Blondeau thus: "kneeling on a sarcophagus is the Genie of Religion; behind, a pyramid with an Ionic scroll, surmounted by a bronze urn. It was made by C." The Church of Ste.-Pélagie was demolished in 1895. Destroyed.

62

Vase

1697–8   Marble
Payment 850 L., *Comptes*, IV, 188, 336. On the balustrade of the Demi-lune des Vents, Marly; see Barois no. 11. cf. Keller-D., II, p. 20. Whereabouts unknown.

64

63

63*
Jules Hardouin-Mansart

1698   Bust   Marble   86 × 73.5 (incl. pedestal: 14)
Signed: COYZEVOX FECIT 1698
Given to the Génovéfains in 1738 by Hardouin-Mansart's daughter (see inscription on the small pedestal); cf. Keller-D., II, p. 20–1.

PARIS, BIBLIOTHEQUE STE-GENEVIEVE

64
Two Fathers of the Church

1698–9   Statues   Stone
Payment 700 L., *Comptes*, IV, 330, 471. Two of the eight Fathers of the Greek and Latin Church carved by C., Poultier, Mazeline and Tuby. On the tribune of the attic inside the Dôme des Invalides. cf. Keller-D., II, p. 23; Félibien des Avaux, *Invalides*, p. 297. Anon. engr.* of the tribune with four Fathers of the Church in Bibl. Ville de Paris, recueil no. 90273. Destroyed during the Revolution.

65–68
Four Groups for la Rivière, Marly

1698–1707   Marble
C. at first rec. c. 19,300 L. for the four groups, *Comptes*, IV, 963, 1071; V, 40, 143; later other works for Marly were incl. in the payments, *Comptes*, V, 240, 253, 340, 431; total payment 71,241 L., *Comptes*, V, 510. The four groups were at the four corners of La Rivière at Marly, cf. Keller-D., II, p. 45–52.

65

66

67

68

71

65*
Neptune

Group   Marble   H: 184
Pendant to Amphitrite, at the upper part of 'la Rivière'. The God sits on a seahorse, attacking its neck with his trident. Removed from Marly in 1795 to the park of the Palais du Corps législatif, then to the Cours Dajot in Brest. Since 1966 in the Louvre.

PARIS, LOUVRE

72

66*
Amphitrite

Group   Marble   H: 184
Pendant to Neptune, no. 65. The Goddess on a dolphin, three little tritons playing around her. The group's history is the same as no. 65, but in Brest it stood near a fountain at the old port.

PARIS, LOUVRE

67*
The Seine

Statue   Marble   H: 270
Pendant to The Marne (no. 68), at the lower part of La Rivière, Marly. The bearded God sits on a rock, in his raised left hand an oar, his right arm resting on an overturned urn. At his feet two infants (only one preserved). Successively in the parks of the Palais Bourbon, Monceau and St.-Cloud. In the Louvre since 1875.

PARIS, LOUVRE

68*
The Marne

Statue   Marble   H: 220
Pendant to The Seine (no. 67), at the lower part of La Rivière. The River Goddess, on a rock, leaning on an urn, wears a crown of wheat-ears and flowers and holds a cornucopia; at her feet two children. The history of the statue is the same as that of Neptune (no. 65).

PARIS, LOUVRE

69
Queen Marie-Thérèse

c. 1699   Bust   Marble
Exh. Salon 1699. cf. Keller-D., II, p. 23. Identical with no. 30 or a repeat? Whereabouts unknown.

70
Unknown Woman

c. 1699   Bust   Marble
Exh. Salon 1699 cf. Keller-D., II, p. 23. Not ident. or disapp. *See appendix.*

71*
Louis XIV

c. 1699   Bust   Bronze   H: 75
Exh. Salon 1699. This is perhaps the bronze now in the Wallace Coll., Inv. S. 165, orig. from the Hertford Coll., cf. Keller-D., II, p. 24–5.

LONDON, WALLACE COLLECTION (?)

73

72
Tomb of Ferdinand-Egon de Furstenberg

c. 1700   Stone and stucco
Orig. in the Church of St.-Germain-des-Prés, acc. to
the *Mém. inéd.*, and the *Descr.* of Paris. The monument
consisted of military trophies and two weeping genies
on a sarcophagus, cf. Keller-D., II, p. 26–7. Engr.★ by
Chaufourier and Pigné in Bouillart, *Hist. de l'abbaye roy.
de St.-Germain-des-Prés*, 1724. Destroyed during the
Revolution.

74

73★
Matthew Prior

1700   Bust   Marble   H: (with pedestal) 83
Acc. to the *Mém. inéd.*, part of the poet-diplomat's
tomb in Westminster Abbey. The artist could have met
his model during Prior's stay in Paris from 1699–1700.
cf. Keller-D., II, p. 28.

LONDON, WESTMINSTER ABBEY

A replica, reduced in size, from a private coll., was
exh. in 1960 at the Mus. des Arts Décor., Paris:
Louis XIV, Fastes et Décors, cat. no. 707.

75

74★
Duc de Richelieu

1700   Bust   Marble   H: 76 (with pedestal: 85)
Formerly Coll. of the Princes de Condé, cf. Keller-D.,
II, p. 28–9.

CHANTILLY, MUSEE CONDE

75★
Angel

1700–6   Bas-relief   Stone   240 × 310
cf. N. Coustou no. 33. The angel, in the cul de four
above the arcade leading to the Chapel of St.-Augustin
in the Dôme, carries a helmet on a pole; cf. Keller-D.,
II, p. 29–30; Félibien des Avaux, *Invalides*, p. 297;
Engr. by Cochin in Pérau, pl. 42. Payment 1500 L.,
Comptes, IV, 611, 727; Arch. Nat., O^I 1665.

PARIS, DOME DES INVALIDES

76

76*
Le Nôtre

After 1700   Bust   Marble   H: 65
Comm. after the death of Le Nôtre in 1700 for his tomb in St.-Roch by Cotton (no. 5*). Returned to the church after an interval in the Mus. des Mon. fr. during the Revolution. cf. Keller-D., II, p. 31–2.

PARIS, CHURCH OF ST.-ROCH

77*   78*
Fame and Mercury

1701–2   Two equestrian statues   Marble   H: 320
Both signed: ANTONIUS COYZEVOX LUGD. SCUL. REG. FECIT 1702
Fame, mounted on a winged horse, sounds a trumpet; Mercury holds his caduceus; the two horses rear above a pile of military accessories. First at the Abreuvoir in Marly; later replaced by G. Coustou's horses (nos. 76, 77); in 1719, trsf. to the entrance of the Tuileries gardens. In 1794, Coustou's horses were put opposite those by Coysevox, at the entrance to the Champs Elysées. cf. Keller-D., II, p. 33–40. Payment 40,000 L., *Comptes*, IV, 734, 851–2, 963.

PARIS, PLACE DE LA CONCORDE

Some of the many small replicas of these famous statues were made during the artist's life-time.

79
Tomb of the Marquis de Nangis

1702   Bonbanc stone, marble and gilded stucco
On 14 Jan. 1702, C. and Marie de Bailleul, widow of the Marquis, signed before a notary the estimate and contract for 3000 L. for the tomb to be erected during 1702 in the chapelle des seigneurs de Nangis in the Church at Nangis. Acc. to the estim., the monument, placed on pilasters and an entablature, was to show two children, one standing, holding a medallion with the portrait of the deceased in profile, the other sitting on a shield; in front, an inscription in gilded letters on a white marble slab, at the side, trophies of arms in gilded stucco. Min. Centr. Arch. Nat., Et. XVI, 619 (Inform. L.-H. Collard). The chapelle de Nangis and its

77

78

82b   *80b*

contents were destroyed during the Revolution. There is no evidence in the old Descriptions to show whether the monument was ever executed.

80
Robert de Cotte

1704–7
  a. *Bust*
Exh. Salon 1704; *Livret*, p. 12. Probably the terracotta model for the two following works. Whereabouts unknown.

b.★ Bust   Marble   H: 55   Signed & dated 1707
Given to the Génovéfains by the architect's widow in 1738. cf. Keller-D., II, p. 53.

PARIS, BIBLIOTHEQUE STE.–GENEVIEVE

c.★ Bust   Bronze   H: 55
cf. Keller-D., II, p. 53.

NEW YORK, FRICK COLLECTION

82c   *80c*

81
Turenne

1704   Bust
Exh. Salon 1704; *Livret*, p. 10. Whereabouts unknown.

82
Vauban

a. *Bust*
Exh. Salon 1704; *Livret*, p. 12. cf. Keller-D., II, p. 41–2.
Perhaps the model for no. 82b. Whereabouts unknown.

b.★ Bust   Marble   Signed: COYZEVOX. F./1706
Inscription on the stump of the left arm 'QUAE NON
MAENIA'. Purchased by George IV at the Watson
Taylor sale, 28 May 1825 for £106.1.0.

WINDSOR CASTLE, ROYAL COLLECTION

c. Several busts of Vauban exist, based on 82b., but
with variants. One, marble, in the Mus. des Plans en
relief, Paris; another, plaster, is still with the family of
Vauban; a third, plaster★, in the Louvre (formerly Coll.
May).

83
Chevalier de la Vallière

1704   Bust
Exh. Salon 1704; *Livret*, p. 12. Keller-D., II, p. 42. Not
ident. or disapp.

84
Madame de la Ravois

1704   Bust
Exh. Salon 1704; *Livret*, p. 10. Keller-D., II, p. 42. Not
ident. or disapp.

85³

85★
Tomb of Henri de Lorraine, Comte d'Harcourt

1704–11   Marble   Signed: ANTOINE COYZEVOX F. 1711
Estim. for 18,000 L., in 1704; designed by R. de Cotte.
The deceased in Roman dress, half reclining on a
sarcophagus in the attitude of the 'mourant assisté', his
hand held by an angel kneeling at his side, who places a
laurel crown on his head. First erected with a large
stucco decor. in the Abbey Church of Royaumont★
(where a fragment of the curtain still remains), it has
only recently been returned there after 150 years in the
Church at Asnière-sur-Oise★. cf. Keller-D., II, p. 63–8.
The great rectangular bas-relief in gilded lead on the
base, repr. the conquest of Turin, has been destroyed.
Engr.★ by Desmaisons.

ABBAYE DE ROYAUMONT
See appendix.

85¹

Detail

85²

86

86*
Marie Serre, mother of the painter Rigaud

1706 Bust Marble H: 81 Signed: MARIE SERRE, MERE DE HYACINTHE RIGAU. FAIT PAR COYZEVOX EN 1706. Comm. and presented to the Acad. Roy. by Rigaud, Keller-D., II, p. 44. Testaments of Rigaud, Min. Centr. Arch. Nat., Et. XCV, 36, 30 May, 1707; LIII, 237, 16 June 1726; LIII, 275, 29 Sept. 1735; publ. by D. Wildenstein, 'Doc. inéd. sur les artistes fr. du 18e s.', 1967.

PARIS, LOUVRE

87
Duc d'Antin

Bust Plaster
C. offered to do a bust of d'Antin for the Acad., *P-V*, IV, p. 67. Mentioned in an Invent. of 1710, cf. Fontaine, p. 215; Keller-D., II, p. 54–5. Not ident. or disapp.

88* 89* 90*
Faun (or Pan) playing the Flute

1708–10 Group Marble H: 184
Signed: A. COYSEVOX F. 1709

Hamadryad or Nymph of the Woods

1708–10 Group Marble H: 180

Flora

1708–10 Group Marble H: 180
Signed: A. COYZEVOX. 1710
These three groups, designed as an ensemble, corresp. to N. Coustou's three groups 'Adonis' and 'Two Nymphs' (nos. 52–4), were comm. in 1708 for two recesses in the Appartements Verts opposite the Pavillon Royal at Marly. Price unknown, because payment together with other works, *Comptes*, V, 240 253, 340, 431, 510. For a short time in Marly, where Piganiol saw them, cf. *Vers.-Marly*, 1713, p. 243; after 1721 in the Tuileries Gardens, Invent. Arch. Nat., O[I] 1969[A], p. 200. The Faun in the Louvre since 1870, the two other groups since 1972; the two latter are damaged.

Sitting on a tree trunk, the faun plays his flute, behind him a young satyr. Hamadryad and Flora, also sitting, listen to him with admiring gestures. Behind them, small cupids. cf. Keller-D., II, p. 57–60.

PARIS, LOUVRE

Several replicas in marble, bronze, terracotta, some reduced in size; among the terracottas:

a. Another large Hamadryad in terracotta, recently bought by the Chât. de Serrant (Maine-et-Loire).

b. Two small terracottas of the Faun and the Hamadryad in the Louvre.

91
Marie-Adélaïde de Savoie, Duchesse de Bourgogne

1710
a.* Statue Marble H: 195 Signed: A. COYZEVOX, 1710. AD. VIVUM
Comm. by the duc d'Antin for his chât. de Petit-Bourg; trsf. to the Grand Trianon, finally to the Louvre. The Princess as Diana the Huntress, a quiver on her back, a hunting-dog at her side. cf. Keller-D., II, p. 61–2.

PARIS, LOUVRE

Of this famous statue, numerous replicas exist in reduced size, from various materials and periods, esp. a large terracotta, recently acq. by the Chât. de Serrant (Maine et Loire).

b.* Bust Marble H: 50 Signed: A. COYZVOX. AD. VIVUM. F. 1710.
Executed at the same time as the statue, with some variations to the head. Exh.: in the bedchamber of Louis XIV at Versailles. Another signed copy is in the Museum of Fine-Arts, Moscow.

VERSAILLES, MUSEUM

There exist a number of marble replicas of this bust.

88

90

89

91b

91a

92*
Jacques Gabriel, architect (c. 1630–1686)

1711 Bust Marble H: 88 Signed: A. COYZEVOX
F. 1711
Hist. and prov. unknown. cf. Vitry, 'Les bustes des
trois Gabriel', in *Mélanges Lemonnier*, 1913, p. 302–5;
Keller-D., II, p. 63. Posthumous portrait.

PARIS, MUSEE JACQUEMART-ANDRE

93*
Charles-Maurice le Tellier, Archbishop of Rheims

1711 Bust Marble H: 75 Signed & dated
Comm. for the Genovéfains; Keller-D., II, p. 68–9.

PARIS, BIBLIOTHEQUE STE.–GENEVIEVE

89

90

92

93

95

94a

94b

96¹

94
François du Vaucel, fermier général
(farmer-general of taxes)

1712
    a.★ Bust   Marble   H: 76 (incl. socle)
Originally in du Vaucel's chât. de La Norville, then in
the Coll. Doucet. Sold in 1912 to Jules S. Bache, USA.
cf. Keller-D., II, p. 72.

PRIVATE COLLECTION

    b.★ *Bust*   Terracotta
Probably the model for the marble bust. In a private
coll. in 1920. Present whereabouts unknown.

96²

95★
Madame du Vaucel

1712   Bust   Marble   Signed: A. COYZEVOX. 1712
Pendant to the bust of her husband, no. 94a. History as
for 94a, but bought by a Mr. Bousquet at the sale of
1912. cf. Keller-D., II, p. 72. Whereabouts unknown.

96
Tomb of Hardouin–Mansart

1712   Bas-relief   Marble   291 × 162
Comm. by the widow, Anne Bodin, and placed in the
Church of St.-Paul against a pillar of the Communion
Chapel; estim. 26 Apr. 1712, Min. Centr. Arch. Nat.,
Et. CV, 1093 for 2600 L. Mentioned in the *Mém. inéd.*, I,
p. 37 and in the *Descr.* of Paris. It showed a marble
figure of Fame holding a medallion with the profile of
the deceased, against a curtain in gilded stucco, engraved
with the Dôme and, on a scroll, the ground-plan of the
Invalides. Above, the family coat-of-arms flanked by
eagles; below, the inscription; underneath a death's
head. In the Mus. des Mon. Fr. during the Revolution.

98

Only the inscription and the medallion★ remain in the Museum at Versailles. cf. Keller-D., II, p. 55–6; F. Souchal, 'Monum. funér. du Duc d'Angoulême et d'Hardouin-Mansart', in *BSHAF*, 1972, p. 158–9. Watercolour sketch★ of the tomb, Bibl. Nat. Ms. Clairambault 945, p. 233. Drawing by St.-Aubin in his copy of Piganiol, *Paris*, 1742, IV, p. 23 (Mus. du Petit-Palais, Paris).

VERSAILLES, MUSEUM (The medallion)

97
Silence and Modesty

1712–13   Models for Bas-reliefs
Intended for a vestibule of the Chapel at Versailles, but not executed. C. was paid 780 L. for the models, *Comptes*, V, 873; Keller-D., II, p. 73. Sixteen 'Virtues' for the Vestibule Haut were carved in stone by other sculptors: pairs of female figures reclining on the arches above the doors and windows. C.'s models were probably connected with this project. Destroyed.

98★
Louis XIV fulfilling the Vow of Louis XIII to the Virgin

1713–15   Statue   Marble   H: 180
Part of the ensemble called 'The Vow of Louis XIII' in the choir of Notre-Dame, Paris; the rest was entrusted to N. Coustou (no. 61) and G. Coustou (no. 38), cf. P. Bertrand no. 28★. Louis XIV, in Coronation robes, kneels in the attitude of oblation. Payment 8100 L.

Comptes, V, 695, 787, 873. During the Revolution in the Mus. des Mon. fr. Returned to Notre-Dame after an interval in the Chapel at Versailles. Keller-D., II, p. 75–6.

PARIS, NOTRE-DAME

99
Louis XV as a Child

c. 1716
a.★ Bust   Marble   H: 41   Signed: A. COYZEVOX F. cf. Keller-D., II, p. 77–8. Acc. to the *Mém. inéd.*, II, p. 38, C. made four busts of Louis XV at different ages, i.e. between the death of Louis XIV in 1715 and 1720, the date of C.'s Biogr. in the *Mém. inéd*. In 1716, C. asked the Acad. roy. to register a bust of the young King, *P-V*, IV, 231. This very fine bust passed into the art trade (Coll. Cormis; Coll. Wildenstein; Coll. Rothschild).

PRIVATE COLLECTION

A replica with slight variations exists, but the signature: A. COYSEVAUX 1717, is doubtful. As different from no. 99a, the young King wears the Order of the St.-Esprit. Collection Burat.

PRIVATE COLLECTION

b. *Bust of Louis XV as a child*   Tonnerre stone
Mentioned as by C. in the Invent. a.d. of Michel Velut de la Crosnière, 24 Apr. 1735, Min. Centr. Arch. Nat., Et. XVII, 690. May be the same as a bust (stone) in the Museum at Valenciennes.

100
Marquis de Louvois

1716   Bust   Marble
Comm. by his son, the Marquis de Courtanvaux. Payment 1000 L., Min. centr. Arch. Nat., Et. XXIV, 576. Transport 4 Jan. 1716, quittance 14 Apr. 1717. cf. Fermel'huis, *Eloge*, p. 34; *Mém. Inéd.*, II, p. 37. Not ident. or disapp.

101★
Maréchal de Villars

1718   Bust   Marble   Signed & dated
cf. Fermel'huis, *Eloge*, p. 34 and *Mém. inéd.*, II, p. 38.

ENGLAND, ROYAL COLLECTION

102★
Cardinal Melchior de Polignac

1718   Bust   Marble   Signed: COYZEVOX F. 1718
Still in the possession of the family. cf. Keller-D., II, p. 78–9.

PRIVATE COLLECTION

99a

101

103
Louis XV as a child

1719
  a.★ Bust   Marble   H: 41
Probably one of four busts noted in the *Mém. inéd.*,
II, p. 38; Keller-D., II, p. 79, pl. 146.

  b.★ Bust   Wax   Signed & dated 1719
Probably the maquette of no. 103a.

VERSAILLES, MUSEUM

PRIVATE COLLECTION

103a

102

103b

104

UNDATED WORKS

104*
Marquis de Louvois

High-relief Bust Marble H: 124
Signed: A. COYZEVOX
Sale P. Gouvert, Paris, 10 May 1960, no. 73.
Profile of the marquis, in state dress, wearing a cloak.
The bust, in a medallion, is surrounded by sham
drapery, mounted on a modern plaque in Comblanchien.
Prov.: supposedly from the Hôtel Louvois. Where-
abouts unknown.

105
Chancellor Boucherat

Bust Plaster
Given by C. to the Acad. roy., acc. to the invent. of
1775. cf. Fontaine, p. 215; Keller-D., II, p. 16. Not
ident. or disapp.

106
Antoine Coysevox

c. 1702
   a.* Bust Marble H: 67
Date probably c. 1702 as suggested by N. Rondot,
Les. sculpts. de Lyon, Lyon-Paris, 1884, p. 49; Keller-D.,
II, p. 32–3. Presented in 1788 to the Acad. roy. by
Charles-Pierre Coustou, C.'s great-nephew.

PARIS, LOUVRE

   b. Bust Terracotta H: 69 (see p. 177*)
The drapery is a later addition. Probably the model for
the marble bust, no. 106a. Prov.: English private coll.;
given by Mr. & Mrs. Grover-Magnin to the De Young
Mus., San Francisco. cf. W. Heil, 'A Bust by Coysevox'
in *GBA*, 1952[2], p. 351–4.

SAN FRANCISCO, USA. M. H. DE YOUNG MEMORIAL MUSEUM

107*
Antoine Coypel

Bust Marble H: 55
Acquired from the original owners, the family of the
sculptors Dumont. cf. Keller-D., II, p. 71.

PARIS, LOUVRE

108

107

106a

108
Gérard Audran (1640–1701)

Bust
Engr.★: by N. Dupuis after C.'s sculpture. Whereabouts
unknown.

109★
Unknown Man

Bust   Terracotta   H: 53
Bought by the Louvre in 1920; wrongly identified as
Gérard Audran (see no. 108).

PARIS, LOUVRE

110
Cardinal de Bouillon

Bust   Marble
cf. Fermel'huis, *Eloge*, p. 34; *Mém. inéd.*, II, p. 37;
Keller-D., II, p. 84. Not ident. or disapp.

111
Gérard Edelinck

Bust   Terracotta
cf. *Mém. inéd.*, II, p. 58. Not ident. or disapp.

112
Jean-Baptiste Fermel'huis

Bust   Marble
cf. Fermel'huis, *Eloge*, p. 32–3. Not ident. or disapp.

109

113*
Unknown Man

Bust   Marble   H: 72 (incl. socle)
Signed on the back: A.C.F.
Perhaps the bust of Fermel'huis, *Eloge*, no. 112. Keller-D., II, p. 86, 91. Galliéra sale, Paris, 29 Nov. 1973, cat. no. 78.

PRIVATE COLLECTION

114*
Charles d'Albert, Duc de Chaulnes

Bust   Marble   H: 70 (without socle)
Mém. inédits., II, p. 38; Fermel'huis, *Eloge*, p. 34. Perhaps identical with a marble bust, not signed or dated, in the sale Chât. d'Albert, 1852, then belonging to the Orléans family; today in the Mus. at Amiens*; was wrongly identified with a bust of the Regent.

AMIENS (Somme), MUSEUM

115
President de Harlay

Bust
cf. *Mém. inéd.*, II, p. 38; Fermel'huis, *Eloge*, p. 34. Not ident. or disapp.

116*
The Duc de Montausier

Bust   Marble   H: 98
cf. *Mém. inéd.*, II, p. 37; Fermel'huis, *Eloge*, p. 34.

PRIVATE COLLECTION

117*
Unknown Man

Bust   Marble   Signed underneath: A. COYZEVOX F.
Does not represent Villars (no. 102), as suggested by Keller-D., II, 99–100.

VERSAILLES, MUSEUM

118*
Unknown Man

Bust   Marble   Not signed or dated
Pres. in 1816 to the Comédie Française by a Mr. Dubief; cf. Keller-D., II, p. 89–90. Wrong inscription on the pedestal; does not represent Lully.

PARIS, COMEDIE FRANCAISE

113

114¹

116

117

114²

118

119

119*
Tomb of Marie le Camus

In the Cabinet des Dessins at the Louvre is a pen and wash drawing, signed by C., for the planned tomb of Marie le Camus (Guiffrey-Marcel, *Invent.* no. 3143), the widow of Michel Particelli, Surintendant des Finances. The deceased, her hands clasped, half-lies on a sarcophagus, flanked by a weeping woman and a man; above, three cherubim on clouds and a glory of sunrays; on the base a coat of arms and an incription. Not known whether the tomb was ever executed. The drawing was acquired at the sale Destailleurs, 15 June 1896, no. 83.

Detail   DEDIEU

DEDIEU, Jean (1646–1727)

b. Arles 1646. Son of Guillaume Dedieu, joiner in that town, and of Marthe Guillaume. Attended the local Jesuit School, cf. 'Annales du Couvent des Minimes d'Arles', Bibl. munic d'Arles, ms. 166, fol. 204. Apprenticed to the sculptor Michel Péru in Avignon, contract 16 Apr. 1664, Arch. de Vaucluse, publ. in Belleudy (see below). Went to Brest during 1667–9 to work at ships' decorations; then supposed to have gone to Rome, but lived in Paris in 1670, rue Montmarte, parish of St.-Eustache, working at Versailles; on 16 June married Jeanne Dantan, Min. Centr. Arch. Nat., Et. XXXVI, liasse 210. Returned to Arles 1673–8; from August 1678–80 at Chartres with his brother Pons, also a sculptor, taking part in numerous surveys of stones in the quarries. Back in Paris he lived in the Vieux Louvre; in 1683 his friend, the sculptor Pierre Puget, came to live with him. His recollections of Puget, written at the request of Père Bougerel, the Oratorian; cf. L. Lagrange, 'Pierre Puget', in *GBA*, 1865–67[1], t. XVIII–XXII. In 1684 he went to Arles to escort to Paris the recently discovered antique Venus, repaired by him (see no. 18), which was to be presented to the King by the Consulate in Arles, *Comptes,* II, 383, 492, 938; Bibl. mun. d'Arles, ms. 547, fol. 192. In 1685 he went to Le Havre in search of the equestrian statue of Louis XIV by Bernini, *Comptes*, II, 759. On the 27 Jan. 1685 he received a gold medal from the Acad., *P-V*, II, 296, but was never made a member, *ibid.*, III, 4, 17, 233, 235, 245, 330; IV, 398; in 1709 his presentation to the Acad. was cancelled, *ibid.*, IV, 78; in 1706 Cronström sounded him about working in Sweden for the King; he was not engaged because of his advanced age and the high fee he demanded; cf. *Corresp. Tessin–Cronström*, 24 Oct. and 24 Nov. 1706. His wife died in 1718, cf. Jal, p. 497. In 1720 he lost part of his coll. of paintings and works of art in a fire at Boulle's studio, cf. letters to his brother Pons, 8 July, 27 Aug., 24 Sept. 1720, Arch. d'Arles, cf. Belleudy, below. Ruined by the bankruptcy of J. Law, he bought a small farm in the Camargue and other land, letter of 29 Oct. 1722; also a house in Arles where he retired in 1726. Died 31 May 1727. cf. Mariette, *ABC*, II, p. 112; T-B, IX, 1913, pp. 277–8 (P. Vollmer); J. Belleudy, 'Jean de Dieu', in *Mém. de l'Acad. Vaucluse*, XXV, 1925, p. 185 ff. His portrait in oils in Mus. Réattu, Arles.*

1*
Saint Christopher

1672   Group   Stone   H: over 200
Carved for the Church of St.-Trophime, Arles, at the expense of Canon Pillier in memory of his father, the lawyer Christophe Pillier; mutilated during the Revolution. cf. J.-J. Estrangin, *Etudes archéol. sur Arles*, 1838; E. Fassin, 'Une Promenade dans Arles', in *Bull. de la Soc. des Amis du vieil Arles*, July 1907, p. 294. The Saint walks with the child Jesus on his right shoulder; on the supporting tree-trunk, traces of the Pillier family coat of arms.

ARLES, MUSEE ARLATEN (B. du R.)

1

3–17
WORK FOR THE HOTEL DE VILLE, ARLES

Bibl.: 'Une promenade dans Arles en février 1795', publ. by E. Fassin in *Bull. de la Soc. des amis du Vieil Arles*, July 1907, p. 290–302; L. Jacquemin, *Guide du voyageur dans Arles*, Arles, 1835, p. 462 ff.; H. Clair, *Les Mon. d'Arles antique et moderne*, Arles, 1837, p. 191–7; J.-J. Estrangin, *Etudes archéol., hist. et statistiques sur Arles*, Arles, 1838, p. 236 ff.; Estrangin, *Descr. d'Arles antique et moderne*, Aix, 1845; E.-L.-G. Charvet, 'L'Hôtel de ville d'Arles et ses huit architectes', in *RSBAD*, 1898, XXII, p. 396–418; J. Boyer, 'J. Hardouin-Mansart et l'hôtel de ville d'Arles', in *GBA*, 1969², p. 1–32.

3*
Two Recumbent Lions

1673   Stone   Length: c. 150
At the foot of the great staircase of the Hôtel de Ville. Payment 150 L. to D. in 1674 and, for repairs, in 1675, Arles, Arch. Comm., CC 691, Comptes, pièces justificatives 172 and CC 693.

ARLES, HOTEL DE VILLE

2
Saint Louis

1673   Statue   Stone   More than life-size
In a niche on the quay at Arles at the corner of the Porte St.-Louis; payment 50 L. by the Consuls of Arles, 13 Sept. 1673. Arch. Comm. d'Arles, série BB, no. 35; Comptes, no. 691. Not ident. or disapp.

4
Eleven Lion Heads

1673   Stone
Above the windows of the ground floor. Total payment 33 L., *ibid.*, CC 691.

ARLES, HOTEL DE VILLE

3

6

5
Several Inscriptions

1673–6   Gilded lettering
One in the vestibule above the door leading to the Plan de la Cour; another on the socle of the Venus of Arles; a third in the Cabinet of the Clock Tower, *ibid.*, CC 691–3. Destroyed.

6★
Arles Coat of Arms

1674   Two bas-reliefs   Stone
On the ground floor above the two main portals leading to the Grande Place and the Plan de la Cour. The escutcheon, decorated with the seated lion of Arles in bas-relief, on a console surrounded by acanthus leaves and cornucopias, supp. by two nude children. Total payment 150 L., receipt 24 July 1674, *ibid.*, Et. Véran, 404 E, liasse 804, fol. 339 and CC 692.

ARLES, HOTEL DE VILLE

7
Four Consoles

1674   Stone
Under the elliptical vault of the Salle Basse on the ground floor of the Hôtel de Ville. Payment 12 L., *ibid.*, Et. Véran, 404 E, liasse 804, fol. 339 v., 340 r.

ARLES, HOTEL DE VILLE

8★
Decoration of the Ten First Floor Windows

1674   Stone
D. carved, on the lintels of six of these windows, bas-reliefs with the monogram of the town of Arles intertwined with palm branches, and above the entablature, medallions in half-relief with heavy folds of drapery on both sides. The medallions showed the portraits of the first six kings of Arles: Bozon, Louis Bozon, Hugues, Rodulphe, Geraldus and Conrad I. Effaced during the Revolution. The lintels of the four other windows show

8

9, 11, 12

the monogram of the King entwined by oak branches. On the entablature two sphinxes* lying opposite each other; the crowns between their paws disapp. during the Revolution. Payment 320 L., *ibid.*, BB 35, fol. 442, CC 692.

ARLES, HOTEL DE VILLE

9–13
SCULPTURES AT THE ATTIC

9*
The Royal Coat of Arms supported by two Figures of Fame

1674　Two groups　High-relief　Stone
On the two façades under the pediment. The two groups were made by D. after one model: two hovering winged female figures support a drapery revealing an escutcheon; one sounding, the other holding a trumpet; behind the escutcheon, foliage. The King's monogram was chipped off during the Revolution; now replaced by the letters 'R F' on one side. Agreed fee 500 L., *ibid.*, BB 80, I, fol. 177, 30 Nov. 1674; BB 35, fol. 442; CC 692.

ARLES, HOTEL DE VILLE

10
Two Captives seated on Trophies

1675　Two high-reliefs　Stone
On either side of the figures of Fame at the Grande Place. Placed in position 16 Oct. 1675, 404 E, liasse 883, fol. 222–3, 650. Fee agreed 27 May 1675, BB 80, fol. 10; payment 700 L. together with the two statues of Might and Justice, CC 693, see no. 11. Destroyed.

11*　12*
Might and Justice

1675　Two statues　Stone　Over life-size
On either side of the figures of Fame facing the Plan de la Tour. Justice, leaning on lictor's fasces, holds a pair of scales in her left hand; Might carries the drum of a column. Payment, see no. 10.

ARLES, HOTEL DE VILLE

13
Two Suns surrounded by Clouds

1675　Two bas-reliefs　Stone
On the pediments of the two façades. Payment 55 L., *ibid.*, E 404, liasse 883, fol. 650 v. and CC 693. Receipt 31 Dec. 1675.

ARLES, HOTEL DE VILLE

14

15

14*
Fifteen Pots-à-feu

1675   Stone
On the upper balustrade. Payment 45 L., *ibid.*, E 404, liasse 883, fol. 650 v.; liasse 884, fol. 198 v.

ARLES, HOTEL DE VILLE

15*
Trophies

1675   Two bas-reliefs   Stone
On both façades of the main building, at the height of the first floor in the arches above the windows. They show a cuirass, flags and various weapons. Payment 120 L., receipt of 18 Mar. 1676, *ibid.*, E 404, liasse 884, fol. 198.

ARLES, HOTEL DE VILLE

16
Trophies, Portraits and Five Heads

1675–6   Stone
Trophies and portraits above the two portals of the vestibule, the Porte du Concierge and the Porte de la Salle Basse; the five heads were carved on the keystones of the arcades. Payment 120 L., *ibid.*, CC 693. Destroyed.

17
Louis XIV

1676   Statue   Pernes stone
Comm. by the Consuls, D. undertook on 13 July 1676 to execute, after his own model, a standing statue of Louis XIV on a stone pedestal in the vestibule of the Hôtel de Ville, *ibid.*, E 402, liasse 401, fol. 432. First payment 360 L., rec. 24 Mar. 1677, E. 402, liasse 402, fol. 312; raised to 500 L., CC 694, BB 80, III, fol. 54. Towards the end of his life D. intended to make alterations to this statue, but died before he could carry them out. Destroyed during the Revolution. *See app.*

19[1]

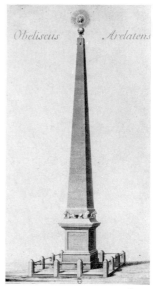

19[2]*–20*

21

21* Tomb of Bishop Gaspard du Laurens

1677 Stone
Trad. attrib. to D., cf. A. Du Mège, *Vues de la cath. d'Arles*, 1829, p. 16; L. Jacquemin, *Hist. des archevêques d'Arles*, Bibl. Munic. d'Arles, Ms. 126, fol. 177–85; L. Jacquemin, *Guide du voyageur dans Arles*, 1835, p. 354–355 ff. The Bishop died in 1630; his tomb, on the rear wall of the Chapelle des Rois in St.-Trophime, was not erected until 1677. Although mutilated during the Revolution, the essential parts are preserved: the sarcophagus, 'à l'antique', with acanthus leaves and two heads on the supporting consoles; a youthful angel lifts the lid, allowing the deceased to emerge, his out-stretched hands clasped; the head has disappeared. Seated on the right, a female figure repr. Charity, with two children; three putti hold the inscription and an escutcheon with the coat of arms of du Laurens.

ARLES, CHURCH OF ST.-TROPHIME

18 Restoration of the Venus of Arles

1676
The 'restoration' of this antique statue—discovered in 1651, at first called 'Diana'—for which D. received a payment, must have consisted of small repairs, because it was Girardon who in 1685 replaced the missing parts and added the attribs. of Venus, before the statue was placed in the Grande Galerie, Versailles.

PARIS, LOUVRE

22 *Saint Mary Magdalen*

Before 1678 Stone
Acc. to local trad. (cf. M. de Truchet, 'Une anecdote sur J. Dedieu', in *Le Musée*, 1876, 2nd ser., no. 29, p. 228–9), comm. by Madeleine Deloste, a woman of Arles. The Saint, penitent, was repr. lying down, leaning on a death's head. Acc. to Truchet, the statue was still in the Roquépine Garden in 1876. Whereabouts unknown.

19* Louis XIV (!) in a Sun (Attrib.)

1677 Lead
Originally surmounting the globe at the top of the Obelisk at Arles. The traditional attrib. to D. is not borne out by the very summary treatment of the King's face, nor by any document; the Arch. mention only payments for iron and woodwork; cf. J.-J. Estrangin, *Descr. d'Arles*, p. 63 ff.; E. Fassin and A. Lieutaud, 'L'Obélisque d'Arles', in *Bull. Soc. des amis du vieil Arles*, Jan. 1909, p. 1–17; Apr. 1909, p. 66–7; July 1909, p. 118–136. Engr.* of the obelisk by Poilly. Brought down from the obelisk in 1792. *See appendix.*

ARLES, MUSEE REATTU

23 Work in the Choir Enclosure, Chartres Cathedral

1678–80
a.* The woman taken in adultery
Group of four figures Stone H: 127
b. Ornaments around the niches Stone
D. carved a scene with four figures: the adulteress standing; a pharisee holding her by the arm; Jesus kneeling, writing on the ground; behind, a second pharisee in a gesture of reproach. It is not clear what else in this enclosure is by D. Payments: between 29 Aug. 1678 and 23 June 1679, D. rec. 2150 L. 5 s. 6 d., comptes du clerc de l'oeuvre, reg. G 424, publ. by Jusselin. A new contract was signed on 29 Aug. 1679 and D. rec. another 553 L. 10 s. The payments stopped on 24 June 1680. cf. F. de Mély, 'La cath. de Chartres', in *RSBAD*, 1890, p. 523–33; C. Jouin, 'Le Tour du Choeur de la Cathédrale de Chartres', in *P-V de la Soc. Archéol. d'Eure et Loir*, XIII, 1919, p. 258–60; M. Jusselin, 'Le Tour du Choeur de la Cathédrale de Chartres', in *Mém. de la Soc. archéol. d'Eure et Loir*, XXI, 1957–61. Other scenes were carved by P. Legros I, Tuby the younger and Mazière.

CHARTRES, CATHEDRAL

20 *Four Crouching Lions*

1676 Stone
In collab. with Antoine Paulet. At the foot of the obelisk on the pedestal. Replaced in 1829 by four bronze lions. Bibl., see no. 19. Payment 120 L., 24 Mar. 1677, *ibid.*, CC 694. Destroyed.

23

24
Two Men and Two Horses

Between 1681–85   Bas-relief   Stone
In a pediment above one of the portals of the small stables at Versailles, next to the Hôtel Conty, acc. to Félibien des Avaux, *Versailles* (Tables) and Piganiol, *Vers.-Marly*, 1730, I, p. 10, I. Disappeared.

26   *27*

25
Copy of the Sarcophagus of Saint Aurelius

1684
The sarcophagus was in the Aliscamps at Arles. D.'s copy, comm. by Louis XIV, was not accepted by the King, who thought the motifs too small; cf. *Ann. du couvent des Minimes d'Arles dit St. Honorat des Aliscamps 1591–1705 par R. P. M. Fabre*, Bibl. Munic. d'Arles, Ms. 166, fol. 204, 1684. Whereabouts unknown.

26*
Bacchante

1684–5   Term   Marble   H: 275
At the north side of the Parterre de Latone. The Bacchante, nude to the waist, her hips draped in a lion's skin, plays a basque tambour. Payment 7000 L., together with the Term of Lysias (no. 27), *Comptes*, II, 441, 625, 990, 1092, 1140, 1175.

VERSAILLES, PARK

27*
Lysias

1685   Term   Marble   H: 275
Design by Mignard; repr. a bearded old man, a cloth draped around his shoulders, in his left hand a rolled-up parchment. Payments 7000 L., together with the Bacchante (no. 26), *Comptes*, II, 625, 990; III, 990, 1121.

VERSAILLES, PARK

28
Guilloche Moulding on the Colonnade, Versailles

1685–6   Stone
Payment 640 L., *Comptes*, II, 625, 950. cf. Cornu no. 17*.

VERSAILLES, PARK

33

29
Ionic Capitals for the Grand Trianon

1687–8   Marble
D. received 1186 L. for the capital of a free-standing column (cf. Coysevox no. 50★), three square pilaster capitals and two corner capitals (cf. André no. 11★), *Comptes*, II, 1175; III, 94.

VERSAILLES, GRAND TRIANON

30
Sculpture for the Place Louis-le-Grand (today Place Vendôme)

1690–91   Stone
  a. *46 capitals*
  b. *44 consoles*
Payment 901 L., *Comptes*, III, 424, 562. The square was redesigned in 1698. Destroyed.

31
Capitals and Consoles

1690–1   Stone
Forty Composite capitals and 8 consoles at the Dôme des Invalides carved by D., Chauveau (no. 4b★), Boutet, Dufour and Jouvenet; payment in several instalm. in 1690–1. Bibl. Nat., Ms. fr. no. 22936, Distr. de toute la sculpture de l'église des Invalides, 24 May 1690 and *Comptes*, III, 422, 559.

PARIS, DOME DES INVALIDES

32
Eight Capitals

1691–4   Stone
For eight Composite capitals for columns and pilasters in one of the chapels of the Dôme, D. rec. four payments total. 1760 L., *Comptes*, III, 559, 701, 844; IV, 329.

PARIS, DOME DES INVALIDES

33
Model for an Evangelist

1691
On 31 Jan. 1691, four evangelists for the pendentives of the Dôme des Invalides were comm. from D., P. Magnier, Lespingola and P. Legros I, Bibl. Nat. Est., Coll. de Cotte, Hc 14, 2★. On 19 Aug. 1691, D. rec. 91 L. "for his clay and wax models" (for one of these?). The project was never followed up. Destroyed.

34
Ornaments for the Panels of the Vault

1692–1700   Stone
D., Jouvenet and others worked from 1692–1700 to decorate the 12 panels of the cupola with roses and carved frames; several payments, *Comptes*, III, 702, 844; IV, 330, 472, 611.

PARIS, DOME DES INVALIDES

35
Angel holding the Ark of the Covenant

1693–9   Stone
This angel, in one of the twelve panels of the cupola of the Dôme des Invalides, was part of Hardouin-Mansart's first programme, abandoned at the end of 1699. D. rec. 1000 L., *Comptes*, III, 844; IV, 329, 469; Arch. Nat., O[I] 1665, 36, 38. cf. N. Coustou no. 11b. Destroyed.

36
Model for the Tomb of Mignard

1697
Estim. before a notary, publ. in *NAAF*, VIII, 1892, p. 242 ff. D. had planned a monument in marble of various colours: on the sarcophagus a reclining allegorical figure of Painting (L: c. 250), accomp. by a child carrying an escutcheon; on the pedestal, a portrait bust of Mignard, to be presented by the Comtesse de Feuquières—this refers to the bust carved by Desjardins (no. 52). A 3-metre high pyramid was to dominate the ensemble, with the coat of arms of the deceased; an urn on top of the pyramid, two lamps and two consoles in gilded bronze. The project was never carried out; later entrusted to J.-B. Lemoyne II. Destroyed.

37
Vase for the Demi-lune des Vents, Marly

1697–8   Marble   H: 130
cf. Barois no. 11★. One of 12 vases for the balustrade of the Demi-lune des Vents, similar to the one by Raon. Arch. Nat., O[I] 2773[5], payments 850 L., *Comptes*, IV, 188, 335. Not ident. or disapp.

39

38

Decoration for the Demi-lune des Vents, Marly

1697–8   Lead
    a. *Two sea monsters*
    b. *Two heads of winds*
cf. Barois no. 12. On the marble retaining wall enclosing the Demi-lune des Vents. The Bassin was compl. in 1703. Reprod. in a water-colour drawing, Arch. Nat., O^I 1470, pl. 12. D. rec. for both works 548 L., *Comptes*, IV, 188, 336. Destroyed.

39*

Work on one of the two Pavilions at the Ménagerie, Versailles

1699   Stone
Each of these two pavilions has two pediments decor. with large shells, each surmounted by two cupids; those in the pavilion at the side of the old Laiterie are by Van Clève, acc. to Mém., Arch. Nat., O^I 1805[101]; those in the pavilion on the right, accomp. by musical instruments, must therefore be by D.; they are badly damaged. Payment to D. 350 L., *Comptes*, IV, 449.

VERSAILLES, PARK

40

Restoration Work on Statues at Marly

1702
In collab. with a team which rec. 4586 L., *Comptes*, IV, 853.

41

Saint Eustacia

1702   Plaster   H: 285
In a niche of the Chapelle St.-Jérôme at the Dôme des Invalides; cf. Félibien des Avaux, *Invalides*, p. 300; Granet, p. 112; Pérau, p. 78. Never exec. in marble; disapp. in 1745, cf. C. Dreyfus, 'Les statues du Dôme des Inval. au XVIIIe s.', in *BSHAF*, 1908, p. 108–9. Pen drawing in Coll. de Cotte, Bibl. Nat. Est., Hc 14, 2; engr.* by Ch.-N. Cochin in Pérau, pl. 105. Destroyed.

42

Works at the Pièce des Vents, Marly

1703–4   Gilded lead
    a. *Two groups of Tritons*
    b. *Shells, Heads of monsters and winds*
cf. N. Coustou no 43*. Payments to D., Flamen (no. 50), Van Clève, Lepautre, Le Lorrain and Lapierre, 11,760 L., *Comptes*, IV, 964, 1072. Destroyed.

43

Repair and Cleaning of the Two Groups of France Triumphant by Marsy and Girardon

1705
In the forecourt of Versailles. Payment 850 L., *Comptes*, IV, 1157; V, 534.

VERSAILLES, PALACE

41

45

44
Work on the outside of the Chapel, Versailles

1704–5   Stone
   a. Five Corinthian pilaster capitals
   b. Two gargoyles
   c. Twenty-five roses
   d. Twenty-five modillions

In collab. with Simony. Estim. for the capitals 1250 L., for the gargoyles 365 L., for the rose and modillions on the cornice 425 L.; Mém., Arch. Nat., O^I 1784; paid in 1704, *Comptes*, IV, 1049.

VERSAILLES PALACE, CHAPEL

45*
Decorations on the Roof of the Chapel, Versailles

1705–7   Lead
In collab. with Poultier, Poirier, Lepautre, François (no. 26), Lapierre, Voiriot, Offement and Berja. In the centre of the ridge was a lantern, with eight columns, eight cherubim heads, eight consoles with plant decoration, the whole crowned by 16 feuilles d'eau. This very heavy lantern has been taken down. The rest of the ornaments, consisting of cherubim, fleurons, fleurs-de-lis, consoles, suns, tassels are still in place along the ridge, on the hips of the roof, and around the dormer windows. In the centre of the sloping roof, terms of cherubim, two in the round, two lying on the ridge, joined by garlands, supporting the royal crown; underneath, a cartouche with the royal coat of arms, the collars of the orders of St.-Michel and St.-Esprit and trophies of arms. This considerable work, incl. cost of scaffolding, erection, workmen's wages and changes in the design was estim. at 79,498 L., Mém., Arch. Nat., O^I 1784; paid in 1710, *Comptes*, V, 412. Engr.* in Blondel, *Arch. Fr.*, IV; pencil drawing* of the lantern in Stockholm, CC 1263.

VERSAILLES PALACE, CHAPEL

46
Young Angels with various Attributes

1708
   a. *Two young Angels carrying a Vase*
Wax model. Rejected
   b. *Three young Angels carrying the House of the Virgin.*
Wax model. Rejected
   c. Two young Angels holding a Mitre
Bas-relief   Stone   L: c. 350
After Van Clève's model. Outside the chapel above the first curved bay of the Petite Cour; very much restored by Croisy in 1875; the missing attribs. were replaced in imitation of the corresp. bas-relief by Tuby at the side of the Cour de la Smalah. Arch. Nat., F^{21} 3474–6. Total estim. 1060 L., Arch. Nat., O^I 1784; paid in 1708 and 1710, *Comptes*, V, 214, 414. Almost completely destroyed.

VERSAILLES PALACE, CHAPEL

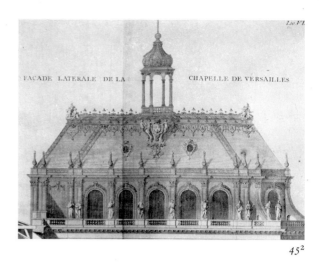

45²

48
Capital for the Salon Haut of the Chapel

1708–10   Bonbanc stone
Corinthian capital of an engaged column. Estim. 340 L.,
paid in 1708 and 1710, *Comptes*, V, 214, 414.

VERSAILLES PALACE, CHAPEL

45³

47
Sculpture at the Chevet of the Tribune

1708
   a.★ Fall of musical trophies
Six bas-reliefs   Stone   454 × 75
   b.★ Plant ornaments
Six bas-reliefs   Stone   162 × 75
Between the columns on the wall at the back of the
chevet; the plant bas-reliefs overhang the musical
trophies. In collab. with other sculptors. Estim. 4920 L.,
Mém., Arch. Nat., O¹ 1784. Paid between 1708–11,
Comptes, V, 217, 320, 527.

VERSAILLES PALACE, CHAPEL

47b

47a

51   52

49
Nymph of Diana

1710

For bibliogr. see Cayot no. 8. D. and nine other sculptors, Flamen (no. 58), Frémin (no. 31), Lapierre, Lepautre, P. Magnier, J.-L. Lemoyne, Mazière, Poultier, Théodon, each rec. on 1 Aug. 1710 200 L. for a Nymph of Diana, *Comptes*, V, 432. For each completed nymph c. 3600 L. were paid, but D. rec. no further payment, so he probably never finished his statue. Drawing★ in the Coll. de Cotte, Bibl. Nat. Cab. Est., Fb 26; the nymph, walking, with a bow and quiver, wears a flowing dress; at her feet, a dog and game. Destroyed. (?)

50
Model for Saint Genest (Saint Genesius)

c. 1726

At the time of the restoration of the Saint's shrine in Arles. Exec. in silver on 14 Feb. 1727 by Bénezet Vinay, silversmith of Avignon, after D.'s model, Arch. de Vaucluse, cf. Belleudy, *op. cit.* (Biogr.); cartulaire du chapitre de la Sainte Eglise d'Arles, Bibl. Munic. d'Arles, Ms. 146, II, fol. 543. Whereabouts unknown.

51
Woman holding her Cloak

Drawing★ in Coll. de Cotte, Bibl. Nat. Est., Fb 26, annot.: 'par le sieur De Dieu'. It is not known to which work this and the following drawing refer.

52
Man holding a Scroll

Drawing★, see no. 51.

49

1

1*

Father Jacques de Sirmond, Counsellor of Louis XIII, Jesuit (1559–1651)

1698   Medallion   Marble   77 × 64   Signed on the edge at the left: ANNO 1698 I. DEFER. SCULPT.
The inscription on the back refers to the comm. of the medallion by the deceased's great-nephew, Matthieu Sirmond. Property of the family until 1801; acqu. by Lenoir for his Museum, cf. Courajod, *Lenoir*, no. 1063, I, p. 161; *Arch. du Mus. des Mon. Fr.*, I, 251; III, 45–6; G. Brière, 'Sculpteurs fr. 17–18ᵉ s.', in *BSHAF*, 1923, p. 68.

VERSAILLES, MUSEUM

2

Joseph's Cup is discovered in Benjamin's Pack

1698   Bas-relief
2nd sculpture prize, *P-V*, III, 241, 246, cf. Guiffrey, *Liste Pensionnaires*. Destroyed.

3

Jacob's Vision in Egypt during his search for Joseph

1699   Bas-relief
1st sculpture prize, *P-V*, III, 277. Destroyed.

4

Hercules chaining up Cerberus

1703
This model was D.'s reception piece for his entrance to the Acad., *P-V*, III, 370. Destroyed.

5

Various Ornaments in the Chapel at Versailles

1707
  a. Ecclesiastical Trophies   Bas-reliefs   Stone

DEFER, Jean-Baptiste (1674–after 1714)

b. Paris 1674, son of Claude Defer, master fellmonger; grandson of Antoine Defer, illuminator and dealer in engravings; cousin of the sculptor Jean Voiriot. D. rec. a second prize (see no. 2); then a first prize (see no. 3) in the Concours at the Acad.; went to Rome, where he stayed from July 1699 to June 1700. In 1703, agréé by the Acad. On 18 July 1707, he married Antoinette Suc. The date of his death is not known, but he was still alive in 1714. cf. Bibl. Nat. Ms., Fich. Laborde 12079 & 16788; Bellier de la Chavignerie, I, 375; T-B, VIII, 1913, p. 536.

7

6

In collab. with other sculptors, cf. Bertrand no. 18b*. Mém., Arch Nat., O^I 1784; payment in 1711, *Comptes*, V, 530.

b. Ornaments   Stone

In collab. with François (no. 20), Girard, Raon, Vigier and others. The ornam., with fleurs-de-lis carved in the lozenges, decor. three faces of the bases of the Corinthian columns and the bases of the pilasters of the Tribune. Some fleurs-de-lis broken off during the Revolution. Payment 14,367 L. 1s. 8d., *Comptes*, V, 214, 529.

VERSAILLES PALACE, CHAPEL

6*
Winged Children outside the Chapel, Versailles

1708   Bas-relief   Stone   180 × c. 345

Two winged children holding laurel wreaths and palms. After a small wax model, from an earlier cancelled project. One of the great bas-reliefs above the big window arches on the north side. Estim. 1000 L., Mém., Arch. Nat., O^I 1784. Total payment 1060 L., *Comptes*, V, 213, 527.

VERSAILLES PALACE, CHAPEL

7*
Ornaments on the Culs de Four of the Aisles

1709   Stone

In collab. with others. Payment 1360 L., *Comptes*, V, 319, 527.

VERSAILLES PALACE, CHAPEL

8   9*
Two Ecclesiastical Trophies

1709   Bas-reliefs   Stone   248 × 35

On either side of the window in the centre of the chevet on the ground floor. Estim. 760 L., Mém., Arch. Nat., O^I 1784. One has a crown of flowers, a cantor's baton, two lamps, a cassolette, a double cross, a palm and a censer; the other, a cross with cherubim heads, a vase, a reliquary, two candle holders, a lamp and a bowl.

VERSAILLES PALACE, CHAPEL

10
Portrait of a Gentleman

Oval medallion   Marble   48 × 34 excl. frame

Zelikine sale, 7–9 May 1908, *Cat*. no. 28. Man with a long perruque, period Louis XIV. Signed on reverse: DE FER. Frame in carved and gilded wood. Prov: Bagatelle sale. Sold for 360 L. Whereabouts unknown.

9

Detail

DESJARDINS, Martin (French vers. of van den Bogaert) (1637-1694)

Son of Jacob van den Bogaert of Breda and Jeanne des Cours; bapt. 11 Nov. 1637 at Breda, cf. G.-J. Rehm, 'De Beeldhouwer M. Desjardins', in *De Oranjeboom* (*Jaarboek van de Geschied en Oudheidkundigekring van Stad an Land van Breda*, vol. 13, 1960). In 1651-2, apprenticed at Antwerp to the sculptor Peter Verbruggen the elder; enrolled in the Antwerp Guild of St. Luke, cf. P. Rombouts and T. van Lerius, *De Liggeren en andere Historische Archieven der Antwerpsche sint Lucasgilde*, II, p. 226, 230. Acc. to Guillet de Saint-Georges, went to France via England, arriving penniless in Paris; well received by the French sculptors, esp. J. Houzeau, Van Obstal, J. Buirette. A rich merchant of gold, silver and silk cloth, Jean Cadaine, took him as lodger into his house at the rue du Cimetière, Par. St.-Nicolas-des-Champs; on 24 Sept. 1661. D. married his daughter Marie, sister of the sculptor Guillaume Cadaine, Min. Centr. Arch. Nat., Et. L, 78. Three children; one of them, Jacques, future Contrôleur des Bâtiments du Roi at Marly, married Marie-Julie Hardouin, niece of Jules Hardouin-Mansart, 15 Aug. 1694 (Bibl. Nat. Ms., Fich. Laborde 120090). The son of D.'s brother Jean, Jacques Desjardins, became Fondeur et Sculpteur des Bâtiments du Roi. D. himself received into the Acad., 28 Mar. 1671; Asst. Prof. 1 Oct. 1672; Prof. 27 July 1675, *P-V*, I, 359, 399; II, 55. In 1679, he lived at rue Neuve-des Deux-Portes, Par. St.-Sauveur; his studio was in the Hôtel de St.-Chaumont, bail (lease) signed 18 Feb. 1679, marché 27 Mar. 1679, Min. Centr. Arch. Nat., Et. LXIX, 94. Asst. Rect. Jan. 1682, *Mercure*, Jan. 1682, p. 207; *P-V*, II, 212; Recteur 27 July 1686, *P-V*, II, 332. In April 1686, he was asked

to give his opinion about the equestrian statue of Louis XIV which the town of Marseilles had comm. from Puget; D. himself had been proposed for this project, cf. L. Lagrange, 'Puget', in *GBA*, 1866[I], p. 266. On 29 April 1693 he lived in rue St.-Marc outside the Porte Montmartre, Par. St.-Eustache, Min. Centr. Arch. Nat., Et. XXX, 129. Died a very rich man, 2 May 1694, in his apartment in the Vieux Louvre; buried on 4 May in St.-Germain-l'Auxerrois, cf. Fidière, *Etat Civ. des peintres, sculpteurs de l'Acad. roy.*, 1883, p. 54; *P-V*, III, p. 145; Invent. a.d. 7 Aug. 1694, Min. Centr. Arch. Nat., Et XXX, 133; partage of his possessions 7 May 1695, *ibid.* XXX, 136. Had two studios, one at the Vieux Louvre, the other near the Porte Richelieu. In recognition of his work, his descendants were ennobled by Louis XIV in 1704, Arch. Nat., O[I] 48, fol. 87. Hyacinthe Rigaud painted portraits of D. and his wife, exh. at the Acad., cf. Guérin, *Descr. Acad.*, p. 113 (now in the Louvre). Many engrs. after Rigaud by Edelinck, Odieuvre, Dupin, Boilly and others. A second portrait of D.⋆ by Rigaud is now in the Mus., Versailles, cf. Guillet de St.-Georges, I, p. 386–401; Fontenai, II, p. 484–5; Jal, p. 487; T-B, IV, 1910, p. 215 (E. de Tayes); L. Seelig, 'L'invent. a.d. de M. Desjardins', in *BSHAF*, 1972, p. 161–82.

I
Work at the Château de Vincennes

1658–70
Acc. to Guillet de St.-Georges, I, p. 387, D. was employed by Houzeau at the Chât. de Vincennes immediately after arrival in Paris; he probably carved ornaments for the interior of the Pavillon de la Reine-mère, which have disappeared, except for the panelling of the walls and ceiling in the Chambre du Grand-Conseil, now in the Louvre; cf. Houzeau. Then, again acc. to Guillet, *ibid.*, the sculptor Van Obstal employed him for work on the figures of slaves in bas-relief on the arch of the new portal built by Le Vau at the south side of the courtyard. In the engravings (Marot⋆ and others), they sit on either side of Mazarin's coat of arms, later replaced by a Sun carved by Houzeau. Van Obstal paid D. during the years 1667–70. The slaves no longer exist. Mostly destroyed.

1

2i

2j

2
Decoration on the Staircase of the Hôtel Salé

c. 1658   Bas-relief   Stucco
Acc. to Guillet de St.-Georges, I, pp. 308, 387, D. and the Marsy brothers worked under the direction of Buirette (see biogr.) on the stucco decorations of the Hôtel d'Aubert de Fontenay (Hôtel Salé).

a.* Eagles, volutes, acanthus leaves
Bas-reliefs in méplat in the arcades under the staircase.

b.* Eight busts in medallions flanked by young Telamones.
The Telamones, standing on pilasters, support the cornice of the ceiling of the great staircase. Beribboned garlands crown the medallions.

c. Ornaments at the cornice.
Rich ornamentation of the moulding, framing the cornice of the great staircase, acanthus leaves, beads, oak leaves.

d.* Four female heads in scallop shells; underneath, eagles on Jupiter's thunderbolts.
These decorate the four corners of the cornice.

e.* A frieze of children at the cornice of the great staircase.

Eight groups of two children sitting in various attitudes on volutes, holding a garland; they frame the initials A & C, of Aubert and his wife Anne-Marie Chastelain.

f. Male head and garlands
Above the arcade of the great staircase opening on to the adjacent vestibule.

g. Ornaments at the mouldings and arcades of the vestibule
Oak leaves underneath the cornice, leaves and masks on the volutes of the cornice, acanthus leaves in the scotia and above the doors.

h.* Six groups of children crowning six busts
Above the doors and windows of the vestibule under the cornice. The busts repr. Mars, Minerva, Diana, Apollo, Ceres, Bacchus.

i.* Jupiter and his eagle
Jupiter, in half-relief, seated, with sceptre and thunderbolt; in the cornice of the vestibule.

j.* Juno and the peacock
Opposite Jupiter.

PARIS, HOTEL SALE, 5, rue de Thorigny

2a

2d

2b

2h

3*
Decoration on the staircase of the Hôtel de Beauvais

c. 1660   Bas-relief and half-relief   Stucco
The whole decoration on this staircase was by D., cf. Guillet de St.-Georges, I, p. 387 and old *Descr.* of Paris. Only the first flights remain.

a.* Four pairs of children
In the cornice on the ground floor. The children are sitting on either side of vases and medallions with the intertwined initials of Pierre de Beauvais and Catherine-Henriette Bellier.

b.* Great eagle on thunderbolts
Above one of the arcades of the staircase.

c.* Two nude children carrying an escutcheon.
In the moulded frame under the vault opp. the entrance to the staircase.

d.* Two lying sphinxes framing the interlaced letters C and B.
On the third flight.

e.* Trophies of arms.
On the arcades of the small vestibule in the back on the ground floor and on the first landing.

f. Ram's heads with garlands, framing crowned initials and oak leaves.
On the first floor

g.* Female head with garlands
Above the arcade on the first floor.

PARIS, HOTEL DE BEAUVAIS, rue François-Miron

3d

4
Figures for Private Apartments

c. 1660   Wood
cf. Guillet de St.-Georges, I, p. 388. Not ident. or disapp.

5
Saint Benedict

c. 1660   Statue   Stucco
For the Church of the Bénédictines du St.-Sacrement in the rue Cassette, built in 1659. cf. Guillet de St.-Georges, I, p. 388. Not ident. or disapp.

3c

3e

3a

3b

3g

7

6
Christ appearing to Mary Magdalen

c. 1660   Group   Terracotta
Acc. to Guillet de St.-Georges, I, p. 388, the two-figure group was in the Carmelite Church in the rue de Vaugirard. Not mentioned in any of the old *Descr.* of Paris. Not ident. or disapp.

7
Work on the Church of Sainte-Catherine-de-la-Couture

c. 1662
cf. Guillet de St.-Georges, I, p. 388–9; Le Maire, *Paris, ancien et nouveau*, 1698, I, p. 424. The church was demolished in 1777.
   a. *Six children carrying the attr. of St. Catherine*
Six statues   Stone
At the top of the façade of the church on either side of the statue of St. Catherine by Houzeau. Each carried an attrib. of the Saint: a book, a crown, a sword, a wheel, a palm, a ring, a bundle of fasces. Engr.* by Patte in Blondel, *Arch. Fr.*, II, Book IV, no. XVI. Destroyed.
   b. *Scenes from the Old Testament*
Four bas-reliefs   Stone
Each above one of the statues of Virtues in the niches of the façade. Above Prudence (by Houzeau), Joseph explaining his dreams to Pharaoh. Above Temperance (by Houzeau), David athirst in the midst of his army, pouring water on the ground; above Justice (by L. Magnier), the judgement of Solomon; above Might (by L. Magnier), Sampson taming the lion. Destroyed.
   c. *Four children carrying the attribs. of St. Genevieve*
Wood (?)
Acc. to Guillet de St.-Georges, "above the wooden screen which served as an enclosure in the chapel of St. Genevieve. Four children in full-relief holding one of the symbols attr. to the Saint, incl. a prayer-book and a candle." This chapel, to the left of the nave, was

handed over on 8 Oct. 1661 to the confraternity of the Jurés mouleurs de bois (officials charged with measuring and supervising the sale of timber), Arch. Nat., LL 1460, cf. Raunié, *Epitaphier*, 1893, II, p. 271, note 2. Destroyed.

8
Tabernacle

1666   Wood
Acc. to the contract 14 Aug. 1666, Min. Centr. Arch. Nat., Et. CVII, 206 (inform. Mr. Seelig), D. copied for a fee of 750 L. the tabernacle of the high altar of Ste.-Catherine-de-la-Couture with its ornaments, figures in gilded wood, initials and coats of arms of SS. Peter and Paul. Destroyed.

9
Tomb of the Champrond Family

c. 1668   Bas-relief   Marble
Acc. to Guillet de St.-Georges, I, p. 390, D. carved for a tomb in the choir of the Church of Ste.-Catherine-de-la-Couture a bas-relief "Grief and one of its genies holding an inscription". cf. Raunié, II, p. 294. This incription mentions that in the tomb are buried: Jean de Champrond, Councillor to the King (d. 3 Aug. 1658); his son Jean de Champrond, also Councillor to the King (d. 11 July 1668), and their wives. J. de Champrond the elder asked in his will, 30 July 1658, that an epitaph should be placed on his tomb (Min. Centr. Arch. Nat., Et. XXVI, 95); his son comm. the sculpture. In 1783, the coffins and the cenotaph were trsf. to the Chapel of St.-Louis in the Church of St.-Paul-St.-Louis; cf. Abbé Mercier, 'Notice sur les tomb. trsf. en 1683.' in *Journ. des Sav.*, 1789. Disapp. during the Revolution, cf. D. de Hansy, *Not. hist. sur la par. St.-Paul-St.-Louis*, Paris, 1842; Guilhermy, *Inscr. de la Fr.*, 1873, I, p. 229. Destroyed.

11

10
Sculptures on the Pediments of the Château de L'Isle-Adam

1669–71   Stone
Acc. to Guillet de St.-Georges, I, p. 388, comm. by the Princesse de Conti, Mazarin's niece, probably during the reconstruction of the Chât. between 1669–71; cf. E. Davras, *Les seign. châtel. de L'Isle-Adam*, 1939, p. 74–5. Destroyed in 1789 during the Revolution.

11
Large Model of a Group of Captives

1670   Plaster
Model for one of four groups of captives on the entablature of the Triumphal Arch of the Porte St.-Antoine, erected after designs by Perrault. Payment 450 L. on 22 Feb. 1671, *Comptes*, I, 504. The coat of arms of France above the four groups was by Lespagnandelle. Engr.* by Babel in Blondel, *Arch. Fr.*, II, Bk. IV, No. XI, pl. I, after a print by S. Leclerc. Destroyed in 1716.

12
Work on the North Façade of the Central Building at Versailles Palace

1670–71
  a.* Thetis
Statue   Stone   H: over 200
  b.* Galathea
Statue   Stone   H: over 200
  c.* Narcissus
Statue   Stone   H: over 200
  d. *Groups of children*
Bas-reliefs   Stone
Acc. to Guillet de St.-Georges, I, p. 385, D. carved statues of Acis (in fact, Thetis), Galathea and two

Detail   12c

Naiads for the second storey. Acc. to Piganiol, *Vers.-Marly*, 1724, II, p. 4, he did Echo, Narcissus, Thetis and Galathea. Stylistically, only Thetis, Galathea and Narcissus can be attrib. to him. Thetis and Galathea are half-nude, Galathea with an oar and a rudder; Thetis with two dolphins between her feet; Narcissus with a dolphin, turns towards the nymph Echo. At the end of the 19th c. Narcissus was replaced by a copy; original now in Versailles, Museum. Thetis partly restored in 1898 by Jonchery, Arch. Nat., F²¹ 3495ᴮ. Each stat. estim. at c. 350 L. Payment 1560 L. in 1670–71, *Comptes*, I, 421, 514. cf. F. Souchal, in *GBA*, 1972ᴵ, p. 78.

VERSAILLES, PALACE

13–14
WORK AT THE COLLEGE DES QUATRE NATIONS (NOW PALAIS DE L'INSTITUT)

Cf. Lemonnier, 'Notes sur la constr. du collège Mazarin', in *Journ. des Savants*, Jan.–Feb. 1915; *Le Collège Mazarin et le Pal. de l'Institut*, Paris, 1921; A. Gutton, 'La chap. du collège des Quatre Nations, la Coupole de l'Institut', in *Mon. Hist. de la Fr.*, no. 1, Jan.–Mar. 1963.

13*
Might and Justice

1670   Two figures in half-relief   Stone   Over life-size.
On the pediment of the first courtyard of the Collège Mazarin, above the south portal. The figures sit at

12a   12b

13

13

either side of a clock; 'Might' on the right, armed with a club; 'Justice', her hand on a sword, indicating the time with her finger. Payment: 1000 L.; rec. 12 May 1670, Arch. Nat., H³ 2822, fol. 75–6.

PARIS, PALAIS DE L'INSTITUT

14
Work at the Chapel of the Palais de l'Institut

1671–3
Compl. in Jan. 1673, Bibl. de l'Institut, reg. des délib., Ms. 368, fol. I; D.'s total estim., 9920 L., brought down to 7100 L. in Girardon's report, was finally reduced to 6900 L.; paid in several instalm. between 12 Nov. 1671 and 24 Mar. 1673. Arch. Nat., *Livre de la despence tenu par Mariage*, H³ 2824, fol. 27 and H³ 2822, fol. 76.

a. *The Beatitudes*
Eight figures in half-relief   Stone
Descr. by Guillet de St.-Georges, I, p. 393: female figures, seated in the spandrels of the four great arcades of the chapel, removed in 1806 by the architect Vaudoyer. The first, repr. the Meek, carried a lamb; the second, the Poor in Spirit, held a hand towards the sky; the third, those Persecuted for Righteousness' sake,

cried over two children with their throats cut; the fourth, the Peacemakers, held up an olive branch, crushing weapons underfoot; the fifth, the Merciful, distributed money; the sixth, those Athirst after Righteousness, held a sword and a pair of scales which a man was trying to seize; the seventh, Mourning, lifted a grief-stricken face towards a ray of light from the sky; the eighth, the Pure in Heart, held up a heart. Engr. by Chevotet in Blondel, *Arch. Fr.*, II, Liv. III, pl. 5, showing a cross-section★ of the church. Destroyed.

14b

b.★ Twelve apostles
Bas-relief   medallions   Stone
On the interior of the drum of the dome between the pilasters. During the restorations of 1960–2, the sculptor Belmondo completely renewed the heads of St. Peter and St. Andrew.

CHAPEL OF THE INSTITUTE

c. *Head of cherubim*
Stone
Acc. to Guillet de St.-Georges, "above the arcades supporting the dome". Destroyed at the same time as the Beatitudes.

15
Tomb of Antoine d'Aubray, Comte d'Offemont

1671   Marble (?)
cf. Guillet de St.-Georges, I, p. 388; in a chapel of the Eglise de l'Oratoire. Descr. by Millin, *Antiq. Nat.*, II,

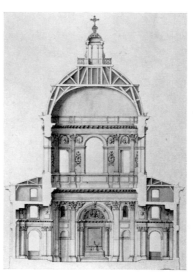

14a

15²

Chap. XIV, p. 11, with engr.* by Ransonnette, pl. IV. Justice, reclining on the tomb, in her right hand fasces and a pair of scales, leans on a shield holding a medallion portrait of the deceased. Trsf. in 1791 by Lenoir to the Mus. des Petits-Augustins, then disapp. There is a plaster cast in the Versailles Mus.*

16*
Hercules Crowned by Glory

1671   Bas-relief   Marble   77 × 74
Recept. piece for the Acad., *P-V*, I, p. 359; Guérin, *Descr.*, p. 85; Guillet de St.-Georges, I, p. 391. Hercules, the skin of the Nemean lion over his shoulder, armed with his club, treads underfoot a dragon; he personifies the heroic virtues of the King and is being crowned by a female figure, seen from the back, who holds a statuette of glory in her left hand; next to her a celestial globe.

PARIS, LOUVRE

15¹

Detail

15³

16

17
Angel for the Funeral Service of Chancellor Séguier

1672   Cardboard
D. made, after le Brun's design, one of the four angels, or genies, receiving the soul of the deceased, for the funeral service of the Chancellor at the Eglise de l'Oratoire on 4 May 1672. The other three angels were by Le Hongre, Houzeau and Massou, see *P-V*, I, 397 and a letter by the Marquise de Sévigné, dd. 6 May 1672. Engr.★ by S. Leclerc. Destroyed.

18
Juno

1672   Statue   St.-Leu stone   H: c. 250
Attrib. to D. in the *Comptes*, I, 618, also by Guillet de St.-Georges, I, p. 395 and Piganiol, *Vers.-Marly*, 1724, I, p. 11. The Goddess with her peacock, standing on the balcony of the Aile Nord des Offices at Versailles, repr. one of the four elements ('Air'), together with 'Iris' by Houzeau and 'Zephyr' by Roger. These statues appear in an engraving by I. Silvestre showing the forecourt of the Château de Versailles in 1674★. Payment 400 L. in 1672, *Comptes*, I, 618. Destroyed when the Offices were demolished in 1771.

17

18

21a   21b   21c

19
Apollo Pursuing Daphne

Before 1673   Bas-relief
Exh: Salon 1673, *Livret*, p. 32. Not ident. or disapp.

20
Justice

Before 1673   Bas-relief
Exh: Salon 1673, *Livret*, p. 32. Not ident. or disapp.
See appendix.

21d

21
Several Fountains in the Labyrinth

1673–4   Lead and tin
   a. *The fox and the crane*
   b. *The crane and the fox*
   c. *The fox and the grapes*
   d. *The mouse, the cat and the little cock*
The sketch-plan of the labyrinth in Tessin's papers in Stockholm, gives D.'s name for all four fountains. Payment 3650 L. in two instalm. in 1673, final payment 2 June 1674, *Comptes*, I, 618, 696, 762. Engr.★ by Leclerc, cf. A. Marie, *Naissance de Vers.*, 1968, I, p. 128–129, 134–5. Destroyed.

22
The Child Mars riding a lion

1673–4   Group   Lead
The group, symbol. 'Might' (Guillet de St.-Georges, I, p. 395), or 'the Spirit of Valour', showed "the child Mars, sword in one hand, shield in the other, sitting on a lion, which crushes a wolf", Piganiol, *Vers.-Marly*, 1764, II, p. 186. The Group stood at the bottom of the Avenue on the right, on one of the fountains of the Théâtre d'eau, with rich sculptural decoration after designs by Le Brun: on the upper fountain 'Cupid on a Dolphin' by G. Marsy; in the theatre itself: 'Two Cupids with a lobster' by Houzeau, 'Two Cupids playing with a Gryphon' by B. Massou, 'Two Cupids playing with a Swan' by Tuby, 'Two Cupids playing the Lyre' by P. Legros I; at the bottom of the Allées de la Cascade: 'The Child Jupiter on an Eagle' by P. Legros I, 'The Child Pluto on Cerberus' by Massou and D.'s group of 'The Child Mars on a Lion'. Sanguine in Stockholm, CC 2733; engr.★ by Lepautre. Disappeared.

22   *28*   *26*

23
Saint Luke and Saint John for the Chapel of the Palais de l'Institut

1673–7   Two groups   Stone   H: c. 350
Models accepted in Jan. 1673, Reg. des délib., Bibl. de l'Inst., Ms. 368, fol. 1. Exec. of large clay models and stone groups betw. Dec. 1676 and end of Mar. 1677, *ibid.*, fol. 191 v°, fol. 204. Two of 12 stone groups on the exterior entablature of the chapel, the Evangelists in the centre, the Fathers of the Church on each side. Le Hongre carved the two other Evangelists; Houzeau, Massou, Jouvenet and Granier, the Fathers of the Church. Payment 1800 L. for the two. Engr.* of the façade of the chapel, with the groups, by Chevotet in Blondel, *Arch. Fr.*, II, Liv. 3, pl. 4. Destroyed.

23

24
Four Masks at Versailles

1674   Stone
At a forepart of the central building, facing the North Parterre on the keystones of the windows. Payment 120 L. on 23 Dec. 1674, *Comptes*, I, 762. Restored or replaced.

25
Work on the Ambassadors' Staircase, Versailles

1674
D. and a team rec. 300 L. in 1674 "on account of the great staircase", *Comptes*, I, 737. Destroyed.

26*
The Conquest of Besançon

1674   Bas-relief   Stone
One of the four bas-reliefs on the Triumphal Arch of the Porte St.-Martin, on the north side to the right. The capture of Besançon is symbol. by the King, seated in the midst of trophies, receiving the keys of the town from a kneeling female figure; above, Fame announces the conquest. The other three bas-reliefs are by Le Hongre, P. Legros I and G. Marsy. Payment 700 L. on 14 Aug. 1676 to D., Arch. Nat., KK 494.

PARIS, PORTE ST.-MARTIN

27
Work in the Octagonal Room in the Appartement des Bains, Versailles

1674–5
   a. *Figure personifying a Month*
Lead and gilded tin   Life-size
Acc. to Guillet de St.-Georges, I, p. 395, D. carved for the Appartement des Bains "two figures of young men holding cornucopias". But the *Comptes* give only one figure to D., one each to P. Legros I, G. Marsy, Regnaudin, Hérard and Houzeau and two each to Girardon, Le Hongre and Tuby. Each fig. estim. at between 1250–1400 L. D. rec. a sum on account in 1674, *Comptes*, I, 762, and his final payment, together with Girardon, in 1676, *Comptes*, I, 831. Destroyed.
   b. *Ornaments*
Payment 700 L. in 1676, *Comptes*, I, 902. Destroyed.

28
Works at the Château du Val

1675–7
In collab. with Le Hongre and Légeret. The sculptures consisted of stone masks and urns outside, wood carvings inside. cf. L. de la Tourrasse, *Le chât. du Val*, 1924. Payment 4688 L. 14 s., *Comptes*, I, 822, 894, 956. Only the masks* remain.

CHATEAU DU VAL (Seine-et-Oise), near St.-Germain-en-Laye

29
Works at the Château de Clagny

1675–82
   a. *Undefined work*
Payment 200 L. in 1675 to D. alone, *Comptes*, I, 845; 8400 L. in several instalm. from 1675–78 to D. and Le Hongre as associates, *Comptes*, I, 846, 917, 982, 1076.
   b. *Work on various models*
1676–80
Payment 72 L. in 1677 to D. "for ornaments on the model", *Comptes*, I, 982; 90 L. in 1682 to D. and Le Hongre "for work in plaster done in 1676 on the large model", *Comptes*, II, 175; 550 L. to D. and other sculptors in 1682 "for work on the wax model for the gallery of the chât.", *Comptes*, II, 174.
   c. *Victory among Trophies*
1678–82   Stone   H: 350
Carvings in the great pediment facing the courtyard, acc. to Guillet de St.-Georges, I, p. 396. Payment 2046 L. in three instalm., *Comptes*, I, 1075, 1190; II, 160.
   d. *Sculpture in the Salon*
1679
Payment 200 L., *Comptes*, I, 1190.
   e. *Work in stucco on the Cornice and the Attics of the Wing*
1679
In collab. with Pâris. Payment 960 L., *Comptes*, I, 1191.

30

   f. *Work on the Pavilion of the Chapel*
1679–80
Payments of 120 L., 100 L., 940 L., *Comptes*, I, 190, 1326.
   g. *Valour and a Lion*
Group   Stone
Above the main entrance to the vestibule, acc. to Guillet de St.-George, I, p. 396. The chât. was demolished in 1779. Destroyed (29a–g).

30*
Diana or Evening

1675–84   Group   Marble   H: over 200
Placed on the fountain of Diana in 1684. The Goddess, wearing a diadem, a quiver on her left shoulder, strides

forward, brandishing a bow; at her side, a greyhound leaping out of a bush. Payment on acc. 3400 L., *Comptes*, I, 831, 902, 964, 1048, 1158; II, 442. Final payment 10,500 L. in 1695 to his heirs, incl. a sum for the 'Artemisia' du Tapis-vert (no. 48), *Comptes*, III, 1086. Engr. by Edelinck and Thomassin, p. 89. *See appendix.*

VERSAILLES PALACE, PARK

31
Work on the Small Model of the Dôme des Invalides

1676–7 Wax
D. worked on this model from Nov. 1676 with Le Hongre, Mazeline, Jouvenet. Mém. de la dépense, Arch. de la Guerre, carton 17, liasse B, pièce no. 4. Receipt for 2221 L., 25 July 1677, paid to the four sculptors. Destroyed.

32
Work on Plaster Model of the Dôme des Invalides

1677–8
The same four sculptors suppl. various models of ornaments for the surround of the lantern, capitals, modillions. Mém. (see no. 31 above), pièce no. 6. Receipt for 1500 L. paid to the sculptors 10 July 1679, incl. other work. cf. no. 33. Destroyed.

33
Work at the Lantern of the Dôme des Invalides

1677–8
   a. *Four fleurs-de-lis*
Lead and tin   H: 120
   b. *Six consoles*
Oak under lead
In collab. with Le Hongre, Jouvenet, Mazeline; Mém.: see no. 31. Put in place provisionally. Destroyed.

37

34
Undefined Work for Versailles

1677
Acc. to the *Comptes*, I, 964, 9 Dec. 1677, D. and others rec. 567 L. "for having re-carved plaster sculptures in stone". Not identified.

35
Work on the Tomb of the Marquis de Vaubrun

1678
   a. Two Corinthian Capitals
Lead and tin
   b. Two Bases
Copper
Contract 14 Apr. 1678 for 1500 L., Min. Centr. Arch. Nat., Et. LXXXIII, 165 (inform. Mr. Seelig), cf. Sainte-Beuve, 'Le Tomb. du M. de Vaubrun', in *GBA*, 1928[I], p. 153. See Coysevox no. 9★.

CHATEAU DE SERRANT (Maine-et-Loire), CHAPEL

36
Work on Chimney Stacks at Versailles

1678
In collab. with Jouvenet. Payment 1640 L. in 1678–81, *Comptes*, I, 1050, 1283. Not identified.

37
Pulpit in the Church of Saint-Louis-en-l'Ile

Before 1679   Wood
Acc. to Guillet de St.-Georges, I, p. 388, D. "worked in wood for this pulpit and carved the figures of the four Evangelists". The pulpit, repl. by a new one under the Concordat, has disappeared. Engr.★: *Chéreau*, Bibl. Nat. Est., Va 255 n. Destroyed. *See appendix.*

38★
Work on Two Pavilions of the Forecourt, Hôtel des Invalides

1679   Stone
Trophies of arms and bas-reliefs in collab. with Le Hongre, Jouvenet, Mazeline. Payment 1600 L. incl. two stoups (see no. 39). Cert. d'expert., 9 Jan. 1680, Arch. de la Guerre, Fonds Inval., cart. 17, liasse B, pièce 8.

PARIS, HOTEL DES INVALIDES

39★
Two Stoups

1679   Hard limestone   H: 142
Against the entrance wall of the Church of St.-Louis. Two large scallop-shells, each supported by a volute. Payment and collab., see no. 38.

PARIS, CHURCH OF ST.-LOUIS DES INVALIDES

38   *38*

40

***Work in the Grand Salon, the Cabinet and the
Queen's Chamber, Versailles***

1679–80   Stucco
In collab. with Le Hongre. Payment 7901 L. 13s. 4d.,
Comptes, I, 1158, 1287. This considerable sum was for a
wall decoration which, acc. to Guillet de St.-Georges, I,
p. 375, consisted of a stucco cornice supported by
caryatides, and flower garlands over the windows.
Destroyed.

41
Louis XIV

1679–83
    a.* Statue   Marble   H: c. 350
Comm. by the Maréchal de la Feuillade for his country
seat, then for Paris. The King, standing, fist clenched on
hip, wears a breastplate 'à l'antique', a cloak over his
shoulders, a commander's baton in his right hand, a
sword at his side; at his feet, a plumed helmet. The

contracts, 13 Jan. 1679 and 10 Apr. 1681 before the
notary De Beauvais, are lost. The marble, worth
10,000 L., was supplied by the King in 1679, *Comptes*, II,
374. A large plaster model was placed in the garden of
the Hôtel St.-Chaumont in 1681, cf. report on the King's
visit in *Mercure Galant*, Dec. 1681, p. 256–9. The statue
was designed to stand on a high pedestal surrounded by
four slaves; on the base four bronze bas-reliefs.
Presented to the King in 1683, moved to the Orangery
at Versailles, *Comptes*, II, 315. Decapitated during the
Revolution. Original drawing* in Berlin, Kunstbibliothek Hdz. 2625a, Blatt 58; engr. by Thomassin,
pl. 86. In 1816 the sculptor Lorta carved a new head.

VERSAILLES PALACE, ORANGERIE

    b.* Statuette   Painted wax   H: 36
Model for the marble statue, cf. Brinckmann, *Barock-
bozzetti*, III, 1925, p. 96.

BAYONNE, BONNAT MUSEUM

39

41a

c.★ Statuette   Gilded terracotta   H: 83
Small-scale model for the marble statue, cf. J. Cordey, 'Note sur la stat. de M. Desjardins repr. Louis XIV', in *BSHAF*, 1935, p. 274.

CHATEAU DE VAUX-LE-VICOMTE, Seine-et-Marne

42
Work on the Grande Ecurie, Versailles

1680
   a.★   Children among trophies
Two bas-reliefs   Stone
On the pediments of the two wings of the Great Stables, cf. Guillet de St.-Georges, I, p. 395. Payment 220 L. in 1680 to 'the sculptor Martin', *Comptes*, I, 1289. Piganiol, *Vers.-Marly*, 1701, p. 5, also attribs. them to 'Martin'.
   b. Masks   Stone
Acc. to Guillet de St.-Georges, I, p. 395, on the pediment of the stables; but more probably some of those on the keystones of the arched windows.

VERSAILLES PALACE, GRANDE ECURIE

43
Four Trophies

1681   Stone
Crowning the north façade of the central building at Versailles. Payment 600 L., 23 July 1681, *Comptes*, I, 1284. Replaced.

44
Virgin and Child

1681–6   Group   Marble   H: 215
On the altar of the Virgin in the Church of the Sorbonne. The altar, designed by Le Brun, compl. in 1685, remained without the statue which, acc. to Brice, 1694,

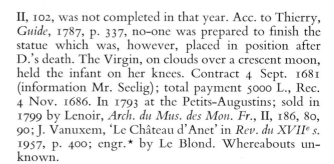

41a

II, 102, was not completed in that year. Acc. to Thierry, *Guide*, 1787, p. 337, no-one was prepared to finish the statue which was, however, placed in position after D.'s death. The Virgin, on clouds over a crescent moon, held the infant on her knees. Contract 4 Sept. 1681 (information Mr. Seelig); total payment 5000 L., Rec. 4 Nov. 1686. In 1793 at the Petits-Augustins; sold in 1799 by Lenoir, *Arch. du Mus. des Mon. Fr.*, II, 186, 80, 90; J. Vanuxem, 'Le Château d'Anet' in *Rev. du XVIIᵉ s.* 1957, p. 400; engr.★ by Le Blond. Whereabouts unknown.

41c

41b

42a

44

45
Work for the Place des Victoires, Paris

1682–5

cf. A. de Boislisle, 'Not. sur la pl. des Victoires et sur la pl. Vendôme', in *Mém. de la Soc. de Paris—Ile de France*, 1888, p. 37–87; R. Josephson, 'M. Desjardins et ses mon. de Louis XIV, in *RAAM.*, 1928, p. 171–91. Modification of the initial project for a monument to the glory of Louis XIV, offered by the Duc de La Feuillade. A square was to be created for this purpose. The contract signed before the notary de Beauvais, 22 Apr. 1682, is lost. On 26 May 1683 further details were added in the form of a simple contract, Min. Centr. Arch. Nat., Et. CXIII, 134. D. designed a pedestal to be made by J. Derbais, contract 9 Feb. 1684, Et. LXXXIII, 184. On 9 Mar. 1685 more modifications were added, in the "Devis et Marché des augmentations des trophées de bronze", total 13,700 L., *ibid.* At the time of D.'s death, 8800 L. remained unpaid, of which only 5000 L. were paid on 1 June 1700, cf. Invent. a.d. 7 Aug. 1694, Et. XXX, 133; partage 7 May 1695, Et. XXX, 136; quittance 1 June 1700, Et. CXIII, 183. The Place des Victoires was inaugurated on 28 Mar. 1686.

45

Turkey   *45b*

Empire   *45b*

Greatly modified later. All of D.'s work dispersed or destroyed. Many old *Descriptions*: Descr. of 1690, cote no. 12755, Bibl. Ville de Paris; Brice; Piganiol; Guillet de St.-Georges, I, p. 396; Beguillet, *Descr. Hist.*, 1779, p. 86; many engr., the most faithful is probably the one by Guérard★.

Spain   *45b*

Holland   *45b*

45c

45d

a. *Louis XIV crowned by Victory*
1682–5   Group   Gilded bronze   H: c. 500
Replacement of the marble statue offered to the King
by the Duc de La Feuillade, see above. Cast in one
piece by D. himself; destroyed 10 Aug. 1792. The group
stood on a pedestal in the centre of the Square; the King,
standing, in coronation robes, sceptre in hands, treads
underfoot Cerberus, a symbol of the Triple Alliance;
behind him Victory, one foot on a globe, a palm in her
hand, crowned him with laurel; at their feet, a shield,
weapons, a club and a lion's skin. Destroyed.

b.★ Four chained slaves
Statues   Bronze   H: c. 350
Cf. J. Hauser, 'Les statues des Captifs aux Invalides', in
Bull. de la Soc. d'Hist. et d'archéol. des VIIè et XVè arr.,
Dec. 1923, no. 26, p. 144–7. Model for the first project
made after 1681, cf. *Mercure Galant*, Dec. 1681, p. 256–
269. Several bronze trophies were added to the statue in
1685, cf. Devis des Augm., 9 Mar. 1685, see above. The
slaves, joined by a gilded chain, were sitting on the four
corners of the pedestal. They symbol. the defeated

nations: a worn out old man repr. the confederation of
the German Empire; an aged man dressed like the
Dacians, repr. Turkey; a man in his prime with an
indignant expression, Holland; a young man in an
imploring attitude, Spain. Removed to the courtyard of
the Louvre, by decree 20 June 1790, Bibl. Ville de Paris,
cote 1873; in 1806, trsf. to the Hôtel des Invalides;
remained there until 1965.

CHATEAU DE SCEAUX, PARK

c.★   The Peace of Nimwegen
d.★   The Crossing of the Rhine
e.★   The Capture of Besançon
f.★   The Predominance of France over Spain
Four rectangular bas-reliefs   Bronze   110 × 158
Models made in 1681, cf. *Mercure Galant*, Dec. 1681,
p. 256–9. Enlarged in 1685, estim. Mar. 1685, cf. supra.
On the four sides of the pedestal between the slaves.
Removed during the Revolution to the Petits Augustins,
Arch. Mus. des Mon. Fr., I, 13; II, 186; III, 180, 183.

PARIS, LOUVRE

45e

45f

45g

45h

45m¹

45m⁴

45m⁵

g.* The Destruction of Heresy
h.* The Abolition of Duelling
Circular bas-reliefs   Bronze   Diam: 82
Added to the lower part of the pedestal base, estim.
9 Mar. 1685, see above. History as for the rectangular
bas-reliefs c–f. The festoons have disappeared.

PARIS, LOUVRE

i. *Four bronze escutcheons with the coat of arms of France
with palms and laurels*
On the upper cornice of the socle. Destroyed.
j. *Eight bronze consoles.* Destroyed.
k. *Four bronze friezes with the King's Device, with
laurel branches.*
On the pedestal; cf. estim. 9 Mar. 1685. Destroyed.
l. *Eight bronze cartouches with inscriptions refer. to the
life of Louis XIV.*
On the foreparts of the lower base, Arch. Nat., H 1831,
fol. 571–8 v°. Destroyed.

m. Medallions on the lanterns
cf. A. Vuaflart, 'Les médaillons de la pl. des Vict.' in
Les Mus. de Fr., 1914, p. 49–50; A. Michel, 'Les
accroissements du départ. des sculpt. au mus. du Louvre'
in *GBA*, 1917, XIII, p. 64–5. Contract 12 Aug. 1686 with
Jean Arnould, sculptor, and Pierre Le Nègre, founder,
for 24 bronze medallions after Mignard's designs for the
four lanterns of the square. Min. Centr. Arch. Nat., Et.
LXXXIII, 186. Only 12 were done in bronze, the 12
others remained in plaster, cf. *Descr.*, 1690, *cit. supra*,
p. 8. Most likely exec. in D.'s own studio where
Cronström saw them in 1685, cf. Josephson, *loc. cit.*;
Cronström asked D. to correct the bas-relief: 'The
Swedes re-established in Germany.' The medallion
repr. the submission of the Doge of Genoa had originally
been comm. from D. for the lower base, contract,
9 Mar. 1685, cf. *supra*. These medallions were hanging
from garlands of oak leaves and laurel held by lion
heads. For the subjects repr. see Boislisle, *op. cit.*, p. 68.
The lanterns were taken down in 1717. During the
Revolution five of the medallions were at Kew Gardens,
London and at the beginning of the 20th c. in Windsor
Castle. Returned to France in 1914. They are (1)* 'The
Re-establishment of Military Discipline' (Diam. 80);
(2)* 'The Pyramid erected in Rome, then demolished
by leave of the King' (Diam. 78); (3) 'Valenciennes
taken by storm, saved from pillage' (Diam. 79);
(4)* 'The Swedes re-established in Germany' (Diam. 84);
(5)* 'The submission of the Doge of Genoa' (Diam. 84).
The others are lost. They may well have been the six
great bronze medallions (diam. c. 75) in the Lapérière
sale, Paris, 19 Apr. 1825, no. 25, sold for 2700 fr. which
repr: 'Pomerania handed over to the Swedes'; 'The
diplomatic mission from Siam'; 'Conquest of a town by
Condé'; 'Victory handing palm branches to the victors';
'The joining of the two seas'; 'Louis XIV ordering the
construction of a building'. It is not known what
happened to the six medallions from the Lapérière sale.

PARIS, LOUVRE (Five medallions only). *See appendix.*

46b

46
**Equestrian Statue of Louis XIV for
Aix-en-Provence**

1687–94 Bronze The horse c. 420 high, the
King c. 390 high
cf. Boislisle, *op. cit.*, and Josephson, *Desjardins et ses
monum. de Louis XIV*, in *RAAM*, 1928, p. 270–91.
a. *Large plaster model*
Contr. 14 July 1687, Arch. Départ. de S.-et-O., publ. by
P. Volk (research by Coural) 'Darstellg. Ludwigs XIV
auf steigend. Pferd', in *Wallraf Richartz Jahrbuch*, 1966,
for 90,000 L., for a bronze statue after a design by
Mansart. At the time of D.'s death, the large statue had
not been cast. D. had already rec. 27,000 L.; his heirs
claimed the rest, the son taking the casting upon himself; cf. Invent. a.d., 7 Aug. 1694, Min. Centr. Arch.
Nat., Et. XXX, 133 and partage 7 May 1695, Et. XXX,
136. The casting was never done, the full-size model was
trsf. to Versailles. It showed Louis XIV in Roman dress,
hair streaming back, on a rearing horse; most of its
weight was supported by the tail, cf. *Les voyages d'étude
de N. Tessin*, Stockholm, 1914, p. 106. Whereabouts
unknown.
b. Small models and reductions
Found in D.'s studio after his death; the full-size
plaster model of the statue for Aix, a half-size wax
model and a smaller plaster model. Invent. a.d., cf.
supra. In 1700, Cronström bought for the King of
Sweden a bronze reduction, cf. *Tessin–Cronström
Corresp.*, p. 282, 318, 334. Also related is a bronze
statuette in a private coll.* publ. by P. Volk, *loc. cit.*, fig.
40; stylistically close to D.'s work, it shows the above-
mentioned details.

47a

47
Equestrian Statue of Louis XIV for the Place Bellecour, Lyons

1688–91

    a. *Statue*   Bronze   c. 390 × 420
Louis XIV in Roman dress, riding a pacing horse.
cf. Artaud, *Arch. hist. et statist. du Rhône*, 1825, II, 348, 419; Boislisle, 'Not. sur la pl. des Victoires et la pl. Vendôme', in *Mém. Soc. hist., Paris, Ile-de-Fr.*, 1888, p. 229–32; L. Galle, 'Projet d'une statue equ. du roi à Lyon', in *RSBAD*, 1903, p. 447; R. Josephson, 'M. Desjardins et ses mon. de Louis XIV' in *RAAM*, 1928, p. 270–91.

Contract signed 20 May 1688, Arch. Munic. de Lyon, DD Invent. Chappe, XIII, p. 300; Renaud, 7, 26, fol. 224, 226 for 90,000 L. Design by Hardouin-Mansart; cast in 1691. At D.'s death the statue was in his studio, the sum of 22,000 L. still being due to him; c. 1400 L. were required "pour la rendre parfaite", cf. Invent. a.d. 7 Aug. 1694, Min. Centr. Arch. Nat., Et. XXX, 133. Trsf. to Lyons in 1700/1, erected in the Place Bellecour on 2 Dec. 1713 on a pedestal decor. with works by N. Coustou (nos. 64, 65) and G. Coustou (nos. 40, 41). Engr. by Audran*, Bernard, Frey etc. Destroyed in 1792. *See appendix.*

    The bronze foot of the King now in Lyons, Mus. historique, cf. Opdycke, 'An equ. statuette of Louis XIV', in *Fogg Art Mus. Annual Rep.*, 1956–7.

    b. Models and reductions
Found in D.'s studio after his death: the full-size plaster model, a half-size wax statue and a smaller plaster model. Cronström bought for the King of Sweden the plaster model (120 high) and a small bronze, 15–18 *pouces* (c. 45) high. The plaster was broken on arrival in Sweden in 1702, but the founder Aubry, then resident in Stockholm, retained the half-size wax model. cf. *Tessin–Cronström Corresp.*, p. 278, 282, 318, 334. Many statuettes have been suggested as models and reductions of the Lyons statue, cf. M. Krohn, *Frankrigs og Danmarks Kunstneriske forbindelse, det 18 Aarh*, Copenhagen, 1922; R. Josephson, *op. cit.*, p. 270–91; Maumené et d'Harcourt, in *AAF*, 1931, XVI, p. 244; J.-G. Mann, *Wallace Coll. Cat.*, 1931, p. 166; J. Rubow, 'Rytter-statuetten af Desjardins', in *Kunstmus. Aarskr.* 1933–4, p. 279–82; R. de Micheaux, 'Deux sculptures du temps

47b

47b

48

48*
Artemisia

1687–94
Statue   Marble   H: over 200
Begun by A. Lefèvre who rec. on acc. 1000 L. in 1687/8,
Comptes, II, 1179; III, 98. Completed by D., whose heirs
rec. the balance, in a combined payment with the fee
for 'Diana' in 1695, *Comptes*, III, 1086. Placed on the
south side of the Allée Royale. The Queen is about to
drink a brew containing the ashes of her husband.

VERSAILLES, PARK

49*
Queen Marie-Thérèse

c. 1690   Bust   Marble   H: 88
Acc. to Guillet de St.-Georges, p. 399, done in collab.
with Girardon for the Chât. de Villacerf, cf.
P. Francastel, *Girardon*, Paris, 1921, p. 89.

TROYES, MUSEUM

de Louis XIV au mus. lyonnais des arts décor.', in *Bull.
Mus. Lyon.*, II, 1953, p. 38–42; L. Opdycke, *loc. cit.*;
P. Volk, *loc. cit.*

The most authentic is the bronze in the Copenhagen
Mus., still with its moulding vents*. In 1754 in the
studio of the sculptor J.-L. Lemoyne, it was bought by
Reventlow for the Danish government, cf. Krohn,
cit. supra. Other probable reductions: the bronze
statuettes in the Metropolitan Mus., New York*; the
Wallace Coll., London; the Fogg Art Mus., Cambridge,
Mass.; the plaster statuette in the Mus. Carnavalet,
Paris.

50
Colbert de Villacerf (1629–99)

c. 1692
  a. *Bust*   Plaster
Offered to the Acad. by Edouard Colbert de Villacerf
on 4 Apr. 1693, *P-V*, III, 110. Disappeared.
  b.* Bust   Marble   H: 105
Inscription under the shoulder: EDOUARD COLBERT,
MARQUIS DE VILLACERF, SURINTENDANT DES BATIMENTS
DU ROI, AGE DE LXIII ANS, FAIT PAR DESJARDINS, SCULPTEUR
DU ROI, RECTEUR DE SON ACADEMIE.

49

50b

Offered by Edouard Colbert de Villacerf to the Acad. on 29 Dec. 1696, *P-V*, III, 201, 203, 211; cf. Guérin, *Descr.* p. 51. Marble copies in the Art Trade.

PARIS, LOUVRE

c. *Bust Bronze*
Mentioned in the Invent. a.d. of 7 Aug. 1694, Min. Centr. Arch. Nat., Et. XXX, 133. Whereabouts unknown.

51
Sculpture for the Louvois Tomb

1693–4
  a.* Vigilance
Statue   Bronze   H: Life-size
  b.* *Model* for the statue of Anne de Souvré, Marquise de Louvois.
The Marquise, a book in her hand, kneels on the sarcophagus beside her husband (carved by Girardon); 'Vigilance', one foot on a globe with the inscr. "Mart Desjardins fecit.", sits on the right, a lamp in one hand, pointing with the other to the open pages of a book. Beside her a crane, standing on one leg (broken off). Girardon's 'Wisdom' forms a pendant to 'Vigilance'. Estim. and contr. 17 June 1693 for 56,000 L. to be divided between D. and Girardon, Min. Centr. Arch. Nat., Et. LXXV, 393. The marble was supplied to the sculptors in 1693, *Comptes*, III, 816. At the time of his death, D. had only done the moulding for Vigilance and the model for the statue of the Marquise. His son, Jacques, made the bronze cast of the first, Van Clève carved the second in marble. cf. Guillet de St.-Georges, I, p. 399. The 56,000 L. were paid to Girardon and Jacques D. in six instalm. between 1693–1703, Min. Centr. *ibid.* Erected in the Church of the Capucines in 1699, cf. Brice, 1706, I, p. 204; Piganiol, 1765, III, p. 46. During the Revolution in Lenoir's Mus., no. 205; *Arch. du Mus. des Mon. Fr.*, II, 32; III, 180. In 1819 trsf. to the Chapel of the Hospice de Tonnerre. Engr.* by Aveline in Brice.

TONNERRE, HOSPICE (Yonne)

51a

51b²

Detail   *51b¹*

54b

52*
Pierre Mignard (1612–95)

Bust Marble H: 63
Offered to the Acad. by the painter's daughter, Comtesse de Feuquières in 1726, *P-V*, V, 17, 18. Used as model for the bust on the tomb, cf. Ph. Huisman, 'Les Bustes de Mignard', in *GBA*, 1958[I], p. 266. Marble copy in Cleveland Museum, USA.

PARIS, LOUVRE

53
Poisson's Tomb in Saint-Sauveur

Acc. to Guillet de St.-Georges, I, p. 390, erected in memory of a young officer killed in the service of the King; attached to a pillar at the entrance to the nave. The family of the famous comedian Raimond Poisson (1630–90) lived in the parish of St.-Sauveur. Acc. to Jal, p. 983, the funeral of "M. Poisson, officer of the King, who died in the rue St.-Denis" took place in this church on 10 May 1690. Destroyed.

54
Model for a Statue of Charlemagne

a. *Large plaster model*
Payment 1150 L. to D.'s widow and heirs in 1703, *Comptes*, IV, 956. Destroyed.
   The statue, exec. between 1701–6 by Coysevox (no. 60) after a different model, was placed on the façade of the Dôme des Invalides as a pendant to St. Louis by N. Coustou (no. 34).
   b.* Esquisse Terracotta H: 60
A statuette repr. Charlemagne may be considered as one of the preparatory models by D., cf. *Cat. de L'Exp. Louis XIV, faste et décors*, Mus. des Arts Décor., Paris, 1960, no. 711.

PRIVATE COLLECTION

55
Victory

Bas-relief Plaster c. 115 × 160
Mentioned in a letter from Tessin to Cronström, dd. 17 May 1693, cf. *Tessin–Cronström Corresp.* Not ident. or disapp.

56
Nude Man holding an Infant in his Arms

Drawing* in Coll. de Cotte, Bibl. Nat., Est. Fb 26, with the note: "par le sieur Desjardins". Not known to which work this refers.

57
Man in Toga apparently making a speech

Ibid.*

58–68
SCULPTURE FOUND IN D.'S STUDIO AFTER HIS DEATH, NOT PREVIOUSLY LISTED

cf. Invent. a.d. 7 Aug. 1694, Min. Centr. Arch. Nat., Et. XXX, 133.

Louis XIV
Bust Bronze
For the Cardinal d'Estrées, val. at 800 L.

52

261

56   57

Model for a Bust of Jabach
Val. at 200 L. "Ready to be cast in bronze". Eberhard Jabach, a French collector of German origin (Cologne, c. 1610–Paris, 1695), sold his coll. of paintings and drawings to Louis XIV in 1671.

Eight Busts
Marble
Val. at 1200 L.

Four Busts
"Ready to be cast in bronze". Val. at 200 L.

Pallas
Bust   Bronze
Val. at 500 L.

The Rape of Proserpina
Group   Bronze
Val. at 2000 L.

The Small Cleopatra
"Ready to be cast in bronze". Val. at 200 L.

Two Statues of Hercules
After antiques, "ready to be cast in bronze". Val. at 600 L.

Two Statues of River-Gods
After antiques; "ready to be cast in bronze". Val. at 500 L.

Two Models of River-Gods
After antiques. Val. at 300 L.

Six Marble Figures
Half life-size. Val. at 3600 L.

DOSSIER, Nicolas (17th c.)

Native of Mailly, near Paris, acc. to Dezallier, *Environs de P.*, 1762, p. 400, who calls him "a little known sculptor"; rec. into Acad. St.-Luc 25 Oct. 1664, J. Guiffrey, *Acad. St.-Luc*, 1915, p. 268. T-B., IX, 1913, p. 501.

1–4
Music, Dance

1671-2   Two Statues (H: c. 200) and two Bas-reliefs
Stone
Payment 1100 L., *Comptes*, I, 514, 671; cf. Piganiol, *Vers.-Marly.*, 1738, II, p. 14. 'Music'* holds a palm-branch, a trumpet and a music scroll. On the corresp. bas-relief* two children deciphering a score. 'Dance'*, crowned with flowers, holding a lyre, and on the bas-relief*, two children with a mask. On the façade of the central building on the Parterre Sud.

VERSAILLES, PALACE

5
Animals for the Labyrinthe, Versailles

1673
Payment 800 L., *Comptes*, I, 697, 762. Not ident. or disapp.

6

1

2

Bibl. Nat. Est., Fb 26; drawings in Stockholm, THC 3748 and 5130. *See appendix.*

VERSAILLES, PARK

6*
Fire

1675–84   Statue   Marble   H: over 200
Total payment 4100 L., *Comptes*, I, 830, 965, 1050, 1161, 1286; II, 197, 335, 442. On the surround of the Bassin de Latone. Woman holding a vase with flames, at her feet a salamander. Drawing by Le Brun, Paris,

7
Work at the Château de Clagny

1676–7
In collab. with La Perdrix, payment 820 L., *Comptes*, I, 918, 933. Destroyed.

4

3

8¹

8*
Horography

1681   Statue   Stone   H: 200
Payment 300 L., *Comptes*, II, 11. Identified through drawing* in Bibl. Nat. Est., Fb 26. 'Horography' (the art of making sun dials), is a richly draped woman, holding a dial, a compass and a square; misinterpreted by later restorations: she now holds a hammer in her right hand. On the south wing. cf. F. Souchal, 'Versailles', in *GBA*, 1972¹, p. 94–95.

VERSAILLES, PALACE

8²

9
Venus de Medici

1684
D. rec. on 30 Sept. 1684 by order of Louvois, two stucco casts of the Venus de Medici, taken from the Salle des Antiques at the Louvre, to make a copy for the Chevalier de Nogent at Meudon. Arch. Nat., O¹ 1964³. Not known whether the copy was ever made.

DROUILLY (or de ROUILLY), Jean (?-1698)

b. Vernon (Eure), son of Jean de Rouilly, master joiner. 16 May 1660 marr. Elisabeth Semellet, daughter of a carpenter, marr. contract in Min. Centr. Arch. Nat., Et. XXXVI, 195. Lived in the rue Pastourelle, parish of St.-Nicolas-des-Champs. Rec. into Acad. St.-Luc 4 Nov. 1668; made juré (sworn expert) at the same Acad., cf. Guiffrey, *AAF*, IX, 1915. In 1669, D. lived in the rue Vieille-du-Temple, contract. 1 Apr. 1669, Min. Centr. Arch. Nat., Et. XXX, 70. Death of his wife 22 Dec. 1673, Herluison, *Actes.*, p. 390. Died Paris 1698, cf. Dezallier, *Environs de P.*, 1762, p. 400; T-B., IX, 1913, p. 582.

I
Work at the Château de Chilly

1669
Contract 1 Apr. 1669 between D. and the joiner Charles Liget for sculpture on a door in the Chât. of the Marshall d'Effiat, for 100 L., Min. Centr. Arch. Nat., Et. XXX, 70. Destroyed.

2
The Cyclops Steropes

1672   Statue   Stone
One of the statues of the pavilions flanking the entrance court at Versailles; symbolised 'Fire'. Payment 400 L., *Comptes*, I, 618. The statues disappeared during later modifications to the pavilions. Piganiol, *Vers.-Marly*, 1730, I, p. 14. Félibien des Avaux, *Versailles* (Table), attribs. to D. the other Cyclops, Bronte. cf. Desjardins, no. 18*. Destroyed.

3
Work for the Labyrinthe at Versailles

1673   Lead
Probably one of the animals of the Labyrinthe; payment 550 L., *Comptes*, I, 697, 762. Not ident. or disapp.

5

4
Work at the Louvre

1674
Payment 1000 L., *Comptes*, I, 743. Not ident. or disapp.

5
Tabernacle

1674   Wood, painted and gilded
On the high altar in the old church of the Monastery des Grands Augustins. Acc. to Lemaire, *Paris, ancien et moderne*, I, 1693, p. 317; Millin, *Antiq. Nat.*, 1791, III, p. 63 and other *Descr.* of Paris, it was given by Father Lambrochon of the Convent. In the Corinthian order, surmounted by a cupola and a globe, with two niches. Engr. view* of the high altar by P. Brissart after Drouilly in Coll. Clairambault, Bibl. Nat. Ms. 1146, fol. I. Destroyed shortly before 1791.

6
Work at the Château de Clagny

1674–80   Lead, stucco, stone, wood
Varied work of great importance; D., alone or with others, rec. more than 25,000 L. His main collab. was Raon. *Comptes*, I, 772, 845, 917, 982, 1075–6, 1189–91, 1326; II, 159, 160. Most of the work, connected with exterior and interior decoration, remains undefined. Named are: 33 lion heads, as water-sprouts; lead ornaments for the dome; stucco cornices for the salons; three figures; marble paving for the bath. Apparently D. also did cabinet work; no reason to doubt that this is the same man. Destroyed.

7
Repair of a Triumphal Arch in Paris

1675
In collab. with Thevenot; payment 476 L., *Comptes*, I, 819. Not ident. or disapp.

8*
The Heroic Poem

1675–9   Statue   Marble   H: 227
'The Poem' is repr. as a male figure, laurel-crowned, holding a trumpet. Payment of 1900 L. in several instalments between 1675–9, *Comptes*, I, 832, 902, 965, 1048, 1161 and 1695, the balance, grouped with other works, *Comptes*, III, 1080, 1129. In the Parterre Nord. *See appendix.*

VERSAILLES, PARK

9
Two Adoring Angels

1677
Made in 1677 for the two pillars above the high altar of the church of the Minimes in the Place Royale, Paris, acc. to Les Annales de l'Ordre des Minimes, Bibl. Nat. Ms. français 23126, p. 100, 156. cf. M.-T. Forest, '*Les Sculptures de Gilles Guérin au Couvent des Minimes à Paris*', in *BSHAF*, 1973, p. 121–9. Probably destroyed during the Revolution.

8

12

14

10
Restoration of the Figures in the Bosquet de la Renommée in the Park at Versailles

1680
In collab. with Buyster, Legros, Massou, Jouvenet, Mazeline; payment 120 L., *Comptes*, I, 1283. Disappeared.

11
Two Vases, Basins, Masks and Shells

1682–3   Metal
Payment 1400 L., *Comptes*, II, 140, 278. In the surround of the Pièce d'eau sous le Dragon, later the Bassin de Neptune. cf. Carlier no. 3★.

VERSAILLES, PARK

12★
Eight Ionic Capitals in the Colonnade

1684–6   Marble
Payment 1808 L., *Comptes*, II, 440, 621, 987. cf. Cornu no. 17★.

VERSAILLES, PARK

13
Saint Michael throwing Lucifer

1684   Group   Stone
For the Choir Vestibule in the Convent Church of the Minimes at the Place Royale, Paris; the stone was supplied by the architect Thevenot, cf. 'Remarques de ce qui s'est passé depuis 1614 au couvent des Minimes de la Place Royale', in *Hist. de la ville et de tout le diocèse de Paris par l'abbé Lebeuf*, ed. H. Cocheris, Paris, 1867, III, p. 519. Destroyed.

14★
Vase

1684–8   Marble   H: 200
Decorated with sun-faces, laurel-branches, palms and rams' heads; Dugoulon made a similar vase, for which he rec. 2500 L. On either side of the central avenue descending from the Parterre d'eau to the Bassin de Latone; D.'s vase on the left. cf. Piganiol, *Vers.-Marly*, 1701, p. 161. Several payments, *Comptes*, II, 440, 1176; III, 94; the balance incl. with payments for other works, III, 1080, 1129. *See appendix.*

VERSAILLES, PARK

16

20

15
Work at the Château de Saint-Germain-en-Laye

1684–5   Stone
   a. *Upper balustrade*. Payment 1782 L., *Comptes*, II, 516, 803. Not ident. or disapp.
   b. *Restoration of existing sculpture*. Payment 546 L., *Comptes*, II, 516, 803. Not ident. or disapp.

16★
Restoration of a Term of Jupiter

1685   Marble   H: of torso 144
An antique statue found in Rome, belonging to the Cardinal de Granvelle in Besançon, cf. Piganiol, *Vers.-Marly*, 1738, II, p. 185 was transformed by D. into a term. Drapery and socle with an eagle on flashes of lightning (later effaced) by D., cf. Thomassin, pl. 178. Payment 1300 L., *Comptes*, II, 621, III, 94. Formerly in the Théâtre d'eau in the park, now in the Louvre. cf. W. Fröhner, *Not. de la sculpt. antique du Louvre*, 1874, p. 63, no. 31.

PARIS, LOUVRE

17
Two Vases and Masks

1685   Languedoc marble
Advance payment 1500 L., *Comptes*, II, 621 "for the petit parc". Not ident. or disapp.

18
Vase

1685   White and red Languedoc marble
Comptes, ibid. Not ident. or disapp. *See appendix.*

19
Three Guillochés

c. 1685   Marble
"To support the windows in the great appartments of the King and Queen". Total payment 11,700 L., incl. nos. 8 and 11, *Comptes*, III, 1080, 1129. Not ident. or disapp.

20★
The Triumph of Venus

1685–8   Plaster model, full-size
In collab. with Le Conte and Légeret, for the centre of one of the Bassins in the Parterre d'eau in Versailles. Payment 8110 L., *Comptes*, II, 621; IV, 4. There was also a full-size model for the other Bassin in the Parterre d'eau (the Triumph of Thetis) by Mazeline, Jouvenet and Hurtrelle, but the project was abandoned. Engr.★ by Dolivar of the Parterre d'eau with the two Bassins. Destroyed.

21
Works at the Colonnade

1686–7
   a. Two masks and a vase   Marble
Payment 1140 L., *Comptes*, II, 987.
   b. Two feet for a basin   Marble
D. had been comm. to carve two statues for the arcades: a young faun and a dryad, Arch. des Bât. Civ., cf. P. de Nolhac, 'Les marbres de Vers.', in *GBA.*, 1911[2], p. 267. The project was abandoned, the statues replaced by 29 marble basins, the feet after a model by Raon. Two of these feet were by D. Payment 800 L., *Comptes*, II, 988, 1175. cf. Cornu no. 17★.

VERSAILLES, PARK

22
Two Pedestals

1686   Marble
Supports for the Chevaux du Soleil in the Bosquet des Dômes in Versailles Park. First payment 650 L., *Comptes*, II, 980. Destroyed.

23
Capitals for Trianon

1687–8   Marble
Capital for a column, two pilaster capitals, two Ionic corner capitals and a half-capital in Composite order. cf. André no. 11★.

VERSAILLES, GRAND TRIANON

24

27

24*
Vase

1687–9   Marble   H: 200
The vase is fluted, with sunflowers in the grooves; a similar vase was carved by de Mélo as a pendant. In the Allée roy. between a vase by Barois and Jouvenet's Hercules. First payment *Comptes*, III, 288; further payments grouped together with other works, *ibid.*, III, 1080, 1129. *See appendix*.

VERSAILLES, PARK

25
Twenty-nine Vases

1688   Stone
Payment 1450 L., *Comptes*, III, 36. Receipt, cf. *NAAF*, 1876, p. 67 'for the roof of the Trianon'. Drawing* in Coll. de Cotte, Bibl. Nat. Est., Va 78 g, 2. Destroyed.

25

26
Two Models of Vases

1689
Payment 75 L., *Comptes*, III, 337, "at the two corners of the façade of the Pavilion of the Salle des Gardes" at Marly. Destroyed.

27*
Tomb of Barthélemy de Gelas, chevalier de Cezen

1689   Marble   95 × 81
Specification signed by D. on 13 June 1689, Arch. Nord 4G 4491; on 2 Oct. 1690 D. rec. 800 florins for the monument. Cezen, governor of Cambrai from 1677–81, was buried in the Chapel of Notre-Dame-de-Grâce in the Cathedral. After the destruction of the Cathedral in 1796, the monument was used as a sopraporte in a private house, then acquired by V. Delattre, and bought by the Museum in 1889. Underneath, a marble slab (disappeared) with engraved inscription (publ. by A. Le Glay, *Recherche de l'église métropolitaine de Cambrai*, 1825, p. 192); on a pedestal with coats of arms and military trophies stands a medallion with the portrait of the deceased held by a cherub (the right arm broken); over the medallion flies a second cherub holding a helmet. V. Delattre, 'Recueil d'épigraphie cambrésienne', in *Bull. Commission hist. Nord*, IX, 1866; Berger et Bruyelle, *Cat. du mus. de Cambrai*, Cambrai, 1893. (Inform. Mr. F. Machelart).

CAMBRAI, MUSEE MUNICIPAL

28
Eight Capitals

1691–8   Stone
Comm. 30 Jan. 1691, Bibl. Nat. Est., Hc 14 a, p. 32 v°. Completed by Roussel in 1698 after D.'s death. Payment 1760 L., *Comptes*, III, 560, 702, 844; IV, 330, 472, 473.

DOME DES INVALIDES

DUMONT, François (1687 or 88–1726)

b. Paris 1687 or 88. Son of Pierre D. (member of the Acad. St.-Luc, sculptor to the Duc de Lorraine), and of Marie Mercier. Brother of the painter Jacques D., called D. le Romain. Pupil of his father. First prize of the Acad. in 1709, cf. no. 9. Made Academician 24 Sept., 1712, *P-V*, IV, 120–1, 131, 155. On 21 Nov. 1712, he married Anne-Françoise Coypel, daughter of Noël Coypel, sister of Antoine Coypel, who was First Painter to the King; marriage contract publ. *NAAF*, 1877, p. 237. Eight children, most of whom died young; the son, Edme, b. 1720, also became a sculptor, *NAAF*, 1877, p. 246. François D. had the title of First Sculptor to the Duke of Orléans, cf. Marriage Contract of Philippe Coypel, 4–6 Mar. 1732, Min. Centr. Arch. Nat., Et. LIII, 260. From April–Dec. 1721, D. lived in Lunéville at the Court of Duke Léopold as First Sculptor to the Dukes of Lorraine, letters patent 30 May 1721, publ. *NAAF*, 1874–5, p. 242. On 29 May 1723, made Asst. Prof., *P-V*, IV, p. 356. He was accidentally killed in Lille on 14 Dec. 1726 when trying to adjust the lead curtain above the tomb of Louis de Melun (no. 27), *NAAF*, 1877, p. 260. Bibl: Fontenai, I, p. 535; Dezallier, *Vie*, p. 313–17; Jal, p. 517; Herluison, p. 124–5; A. Dumont, 'Doc. sur les Dumont sculpteurs', in *NAAF*, 1874–5, p. 242–3; G. Vattier, *Une famille d'artistes, les Dumont*, 1890, p. 9–34; T-B., IX, 1913, p. 128 (J. Locquin); J. Claparède, 'Le Mausolée Bonnier de la Mosson, par F. Dumont', in *Rev. des Arts*, 1959, p. 71–9; F. Souchal, 'F. Dumont, sculpteur de transition', in *GBA*, 1970[I], p. 225–50.

1–8
WORK IN THE CHAPEL AT VERSAILLES PALACE

1
Sculptures on the Royal Tribune

1708–9
Mém. of the sculptors in Arch. Nat., O[I] 1784; *Comptes*, v, 213. cf. P. Bertrand no. 21.

VERSAILLES PALACE, CHAPEL

2

3

2*
Ecclesiastical Trophies

1708–9   Bas-relief   Hard limestone   250 × 54
On the first pillar of the nave, to the right from the entrance. Estim. 650 L., Mém., *ibid.*; payment grouped with other work, *Comptes*, V, 318, 413, 530. A crucifix, a sun held up by a figure, an incense burner, a chalice, a stole, vines, ears of corn, pitchers, lamps, candlesticks etc., are fastened by a ribbon to a clasp.

VERSAILLES PALACE, CHAPEL

3*
Two Candelabra

1708–9   Bas-reliefs   Hard limestone   250 × 48
On the south side, on either side of the niche at the west end. Estim.: 400 L. for one, 350 L. for the other, Mém., *ibid.* The two designs differ. Various ornaments, cherubim heads and entwined dolphins are arranged along an vertical stem resting on a cul-de-lampe, crowned by a flaming censer.

VERSAILLES PALACE, CHAPEL

4

4*
Allegory of Jesus before Pilate

1708–10   Bas-relief   Stucco   L: 180
On the south wall of the nave, in the first arcade below
the Royal Tribune, cf. P. Bertrand no. 22. Roughly
sketched out in bonbanc stone, it was demolished to
make room for culs-de-lampe (cf. no. 1), but re-
modelled by D. in stucco imitating stone. Estim.
2475 L., Mém. and *Comptes, ibid.* An angel, seated on
clouds; at his side, a young angel holding a platter
pours water over the hands of another small angel, an
allegory of Pilate's action.

VERSAILLES PALACE, CHAPEL

5*
Ecclesiastical Trophy

1709   Bas-relief   Limestone   250 × 121
Below no. 4; Mém. *ibid.* Estim. 650 L. The motifs
belong to the same theme: a platter, a pitcher, the Book
of Divine Law, weapons, olive branches, a birch-rod and
a crown of thorns, all hanging from a beribboned clasp;
cf. P. Bertrand no. 23.

VERSAILLES PALACE, CHAPEL

5

6

7

6*
Cherubim Heads on Clouds

1709   Stone
On the keystone of the first arcade in the south wall of the nave. Estim. 225 L., Mém. *ibid.*

VERSAILLES PALACE, CHAPEL

7*
Sculptures in the Vault of the Ambulatory

1709
Together with Laisné, Bercher, Lelong, Rousseau du Louvre and Rousseau de Corbeil, D. decor. the three sections of the ambulatory vault after designs by R. de Cotte. The decor. consists of several oval mould-

ings with stylised plant motifs and the King's coat-of-arms on a mosaic background embellished with roses. Estim. 16,548 L., Mém. *ibid.* and *Comptes*, V, 319.

VERSAILLES PALACE, CHAPEL

8*
Twenty-two Ecclesiastical Trophies

1709   Bas-reliefs   Stone
On the bases of the Corinthian columns supporting the Tribune at the side of the Nave. Rectangular bas-reliefs decor. with various liturgical motifs. D., Dugoullon and Tuby rec. 300 L. for this work, *Comptes*, V, 318, which does not appear in the sculptors' Mém.

VERSAILLES PALACE, CHAPEL

9
David forgiving Abigail

1709   Bas-relief
First Acad. prize; cf. Guiffrey, *Liste pensionnaires*, and *P-V*, IV, p. 92. Whereabouts unknown.

10
Ornaments on the Ceiling of the Salon Bas

1710
D. and a team carved various ornaments on the flat mouldings and cornices; they also repaired the Ionic capitals. Estim. 8702 L. 10s., Mém., *ibid.*, *Comptes*, V, 529. cf. André no. 13a.

VERSAILLES, PALACE

11
Prometheus

1710
a.*   Group   Bronze   78.8 × 62.5
Signed & dated: F. DUMONT FECIT 1710
Bought in Paris by Lord Yarmouth for King George IV of England, Jan. 1818. Exh.: *George IV and the Arts of*

8

11a

Drawing, no. 49, London, Buckingham Palace, 1966. D. showed in the Salon, 1725, a group with the same theme and dimensions, *Mercure*, Sept. 1725, p. 2270. Prometheus, nude, chained to a rock (Mount Caucasus), attacked by a vulture.

ENGLAND, ROYAL COLLECTION

12

b. *Four groups*   Plaster (one of them, bronzed)
Invent. a.d., partly publ. in G. Vattier, *Une famille d'artistes, les Dumont*, 1890. Whereabouts unknown.

12*
Titan struck down

1711–12   Marble   H: 66
Reception piece for the Acad.; sketch and model, 1711; marble, 1712, *P–V*, IV, 120–1, 131, 155. cf. Guérin & Dezallier, *Descr.* p. 63 and 135; Fontaine, p. 162. The titan Urites, struck down by lightning, is lying nude on a pile of rocks.

PARIS, LOUVRE

13
Sculptures on the Rood-screen of the Church of Saint-Pierre-en-Chastres

1713   Stone
   a.* Groups of Cherubim
Stone
D.'s letters, cf. G. Vattier, *op. cit.*, refer to work in the Beauvaisis in 1713. J. Philippot, 'Deux oeuvres de F. Dumont', in *BSHAF*, 1934, p. 49–59, identified what remains of D.'s rood-screen in the ruins of the Celestine Priory, St.-Pierre-en-Chastres in the forest of Compiègne. Four Composite pilasters divide the wall into three parts with a great arch in the centre and niches in the two side parts. On the three keystones D. has carved heads of cherubim in clouds.

PRIORY OF ST.–PIERRE–EN–CHASTRES (near Compiègne)

   b.* St. Peter and St. Paul
Two Statues   Stone   H: c. 200
Acc. to J. Philippot, *op. cit.*, the two statues, to-day placed against the inside wall of the façade of the Church of St.-Jacques of Compiègne, stood originally in the niches of the rood-screen in the Chapel of the Priory St.-Pierre-en-Chastres. Donated to St.-Jacques in 1820 by the owner of the Priory. St. Peter, holding his keys, puts his left hand to his chest; St. Paul holds the Holy Book pressed against his hip, his left hand on the hilt of a sword (the blade is broken off).

COMPIEGNE, CHURCH OF ST.-JACQUES

14
Work at the Hôtel de Toulouse

1713–15
Acc. to Brice, *Descr.*, 1717, D. carved the greater part of the decor. on the stair-head in the Hôtel de Toulouse, work "of a very special finish". Carried out under the direction of R. de Cotte. The staircase has been demolished. Drawing* of the stair-head of the Hotel in Coll. de Cotte, Bibl. Nat. Est., Va 232 e.

13

13a

13a

13b

13b

14

15

15
Crowning of the Portal of the Hôtel de Clermont

1714   Stone
cf. Brice, *Descr.*, 1752, IV, p. 30; J.-F. Blondel, *Arch. Fr.*,
I, p. 209 ff.; Dezallier, *Paris*, 1778, p. 369. The Hôtel,
built by the architect Le Blond, stood in the rue de
Varennes. D.'s contract is dated 15 Jan. 1714 for 850 L.,
Min. Centr. Arch. Nat., Et. I, 254, publ. by Rambaud, II,
p. 722. D. carved for the top of the portal the coat of
arms of the Clermont-Lodève family, supported by
unicorns and genie. Acc. to Brice, *Descr.*, D. also
carved the greater part of the decoration in the Hôtel.
Engr.* of the portal, with modifications, in Mariette,
Arch. Fr., pl. 196. Decor. later changed; then destroyed.

16
Work at the Hôtel d'Evreux (today the Palais de l'Elysée)

1718
    a. *Pediment on the façade*   160 × 840
    b. *Pediment on the stables*   113 × 518
Acc. to D.'s Mém. publ. in *NAAF*, 1874/5, p. 237–8, his
work consisted of the carving of the pediment on the
façade with a cartouche with the coat of arms of the
Duc d'Evreux, Henri-Louis de La Tour d'Auvergne,
supported by two griffins and framed by attribs. of war.
On the pediment of the stables, three horses' heads and
oak branches. D. rec. 1000 L. Destroyed after 1752.

17
Work on the Château de Petit-Bourg

c. 1718
Acc. to Dezallier, *Vie*, p. 313–7, D. carved bas-reliefs for
the Château of the Duc d'Antin, reconstructed by
Lassurance. Destroyed.

18
The Triumph of Galatea

c. 1718   Bas-relief   Model   Terracotta   L: 150
Galatea   Height: 270
Exh.: Salon 1725, cf. *Mercure*, Sept. 1725, p. 2270. Model
of a pediment for the Peterhof Palace, Russia. Acc. to
Mercure, the bas-relief consisted of nine figures, among
them Galatea "in her chariot, accomp. by Tritons and
Nereids". Destroyed.

20

19
Decoration for the Funeral Service of the Duchesse de Berry in Saint-Denis

2nd Sept., 1719
In collab. with S. Slodtz, after Berain's design. D. rec. 220 L., Arch. Nat., O^I 2849, fol. 118–9, publ. in *NAAF*, 1887, p. 332; cf. F. Souchal, *Les Slodtz*, 1967, p. 604. Destroyed.

20
Tomb of the Demoiselles Bonnier

1719   Marble
Contract 1 Nov. 1719, publ. *NAAF*, 1874–5, p. 239–42: *Documents sur les Dumont*. A slab of black marble with inscription, on a white marble pedestal; a death's head and escutcheons; two gilded lions supporting the black marble tomb; above it, the two little girls; the older one, 5 years old, kneels, stretching out a hand to her sister "à l'âge de naissance", who stands on clouds. Behind, a pyramid with urn. Estim. 10,000 L. For the Bonnier Chapel in the Church of the Récollets of Montpellier, destroyed during the Revolution. J. Claparède, 'Le mausolée de mesdemoiselles Bonnier de la Mosson par F. Dumont', in *Rev. des Arts*, 1959, p. 71–9, has discovered the mutilated figure of the 5-year old girl* in the Mus. at Montpellier.

MUSEUM, MONTPELLIER (Fragment)

21
Work at the Château of Lunéville

1721
   a. *Pediment*
   b. *Keystones for the Arcades*
   c.* Sopraportes
From his letters (publ. Vattier, *op. cit.*), we know that D. carved the great pediment of the wing, 550×390, with two slaves and several trophies of arms; he also carved "three heads for the arcades, then 18–19 heads in sandstone". Finally, he carved in the Salon (today the

21c

23b

Salle des Trophées) four sopraportes (extant), with "the coat-of-arms of his Royal Highness on a shield, on one side a child, on the other an eagle, the whole accomp. by trophies of arms".

CHATEAU OF LUNEVILLE (only the sopraportes)

22
Models for the Park of the Château de Lunéville

1721
Acc. to his letter, *ibid.*, D. made models for a Mercury, a Venus, a Hercules and a Minerva. Not ident. or disapp.

23
Work at the Chapel of the Château de Lunéville

1721
   a. *Full-size model of an altar*
Plaster
cf. D.'s letters, *ibid.* Destroyed.
   b.* Groups of cherubim heads in clouds
Stone
On the keystones of the arcades. cf. D.'s letters, *ibid.*

CHATEAU OF LUNEVILLE, CHAPEL

24
Work at the Château de Chantilly

1722
Acc. to Vattier, *op. cit.*, p. 14, D. did "in the course of 1722, in association with a Mr. Thibaut, important work for M. le Duc in his Château of Chantilly". Not ident.

25
Models for a Term of Ceres

1724–5   Plaster and wax   H: c. 280
Payment 2500 L., Arch. Nat., O^I 2225, publ. Furcy-Raynaud, *Invent.* After D.'s death, the marble was carved by G. Coustou (no. 64*), cf. Barois nos. 3, 4. Not ident. or disapp.

26a¹
b¹

26c¹
c²

26d¹
d²

26e, f

The two groups framed the pediment of the north portal; engr.* in J.-F. Blondel, *Arch. fr.*, II, liv. III, no. V, pl. 3. Removed in 1785. Destroyed (e & f).

27
Tomb of Louis, Duke de Melun

1725–6   Marble & bronze
In the first chapel to the right of the altar in the Church of the Dominicans at Lille. J.-B. Descamps, *Voyage pitt. de la Flandre et du Brabant*, 1769, p. 10, new ed. 1838. Contract for 25,000 L., see Vattier, *op. cit.*; Descr. and engr.*, cf. Millin, *Antiq. Nat.*, V, Chap. LVI, p. 3. On the sarcophagus, two figures of Piety and Glory seated on either side of a pyramid with a funeral urn at the top; an escutcheon with the coat of arms of Louis of Melun and military trophies. Framed by two great lead curtains, held back by skeletons, the one on the left holding an hour-glass. Destroyed.

28
Two Lion Heads

Life-size
These appear in the Invent. a.d. of the sculptor, Antoine-François Vassé, 6 Feb. 1736, Min. Centr. Arch. Nat., Et. CXIII, 344, publ. in Rambaud, I, p. 705. Not ident. or disapp.

WORKS MENTIONED IN THE INVENT A.D. OF DUMONT, not previously listed.

cf. Vattier, *op. cit.*
Two Terracotta Sphinxes; Six Busts of Fauns and Bacchantes; Torso of Venus; Two Terracotta Models of Apollo and Diana; Two Children, Plaster.
Not ident. or disapp.

26
Sculptures for the Church of Saint-Sulpice

1725
  a. St. Peter and a child
    I* Group   Stone H: 300
    II *Maquette*   Terracotta
  b. St. Paul and a child
    I* Group   Stone H: 300
    II *Maquette*   Terracotta
  c. St. Joseph
    I* Statue   Stone H: 300
    II* Maquette   Terracotta
  d. St. John the Baptist
    I* Statue   Stone H: 300
    II* Maquette   Terracotta

Acc. to Dezallier, *Vie*, and other *Descr.* of Paris, the stone groups and statues were in 1725 put into niches at the side of the portals of the transept: St. Peter and St. Paul at the north side; St. Joseph and St. John the Baptist at the south side. St. Peter is accompanied by a child carrying the keys; St. Paul holds the Book of Epistles; his sword is held by a child. St. John the Baptist held rushes in the shape of the Cross, St. Joseph a lily (rushes and lily have disappeared).

PARIS, CHURCH OF ST.-SULPICE

The four maquettes are mentioned in D.'s Invent. a.d., cf. Vattier, *op. cit.*; D.'s grandson, Augustin D., discovered St. Joseph and St. John the Baptist in the trade; today in the Mus. Carnavalet.

PARIS, CARNAVALET MUSEUM (two maquettes)

  e. *Two angels carrying a Crozier*
Group Stone
  f. *Two Angels carrying a Cross*
Group Stone

27

FLAMEN, Anselme (1647-1717)

b. St.-Omer 2 Jan. 1647, son of Jean Flamen, merchant, and Jeanne Dumont. In 1669, pupil of G. Marsy in Paris. In 1673, 3rd sculpture prize (see no. 1). Between 6 Apr. 1675 and 1679, pensionnaire of the French Acad. in Rome, *NAAF*, 1879, 365. In 1677, 2nd sculpture prize at the Acad. St.-Luc, Rome (see no. 6). 2 Feb. 1680 married Louise Blart before notary Debeauvais. Charles Le Brun acted as witness because the bride, daughter of Marie Le Bé, was his first cousin and pupil. Thirteen children, one of whom, Anselme II, was a sculptor in Paris (1680–1730), Bibl. Nat. Ms., Fich. Laborde, 26974, 27009–17, 27030–32. In 1681, made Academician (see no. 9); Asst. Prof., 30 Oct. 1694; Prof., 6 Aug. 1701, *P-V*, III, 150, 322. Lived in the Vieux Louvre until his death on 16 May 1717, cf. Piot, *Etat Civil*, 1873, p. 47. T-B, XII, 1916, p. 67 (H. Vollmer).

Anselme II was made Academician in 1708. His reception piece was a marble statuette: 'Plutus, dieu des richesses' (Louvre), *P-V*, IV, 41, 50, 70.

9

1
The Crossing of the Rhine

1673
3rd Acad. Sculpture prize, *P-V*, II, 7, 47; *AAF*, V, 277. Not ident. or disapp.

2
Anatomical Study

1675–9   Bas-relief
Listed in the Invent. of Sculptures at the Acad. in Rome which Errard handed over to La Teulière, dated 6 Dec. 1684, *Corr. Dir. Acad. Fr. Rome*, I, 133. Not ident. or disapp.

3
Mars and Venus

Bas-relief
Listed in the Invent. (see no. 2), "de l'invention du sieur Flamen". Not ident. or disapp.

4
River

1675–9   Terracotta model
Listed in the Invent. (see no. 2). Part of an allegorical monument to the glory of Louis XIV, done by the pupils in Rome under the direction of Errard after his design. Not ident. or disapp.

5
Faun carrying the Child Bacchus

1676–9   Group   Marble
Copy of an antique group called the Borghese Faun. Acc. to the Invent. (see no. 2) it was sent to France. None of the numerous copies of this famous antique has been identified as by Flamen.

6
The Creation of Man

1677   Bas-relief
2nd Sculpture Prize, Acad. St.-Luc, Rome; 1st prize went to the sculptor S. Hurtrelle. cf. G.-J. Hoogewerff, *Bescheiden in Italie, II, Rome, Archieven van Bijzondere instellingen*, 1913, p. 75. Not ident. or disapp.

7
Trophies on the Façade, Versailles

1679–80   Bas-reliefs   Stone
Above the windows of the Grande Galerie; exec. during Hardouin-Mansart's alterations to the façade, facing the Parterre d'Eau. Total payment, incl. the masks on the same façade, 7875 L., *Comptes*, II, 1288; III, 158.

VERSAILLES, PALACE

8
Masks on the Façade, Versailles

1679–80   Stone
On the keystones of the arched windows on the ground floor, probably in the centre part of the building. Payment, cf. *supra*.

VERSAILLES, PALACE

9*
Saint Jerome

1680–81   Oval Bas-relief   Marble   65 × 50
Reception piece for the Acad. Model chosen Jan. 1680, *P-V*, II, 160, 162; F. was received in Apr. 1681, *ibid.*, II, 187, cf. Guérin, *Descr.*, p. 44. During the Revolution, trsf. to the Dépôt de Nesle; in 1815, given to the Church of Notre-Dame, Versailles, cf. Fontaine, p. 166. The

Saint, half-figure, nude, strikes his breast with a stone, gazing at a crucifix which he is holding tightly in his arms.

VERSAILLES, CHURCH OF NOTRE–DAME

10
Restoration of Eighteen Antique Statues

1680
Payment 1419 L. and 1606 L. in 1680–1, *Comptes*, I, 1288; II, 20. Until 1704 the antiques were in the Galerie d'Eau, Versailles (today Salle des Marronniers), but were then dispersed.

11
Work at the South Wing, Versailles

1681
 a. *Unspecified Work*
Payment 900 L., *Comptes*, II, 10.
 b.★ Trophies Bas-reliefs Stone
On the arches of the windows of the Grande Aile. On account, 500 L., *Comptes*, II, 55.

VERSAILLES, PALACE

12★
Erato

1681–2 Statue Tonnerre stone H: over 200
In the group of Muses on the attic storey of the South Wing. A drawing in the Coll. de Cotte, Bibl. Nat. Est., Fb 26 shows the name of F., who actually rec. payments for work on the Great Wing, *Comptes*, II, 136–7, 301; average payment for each statue 500 L., cf. F. Souchal, 'Versailles', in *GBA*, 1972[I], p. 88. The original, now in store, has been replaced by a copy★. The Muse of Lyrical Poetry, accompanied by a little cupid, plays her lyre.

VERSAILLES, PALACE

Detail   12

Copy   12

11b

13

17

13
Model for the Fontaine de la Renommée

1681   Plaster
One of many full-size models submitted between 1676 and 1684 for this fountain in the park at Versailles. It disappeared when the group 'Apollon servi par les Nymphes' was trsf. to this bosquet. Descr. in Piganiol, *Vers.-Marly*, 1764, II, p. 170. Payment 147 L. in 1681, *Comptes*, III, 20. Many contemporary engr. of the Bosquet de la Renommée with the fountains, incl. one "chez Langlois"*. Destroyed.

14
Two Vases, Four Shells, Two Masks for the Bassin Sous le Dragon

1682–4   Metal
F. rec. 300 L. on account for two vases in 1682, *Comptes*, II, 140, and 1600 L. in 1683 "for the vases and basins in metal, the masks and shells and the models", *ibid.*, II, 277. The total payment of 25,200 L. in 1694 mentions (in addition to two basins, four shells and two masks),

Cyparissus, the Faun with the Kid and Boreas and Orithya, *ibid.*, III, 947. The decor. for the Bassin Sous le Dragon, later the Bassin de Neptune, was exec. by a large team; later restored. cf. Carlier no. 3*.

VERSAILLES, PARK

15
Vase

1683   Marble
In 1683, initial payments of 200 L. each were made to several sculptors for white marble vases, $7\frac{1}{2}$ pieds high, intended for the park at Versailles: to Flamen and Tuby for one vase each, to Girardon and Regnaudin for two vases each, *Comptes*, II, 335–6. After that the payments were discontinued; probably the project had been abandoned. Not ident. or disapp.

16

16*
Two Children holding a Trophy

1683   Group   Gilded stucco
The payment of 750 L. to F. for a trophy in the Grande
Galerie, *Comptes*, II, 313 refers to one of the 24 groups of
children seated on the cornice of the Grande Galerie,
made after Le Brun's designs which replaced the rectangular windows with arched ones; cf. P. de Nolhac,
Hist. du chât. de Vers., 1911, II, p. 131–6.

VERSAILLES, PALACE

17
Tomb of the Duc Anne de Noailles

1683   Marble and bronze
The Duc de Noailles died in Paris on 15 Feb. 1678 and
was buried in the Church of St.-Paul. His widow,
Louise Boyer, comm. a monument from G. Marsy.
Marsy died a year later, leaving some partly carved
marbles and a contrat de société for F. to complete the
work; cf. Invent. a.d. of G. Marsy, 29 Jan. 1682, Min.
Centr. Arch. Nat., Et. CXII, 385a. After a survey of the
work in progress by Girardon and Desjardins on 15
July 1682, F. made a new estim. on 18 Dec. 1682, Min.
Centr. Arch. Nat., Et. LXXXIII, 177. Marsy had already
rec. one-third of the total of 12,723 L. In a contract signed
on the same date, it was agreed that F. should rec. 8000 L.
for the tomb, to be finished by the end of June 1683.
Acc. to the survey, Marsy had already done half of the
principal marble group and part of the architecture and
the ornaments. The tomb, erected in the Communion
Chapel of the Church of St.-Paul, no longer exists.
Drawing* in Coll. Gaignières, Bibl. Nat. Est., no. 4770;
descr. in Dezallier, *Paris*, 1752, p. 182; Piganiol,
Descr., 1765, IV, p. 165; Thiery, 1787, I, p. 694. The
sarcophagus, decorated with the coat-of-arms of the
deceased, standing on a socle with an inscription supports
the main group; the marshal, in the arms of Religion,
leans against the Cross, worshipping with clasped hands
the Holy Sacrament. An angel holds up the Holy Book.
Behind, the winged figure of Death carries the mantle
and the ducal coronet towards heaven. Various military
trophies in bronze on the socle. Destroyed.

18*
La Rosée and Zephir

1684 (?)–1717   Group   Marble   H: 180
Descr. in the Invent. of 1733 of the Salle des Antiques,
Louvre, where it stood next to P. Lepautre's 'Clytia';
begun by Massou, continued by F. after Massou's
death in 1684 and completed by Rebillé, Arch. Nat.,
O¹ 1965⁴. In the Invent. of 1754, O¹ 1965⁸, wrongly attr.
to Le Lorrain. In 1762, Dezallier, *Env. de P.*, p. 14, it was
in the park of La Muette, where it was restored in 1783,
Arch. Nat., O¹ 1582, fol. 365. In 1791, Pajou repeated the
wrong attr. to Le Lorrain, *NAAF*, 1901, p. 268. cf.
U. Middeldorf, *Sculptures Kress Coll.*, London, 1976,
p. 100.

WASHINGTON, D.C., NATIONAL GALLERY OF ART

18

19*
Boreas abducting Orithya

1684–7
  a. Group   Marble   H: 260
Begun by Marsy, who in 1677 rec. 1400 L. on account,
Comptes, I, 964. Intended for one of the corners of the
first Parterre d'Eau at Versailles; acc. to Le Brun's plan
the three other corners were also to be filled by
'Abductions': Coronis by Neptunus, Cybele by
Saturnus, Proserpina by Pluto. After Marsy's death,
F. was comm. to complete the group and rec. on
account four payments of 1100 L., 1400 L., 1500 L., and
1500 L., in 1684–5–6–7; the final payment in 1694 of
25,200 L. incl. other works, *Comptes*, II, 441, 628, 995,
1176; III, 947, 1004. The completed work was placed
in the Parterre de l'Orangerie at Versailles in 1687,
Comptes, II, 1188, as a pendant to Regnaudin's 'Rape of
Cybele', *Comptes*, II, 1101; pictures by Cotelle and
J.-B. Martin in the Soulié *Cat.*, nos. 728 & 750. But acc.

to the Invent. drawn up in 1722–3, Arch. Nat., O^I 1969^A, p. 200, the two groups have been in the Tuileries Garden since 1716; in the Louvre since 1972. There are a number of descriptions in the invents. of the royal collections of Paris and the old *Descrs.* of Paris. Like the three other 'Abductions' this is a group of three figures forming a pyramid; Boreas, winged and nude, a symbol of the North wind, holds Orithya tightly with the help of a drapery, the end of which is held by a male figure, prostrate under their feet, symbolising one of the winds. *See appendix.*

PARIS, LOUVRE

b. Numerous bronze versions with variants in the base and drapery; one in the Royal Coll., Invent. 1707, Arch. Nat., O^I 1976^A, p. 865, then in the Coll. of the Marq. de Marigny in St.-Cloud, today in Versailles Mus.; others in the Louvre; Fogg Art Mus., Cambridge, Mass.; Wallace Coll., London; former Coll. of Augustus the Strong, Dresden★ (today Grünes Gewölbe).

19b

20

Work at the Colonnade, Versailles

1685
  a. Three Masks
  b. Two Vases
F. had been comm. to carve two statues for the arcades of the Colonnade: a faun and a Hamadryad, Arch. des Bâtiments Civils, cf. P. de Nolhac, 'Les Marbres de Vers.', in *GBA*, 1911^2, p. 267. The project was abandoned, the statues replaced by marble basins. On the keystones of the arcades, masks, three of them by F., who also produced two of the vases on the cornice. Payment 1290 L. in two instalm. in 1685, *Comptes*, II, 628, 995. cf. Cornu no. 17★.

VERSAILLES, PARK

19a

21

21

21*
Faun with a Kid

1685–6   Group   Marble   H: over 200
Exact copy of the antique original in the Coll. of
Queen Christina of Sweden (today in the Mus.
Archeologico, Madrid). Payments in 1685–6–7, *Comptes*,
II, 628, 995, 1175 amounting to 2600 L. and a final pay-
ment in 1694 together with several other works, *ibid.*,

III, 947. The statue has always stood on the south side of
the Allée Royale. It repr. a nude young man, walking,
with a kid on his shoulders. Drawings in Stockholm,
THC 2730 and in Paris, Bibl. Nat. Est., Fb 25. *See app.*

VERSAILLES, PARK

22
Gladiator

1686
On 16 Aug. 1686, Louvois sent a plaster cast of the
gladiator in the Salle des Antiques to F. to be copied,
Arch. Nat., O^I 1964³. Nothing further is known. Not
ident. or disapp.

25

23

23*
Cyparissus

1687   Group   Marble   H: over 200
Comm. for the north ramp of the Allée Royale. Exec.
after a small model by Girardon, Arch. Nat., O^I 2772.
F. rec. 1500 L. for the full-size model in 1687–8,
Comptes, II, 1175; III, 94; there are receipts for 300 L. in
1687–8, publ. in *NAAF*, 1882, p. 19, and a final payment
grouping several works together in 1694, *Comptes*, III,
947. The young shepherd is repr. before the involuntary
killing of the stag and before his own metamorphosis
into a cypress; he is putting a garland of flowers round
the neck of his favourite animal, caressing it. Drawing
Stockholm THC 3733; Paris, Bibl. Nat. Est., Fb 25.

VERSAILLES, PARK

24
Ionic Capital for the Grand Trianon

1687–8   Marble
F. carved the capital for a single column (cf. Coysevox
no. 50*) and three pilaster capitals (cf. André no. 11*)
for the peristyle and the façade of the Palace. Total
payment 725 L., *Comptes*, II, 1176; III, 94.

VERSAILLES, GRAND TRIANON

29

30

25
Model for the Arcade at the back of the Sanctuary, Dôme des Invalides

1690
F. was comm. to decorate the arcade for a fee of 800 L., Bibl. Nat. Est., Hc 14, 2. The full-size model was altered by Hardouin-Mansart. It repr. the radiant Dove of the Holy Spirit and young angel-musicians playing and worshipping. Drawing★ in Coll. de Cotte, *ibid.* Payment in 1690, *Comptes*, III, 423, Arch. Nat., Oᴵ 1665a, 36; Bibl. Nat. Ms. fr. n.a. 22936. Demolished when the arcade was enlarged.

26
Virtue for the Lantern of the Dôme des Invalides

1691   Statue   Lead
One of the four statues above the lantern, cf. Bourdy no. 3★; Félibien des Avaux, *Invalides*, p. 301. Payment 452 L., *Comptes*, III, 558. F.'s Virtue was holding a sceptre (Félibien). Melted down in 1793.

27
Cherubim Head

1691   Stone
On the façade of the Church of the Dôme des Invalides,

above the niche with Charlemagne (no. 31). Payment 40 L., *Comptes*, III, 556. cf. Félibien des Avaux, *Invalides*, p. 19–20 (descr. without attrib.). Destroyed.

28★   29★   30★
Three Groups of Prophets

1691–9   Bas-reliefs   Stone   260 × 370
cf. N. Coustou, no. 10. On the cornice in the round chapels of the Dôme des Invalides. Payment 1200 L. i.e. 400 L. for each group, *Comptes*, III, 556, 702; IV, 470.
28 Two prophets on the east side of the Chapel of St.-Jérôme. cf. Félibien des Avaux, *Invalides*, p. 301.
29, 30 Two prophets on the east side and two prophets on the south side of the Chapel of St.-Augustin. cf Félibien des Avaux, *op. cit.*

PARIS, DOME DES INVALIDES

31
Charlemagne

1692   Model   Plaster   Full-size
For the niche on the right-hand side of the great portal, Dôme des Invalides. Payment 150 L., *Comptes*, III, 702. Carved in stone by Coysevox (no. 60) between 1695–1706. cf. no. 27. Destroyed.

28

32*
Diana

1693   Group   Marble   H: 182
Signed: ANSELME FLAMEN NATIF DE SAINT-OMER
Payment 2850 L., *Comptes*, III, 1006; placed in the lower
part of the park at Marly in the centre of a bassin, on a
socle decorated with rock-work, under a parasol pine;
cf. the watercolour drawing of the Bosquet de Diane,
Arch. Nat., O^I 1471, p. 21. Descr. in the Invents. of
1695, 1707, 1722 etc., Arch. Nat., O^I 1460^{126}, O^I 1976^A,
O^I 1969^A etc.; also in Piganiol, Dezallier etc. Disappeared at the end of the 18th c.; in 1907 in the Coll.
Hoentschel, then Coll. Seligman. Acq. by the Louvre in
1970 at the Vigier sale, no. 100. The goddess wears a

32²   *32³*   *32¹*

35

III, 846; IV, 47, 330. Destroyed in 1699, Arch. Nat., O^I 1665, 38.

35*
Callisto

1696   Group   Marble   H: 186
One of Diana's Companions, comm. for Marly; for. bibl. see Cayot no. 8. Placed in 1696 between the Pavillon Royal and Les Gerbes, cf. Piganiol, *Vers.-Marly*, 1701, p. 379. Payment 2850 L., *Comptes*, IV, 8, 63. The small bronze model was cast by Roger, *Comptes*, IV, 48, 190. In 1705 the marble was sent to the Bosquet des Dômes, Versailles. Fitted with a marble pedestal by the sculptors Armand and Monthéan, *Comptes*, IV, 1184. Descr. in Invent. of 1707, Arch. Nat., O^I 1976^A, p. 318–19. Trsf. to St.-Cloud in 1844, but returned to the Bosquet des Dômes, Versailles, where it still stands. Callisto, a scrip over her left shoulder, walks, a greyhound gambolling on her right. In her right hand she held a small horn (disappeared).

VERSAILLES, PARK

36
Decoration on the Bassin of the Demi-Lune des Vents in Marly

1697   Lead
Two gryphons, a great shell, a mask
For the first Bassin of the Demi-Lune. Models in 1697, letter by Villacerf, Arch. Nat., O^I 1465. Payment to F. 1500 L., *Comptes*, IV, 189, 339; Arch. Nat., O^I 2773^5. cf. Barois no. 12. Pendant to a similar group by Van Clève. The two groups stood on either side of two sea-horses by Mazeline. The decor. was dismantled in 1703 and the Bassin re-arranged. Destroyed.

37
Vase for the Demi-lune des Vents, Marly

1697–8   Marble   H: 130
One of 12 vases comm. by Hardouin-Mansart, see Barois no. 11*. F.'s vase was similar to that by Mazière; payment 850 L., *Comptes*, IV, 189, 337. Disappeared.

38
Statue for the Hôtel Le Juge

Before 1698
Mentioned in Brice, *Descr.*, 1698, I, 266, but not in the 1694 edition. Decor. for a fountain in the garden of François Le Juge, Fermier Général, rue du Grand Chantier, Paris. Not ident. or disapp.

39
Patriarch for the Dôme des Invalides

1698   Full-size model   Plaster
cf. Barois no. 10f.* F.'s statue was to be grouped with that by Poultier. The models were probably put in place, but never exec. in stone. cf. engr. in Pérau, p. 87, pl. 21; Bibl. Nat. Est., Hd 135d, pet. fol. Estim. for a group of two Patriarchs: 600 L. Destroyed.

crescent-shaped diadem and a short tunic; she carries a quiver on a bandolier, holds a bow (broken off) and caresses a greyhound standing on its hind legs (the dog's head has been wrongly restored); behind her a tree-trunk draped with a net. cf. M. Beaulieu, 'La Diane d'A. Flamen et ses compagnes' in *Rev. du Louvre*, 1973, p. 83–88. The drawing* in Berlin, Kunstbibliothek Hdz. 2625a 17 is probably a sketch for this statue.

PARIS, LOUVRE

Several copies: one in marble, formerly Maisons-Laffite, sale 21 June 1877, cat. p. 9; two small bronze versions in the Mus. at Charleston, South Carolina,* and in the Pushkin Mus., Moscow, both with variants.

33
Jupiter

1693   Term   Marble
F. rec. only one payment of 700 L. on account, *Comptes*, III, 1693. The work must have been rough-hewn only and then abandoned, as a marble term for Versailles was usually valued at c. 3500 L. Whereabouts unknown.

34
Angel supporting the Piscina

1693–8   Bas-relief   Stone
Decoration on one of the twelve panels of the cupola of the Dôme des Invalides, part of Hardouin-Mansart's first plan, Arch. Nat., O^I 1665, 36. cf. N. Coustou no. 11 b. Payment 1000 L. in three instalm., *Comptes*,

44a

44b

40
Six Large Frames for Marly

1699   Stone   Circumf. 1300; thickness 25
Jouvenet, N. Coustou (no. 20b) and F. together rec.
1452 L. 6s.3d. for six large frames for Van der Meulen's
paintings in the vestibules of the Pavillon Royal at
Marly. Disapp. in 1758 during alterations by Gabriel.
Destroyed.

44c

41   42
Two Small Busts

1699   White marble
Salon 1699, *Livret*, p. 12; cf. Florent le Comte, *Cabinet*,
1700, III, p. 247: "Jeunes têtes". Not ident. or disapp.

43
Model for a Group of Children for Meudon

1699   Plaster
Four large plaster models of groups of children, to be
placed on pedestals in the middle of the Cascades de
l'Artelon, were comm. from F., Hardy, Mazière and
Raon, Arch. Nat., O¹ 1473, p. 142, no. 52. Payment for
each model 800 L., *Comptes*, IV, 480, 618; V, 538.
Intended to be exec. in marble (F. actually rec. a marble
slab for his group, *Comptes*, IV, 302), but finally cast it
in lead. Probably destroyed.

44
Work at the Hôtel Le Brun

1700   Stone
   a.★ Pediment on the garden side
   b.★ Pediment in the courtyard
   c.★ Four masks
The Hôtel was probably built by Boffrand for the

46a

nephew of Charles Le Brun, first painter to the King, in honour of his uncle. Acc. to Brice and Piganiol, the carved decorations were by Flamen. The pediment on the garden side repr. a winged genie, standing, and a seated and helmeted Minerva, holding a medallion with the painter's profile; on the left, a little satyr holding a mask unveils a vase; to the right, a small cupid holds a drawing-board. Underneath the pediment, carved sun-heads between triglyphs decorated with fleurs-de-lis.

On the pediment in the courtyard, two unicorns flanking an escutcheon with the Le Brun coat-of-arms, the head of the sun above waves. Four masks on the arches above the doors: Apollo, Bacchus, a satyr and a silenus.

PARIS, HOTEL LE BRUN, 49, rue du Cardinal-Lemoine

45
Charles le Chauve

1700–1 Medallion Stone Diam.: 100
One of twelve medallions repr. the Kings of France on the drum inside the cupola. A previous project, not carried out, envisaged twelve bas-reliefs illustr. the history of France. F. was to carve "Louis VIII, père de

45

St. Louis, offrant les dépouilles des Albigeois sur un bouclier attaché à un palmier de Albigensibus", Arch. Nat., O¹ 1665, fol. 42. The medallions of the Kings of France were est. at 500 L. each, Bibl. Nat. Est., Hd 135d, pet. fol., but F. rec. only 400 L., *Comptes*, IV, 610, 727 and *NAAF*, 1876, p. 77 for this medallion and an adjoining mosaic of fleurs-de-lis; Félibien des Avaux, *Invalides*, p. 301; Granet, p. 108; Pérau, p. 84; engr.* by Cochin in Pérau, pl. 44. (A copy of F.'s medallion was made by Cartellier in the 19th c., *Rich. Art Fr.*, *Mon. Rel.*, III, p. 238.) Destroyed during the Revolution.

46
Decoration in the Salon de l'Oeil-de-Boeuf, Versailles

1701
a.* Frieze with playing cupids
Bas-relief Stucco, gilded
F., Van Clève and Hurtrelle rec. 2100 L. for this work, designed by Hardouin-Mansart for the new Grand Salon du Roi, *Comptes*, IV, 709; V, 526; order of the King to Hardouin-Mansart 24 April 1701, Arch. Nat., O¹ 1809, fol. 72. Another team, incl. Hardy, Poirier and Poultier, rec. the same sum for another part of this frieze. P. de Nolhac attribs. the frieze at the side of the Grande Galerie to F.'s team, because of its livelier style, *Hist. du Chât. de Vers.*, II, 172. The frieze shows cupids playing against a background of mosaic work.
b.* Two young genies with a garland
Bas-relief Stucco, gilded
On either side of the oval attic window above the fireplace, executed by Van Clève and F. for 400 L., *Comptes*, V, 526.

VERSAILLES, PALACE

47*
Angel carrying the Sacred Ampoule

1701–5 Bas-relief Stone 240 × 310
On one of the four piers supporting the drum of the cupola, in the tympanum over the entrance leading to the Chapel of St.-Grégoire; cf. N. Coustou no. 33.

46b

Originally comm. from Lespingola, Arch. Nat., O[I] 1665, 47, it was done in 1701 by F., who rec. 1050 L. in 1701 and 1705 and possibly the rest in 1709, *Comptes*, IV, 727, 1177; V, 349; a similar angel by N. Coustou had been estim. at 1500 L. F.'s angel holding the ampoule is accomp. by two child angels carrying a crown and a sceptre. Félibien des Avaux, *Invalides*, p. 301; Granet, p. 108; Pérau, p. 82, incl. engr. by Cochin, pl. 42.

PARIS, DOME DES INVALIDES

47

48
Vase

1702–6 Marble H: 156
One of four vases, after a single model by Mazeline, for the steps descending to the Bassin des Nappes at Marly; the other three by N. Coustou (no. 39★), Poirier and Mazeline himself. Descr. in the Invent. Arch. Nat., O[I] 1969[A]. F. rec. several payments, total at least 3360 L.,

Comptes, IV, 734, 852, 963, 1184; V, 538. Payments for the three other vases only 2500 L. each. The extra payment to F. could therefore cover another vase done at the same time, but at first intended for Marly, see no. 49.

PARIS, TUILERIES GARDEN

49★
Vase

1702–6 White marble H: 124
Mentioned by Piganiol, *Vers.-Marly*, 1707 et seq. as in the park at Trianon, together with three other vases by Jouvenet, François (no. 22) and Mazeline. Payment, together with no. 48 above (?). Acc. to the Invent., Arch. Nat., O[I] 1976[A], p. 764–5, which wrongly attribs. all four vases to Jouvenet, they were all similar:

49

51

the body undecorated, the grooves with floral orna-ments at the base, the mouldings and the neck carved. All four now in the Tuileries Garden.

PARIS, TUILERIES GARDEN

50
Work for the Pièce des Vents, Marly

1703   Groups in gilded lead   H: c. 200
    a. *Tritons carrying fishes*
    b. *Shells, Heads of monsters and winds*
cf. N. Coustou no. 43★. 11,760 L. were paid for this work to F., Van Clève, Dedieu (no. 42), Lepautre, Le Lorrain and Lapierre, *Comptes*, IV, 964, 1072. The Pièce des Vents was destroyed at the end of the 18th c. There is a water-colour drawing of the Bassin, Arch. Nat., O^I 1472, p. 8. Destroyed.

51
Nymphs and Children

1703–7   Group   Marble   H: 260
"A group of two female figures seated on rocks, repr. two rivers. One of them holds in her left hand a large bunch of water-plants and in her lowered right, a cornucopia with corn sheaves and fruits; her hair is decorated with rushes; behind her a little girl lies on the rocks; she leans on her right hand and dips her left in the water flowing from underneath the rock covered with large plants and shells; the other figure, also almost nude, rests her right hand on the shoulder of the first one, holding an oar in her lowered left arm, her hair also decor. with rushes and large leaves; behind her a child holding a fish, apparently frightened by it . . . , by Flamen", Invent., Arch. Nat., O^I 1969 A, p. 168. Pendant to Hurtrelle's 'Nymphs' in the Pièce des Nappes, Marly. The two other corners of the Bassin were decorated with 'The Seine and the Marne' by N. Coustou (no. 22) and 'The Loire and the Loiret' by Van Clève. Payment 14,000 L., *Comptes*, IV, 963,

1072, 1184; V, 40, 538. The two groups by F. and Hurtrelle remained in position throughout the 18th c. (descr. by Piganiol, *Vers.–Marly* and Dezallier, *Environs de P.*, all eds.), until the Revolution. Either F.'s or Hurtrelle's group was stored at the Palais du Corps Législatif; then, in 1800, in the Mus. des Mon. Fr., *Arch. du. Mus. des Mon. Fr.*, II, 454–6, nos. 10, 11, 13, 15; after that, its traces are lost. Drawing in Stockholm, THC 5129★ and Berlin, Kunstbibliothek, Hdz. 2625a, bl. 32. Whereabouts unknown.

52
Diana

1704 or earlier   Bronze
Exh. Salon 1704, *Livret*, p. 34. Not ident. or disapp.

53
Head of Flora

1704 or earlier   Bronze
Exh. Salon 1704, *Livret*, p. 34. Not ident. or disapp.

57

55

56

54
Cupidon

1704 or earlier   Statue   Marble
Exh. Salon 1704, *Livret*, p. 37. Not ident. or disapp.

55–57
Statues for the Chapel, Versailles

1707
55* St. Philip
Tonnerre stone   H: 290
The Saint carries a cross, instrument of his martyrdom.
Mém., Arch. Nat., O^I 1784.
56* St. Bartholomew
Tonnerre stone   H: 290
The Saint carries "his flayed skin and a cutlass, which is
also the instrument of his martyrdom", Mém., *ibid.*
57* St. Irenaeus
Tonnerre stone   H: 290
"Dressed as a Greek Father, holding a book indicating
his piety and his eloquence", Mém., *ibid.* Hurtrelle had
made a model for the Saint: "Il est bon que l'on scache
que j'ay fait deux modèles pasablement grand, asses
finis apres des abis grecques qu'il me falut trouver, on
m'en a hauté une", Mém., *ibid.* Payment for each
statue, 1000 L., *Comptes* V, 123, 526.
The statues stand on the exterior balustrade of the
chapel, on the north side.

VERSAILLES PALACE, CHAPEL

58*
Companion of Diana

1710–14   Group   Marble   H: 150
Signed: FAIT PAR ANSELME FLAMEN NATIF DE SAINT OMER
1714
For bibliogr., see Cayot no. 8. F. rec., together with

nine other sculptors (see Dedieu no. 49), a first payment
on account of 200 L. for a Companion of Diana for the
park at Marly, *Comptes*, V, 432. Completed in 1714;
total payment 3600 L., incl. two other instalments,
Comptes, V, 787, 874. In 1722 in the Bosquet du

58

61

Parnasse at Marly, Invent., Arch. Nat., O^I 1769^A, O^I 1976^B, p. 203. During the Revolution, trsf. to Malmaison, then temporarily in the Louvre. Since 1884, in the Bosquet de la Reine at Versailles. Drawing Coll. de Cotte, Bibl. Nat. Est., Fb 26. Resting on her left leg, she lifts her right arm, looking at the (disappeared) bird on her hand; on her left, a hunting dog on its hind legs, which she holds on a leash.

VERSAILLES, PARK

59 60
Silence and Eloquence

Before 1711 Two statues Tonnerre stone
Although intended for the niches in the Salon Haut of the Chapel, Versailles, they were actually put in the Salon of the Château Neuf at Meudon. Since then they have disappeared. Payment 1000 L. for each, Mém., Arch. Nat., O^I 1784; *Comptes*, V, 526. Not ident. or disapp.

61*
Angel with Lance

1712–13 Statue Bronze H: 182
Payment 200 L. for the model, 400 L. for the bronze, *Comptes*, V, 610, 787. One of six angels carrying the instruments of the Passion for the choir of Notre-Dame; erected in acc. with the vow of Louis XIII. cf. P. Bertrand no. 28.

PARIS, NOTRE-DAME

62
Companion of Diana, *also called 'La Chasse au Cailleau' (The Quail-hunt)*

1714 Group Marble
For bibliogr., see Cayot no. 8. Made for Marly; put up in 1714, payment 3600 L. in 1716, *Comptes*, V, 874; c. 1722, temporarily stored in the Louvre, Arch. Nat., O^I 1976^B, p. 332; then in 1746, in the Chât. de la Muette, Arch. Nat., O^I 1583, where Dezallier mentions it as 'Nymph returning from Fishing' *Environs de P.*, 1762, p. 15. Since then, lost. Drawing*, Coll. de Cotte, Bibl. Nat. Est., Fb 26. The nymph held in both hands a hunting-net with captured birds. Whereabouts unknown.

UNDATED WORK

63
The Annunciation

Bas-relief Gilded bronze
Composed of two parts; decorated the retable of the High Altar of the Carmélites Déchaussées in the rue St.-Jacques, where it replaced a painting by Guidi, cf. Brice, *Descr.*, 1725, III, p. 98; Dezallier, *Paris*, 1752, p. 265; Thiery, *Guide*, 1787, II, p. 253. This is the only work F. did for the convent, cf. J. Vanuxem, 'Les sculptures de l'église des Carmélites', in *BSHAF*, 1939, p. 57–74. On 28 Sept. 1792 the bas-relief was sent to the Petits Augustins, A. Lenoir, *Catal. Dépôt provisoire des Petits Augustins*, 1793, no. 115. In 1798, sent to be melted down, Lenoir, *Descr. hist. des mon. de sculpt. au Mus. Mon. Fr.*, 1798, no. 262. Arch. Mus. Mon. Fr., 11, 60, 191.

62

FONTELLE, François (?–before 1695)

Active between 1671 and 1688; died before 1695. Sculpteur-décorateur, employed for the Menus Plaisirs of the King. Maintenance and restoration in the Park and Palace, Versailles, *Comptes*, I, 1161, 1287; II, 20, 180, 181, 197, 207, 315, 335, 347, 438, 463, 472, 616–17, 891; added vine leaves to several statues, *Comptes*, II, 1116. cf. Dussieux, *Le chât. de Vers.*, 1881, II, p. 208. His work in Versailles is often not clearly identifiable, *Comptes*, II, 59, 163, 890–1; III, 36. T–B, XII, 1916, p. 192.

1
Cornice at the attic of the Palace, Versailles

1671–2   Stucco
Payment 3290 L. 11s.8d. in two instalm., *Comptes*, I, 514, 615. Not identified.

2
Work at the Hôtel de Condé, Paris

1676
cf. Mâcon, *Les Arts dans la Maison des Condé*, Paris, p. 20. Contract 29 Apr. 1676, with F. "for work in the grotto de Rocaille, stucco and sculpture work to be done in the Appartment of the Prince in the Hôtel de Condé, amounting to 1100 L." Destroyed.

3
Vases and Consoles for the Palace, Versailles

1679–84
F. rec. "for the vases he made at the side of the grotto", 300 L., *Comptes*, I, 116. "For several vases and consoles he made at the right wing of the forecourt of the Palace", 675 L., *Comptes*, I, 1287. "For the vases and consoles in St.-Leu stone for the Petit Château at Versailles", 200 L., *Comptes*, II, 438. Destroyed.

4
Trophies for the Swiss Guards, Versailles Palace

1680
Payment 1000 L., *Comptes*, I, 1287. Destroyed.

5
Ornaments in the Grand Vestibule facing the Parterre d'Eau, Versailles Palace

1680
Payment 1000 L., *Comptes*, I, 1287. Not ident. or disapp.

6
Work on the Cornices of the Palace, Versailles

1680
Payment 500 L., *Comptes*, I, 1287. Not ident. or disapp.

7
Consoles for Benches in the Petit Parc

1680–1   Marble
Payment 1299 L. 10s. in three instalm., *Comptes*, I, 1287; II, 20, 64.

VERSAILLES, PARK

8
Work at the Appartement des Bains, Versailles

1681–3   Stucco and plaster
Payment 105 L., *Comptes*, II, 15; and 1596 L. 16s. together with Raon, *Comptes*, II, 317. Destroyed.

9
Work at Queen's Chapel, Versailles

1681–2
Payment 825 L., *Comptes*, II, 23, 158. Not ident. or disapp.

10
Work at the Church of Notre-Dame, Versailles

1681
Payment 101 L., *Comptes*, II, 203. Not ident. or disapp.

11
Two Trophies at the South Wing, Versailles

1681–2   Stone
Payments 500 L. and 300 L., *Comptes*, II, 10, 158. Probably large trophies, standing on the balustrade of the roof. Destroyed.

12
Four vases for the South Wing, Versailles

1682   Stone
Payment 760 L., *Comptes*, II, 170. Between the large trophies, cf. no. 11. Destroyed.

13★
Work in the Salle de Bal, Versailles Park

1682
   a.★ Four mortars
Lead and tin
Payment 1800 L., *Comptes*, II, 139, 314.

VERSAILLES, PARK

   b. *Model for a pedestal table*
Payment 573 L., *Comptes*, II, 204. Disappeared. The tables★, in rock-work, are extant.

13a

13b

14
Three Carved Frames for Versailles Palace

1682
Above the mantel-pieces in the Apartment of the Marquise de Seignelay. Payment 130 L., *Comptes*, II, 205. Not ident. or disapp.

15
Work at the Bassin Sous le Dragon

1682–6
  a. Two Vases
  b. Two Shells, Two Basins and Two Masks
Payment 5408 L. 18s., incl. two vases in white marble, cf. no. 16., *Comptes*, II, 140, 278–9; IV, 7, 62. cf. Carlier no. 3*.

VERSAILLES, PARK

  c. *Model Plaster*
In collab. with Mazière. Payment 862 L., *Comptes*, III, 1093, 1140. Disappeared.

16
Two Vases

1682   Marble
For the Petit Parc, Versailles, cf. no. 15. First on the balustrade of the Orangery; in 1692 trsf. to the Bassin du Grand Jet in the Park at Marly, cf. Invent. 1695, Arch. Nat., O^I 1460^{126}. Not ident. or disapp.

17
Work for the Funeral Service of Queen Marie-Thérèse in Notre-Dame, Paris

1683   Cardboard and plaster
F. supplied all the decor. for the catafalque of the Queen: the four Virtues of Faith, Hope, Charity and Religion at the four corners, 30 death's-heads in the tympanums between the pyramids, 50 heads to carry the obelisks,

13

17

19

20

consoles, and coats-of-arms of the Queen and the royal crown, lions' paws under the coffin and four death's-heads on the coffin, cf. Arch. des Menus Plaisirs, Arch. Nat., O^I 2218, 19, 20, publ. in Chennevière, *NAAF*, 1886, p. 162–5. Fee 600 L. Engr.★ in Bibl. Nat. Est., Coll. Hennin, 5315, p. 32. Destroyed.

18
Ornaments on Two Dormer Windows, Versailles Palace

1685   Lead
Comptes, II, 617. Payment 300 L. Not ident. or disapp.

19

1686   Medallion   Marble   71 × 60   Signed on the back: F. FONTELLE. FECIT. 1686

VERSAILLES, MUSEUM

20★
Portrait of Antoine Meusnier, Painter

1688   Medallion   Marble   60 × 45
From the Mus. des Mon. Fr. On the back: ANTONIUS. MEUSNIER PICTOR. III. IIIIII REGIUS.LUDVICO MAGNO ACCEPTUS ILSCUT PLAIRE. AU PLUS GRAND DES ROYS F. ^{S}FONTELLE .FECIT. 1688.
cf. G. Brière, 'Sculpt. fr. des XVIIe et XVIIIe s. au Mus. de Vers.', in *BSHAF*, 1923, p. 67.

VERSAILLES, MUSEUM

21
Two Groups of Children

Lead
Acc. to the Invent. of the Statues at Marly, 15 July 1695, Arch. Nat., O^I 1460^{126}, six groups of children, two of them by F., from the Allée de la Pyramide, Versailles, were placed around the Bassin du Grand Jet. Not ident. or disapp.

FRANÇOIS, Louis (1641?-?)

Son of Nicolas François, joiner, painter and sculptor, and Marguerite Cochy, who lived in the rue Beaubourg, contract of 6 Jan. 1633 in Min. Centr. Arch. Nat., Et. XX, 206 (inform. Mlle. Rambaud). Baptised 18 Aug. 1641, Bibl. Nat. Ms., Fich. Laborde 28010. Member of the Acad. St.-Luc from 1675, cf. Guiffrey, *St.-Luc.*, IX. Married Geneviève Asseline; one son, Pierre, born in 1666, also a sculptor, who became Director of the Acad. St.-Luc, Bibl. Nat., *ibid.*, 28034, 28037. T-B., XII, 1916, p. 374.

FRANÇOIS, Jean (1643?-1714/19)

Younger brother of Louis. Lami thought he was identical with a Jean-Nicolas François who in 1681-3 worked in the Salle du Conseil of the Town Hall at Dijon, Arch. Comm. de Dijon, M 257, fol. 687. A Nicolas François, younger brother of Louis F., was baptised on 16 Aug. 1643, Bibl. Nat., *ibid.*, 28011. On 29 May 1676, Jean F. was sculptor at the Acad. St.-Luc, cf. J. Guiffrey, *St.-Luc*, IX. Jean F. married Marie-Anne Thibault; they had three daughters. He died between 1714-19, cf. Bail (lease) of 22 May 1703, Min. Centr. Arch. Nat., Et. I, 222 and quittance of 15 Oct. 1719, Et. II, 55 (inform. Mlle. Rambaud). T-B., XII, 1916, p. 372.

Abbreviations:
L = work by Louis François
J = work by Jean François
LJ = work done in collaboration
U = work which may have been done by either

I (L)
Cornices in the King's Apartment, Versailles Palace

1671-3   Stucco
Under the direction of Le Vau. Payment 1606 L. 10s. in two instalm., *Comptes*, I, 514, 697. Not ident. or disapp.

2 (U)
Six Vases for Versailles

1672
In collab. with Leclerc. Payment 450 L. *Comptes*, I, 618. Not ident. or disapp.

3 (U)
Consoles for the Château de Clagny

1679   Stone
Payment 60 L. on account, *Comptes*, I, 1191. Destroyed.

4 (J)
Great Portal of the Hôtel Royal des Invalides

1680   Wood
Mém. of work begun 15 July 1680, Arch. de la Guerre, Fonds Invalides, Carton 17, Liasse C. Design by Hardouin-Mansart. Estim. 1460 L. Decoration: in the soffit. Minerva sitting on trophies, and a winged child with a laurel branch, holding a medallion with the coat-of-arms of France⋆; on each of the two panels of the half-doors, under the transom, two seated winged children holding a helmet⋆; underneath, two friezes with trophies of arms and laurels⋆.

PARIS, HOTEL DES INVALIDES

4[1]

4²

4³

5 (J)
Work for the South Wing

1682
    a. Statue   Stone
    b. *Undefined work*
In collab. with Couet. Total payment 960 L. in three instalm., *Comptes*, II, 12, 136, 178. Not ident.

VERSAILLES, PALACE
See appendix.

6 (J)
Work at the Château of Saint Germain-en-Laye

1684–5
Payment 811 L., *Comptes*, II, 516, 803; on the balustrade of the Château and the Queen's Pavilion. Not ident. or disapp.

7 (L)
Work on the Colonnade

1684–7
    a. Eight Ionic capitals   Marble
Payment 1808 L. in three instalm., *Comptes*, II, 442, 623, 989.

    b. Guillochés for two arcades
Payment 640 L. in two instalm., *Comptes*, II, 623, 989.
    c. Foot for a bassin   Marble
Payment 400 L. in two instalm., *Comptes*, II, 989, 1175.
cf. Cornu no. 17*.

VERSAILLES, PARK

8 (J)
Two Ionic Pilaster Capitals

1686   Marble
Payment 280 L., *Comptes*, II, 1175; III, 94.

VERSAILLES, GRAND TRIANON

9 (L)
Two Ionic Pilaster Capitals

1686   Marble
Payment 345 L., *Comptes*, II, 1175; III, 94. cf. André no. 11*.

VERSAILLES, GRAND TRIANON

10 (L)
Six Great Cassolettes

1688   Stone
For the corners of the balustrade on the roof of the Grand Trianon. cf. Cornu no. 20. In collab. with Dufour. Payment 1200 L., *Comptes*, III, 37. Drawing in the Coll. de Cotte, Bibl. Nat. Est., Va 78 g, 2. Destroyed.

11 (LJ)
Work for the Twelve Pavilions at Marly

1688–9
    a. *Vases*
Payment 7237 L. in three instalm., *Comptes*, III, 167, 337, 472.
    b. *Forty-eight carved Ornamental Copings*
In collab. with Vigier and Roussel. Payment 5280 L., *Comptes*, III, 167, 337. Pavilions built after Le Brun's design.
Destroyed.

12 (J)
Woodwork in the Salon of the Château de Chantilly

1689
In collab. with Noël Briquet. Payment 1505 L. 15s; receipts 5 Feb. and 15 May 1691, Arch. du Mus. Condé, *Comptes*, 1690, fol. 114; 1691, fol. 121 vo., cf. A. Vial, *Les artistes décor. du bois*, 1922, I, p. 198; Mâcon, *Les Arts dans la maison de Condé*, p. 43–4. Destroyed.

13 (LJ)
Woodwork in the Church of Chantilly

1690–1
Contract "sous seing privé" (private contract) 9 June, 1690, payment 850 L. in two instalm., Arch. du Mus. Condé, Comptes, 1690, fol. 116; 1691, fol. 121. Not ident. or disapp.

DECORATIVE SCULPTURE ON THE DOME DES INVALIDES

14 (U)
Sculptures above the windows of the Aisles in the Church of the Invalides

1690   Stone
Payment 330 L., *Comptes*, III, 423; there are probably garlands above the first storey windows on both exterior side walls.

PARIS, DOME DES INVALIDES

15 (J)
Great Cornice and Architrave inside the Dôme des Invalides

1691–9   Stone
In coll. with Massou and others, after Jouvenet's design; work on the cornice, 109 toises long (213 metres), 263 roses, 287 modillions. Payment 4555 L. 5s. in several instalm., *Comptes*, III, 558, 702; IV, 331, 472, V, 349.

PARIS, DOME DES INVALIDES

16 (J)
Sculpture on Ten Transverse Ribs in the Dôme des Invalides

1691–1700
   a. *Work on a Model of the Transverse ribs*
In collab. with a team; payment 136 L. 4s. 2d., *Comptes*, III, 560. Destroyed.
   b. Sculpture in stone on the Transverse Ribs
In collab. with a team which rec. 5250 L. in six instalm., *Comptes*, III, 560, 704, 843; IV, 331, 472, 612. Arch. Nat., O¹ 1665, 32.

PARIS, DOME DES INVALIDES

17 (U)
Sculpture on Two Pendentives

1700–03
Model by F. and Lespingola, payment 280 L. in 1700, *Comptes*, IV, 511. Executed in stone by F., Lespingola and J. Desjardins. Payment 3524 L. in several instalm., *Comptes*, IV, 610, 727; V, 34.

PARIS, DOME DES INVALIDES

18 (U)
Ornaments on the Dôme des Invalides

1703
In collab. with Hardy and Lespingola. Payment 420 L., *Comptes*, IV, 956; V, 349. Not ident. or disapp.

19
Corinthian Capitals

1702   Stone
   a. Capital for the Tribune (J)
For a column inside the Chapel. Payment together with other work, *Comptes*, V, 415.
   b. Three groups of Capitals in the Interior (U)
Estims. for 706 L., 353 L., and 1000 L. Payments from 1702–9, *Comptes*, IV, 828, 939, 1049; V, 321.
   c. Four Pilaster Capitals on the Exterior (U)
Estim. 1000 L. Paid in 1708–9, *Comptes*, V, 214, 321.

VERSAILLES PALACE, CHAPEL

20 (J)
Two Mosaic Panels

1702   Stone
Under the window-ledges in the Chapel of the Virgin, *Comptes*, V, 415.

VERSAILLES PALACE, CHAPEL

21 (U)
Saint Monica

1705   Statue   Plaster
Payment 600 L., *Comptes*, IV, 1176; V, 234. In a niche of the Chapel of St.-Augustin in the Church of the Dôme des Invalides. Originally comm. from G. Coustou; drawing in the Coll. de Cotte, Bibl. Nat. Est., Hc 14, 2. Engr.* by Cochin in Pérau, pl. 91; cf. Dezallier,

21

Paris, 1749, p. 274; Félibien des Avaux, *Invalides*, p. 302; Granet, p. 111; Pérau, p. 81. Replaced by a marble statue of the Saint by Houdon. Destroyed. *See appendix.*

22 (U)
Vase

1703   Marble   H: 124
Payment of 950 L., *Comptes*, IV, 963, 1074; V, 42 for a pendant to a vase by Jouvenet at the Cascade Rustique, Marly. Later trsf. to the Parterre haut at the Trianon, where Piganiol, *Vers.-Marly*, 1707 p. 377, noted it together with two other vases by Flamen (no. 49★) and Mazeline. Descr. in Invent., Arch. Nat., O^I 1976^A, p. 764–5 where all four are wrongly attrib. to Jouvenet. All were made after the same model. Now in the Tuileries Garden.

PARIS, TUILERIES GARDEN

23 (U)
Sculpture at the Bassins des Carpes, Marly

1704
In collab. with Hardy, Lespingola, Poirier, Thierry, Armand, Poultier, J.-L. Lemoyne, Lapierre, Monthéan, Voiriot, Offement. Payment 14,500 L., *Comptes*, IV, 1101. Destroyed.

24 (J)
Four Gargoyles

1704   Stone
In collab. with Hardy, Lespingola and Poirier. Payment 720 L., *Comptes*, IV, 1049 and Mém., Arch. Nat., O^I 1784.

VERSAILLES PALACE, CHAPEL

25 (J)
Ornaments on the Cornice of Versailles

1704   Stone

In collab. with Hardy, Lespingola and Poirier. Payment on account 500 L., *Comptes*, IV, 1049.

VERSAILLES, PALACE

26 (LJ)
Roses and Modillions

1704–5   Stone
L.F. carved 50 roses, estim. at 300 L., and 50 modillions estim. at 753 L., Mém., Arch. Nat., O^I 1784; *Comptes*, IV, 1048, 1158; J.F. carved 100 roses, estim. at 600 L., and 100 modillions, estim. at 2500 L., in collab. with a team, Mém., Arch. Nat., O^I 1784; *Comptes*, IV, 1157.

VERSAILLES, PALACE

27 (U)
Decorations on the Roof of the Chapel

1705–7   Lead
In collab. cf. Dedieu no. 45★. *Comptes*, V, 412.

VERSAILLES PALACE, CHAPEL

28 (U)
Two Vases for the Park, Versailles

1706   Marble
In collab. with Poirier and Lespingola. Payment on account 500 L., *Comptes*, V, 41. Not ident. or disapp.

29 (J)
Fifty-three Metopes

1707–09   Stone
For the frieze of the great external cornice. In collab. with Rousseau de Corbeil. Several payments, 500 L., 920 L., 300 L., 1600 L., the latter incl. work listed below, *Comptes*, V, 215, 316, 528.

VERSAILLES PALACE, CHAPEL

31

30 (J)
Sculptures on the Bases of Columns, Capitals and Pilasters

1708   Stone
In collab. with Rousseau de Corbeil, *Comptes*, V, 215.

VERSAILLES PALACE, CHAPEL

31 (J)★
Child Angels playing Trumpet and Triangle

1708   Bas-relief   Stone   L: 356
On the exterior of the Chapel at Versailles, above the arch of a window, cf. Mém., Arch. Nat., O^I 1784. Estim. for the bas-relief 1000 L., payment together with other works, *Comptes*, V, 215, 415. Very much restored, if not entirely re-carved, at the end of the 19th c., Arch. Nat., F^{21} 888, F^{21} 3474^c.

VERSAILLES PALACE, CHAPEL

32 (U)
Ornaments at the Bases of Columns and Pilasters of the Tribune

1708   Stone
With a team, cf. Defer, no. 5 b. Payment 15,576 L., in 1711, *Comptes*, V, 529.

VERSAILLES PALACE, CHAPEL

33 (U)
Work at Meudon

1709
Payment 20,300 L. to a team, for undefined work at the "Bâtiments" at Meudon, *Comptes*, V, 300. Destroyed.

34 (U)
Ornaments on the Ceiling of the Salon Bas

1710
Various ornaments on the flat mouldings and cornices, repair of Ionic capitals, team-work estim. at 8702 L. 10s., Mém., Arch. Nat., O^I 1784; *Comptes*, V, 529. cf. André no. 13a.

VERSAILLES, PALACE

35 (U)
Sculpture on the Window Frames

1711
In collab. with Dugoullon and others. Total payment 5394 L., *Comptes*, V, 531.

VERSAILLES PALACE, CHAPEL

FREMERY, Nicolas (?-after 1687)

b. and d. in Paris, acc. to Piganiol, *Vers.-Marly*, 1701, p. 408. Little is known about his life: on 28 Dec. 1680, he rec. a 2nd prize from the Acad. (see no. 1), and went for at least four years to Rome, *Corr. Dir. Acad. Fr. Rome*, I, 102, 122. Between 1684-7, he worked at Versailles. Lived in the parish of St.-Hippolyte; married Charlotte Canonville; two children, born in 1675 and 1676, Bibl. Nat. Ms., Fich. Laborde 28145-6-7. T-B, XII, 1916, p. 416-17.

We do not know how he was related to the sculptor Martin F., who lived in the same parish, and was Menuisier des Bâtiments du Roi. Martin F. worked in 1655 in St.-Germain-des-Prés (Min. Centr. Arch. Nat., Et. CX, 97, estimate for choir-chairs 17 Feb. 1655); in St.-Etienne-du-Mont (work on the pulpit, Bibl. Nat. Est., Va 259c); in 1666-8 in the Tuileries, *Comptes*, I, 126-7, 185, 245; in 1673 at the Château de Saverne as architect and supervisor, Arch. Bas-Rhin, Fonds Saverne, fasc. 107, cf. H. Wollbrett, *Le chât. de Saverne*, 1969, p. 31; in 1678 in Clagny, *Comptes*, I, 1076; in 1685, he built the high altar of the cathedral in Strasbourg, cf. Dacheux, *La cathédrale de Strasbourg*, 1900, p. 121. Before 1655, Martin F. had married Jeanne Pillon and had several children, whose names, known from a document dated 1693, do not include Nicolas, who might have been dead at that date, Bibl. Nat. Ms., Fich. Laborde 28148 and Min. Centr. Arch. Nat., Et. XXIII, 369.

1
The Fratricide of Cain

1680
2nd Acad. prize, *P-V*, II, 172; Duvivier, *AAF*, Documents 1857-8, p. 278; Guiffrey, *Liste des Pensionnaires*, 1908. Not ident. or disapp.

2★
Urania

Before 1684   Statue   Marble   H: c. 200
Copied in Rome after the antique at the Capitol. Sent to Versailles; placed on the north ramp of the Parterre de Latone. Urania holds a telescope and a parchment roll, with the signs of the zodiac, cf. *Corr. Dir. Acad. Fr. Rome*, I, 130; Piganiol, *Vers.-Marly*, 1701, p. 198.

VERSAILLES, PARK

3★
Faustina

Before 1684   Statue   Marble   H: over 200
Copied in Rome after the antique; placed on the far side of the Bassin de Neptune in Versailles; Piganiol, *ibid.*, p. 183.

VERSAILLES, PARK

4
Apollo

Before 1684   Statue   Marble
Copied after the Medici Apollo, cf. *Corr. Acad. Fr.
Rome*, I, 129. Placed in a green arbour to the west of
the Château de Marly, cf. Piganiol, *ibid.*, p. 390 and other
editions. Not in the Invent. of 1722. Not ident. or disapp.

5*
Venus de Medici

1687   Statue   Marble   H: over 200
Begun by Monnier, finished after his death by F., who
rec. 300 L., *Comptes*, II, 1175. Placed on the north ramp
of the Allée Royale.

VERSAILLES, PARK

5

2

3

Detail

FREMIN, René (1672-1722)

b. Paris 1 Oct. 1672, son of Jean Frémin, master gold-smith, living at the Quai des Orfèvres at the Pont au Change, and of his second wife, Marguerite Tartarin, niece of the painter Charles de La Fosse, director of the Acad. in 1700. Two of F.'s brothers, Jean and Antoine, also became goldsmiths; two others, Jacques and Léon, entered the church. About F.'s family, see Bibl. Nat. Ms., Fich. Laborde 28166, 28168, 28187 and Min. Centr. Arch. Nat., actes notariés de l'Et. X, liasses 244, 245, 248, 300, 350, 376/8, 381, 387, 393, 429, 445, 448/9. F. was a pupil of Girardon and Coysevox, *Corr. Dir. Acad. Fr. Rome*, II, 158, 168, 205. In 1694, a first sculpt. prize, see no. 1. Went to Rome in April with the painters Favanne and Cartaud; stayed until the end of 1699, working for the Jesuits at Gesù, then at the Acad. for the King, *Corr. Dir. Acad. Fr. Rome*, II, 128 ff., 205 ff., 301 ff., 403 ff.; III, 2. After his return to Paris, he lived at the Quai des Morfondus. Pres. to the Acad. 24 Apr. 1700, made Academician 27 Aug. 1701, *P-V*, III, 293, 295, 324. From 1704-7, lived in Les Fossés Mr.-le.Prince, then, in 1707, in the Quai de l'Horloge du Palais. Became Asst. Prof. 30 Dec. 1706, *ibid.*, IV, 36. Married on 22 Nov. 1707 Suzanne Cartaud, daughter of the architect Sylvain Cartaud and Marguerite Dubugra, Bibl. Nat. Ms., Fich. Laborde 28188; of their two sons, Jean-Sylvain became conseiller du roi, maître en sa Chambre des Comptes; Claude-René, Secrétaire du Roi, maison et couronne de France, et de ses finances, Min. Centr. Arch. Nat., Et. X, 447, comptes du 30 Mar. 1739. In 1716, F. lived in the Galeries du Louvre, *NAAF*, 1873, p. 83. Invited by Philip V of Spain to work at his Palace at La Granja de San Ildefonso, near Segovia, F. rec. permission on 14 Jan. 1721, *NAAF*, 1878, p. 20, *P-V*, IV, 314; Min. Centr. Arch. Nat., Et. X, 352, procuration 8 May 1721. The sculptor J. Bousseau agreed to complete F.'s unfinished work in Paris and Versailles, contract 22 April 1721, Min. Centr. Arch. Nat., Et. X, 352. F. departed on 13 May, with the sculptor Thierry, *Mercure*,

May 1721, p. 141. Philippe V appointed him director of the workshop at Valsain, salary 4000 L., *Mercure*, June 1721, p. 129. His wife, Suzanne Cartaud, died in Paris 4 Nov. 1730, Min. Centr. Arch. Nat., Et. X, 428; Invent. a.d. 13 Jan. 1734. He was made First Sculptor to the King of Spain on 28 Sept. 1733 with a salary of 2000 ducats and letters patent of nobility for himself and his children; while on leave in France, he bought the office of 'Secretaire du roi du Grand Collège'; he finally returned to France in 1738. During his stay in Spain, F. accumulated an immense fortune (cf. Mariette, *ABC*, II, 272), increased by numerous inheritances from his father, his mother, his sister Elizabeth, his aunts, his mother-in-law (Min. Centr. Arch. Nat., Et. X, 248, 300, 350, 429, 447, 449; XXIV, 659). He invested this money, Min. Centr. Arch. Nat., Et. X, 300, 337, 339, 447, 453, 473, made numerous loans, bought houses. On 7 July 1742, the Acad. appointed him Director, then on 31 Jan. 1744 Recteur in place of Rigaud, *P-V*, V, 324, 346, 351, 360. He died in the Louvre on 17 Feb. 1744, Testament dated 30 April 1742, deposited 18 Feb. 1744 and Invent. a.d. 27 Feb. 1744, Min. Centr. Arch. Nat., Et. X, 465; partage de ses biens, *ibid.*, 466. cf. Mariette, *ABC*, 1853-4, II, 272; Chevalier de Valory, *Mém. inéd.*, II, 201-9; Fontenai, I, p. 612; Dezallier, *Vie*, II, p. 232; Jal, p. 614-15; Herluison, p. 146; 'Essai d'armorial des art. fr.', in *RSBAD*, 1904, p. 619; T-B, XII, 1916, p. 417-18.
Several portraits of Frémin: 1.) Oil painting by Autreau, 1741 (Louvre). 2.) Pastel by M. Quentin de La Tour (Louvre). Engr. by P.-L. Surugue★, 1747. 3.) A smaller pastel, also by La Tour, cf. A. Besnard and G. Wilden-stein, *La Tour*, 1928, no. 153.

1

Lot and his Daughters leaving the Town of Sodom

1694   Bas-relief
1st Sculpture prize, Acad.; *P-V*, III, 149, 152; *AAF*, V, 1857/8, p. 282. Not ident or disapp.

2

Work for the Altar of Saint-Ignatius in Gesù, Rome

1695-6   Two models for bronze bas-reliefs   H: c.100
   a.★ Invocation of St. Ignatius to extinguish a fire.
   b.★ Healing of the maimed and the sick with oil from a lamp burning before the shrine of the saint.
Comm. by the Jesuits first from Le Lorrain, then from F. who supplied models in terracotta after an oil painting by Father Pozzo. The first cast by G. Piserone, the second by A. Cordier. These are the first and sixth reliefs from the left incorporated in the base of the altar, *Corr. Dir. Acad. Fr. Rome*, II, p. 168, 172, 175-6, 184, 189, 191, 205-6, 211, 216, 223; cf. F. Titi, *Studio di pittura, scultura nelle chiese di Roma*, 1721, p. 190; A. Nibby, *Roma nell'anno 1838*.

ROME, GESU

2a

2b

3
Draped Figure leaning on a Vase

1697–9   Marble
Carved at the Acad. Fr. in Rome after an antique; for
the park at Versailles, *Corr. Dir. Acad. Fr. Rome*, II,
p. 296 ff., 301 ff., 403 ff. Not ident. or disapp.

4
Saint celebrating Mass

Before 1699   Bas-relief
Known through a red chalk drawing★ by Bouchardon,
done in Rome, Louvre, Cab. Dessins inv. 23914, cf.
Guiffrey–Marcel, *Invent.*, no. 514. Not ident. or disapp.

5   6
Alpheus and Arethusa

Between 1700–06   Two statues   Stone
Comm. by Fleuriau d'Armenonville, owner of the
estate of Rambouillet, for 1587 L. Two recumbent
figures repr. a river and a stream, framed the landing-
stage of the canal in the park at Rambouillet, cf. Arch.
de Rambouillet, Invent. des gros meubles laissés par
M. d'Armenonville; A. Moutié, *Notice hist. sur le chât.
de Rambouillet*, 1850, p. 74 and Longnon, *Petite monog.
de Rambouillet*, undated, p. 29. Disappeared.

4

7

7*
Time revealing Truth

1700–1   Bas-relief   Marble   95 × 80
Reception piece for the Acad. 27 Aug. 1701, *P-V*, III, p. 295, 324. cf. Guérin, *Descr. de l'Acad.*, 1715, p. 42. During the Revolution, removed to the Mus. des Mon. Fr., *Arch. du Mus. des Mon. Fr.*, 1897, III, p. 327. Time, a winged old man, and the small genie of the arts, holding a scythe, lift the cloth covering a nude, half-reclining young woman, repr. Truth.

8

Still extant today: 1.) Two fragments of the original marble, one with the figure of Time and the small genie; the other with the bust of Truth; Inv. p. 147. 2.) A painted plaster cast* of the original was taken before it was broken up (95 × 80); Inv. 7610.

PARIS, ECOLE DES BEAUX-ARTS

8
Saint Sylvia

1702   Statue   Plaster
Payments of 200, 250, 200 L. in 1705 and 1709, *Comptes*, IV, 1177; V, 348. Formerly in a niche in the Chapel of St.-Grégoire in the Dôme des Invalides. cf. Félibien des Avaux, *Invalides*, p. 302; Granet, p. 110; Pérau, p. 77. Replaced by a marble statue of the same subject by J.-J. Caffiéri, cf. C. Dreyfus, 'Les statues du Dôme des Inval.' in *BSHAF*, 1908. Pen drawing in Coll. de Cotte, Bibl. Nat. Est., Hc 14, 2. Engr.* by C.-N. Cochin in Pérau, pl. 91. Disappeared.

9*
Hercules abducting Deianera

c. 1704   Group   Stone   H: c. 300
Exh. Salon 1704, *Livret*, p. 31. Forty years later in the parterre in front of the Chât. de la Muette, cf. Invent. des sculpt., 1746, Arch. Nat., O^I 1583, publ. in *NAAF*, VIII, 1892, p. 359, descr. as 'in stone'. Probably acqu. by the Condé family between 1816–30; today in the park of the Château de Chantilly in the grass-covered northern amphitheatre. cf. Lemonnier, 'A propos d'un groupe de Frémin à Chantilly', in *RAAM*, 1920, I, p. 183–6. Hercules, in lion's skin, carrying Deianera in his arms, steps over the defeated Achelous, lying on the ground.

CHATEAU DE CHANTILLY, PARK

10
Mercury abducting Pandora

c. 1704   Group
Exh. Salon 1704, *Livret*, p. 29. Probably, like no. 9, in stone, of large dimensions. Disappeared.

11   12
Portraits of the Architect Cartaud and his Wife

c. 1704   Two busts
Exh. Salon 1704, *Livret*, p. 27, repr. either the architect Sylvain Cartaud (died 1703) and his wife Marguerite Dubugra, whose daughter F. married in 1707, or Jean-Sylvain (1675–1758), Sylvain's son, also an architect, and his wife Jeanne Bailly, whom he had married at the end of 1702. Disappeared.

9

Revolution; in the Palais Bourbon from 1797–1800, then in Malmaison; finally to the Louvre in 1877; cf. F. Boyer, 'Les stat. de Marly au Pal. Bourbon sous le 1er Empire', in *Rev. de l'hist. de Vers. et de S. et O.*, 1936, p. 165.

PARIS, LOUVRE

9

13
Decoration for the Small Baldachins of the Bains d'Apollon in the park at Versailles

1705 Lead
In collab. with a team, cf. P. Bertrand no. 12★. Total payment 1802 L., *Comptes*, V, 538. The small baldachins protected the groups of the sun-horses in the Bosquet du Marais from 1705–78. Demolished by Hubert Robert.

14
Flora

1706–9
a.★ Statue Marble H: 166 Signed: FREMIN AN⁰ 1709
One of the six statues at the Cascade Champêtre, Marly, cf. Barois no. 18. Payment 2200 L. in several instalm. from 1706 onwards, *Comptes*, V, 40, 72, 240 and 365. Descr. in the Invent., Arch. Nat., O^I 1969 A: "Half-covered, hair dressed with flowers, repr. Spring. In her right hand a bunch of flowers (broken off) and in her left, a flower garland connected to the tree-trunk which supports her". Saved by Lenoir during the

14a

14d

b. *A plaster version* of the statue was in the park of the Chât. de la Muette, Arch. Nat., O^I 1583, quoted in *NAAF*, XIV, 1892. Disappeared.

c. *Statue* Terracotta
Sale 15–16 May 1942 in the manor house of Belgrano, Switzerland, cat. no. 49 (reproduced). Whereabouts unknown.

d.* *Statue* Bronze H: 126
Kraemer sale, 28–29 April 1913, no. 120; version with variations. Attrib. to Frémin, certainly inspired by the marble statue. Disappeared.

e. Statue Marble
Coll. William A. Clark, 26702; probably a copy.

WASHINGTON, THE CORCORAN GALLERY OF ART

15
Group of Children

1707 Lead
In collab. with others, cf. P. Bertrand no. 17; after a model by Lepautre and G. Coustou. One of two groups

at the ends of the ridge of the chapel roof. Payment 3500 L., *Comptes*, V, 124.

VERSAILLES PALACE, CHAPEL

16
Cherub Heads

1707 Stone
In collab. with the same team, cf. P. Bertrand no. 16. On the keystones of the high windows of the chapel. Payment 700 L., *Comptes*, V, 124.

VERSAILLES PALACE, CHAPEL

17a
Father of the Church

1707 Medallion Bas-relief Hard stone, gilded, Diam: 62
One of six medallions; cf. P. Bertrand no. 18a*. Payment 150 L., *Comptes*, V, 124, 321, 531.

VERSAILLES PALACE, CHAPEL

17b
Ecclesiastical Trophy

1707 Bas-relief Hard stone, gilded 62 × 57
cf. P. Bertrand no. 18b*. *Comptes*, V, 124, 530–1.

VERSAILLES PALACE, CHAPEL

18*
Mortification and Moderation

1708 Bas-reliefs Bonbanc stone L: 194
Two female figures, seated, on the right of the Tribune; cf. P. Bertrand no. 19. Estim. 1600 L., *Mém.*, Arch. Nat., O^I 1784; *Comptes*, V, 214. 'Mortification' holds a lash, 'Moderation' an hour-glass and a bridle.

VERSAILLES PALACE, CHAPEL

18

(Bertrand 22)

Frémin 19

(Bertrand 23)

Frémin 20

19*
Allegory of the Crowning with Thorns

1709   Bas-relief   Bonbanc stone   195 × 270
In the spandrels of the arcade supporting the Royal
Tribune, as a pendant to Bertrand nos. 22, 23*. Estim.
1200 L., Mém., Arch. Nat., O^I 1784. Payment in 1709–
10, *Comptes*, V, 318–19, 413. A young angel sitting on
clouds, holds the crown of thorns, accomp. by a praying
child angel and three cherub heads.

VERSAILLES PALACE, CHAPEL

20*
Trophy, related to the Crowning with Thorns

1709   Bas-relief   Limestone   250 × 73
On the pillar underneath the great allegorical relief; see
P. Bertrand no. 23*. Two child angels above and below
a cartouche with an allegorical representation of the
Crowning with Thorns; one holds a crown of thorns,
the other a vase. Estim. 800 L., Mém. and *Comptes*, *ibid*.

VERSAILLES PALACE, CHAPEL

21*
Two Cherubim Heads in Clouds

1709   Bonbanc stone   145 × 56
In the centre of the arcade, below the Royal Tribune.
Estim. 250 L., Mém and *Comptes*, *ibid*.

VERSAILLES PALACE, CHAPEL

22
Decoration of the Vault of the Cul-de-Four

1709   Stone
At the second north traverse on the ground floor. The
decor. consists of a rose as a cul-de-lampe, enclosed in an

307

oval moulding and four panaches or pendentives with the royal cypher and other ornaments. Estim. 1960 L., Mém., Arch. Nat., O¹ 1784.

VERSAILLES PALACE, CHAPEL

23
Rose as Cul-De-Lampe and Cordon

1709   Stone
In collab. with Mazière, for one of the small chapels of the Tribune. Estim. 875 L. 10s., see Mém. *ibid.*

VERSAILLES PALACE, CHAPEL

24
Angels carrying the Royal Crown

1709   Models in wax and plaster
In collab. with Mazière, F. supplied the models for one of the culs-de-lampe for the Royal Tribune. Inside a cartouche, two angels carrying the royal crown; around them, three small children on clouds, holding palm and laurel branches. Estim. for the models 300 L., Mém. *ibid.*; payment 200 L., *Comptes*, V, 215. Not exec. in stone. Disappeared.

25
Work for the Hôtel de Ville, Paris

1708–10
  a. *Portraits of the Governor of Paris and the members of the Town Hall Administration*
1708   Nine medallions   Marble
Payment 2700 L., receipt 24 Dec. 1708. These medallions decorated the spandrels of the arcades in the courtyard of the Town Hall, at the side of the Greffe. An inscription in gilded bronze letters around the portraits commemorated the Patents of Nobility granted by the King, Arch. Nat., KK 461, fol. 527 and Lucien Lambeau, *L'Hôtel de Ville de P.*, 1920, p. 37. Disappeared when the Hôtel de Ville was destroyed by fire in 1871.
  b. *Repairs to figures, ornaments and attributes on two fireplaces in the Grande Salle*
1708
ibid. Disappeared.
  c. *Cartouche of the arms of Digeon*, provost of the merchants. Mém. of F., 12 Aug. 1710. Payment 70 L., receipt 29 Jan. 1711. The cartouche was on the cornice of the courtyard, Arch. Nat., KK 462, fol. 729. Disappeared.

26
Two Models for the Church of the Dôme des Invalides

1709   Plaster
Payment 70 L., *Comptes*, V, 348. Disappeared.

27
Work in the Vestibule of the Chapel

1712   Stone
In collab. Payment 588 L. in 1712, *Comptes*, V, 590. Not mentioned in the mém. of the sculptors.

VERSAILLES PALACE, CHAPEL

28
Prudence and Temperance

1712–13   Bas-relief   Gilded lead
Decor. for the panels above one of the arcades in the choir of Notre-Dame, Paris. cf. P. Bertrand no. 28. Payment for each group 450 L., *Comptes*, V, 610, 695. Melted down during the Revolution.

29
Zephyr and Flora

1713–21   Group   Marble
Begun in collab. with P. Bertrand (see no. 29★). The half-finished group was completed by Jacques Bousseau, Traité et convention, 22 April 1721, Min. Centr. Arch. Nat., Et. X, 352. See also no. 32.

PRIVATE COLLECTION

30
The Samaritan Woman

1714–15   Statue   Lead   Over life-size
For the façade of La Samaritaine, the pump-house on the Pont Neuf; part of a group exec. together with P. Bertrand (no. 32★) to replace an older group by Blanchard (nos. 2 & 3). The two sculptors rec. 15,278 L. in 1714–15, *Comptes*, V, 786, 874. Destroyed together with the pump-house in 1813.

31
Companion of Diana

1714–17
  a.★ Statue   Marble   Signed & dated: FREMIN 1717. H: 176
Comm. in 1710 for Marly with nine other Nymphs of Diana, see Dedieu no. 49. Payment on account of 200 L. to each sculptor, *Comptes*, V, 432. Final payment in 1715, 3600 L. each, *Comptes*, V, 874. Not in the 18th c. Invent; reappeared in the 19th c. in the Bosquet des Dômes at Versailles, cf. Soulié, *Mus.-Vers.*, III, p. 520. Trsf. to the Louvre in 1884. Drawing in the Coll. de Cotte, Bibl. Nat. Est., Fb 26. For Bibl., cf. Cayot no. 8.

PARIS, LOUVRE

21

b.★ Statue   Terracotta   H: 176
Signed: FREMIN F[I] 1717
Exact replica of a., except for the socle, which here is
circular. Bought by the Arras Museum in 1934.

ARRAS, MUSEUM

c. *Statue*   Terracotta   1717
Sold in Paris at Drouot, 11 Feb. 1933, *Cat.* no. 139.
May be the same as b.

d. *Statue*   Oise sandstone
Exact replica of a. Sold at Drouot in July, 1927, no cat.,
cf. L. Dimier, 'Tableaux qui passent', in *GBA*, 1928[I],
p. 317–18. Whereabouts unknown.

31b

31a

36

32
The Assumption of the Virgin

1719–21   Bas-relief   Bronze
F. and several sculptors were approached for the decor. of the chapel of Cardinal de Noailles in Notre-Dame, Paris, but F.'s design was not accepted, cf. Bibl. Nat. Est., Hd 135a, pet. fol., 684. Yet he apparently did a great bas-relief in gilded metal repr. 'The Assumption of the Virgin surrounded by a Group of Angels' for the altar above a bas-relief by Vassé; cf. Piganiol, *Descr.*, 1765, I, p. 364; Thiery, *Guide*, 1787, II. p. 106; Dezallier, *Paris*, 1752, p. 6, etc. and 'Etat des objets d'art placés dans les mon. de P.', 18 Nov. 1790, publ. in *NAAF*, 3è série, VI, 1890, p. 18. Only half-finished at the time of F.'s departure to Spain in 1721, the work was incl. in the contract with Bousseau (see no. 29). Melted down during the Revolution.

33–36
The Four Continents

33. *Europe*
34. *Asia*
35. *Africa*
36.* America

Four Busts   Marble   H: 70
Coll. of the banker Beaujon; Sales cat. etc., 25 Apr. 1787, sold as no. 162 for 1730 L. to Lambelin.

EUROPE, ASIA, AFRICA: Disappeared
AMERICA: Private Collection

37–38
Work for the Canons of Saint-Maur

1719
37. *High altar*   Marble
38. *Angel holding a hanging lamp*   Lead
Comm. by the canons of St.-Maur, probably after the visit to St.-Maur on 19 May 1719 of Cardinal de Noailles, who gave permission for a new high altar in the crossing of the transept, cf. Lebeuf, *Hist. du Diocèse de P.*, ed. 1883, II, p. 436. F.'s angel replaced the gold dove still descr. in 1718 by Lebrun des Marettes in his *Voyage liturgique*, p. 179. Trsf. in 1743 to the new Church of St.-Louis-du-Louvre because of the merger of the chapter of St.-Maur with those of St.-Nicolas and St.-Thomas-du-Louvre; cf. Piganiol, *Descr.*, 1765, II, p. 353–62; Hurtaut & Magny, 1779, III, p. 423; Thiery, 1787, I, p.231; 'Etat des objets d'art dans les mon. de P., 18 June 1791' in *NAAF*, 3è série, VI, 1890, p. 75. Disappeared.

39–198
WORK FOR PHILIP V OF SPAIN

1721–38
For F.'s activities at the court of Philip V, cf. mainly J. Digard, *Les jardins de la Granja et leurs sculpt. décoratives*, Paris, 1934. Digard used the original sources (royal accounts, inventories, descr., etc.) to establish an exact catalogue. Her conclusions have been accepted by Y. Bottineau in *L'art de cour dans l'Espagne de Philippe V, 1700–46*, Bordeaux, s.d., with some mods., due to more recently discovered sources and research (Hubert Dumandré's *Invent.* of 15 June 1746: Inventario de las estatuas, bancos y jarrones de marmol y planos de los jardines, Arch. del. Palacio, Inv. Casa 14.)

39*
Philip V of Spain (1683–1746)

c. 1721   Bust   Marble   H: (without pedestal) 78 × 83
The King, turned to the right, in armour, wears the insignia of the orders of the Golden Fleece and the Saint-Esprit. In the 18th c. the bust was in La Granja as a pendant to that of his wife, Elizabeth Farnese, no. 40. cf. A. Ponz, *Viaje de España*, Madrid, 1772; Bottineau, p. 434 and no. 191.

MADRID, ROYAL PALACE (Great Staircase)

40*
Elizabeth Farnese, Queen of Spain (1692–1766)

c. 1721   Bust   Marble   H: (without pedestal) 85 × 68
The Queen, turned to the left, in an embroidered coat with ermine facings, a flower at her bosom and fruit in her hair. The portrait, slightly idealised, is a good likeness. Pendant to no. 39.

MADRID, ROYAL PALACE (Great Staircase)

41*
Louis I, Prince of the Asturias (1707–1724)

Between 1722–24   Bust   Marble
H: (without pedestal) 64 × 68
Probably done on the occasion of his marriage with Louise-Elizabeth of Orleans in Jan. 1722 or at the time of his accession to the throne after the abdication of his

La Granja

father Philip V. The Prince, aged between 14 and 16, wears the insignia of the orders of the Golden Fleece and the Saint-Esprit. Pendant to no. 42, cf. Bottineau, p. 434 and no. 190.

LA GRANJA, PALACE

42★

Louise-Elisabeth of Orleans, Princess of the Asturias (1709–42)

Between 1722–24   Bust   Marble
H: (without pedestal) 60 × 59
The Princess, daughter of the regent Philip of Orleans was aged between 13 and 15, cf. Bottineau, *ibid*. Pendant to no. 41.

LA GRANJA, PALACE

40

39

41

42

WORKS IN THE PARK OF LA GRANJA PALACE

43–122
Sculptures for the Parterre of the Palace, the Cascade Nouvelle, the Rond-point of the Three Graces, the Cenador, the Petit-pont and the Rond-point of Andromeda
Between 1721–8
In collab. with Thierry, therefore before 1728, when Thierry returned to France.

LA GRANJA PALACE, PARTERRE

199

43

45

43–63
THE PARTERRE OF THE PALACE

43*
Africa

Statue   Marble   H: c. 200
On the north ramp of the parterre. A young woman
holding an elephant's head, her foot on a cornucopia.
The old sources, also Digard no. 26, and Bottineau,
p. 429 and no. 160 hesitate between F. and Thierry; here
attrib. to Frémin because of the elegance and liveliness
of the movement, so characteristic of his style.

44*
Milo of Crotona

Statue   Marble   H: c. 200
On the north ramp. Milo about to be devoured by a
lion; inspired by Puget's 'Milo of Crotona' (Louvre).
Old sources divided in attrib. between F. and Thierry.
Digard 28: attrib. to Thierry; Bottineau, p. 431 and no.
174 to F. Here attrib. to F. (see no. 43).

45*
Fidelity

Statue   Marble   H: c. 200
On the north ramp. A female figure holding a heart in
her right hand; a dog sleeps at her feet. Digard 30;
Bottineau p. 431 and no. 174. Unanimously attrib. to F.

44

46

48

50

51

52

53

54

56

60

62

60

61

68

46–63
Eighteen Vases, with Bas-reliefs

Lead, painted white   Av. H: 200
Attrib. to F. and Thierry without clear distinction. Digard inclines more towards Thierry, Bottineau gives no attrib. In similar pairs, facing each other along the east-west axis of the parterre.

46 ⋆ 47
Two Vases, decorated with dolphins
Digard 13 & 25

48 ⋆ 49
Two Vases, on one side Jupiter on his eagle, on the other Cybele on a lion
Digard 15 & 27

50 ⋆ 51⋆
Two Vases with masks of heads of Flora and Bacchus, the handles decorated with lion heads
Digard 17 & 29

52 ⋆ 53⋆
Two Vases with scenes of children playing with a dog
Digard 19 & 31

54 ⋆ 55
Two Vases with hunting trophies, on the handles female heads
Digard 20 & 32

56 ⋆ 57
Two Vases with cornucopias, on the handles heads of satyrs
Digard 21 & 33

58   59
Two Vases with musical trophies, on the handles female heads
Digard 22 & 34

60 ⋆ 61⋆
Two Vases with masks of satyrs and female heads
Digard 23 & 35

62 ⋆ 63
Two Vases with masks, on the handles billy-goat heads
Digard 24 & 36

64–86
LA CASCADE NOUVELLE

64–74
Groups in green-bronzed Lead around the Cascade

Bottineau p. 431 and no. 175. Unanimously attrib. to Frémin.

64⋆
Two Children playing with a fish

Square base: 82   H: 103
On the south side at the bottom of the Cascade. Digard 53.

65⋆
Two Children playing with a fish

Square base: 87   H: 90
On the north side at the bottom of the Cascade opp., but different from no. 64. Digard 63.

64

65

66

67

70

71

66*
Two Children playing with a pheasant and a bow

Square base: 84   H: 91
On the south side above the Cascade. Digard 62.

67*
Two Children playing with a dead rabbit and a boar-spear

Square base: 84   H: 91
On the north side opp. no. 66. Digard 72.

68 * 69
Child riding a sea-horse

Two similar groups, 185 × 125
Above the Cascade. Digard 48, 49.

70*
Lion fighting with a boar

170 × 120
On the south side, above the Cascade. Digard 50.

71*
Dog fighting with a stag

170 × 120
On the north side, opp. no. 70. Digard 51.

72* 73 74
Three head masks of sea monsters

Above the Cascade. Digard 52. Probably by F.

75–78
Marble Statues on the north and south ramps on either side of the Cascade Nouvelle.

75*
Architecture or Magnificence

H: c. 200
On the south side. Attrib. by the old sources to F. or Thierry; by Digard 54 to Thierry; Bottineau p. 429 and no. 160 to Frémin or Thierry. For stylistic reasons, here attrib. to F.

76*
Shepherd

H: c. 200
On the south side. Behind him a kid on its hind legs, trying to snatch leaves which he holds in his hand. Attrib. by the old sources to F. or Thierry, by Digard 58 to Thierry; Bottineau p. 429 and no. 160 hesitates between the two. For stylistic reasons here attrib. to F.

77*
Nymph of Diana

H: c. 200
On the south side. Accomp. by a greyhound on its hind legs. Attrib. by all sources to F. Digard 60; Bottineau p. 431 and no. 174.

78*
Asia

H: c. 200
On the north side. A young woman wearing a crown, holding an incense burner. Attrib. by all sources to F. Digard 66; Bottineau p. 431 and no. 174.

79–86
Eight Vases with Bas-reliefs

Lead, painted white   Av. H: 200
On the ramps, in similar pairs, alternating with the marble statues. Attribution between F. and Thierry not clearly definable.

79 * 80
Two Vases with musical instruments. On the handles female heads. Digard 55 & 65.

81 * 82
Two Vases: on one side a dog fighting a boar, on the other, a dog attacking a stag. On the handles, the heads of bearded old men. Digard 57 & 67.

83 84
Two Vases with sunflowers. Digard 59 & 69.

72

75

76

77

78

79   81   85

80

85*   86
Two Vases, with three children killing an eagle, on the other side three children playing with a goat. On the handles, faces of men. Digard 61 & 71.

87*
ROND-POINT OF THE THREE GRACES

At the summit of the great east–west perspective in front of the Palace.
Fountain of the Three Graces   Lead
In collab. with Thierry. In the middle of a circular basin, diam. 17 m. The fountain, resting on rocks (white-painted lead), consists of two super-imposed basins, the first held up by two naiads and two tritons, the second by three standing graces. At the top, a child holding a great fish in its arms. Attrib. by the old sources to F. or Thierry. Digard no. 73 and Bottineau p. 428 & no. 158 assume collab. between F. and Thierry.

88–112*
THE CENADOR

Pavilion in the shape of an octagonal temple. Digard 74, Bottineau p. 429 and no. 161. The sculptures by F. in collab. with Thierry are:

On the outside:

88–91
Four Pediments above the four axial portals, with bas-reliefs.

East and West: the escutcheons of the houses of Bourbon and Farnese, surmounted by the royal crown, flanked by two lions.
North and South: the cypher of Philip V and Elizabeth Farnese, with a crown, a cornucopia, coins and fruit.

87 *Detail*   87

Detail   87

88

100

92–95
Four masks repr. the four Seasons on the keystones of the arches above the four doors: Spring, Summer, Autumn★, Winter★.

96–99
Four Trophies in bas-relief, symbol. the four Continents, on the angled sides of the Cenador. 456 × 165

North: Europe★; South: Africa; East: America; West: Asia★.

100★
Cupid holding Laurel and Palm-leaves

Statue   Lead, painted white
Standing on the top of the Cenador.

On the inside:

Decorations in gilded stucco, in collab. with Thierry. Coats-of-arms of the Bourbons at the keystones above the doors, Decorations on the Capitals, Trophies on the frieze, Consoles, Geometrical and Vegetable Motifs★ in the centre of the cupola. Also:

101–104
Four groups of Child Angels on clouds, symbols of the Cardinal Virtues.

High reliefs above the cornice:

101★
Two Angels carrying the sun, a sword and scales, attributes of Justice.

102★
Two Angels with key, club, lion's skin and crown of oak leaves, attributes of Might.

100

94

95

96

97

101

102

103*
Two Angels with mirror and serpent, attributes of Prudence.

104
Two Angels with chalice, radiant host and bridle and bit, attributes of Temperance.

105–108*
Four Angels with the arms of the sovereign on shields

Half-reliefs on false marble in the four angled sides of the temple.

109–112
Four Female Statues with Musical Instruments

Marble   Slightly over life-size
In the four niches.
Bottineau, p. 578 and no. 153; acc. to the Invent. of 1746, F. most likely supplied the lead models. The two with trumpet* and mandolin* are by H. Dumandré; the two with violin* and triangle*, by Pitué.

103

106

109 *110* *111*

113–116
LE PETIT PONT

To the north of the palace, behind the Esplanade de la Gerbe.

Four groups of children in bronzed and gilded lead, on the parapet of the small bridge. Bottineau p. 428 and no. 159. The old sources, also Digard and Bottineau, attrib. these groups to F. and Thierry in collab.

113*
Two children capturing a hind

110 × 192
Digard 86

114*
Two children killing a stag

110 × 192
Digard 87

112

113

114

115

116

Detail   *117*

117

115*
Two children cutting the throat of a wild sow

130 × 192
Digard 88

116*
Two children tying up a trapped wolf

130 × 192
Digard 89

117–122
ROND-POINT OF ANDROMEDA

117*
Perseus liberating Andromeda

Fountain Lead Pyramid-shaped
In the centre of a great round basin, diam. 400. On a pyramid of rocks in white painted lead, sitting on a big fish, Andromeda, half-nude, shackled; a cupid is about to undo her chains. Underneath, Perseus, in armour, sword in hand, attacking the dragon whose head emerges below; behind, seated, Minerva, with helmet, lance and shield, watching and advising. All figures in bronzed and gilded lead. The old sources attrib. the whole group to F.; Digard (no. 104) agrees, but gives the dragon to Thierry; Bottineau (p. 431 and no. 178) attribs. the whole to F.
Around the basin eight statues in a half circle, five, acc. to the old sources, by F.

Detail   *117*

327

Detail   *120*

118

119

120

121

122

123

118*
Earth or Cybele

Statue   Marble   H: c. 200
Wearing a mural crown, holding a globe and an inverted cornucopia. Digard 108; Bottineau p. 431 and no. 177.

119*
Fire or Jupiter

Statue   Marble   H: c. 200
Bearded, with an eagle; holding tongues of flame. Digard 109; Bottineau p. 431 and no. 177.

120*
Water or Nereide

Statue   Marble   H: c. 200
Her foot rests on a dolphin; she pours water from a jug. Digard 110; Bottineau p. 431 and no. 177.

121*
Air or Aeolide

Statue   Marble   H: c. 200
A young woman, standing on clouds, holding her cloak; at her feet, two heads, blowing. Digard 111; Bottineau p. 431 and no. 177.

122*
Satirical poem or Silenus or Bacchus

Statue   Lead, painted white   H: c. 200
Holding a tyrsus and a parchment roll. Digard 113; Bottineau p. 431 and no. 177.

123–155
Sculptures in the Parterre of Andromeda, the Bassin of Aeolus and the Parterre of Fame

Probably between 1728–34
Sole artist Frémin, acc. to the old sources, Digard and Bottineau, p. 431 and no. 176.

123–34
PARTERRE OF ANDROMEDA

Four statues   Marble   H: c. 200

123*
Amphitrite or Juno

Walking on the water, holding a sceptre. Digard 116.

124*
Neptune

A bearded old man with a trident, standing on an enormous shell, one foot on a dolphin. Digard 117.

124

125

126

125★
Ismena

A young woman, plumes in her hair, in a short tunic, embroidered coat and high boots; she plays a flute (disappeared). Digard 118.

126★
Saturnus

A bald old man, bearded and winged, holding an hourglass and a scythe (broken). Digard 119.

127–134
Eight Vases in white-painted lead attrib. to F. by the Invent. of 1746, Digard and Bottineau, p. 641.

127–130
Four Vases with handles in the shape of winged dragons, decorated with seated cupids holding garlands. Digard 120–123.

131★
Vase with dolphin handles, on the body a bas-relief, Orion on a dolphin, playing his lyre. Digard 124.

132
Vase of the same shape, with bas-relief repr. Thetis seated on the water. Digard 125.

133 ★ 134
Two similar Vases with bacchantes as handles and a bas-relief repr. three people dancing. Digard 126–7.

127

131

133

135–143
BASSIN OF AEOLUS

Circular. Diam: 170

135*
Aeolus and the Chained Winds

Group in the centre of the bassin   Bronzed lead
On a mass of rocks, King Aeolus, crowned and bearded, with great wings, his face turned towards the sky; he holds chains and sceptre, around him a winged child and child heads of winds. By F., acc. to the old sources, Digard 128 and Bottineau p. 432 & no. 184.

136–143
Eight Masks around the bassin

Lead

144–155
PARTERRE OF FAME

144*
Daphne pursued by Apollo

Statue   White marble   Life-size
On a sculpted marble socle. By F., acc. to Digard 163 and Bottineau p. 428 & no. 153.

145*
Apollo pursuing Daphne

Statue   White marble   Life-size
On a sculpted marble socle. By F., acc. to Digard 164: Bottineau, *ibid.*

135

144

145

146

150

152

146*–149
Four Vases

Lead, painted white
With the coats-of-arms of the houses of Bourbon and Farnese, united by the ribbons of the orders of the Golden Fleece and of the Saint-Esprit. Volute-shaped handles with lions' heads below, crested helmets above. By F., acc. to Digard 165–8 and Bottineau p. 433 & no. 186.

150 * 151
Two Vases

Lead, painted white
On the cover, a hunter with a cock, a huntress with a trumpet; on the body, a bas-relief of hounds attacking a stag. Volute-shaped handles ending in stags' heads. By F., acc. to Digard 169/70 and Bottineau, p. 433 & no. 186.

152 * 153
Two Vases

Lead, painted white
On the rim, two seated figures holding a great net spread over the body; carved boar and roebuck heads, hunting implements. By F., acc to Digard 171–2 and Bottineau, *ibid.*

154

155

Detail   155

156

154*
Lucretia

Statue   White marble   Life-size
On a sculpted marble socle. Leaning on a pilaster, holding a knife, about to kill herself. Attrib. by Digard 178 to Bousseau, but acc. to the Invent. of 1746, by F. cf. Bottineau p. 433 and no. 185.

155*
Diana, or Atalanta

Statue   Marble   Life-size
On a sculpted marble socle, holding a bow, at her side a quiver, a slain boar under her feet. Attrib. by Digard 179 to Carlier, but acc. to Invent. of 1746, by F. cf. Bottineau, p. 428 and no. 154.

156–177
Sculptures on the esplanade of the Palace, the Rond-point of Fame and the Carrefour of the Eight Avenues

Between 1728–40
Mostly by F., completed by Pitué and Dumandré; Thierry did not collab.

165

160

158–163*
Six lying Chimaeras

Lead, painted white   78 × 140
Digard 2, 3, 6, 7, 10, 11. Facing each other in pairs, with female heads and upper torsos and lions' bodies, like the sphinxes. The chimaeras, Digard 6, 7, differ from the four others. Entirely by F.

156–157
ESPLANADE OF THE PALACE

cf. Bottineau, p. 430 & no. 173 and p. 577.

156 * 157
Children mounted on a Sphinx

Two groups   Lead, painted white   89 × 140
Two children in various attitudes, holding laurel crowns. Attrib. to F. by Digard 1 & 12; after F.'s departure, completed by Dumandré.

164
Boy and Girl playing with hunting implements

Group   Lead, painted white   88 × 140
The children, leaning on a greyhound, with a hunting horn, a quiver, slain birds. Digard 4, entirely by F.

167

168

168

Detail

168

Detail   *168*

165*
Boy and Girl playing with a deer

Group   Lead, painted white   84 × 140
Digard 5, entirely by F.

166
Boy and Girl playing with a bow and a small eagle

Group   Lead, painted white   84 × 140
Digard 8, entirely by F.

167*
Boy and Girl playing with masks

Group   Lead, painted white   84 × 140
The girl has a likeness to Marie-Louise of Savoy, first
wife of Philip, as she appears in no. 199. Digard 9,
entirely by F.

Detail   *168*

ROND-POINT OF FAME

168*
Fountain of Fame

In the centre of a great circular bassin, diam. 320.
Monumental fountain in the shape of a pyramid of
rocks, in lead; on top, on the wings of Pegasus, the
figure of Fame sounding a trumpet. On the rocks, four
defeated warriors, falling. Below, seated, four river gods,
two old men and two women, pouring water out of an
urn, repr. the Rivers Tagus, Guadalquivir, Douro and
Ebro. In the bassin four groups of children each mounted
on a fish. Digard 173–7; Bottineau, p. 433 and no. 187.
Designed and begun by F., completed by Dumandré
and Pitué after F.'s departure towards the end of
Philip V.'s reign.

Detail   *168*

170

176

169

169–173
CARREFOUR OF THE EIGHT AVENUES

Bottineau p. 432 and no. 182. The marble was bought c. 1732. The sculpture by F.; Juan la Costa helped with the ornaments. Some fountains completed by Dumandré.

In the centre of the Carrefour:

169*
Mercury abducting Pandora (or Psyche)

Group   Lead, with green bronze
Mercury, in his winged helmet, holding his staff, lifts up Pandora, who holds a flask; a Zephyr at their feet, supports them. Digard 144; entirely by F.

Eight great Fountains around the Carrefour:

170*
Fountain of Saturnus

Lead and marble
Repeat of the statue in the Parterre of Andromeda (no. 126). On either side of the bassin, a fallen stag and, as in each of the eight fountains, a winged child riding a swan. Digard 145; completed by Dumandré.

177

172

171
Fountain of Minerva

The Goddess seated on a central pedestal, helmeted and armed, surrounded by the attribs. of science. On each side volutes with shells. Digard 146.

172*
Fountain of Hercules

Hercules, nude, holding his club, seated on a lion's skin with the attribs. of 'Might' (oak branch) and of the Hunt (quiver). On either side of the pedestal, volutes with shells. Digard 147.

173
Fountain of Ceres

Ceres holding a great sheaf of corn, on a marble basin surrounded by winged dragons. Digard 148.

174
Fountain of Neptune

Neptune, trident in hand, stands in front of a shell, pointing his forefinger. At his feet, a dolphin; on either side of the basin, a sea-horse. Digard 149.

175
Fountain of Victory

Seated on a pedestal, holding a laurel-crown and palms. On either side, shells and marine animals. Digard 150.

176*
Fountain of Mars

The god seated, armed and helmeted, leaning on his shield. The ground at his feet strewn with weapons. On either side of the pedestal a shell. Digard 151; probably completed by Dumandré.

177*
Fountain of Cybele

The Goddess standing on the basin, veiled, in an imploring attitude. On either side of the basin, a lion overturning a cornucopia. Digard 152.

On each side of the fountains, a putto riding a swan.*

170–177

170–177

170–177

178–195

Sculptures in the Long Avenue, the Bosquet of the Eight Avenues and the Bath of Diana

Completed after 1738 by Bousseau, Pitué and Dumandré.

178–187
THE LONG AVENUE

Bottineau, p. 578 and no. 155 ff. Acc. to the Invent. of 1746, F. 'invented' (i.e. supplied) the models (*disappeared*) for the ten following statues, exec. after his departure by Bousseau:

Ten statues   Marble   H: c. 180

178*
Apollo defeating the Serpent Python

Laurel-crowned, holding a sceptre, crushing the serpent under his foot. Digard 130.

179*
Clio

Holding a small trumpet and a book. Digard 131.

180*
Melpomene

Digard 132.

181*
Urania

Holding a globe. Digard 133.

182*
Calliope

Holding three books in one hand, a laurel branch in the other. Digard 134.

183*
Polyhymnia

Holding a roll of parchment. Digard 135.

184*
Terpsichore

Dancing, beating a tambourine, her foot on a lyre (right forearm missing). Digard 136.

185*
Thalia

Dancing, holding her coat with the right hand, lifting her right foot (broken off). Digard 137.

186*
Erato

With a cupid, holding a torch; in her right hand, a lyre. Digard 138.

187*
Euterpe

Crowned with roses, in her hand a flute, her right foot on a tambourine. Digard 139.

170–177

179

178

180

182

181

183

Detail 185

185 187

184

186

188

188–193
BASSINS OF THE BOSQUETS OF THE EIGHT AVENUES

188 * 189
First and Second Bassins of the Dragons or Fountains of the Tripod of Apollo

In the middle of the bassin (diam.: 160), the fountain in painted lead: four dragons on rocks, supporting four consoles with an urn, surrounded by infant tritons. The foot of the urn formed by dolphins, with intertwined tails. Digard 153–4; Bottineau p. 432 and no. 180; entirely by F.

190 * 191 *
First and Second Bassins de la Vasque

In the middle of the bassin (diam.: 160), an octagonal lead pedestal, supporting a circular bassin; on top of it a triton lifts up a nereide. Around the bowl, four children pouring water out of urns. The pedestal framed by four volutes with four sirens above the first bassin and four tritons under the second, supporting shells with their lifted arms. Masks and ornaments. By F., acc. to Digard 155–6 and Bottineau, *ibid.*

346

191

Detail 190[1]

Detail 191[1]

Detail 1902

Detail 1903

192*
Bassin of the Basket

In the middle of the bassin (diam.: 340), a group in lead of four swans supporting a fruit basket with their open wings. Around the basket a large wreath with two tritons and two sirens holding on to it. By F., acc. to Digard 158; Bottineau p. 432 and no. 181.

193*
Bassin of Latona or of the Frogs

A white marble group of Latona and her two children, Diana and Apollo, in the centre of a circular bassin (diam. 230). The group is placed high on a pedestal supported by a lead socle in two octagonal tiers (painted to imitate white marble). On the socle, masks,

192

Detail   193

193

consoles and frogs. In the bassin eight figures, half-man,
half-frog and sixteen groups of frogs and rushes.
Digard 157; acc. to Bottineau, p. 557 and no. 151,
F. conceived the ensemble. For the central group of
Latona and her children, there was first a model and a
group in lead by F., replaced in 1744 by the marble.
Exec. by Bousseau between 1738–40, completed by
Pitué.

Detail   192

Detail 193

Detail 193

Detail 193

Detail 193

Detail 193

194

194*
BATH OF DIANA

Monumental architectural ensemble, various ornaments and groups of figures in lead; the original project very likely by F., execution by Bousseau, completed in 1742, ornaments by Dumandré and Pitué. Digard 190; Bottineau p. 579 and no. 166–7.

195*
Benches in the Park

Marble
Sculpted feet, mostly by F.; Bottineau p. 643.

195

Detail 196

196

Detail 196

196–198
WORKS OF UNKNOWN DATE INSIDE THE
PALACE

196[star]
Fountain of the Corals or of the Conchas

After 1732   Marble and lead   160 × 190
Placed against a background of rock-work on the
ground floor of the South-West Pavilion. Amphitrite
sits on a large shell held up by two tritons (lead);
three children are playing with dolphins. The old sources
give no attribution. Digard 106–7, attribs. the very
French conception to Thierry but, acc. to Bottineau, p.
430, the pavilion dates from 1729–32, when Thierry had
returned to France, so the work is more likely by F. or
Bousseau. Close to F.'s style in the Fountain of the Three
Graces and the Bassins des Vasques (nos. 87, 190, 191).

197[star]
Faith

Before 1738   Statue   Marble   H: 181
Woman with veiled face holding a chalice. cf. Ponz,
Viaje de España, 1772; Digard 42; Bottineau p. 434 and
no. 190.

LA GRANJA, PALACE

198
Apollo, seated, holding a Lyre

Before 1738   Statue   Marble
In the Palace, acc. to Ponz, *ibid.*; Bottineau p. 434 and
no. 191. Disappeared.

199[star]   See p. 312[star]
Marie-Louise of Savoy, Queen of Spain (1685–1714)

Bust   Marble   H: 72 (incl. socle)   L: 45
The first wife of Philip V, whom he had married in
1701. The work here attrib. to F. because very similar
in style to the other busts of the royal family by
F. (nos. 31–42). It would in this case be posthumous,
perhaps ordered by Philip V during 1720–25.

LA GRANJA, PALACE

197

APPENDIX

Errata and Addenda

ANDRE

8. Tiridates

Estim. 3000 L., 15 Aug. 1692, Arch. Nat., O^I 1964^4.

ARCIS

43. *Angel for the Church of the Sorbonne, Paris*

The sculptor of the adoring angel on the High Altar, opposite the one by Van Clève, was not Arcis but Etienne Le Hongre. cf. Guillet de St.-Georges, *Mém. inéd.*, I, p. 372 and the contract signed 25 June 1686 between the sculptors Le Hongre, Van Clève and the priors of the Sorbonne, Min. Centr. Arch. Nat., Et. LXXIII, 536.

44. Vase

Estim. 1800 L., 15 Aug. 1692, Arch. Nat., O^I 1964^4.

BAROIS

5. Vase

Estim. 1400 L., 15 Aug. 1692, Arch. Nat., O^I 1964^4.

BERTIN

10.11. *Aristaeus* and *Eurydice*

Aristaeus only (not Eurydice) is mentioned under the heading of 'Roman General' in several inventories of the 19th c., Arch. Louvre 35 DD 4, 35 DD 5, 35 DD 25, 1 DD 132; in 1820 the damaged statue was still in the Trianon, invent. no. 1464; in 1846 in the store at Versailles, invent. no. 1759.

BERTRAND, David

Addition to Biography:
Son of Jean B., native of Metz, and Marie Adam. Married Judith Meusnier in July 1658; ten children, one of them the sculptor Philippe. About the family B., see Haag, 'Etat civil des Protestants en France', Ms. 892 of the Bibl. de la Soc. de l'hist. du Protestantisme français.

1. *Work in the Hôtel de Luynes* 1669

The hôtel was built by Le Muet in the old rue St.-Dominique, faubourg St.-Germain, today Square de Luynes. The works undertaken for Louis-Charles d'Albert, Duke of Luynes (1620–90), husband of Anne de Rohan, were valued by Gilles Guérin at 3681 L.; valuation 19 Feb.–19 June 1669, Arch. Nat., Z^{IJ}302. They consisted of:

a. Stone sculpture at the carriage gateway: 2 children, their bodies ending in foliage; 2 masks; 3 consoles decor. with festoons.

b. Plaster consoles in the courtyard.

c. Several mantel-pieces in the apartments decor. with bas-reliefs repr.: 1. In the great hall: Pallas Athene with 3 children and at the lower frieze, the Rape of the Sabines. 2. In the great Chambre à alcôve: the coat of arms of the Luynes family, with children holding a helmet and a Connétable's sword and a child symbolising Victory, seated on trophies. 3. In the bedchamber opening on to the courtyard: the Judgement of Paris.

d. In the great Chambre à alcôve: four sopra-portes illustrating the four seasons.

e. Various ornaments on the cornices, pilasters and ceilings, also for the pavements.

The beauty of these apartments praised in Brice, *Descr.*, 1687, p. 217. The hôtel was altered in the 18th c. and demolished in 1900.
Destroyed.

5. *Work in the Apartment of Philippe de Lorraine in the Palais Royal* 1674

Under the direction of A. Lepautre and in collab. with the sculptor Sébastien Picard. B. received 343 L. Invent. des papiers de A. Lepautre (Inform. J.-M. Thiveaud, *A. Lepautre*, typewritten thesis, Ecole des Chartes, 1970). The apartment, famous for its luxurious furnishings, was situated in the second courtyard beyond the Galerie des Hommes Illustres. Destroyed.

6. *Work in the château of St.-Germain-en-Laye* 1675

In the apartment of Louis de Lorraine, Count of Armagnac, under the direction of the architect A. Lepautre. Works of sculpture were assessed on 1 Feb. 1675, Arch. Nat., Z^{IJ}327 (Inform. J. M. Thiveaud, *A. Lepautre*, see no. 5 above). B.'s estim. of 1087 L. was reduced to 714 L. The work consisted of:

a. In the Cabinet: The cornice decor. with acanthus leaves, a bas-relief over the buffet-table with a frieze of children, above them a garland of vine-leaves forming an arch, supporting a cross of Lorraine under a crown; two children in round-relief, each holding one end of the garland and a sword; the buffet-table, surrounded by wooden icicles, stood on lion-feet; above the chimney-piece which B. repaired, he sculpted a round bas-relief (diam. 138), repr. the Sacrifice to Apollo.

b. In the Bedchamber: B. sculpted above the chimney-piece, which he also repaired, a rectangular bas-relief (146 × 94), repr. the Sacrifice to Minerva. In niches on either side of the fire-place, two figures surmounted by square bas-reliefs; above an arched frame decor. with roses, in the arch a bust of Louis XIV against a background of trophies; upon the arch two children in round-relief holding laurel wreaths.
Destroyed.

7. *Work in the Hôtel d Elbeuf* 1681–2

This hôtel at 56 rue de Vaugirard, former hôtel de Kerveno, once belonged to Henri, Duke of Lorraine, whose half-brother Charles of Lorraine, and father Charles of Lorraine, Duke of Elbeuf, lived there; when it was seized B. demanded a valuation of the works of sculpture he had done there (expertise by J. Houzeau and D. Martin, 25 Oct. 1686, Arch. Nat., $Z^{1J}375$). They were:

a. In the Duke's apartment: 2 bas-reliefs above the doors repr. 1. the Rape of Helen; 2. children holding helmets and banners.

b. In Madame's apartment: 3 mantel-pieces, sculpted marble and stone; 1. In the ante-chamber, a bas-relief held by two sphinxes, repr. Fame inscribing the names of the Virtues, surmounted by children holding a basket of flowers. 2. In the chamber, an oval bas-relief repr. the Holy Family, under a frieze showing the Adoration of the Infant Jesus by St. John and angels, surmounted by children holding a crown. 3. In one room: 2 large figures and 3 children, underneath the head of Apollo.

c. In the same room: two sopraportes repr. 1. The Sacrifice to Diana copied from the Arch of Constantine in Rome; 2. a conquest by Louis XIV.

The whole of these works, incl. repairs and floors, estim. at 2900 L. The hotel, altered in the 18th c., was demolished in 1953. Destroyed.

8. *St. Benedict, St. Scholastica and two Vestal Virgins*

1686   Four statues   Limewood   H: c. 195
Exec. by B. for the cabinet-maker Jean Justine. Valuation 14 Oct. 1686 by J. Raon and L. Magnier, Arch. Nat., $Z^{1J}375$. The two statues of the saints were judged badly done and unacceptable; the two vestal virgins, incl. the models, were estim. at 120 L. and 60 L. Not ident. or disapp.

9. *Works at the Hôtel de Mailly* 1687

By order of Louis II of Mailly, colonel of the regiment of Condé (1652–88) and his wife Marie de Coligny, whom he had married on 26 April 1687, the Hôtel de Mailly-Nesle, built in 1633 at the corner of the present Quai Voltaire and the rue de Beaune, was entirely refitted with paintings by Jean I. Berain and Camot, partly still extant (cf. A. Weigert in *L'Architecture*, 15 Jan. 1932) and sculptures by David B. The sculptures valued 18 Oct. 1687 at 802 L., by J.-B. Tuby and P. Mazeline, Arch. Nat., $Z^{1J}381$, consisted of:

a. Stone sculpture on the façade in the courtyard: a great pediment with arms, books, trophies; underneath a small arched pediment; two consoles.

b. In the 'Cabinet' of Louis de Mailly: a fireplace decorated with the coat of arms of the Mailly family, books, trophies, a bas-relief repr. the conquests of Louis XIV and as a frieze depicting the battle of Seneff, where in 1674 the colonel's leg was shattered by a musket-shot.

c. Models of a cornice for the great salon.
Destroyed.

BUIRETTE

Between
9 & 10. *Works at the Hôtel d'Effiat, Paris* 1684–5

B. rec. 87 L. for works at the old Hôtel d'Effiat, 26 rue Vieille-du-Temple, which in 1682 became the property of the Hôtel-Dieu, cf. *Invent. des Archives Hospitalières antérieures à 1790*.

Hôtel-Dieu, II, p. 237 (6831, layette 234, liasse 1452). It is not known what these works consisted of. The Hôtel was sold to Claude Le Peletier in 1692 and demolished in 1882.

10. Amazon

Estim. 5000 L., 15 Aug. 1692, Arch. Nat., O^I 1964[4].

11. Vase

Estim. 3300 L., 15 Aug. 1692, Arch. Nat., O^I 1964[4].

CARLIER

7. Urania

Estim. 3250 L., 15 Aug. 1692, Arch. Nat., O^I 1964[4].

8. *Venus de Medici*

Estim. 3800 L., 15 Aug. 1692, Arch. Nat., O^I 1964[4].

9. Papirius

Estim. 7000 L., 15 Aug. 1692, Arch. Nat., O^I 1964[4].

CHAUVEAU

25. *Three carved pediments, Château de Roissy-en-France*

One of the three pediments★ is still extant, although in a very bad state.

25

36a

36b

36c

36. Work at the Château de Frascati

Several of C.'s drawings for the decor. of the chapel, from the Coll. de Cotte, are preserved in Bibl. Nat. Est., Va 57, 6; among them:
    a. The elevation of the façade and the entrance-door★.
    b. Cross-section of the chapel and elevation of the high altar with a retable in relief repr. the Baptism of Christ and, on either side, the four Evangelists★.
    c. Cross-section of the chapel and reverse of the façade★.
    d. Sopraporte with coat-of-arms of Mgr. de Coislin★.

CLERION

Biography: Marriage contract of C. with Geneviève Boullongne, 20 Sept. 1680, Min. Centr. Arch. Nat., Et. XXXV, 450.

15. Venus Callipygos

Estim. 3450 L., 15 Aug. 1692, Arch. Nat., O^I 1964^4.

18. Juno

Estim. 3000 L., 15 Aug. 1692, Arch. Nat., O^I 1964^4.

COLLIGNON

3. Tomb of Julienne le Bé

Acc. to the valuation of 4 July 1690, quoted by Dumolin (1200 L., Arch. Nat., Z^{IJ}401), the tomb was completed in 1686.

Between
11 & 12. Models for Andirons 1686

Made for Simon des Ormeaux, goldsmith; val. at 50 L. by Drouilly and Houzeau, 1 Aug. 1686, Arch. Nat., Z^{IJ}369. They consisted of a decorated vase on a socle, supported in the first model by two winged sphinxes, in the second by two consoles.

36d

Collignon 15

15. *Model for a tomb,* *Undated*

Known through a drawing★ by B. Picart (1673–1733), preserved in the National Museum, Copenhagen, with the handwritten note: "Drawn by B. Picart after a model by Collignon"; cf. M. Sainte-Beuve, 'Le tombeau du Marquis de Vaubrun', *GBA*, 1928[I], p. 153. The monument consists of a pyramid rising above a sarcophagus, supported by a base decor. with volutes and winged death's heads; on either side of the pyramid seated figures repr. Religion and Hope; above them an angel holding a medallion with a double portrait in profile of the deceased and his wife. No coat of arms on the blason, no inscription on the tablet.

COTTON

6. *Works for C. Tribouleau* 1701

Claude Tribouleau, conseiller and secrétaire du roi, had not paid C. for works carried out at his house in Bondy; at the request of Cotton's wife, Madeleine Molin, valuations were made on 20 April and 15 May, 1702, Arch. Nat., $Z^{IJ}459/60$. The works were:

a. Equestrian statue of Louis XIV in stucco for a blind arcade behind a staircase. The King, H: 195, in Roman dress, being crowned with laurels by an infant with a quiver, stretched out his right arm in a gesture of command; his horse, L: 225, reared up above trophies and weapons. Because of faulty proportions, the work was only valued at 600 L. by the first expert, 1800 L. by the second, and 800 L. by a final valuation.

b. Model for a vase for the sideboard in the dining-room;

c. sketch for the head of a faun for the window in the dining-room.

Destroyed.

COUSTOU, G

7. **Hercules on the Funeral Pyre**

b[2].★ Statuette Terracotta 27 × 40

Another version with important variations from the marble.

PRIVATE COLLECTION

$7b^2$

Between
51 & 52. Louis XV. c. 1724 Bust

For the Hôtel de Ville. Acc. to a letter of R. de Chateauneuf to
the architect Beausire, Arch. Seine D4 A2, 768, the bust was put
into the room used as an office by the municipal magistrates, in
1724. Acc. to a handwritten note by C. himself (destroyed in
1871, publ. by A.-J.-V. Lecoy de Lincy and V. Calliat, *Hist. de
l'Hôtel de Ville de Paris*, 1844, p. 14) this happened in 1734, not in
1724; probably a transcription error by Lecoy.

74.★ Cardinal Armand-Gaston de Rohan

Engr. in Boffrand, Livre d'Arch., 1742   74

NICHOLAS COUSTOU
Litho after an 18th c. sanguine
Bibl. Nat. Est., Ef 367–petit fol.

COUSTOU, N

22.★ The Seine and the Marne   *Another view of this group*

COYSEVOX

26. *Sopraporte in the Cabinet des Bijoux, Versailles*

A drawing in the Arch. Nat., O^I 1778 shows that the bas-relief was arched and repr. a woman sitting on a cornucopia beside an ewer, between two cupids, one holding a vase, the other a basket of fruit. cf. A. Marie, *Mansart à Vers.*, 1972, II, p. 412.

54. **Sculptures on the Façade, Dôme des Invalides**

The four statues d–g were carved by C. and Tuby. Fee for each statue 350 L., Bibl. Nat. Ms. fr.n.a. 22936.

Between
70 & 71. *The Grand Dauphin* c. 1699 Bust Marble

Exh. Salon 1699, cf. Keller-D., II, p. 23. It may be the bust in the Nat. Gall. of Art, Samuel H. Kress Coll., Washington DC.

Between
85 & 86. *Models for the Sculptures at the entrance to the Hotel Soubise* 1705

Estim. and contract 14 July and 21 Nov. 1705, Min. Centr. Arch. Nat., Et. XCIX. Exec. in stone by P. Bourdict (no. 5) and G. Coustou (no. 9).

DEDIEU

17. *Louis XIV*

Acc. to the description in C. C. G. du Vertron, 'Ludovicus, vir immortalis. Serenissimo Delphino. Carmen', 1687, publ. in *Rev. Universelle des Arts*, XXIII, 1866, p. 117, Louis XIV was repr. "in military dress, Roman style, with an Emperor's cloak trailing on the ground . . . crowned with laurels . . . in his right hand a commander's baton, the other hand turned, resting on his left hip".

19. **Louis XIV in a Sun**

Attrib. to Dedieu by du Vertron, see no. 17.

DESJARDINS

After **20.** *Sculptures in the Hôtel de Monsieur, Versailles* 1673

The Hôtel Condé, bought on 6 October 1672 by Philippe d'Orléans, the King's brother, was the subject of extensive redecoration. The sculptoral works, entrusted to Desjardins, Coulon and Samson, were assessed in 1673. D.'s work in the interior of the hôtel consisted of:
   a. *44 Plaster consoles*, decorated with "feuilles de refend, balustres et fleurons". Height 65; estim. 176 L.
   b. *Oval garland of flowers and leaves*, perimeter 1100; estim. 170 L.
   c. *A bas-relief above a mantel-piece*, in the bedchamber on the first floor. It repr. a figure of Fame seated on a globe together with a child; enclosed by an oval border of laurels, surmounted by trophies and festoons. Estim. 230 L.
   d. *Two bas-reliefs in the Chambre des Bains*, height 120, repr. children with vases and garlands. Estim. 230 L. cf. Arch. Nat., Z^{IJ}320, assessment 21 May 1673; Z^{IJ}321, assessment 5 July 1673 (inform. J.-M. Thiveaud, *A. Lepautre*, op. cit. p. 355).
   This is probably the hôtel at 2, place Gambetta, Versailles, whose ancient decoration has entirely disappeared.

30. *Diana*

Estim. 5500 L., 15 Aug. 1692, Arch. Nat., O^I 1964^4.

37b. **Decorative Sculpture in the Choir of St.-Louis-en-L'Ile** 1678 Stone

   a. 37 roses on the arches supporting the vault.
   b. 60 modillions and 60 roses on the cornice around the choir.
   c. 4 consoles on the keystones of the arcades.
   d. 10 Corinthian capitals.
Contract between the churchwardens and the sculptor signed 16 June 1678, amounting to 2000 L., Min. Centr. Arch. Nat., Et. XII, 175. The roses and capitals decor. with olive leaves in memory of the Passion of Christ and the crown of thorns which St. Louis, patron of the church, went to seek in the Holy Land. Acc. to Brice, *Descr.*, 1687, I, p. 242, the designs for the architectural ornaments were done by the painter J.-B. de Champaigne, then honorary warden; the work was directed by the architect Le Duc. At the same time the woodcarver and sculptor, François Hinault, exec. the woodwork in the choir (stalls, high altar and retable), the door at the side of the rue Poulletier and the panelling in the new vestry; contracts 13 June and 14 Nov. 1678, 20 and 27 April 1680, Min. Centr. Arch. Nat., Et. XII, 175–6, 180.

PARIS, ST.-LOUIS-EN-L'ILE

45m^3★ **Work for the Place des Victoires, Paris**

Medallions on the lanterns

Valenciennes taken by storm, saved from pillage 43m^3

47a. *Equestrian Statue of Louis XIV*

See also L. Seelig, in *BSHAF*, 1973, p. 176, 180 and G. Gardes, 'La Décor. de la Place royale de Louis-le-Grand (Place Bellecour) à Lyon, 1680–1793' in *Bull. des Mus. et Mon. Lyonnais*, 1974, nos. 1 & 2, p. 185–207, 219–29. Length of horse: 550 (acc. to Gardes). Full-size plaster model by J. Robert in 1691; the bronze was cast in 1693–4 by R. Scabol. In 1710 the town of Lyons still owed 20,000 L. to the heirs. The marble decor. of the pedestal exec. by Chabry in 1716–17, that in bronze by the brothers Coustou.

DOSSIER

6.   The Fire

Estim. 3200 L., 15 Aug. 1692, Arch. Nat., O^I 1964^4.

DROUILLY

8.   The Heroic Poem

Estim. 4000 L., 15 Aug. 1692, Arch. Nat., O^I 1964^4.

14.   Vase

Estim. 2500 L., 15 Aug. 1692, Arch. Nat., O^I 1964^4.

18.   *Vase*

Estim. 800 L., 15 Aug. 1692, Arch. Nat., O^I 1964^4.

24.   Vase

Estim. 1400 L., 15 Aug. 1692, Arch. Nat., O^I 1964^4.

FLAMEN

19.   Boreas abducting Orythia

Estim. 13,000 L., 15 Aug. 1692, Arch. Nat., O^I 1964^4.

21.   Faun carrying a Kid

Estim. 4300 L., 15 Aug. 1692, Arch. Nat., O^I 1964^4.

FRANÇOIS

Between
5 & 6.   *Notre-Dame-des-Sept-Douleurs*

1682   Statue, painted wood   H: c. 195
Acc. to the Ms. of the Père Isidore de Ste.-Madeleine (copied in
Ms. CP 3548, Bibl. de la Ville de Paris), F. exec. for the retable
of the Chapel Notre-Dame-des-Sept-Douleurs in the church of
the Convent des Petits-Pères, today Notre-Dame des Victoires,
a statue of the Virgin, her heart pierced by a sword; payment 150
or 200 L. Replaced in 1729 by a painting. Not ident. or disapp.

21 (U)   *Saint Monica*

cf. Dreyfus, 'Les statues du Dôme des Invalides au XVIIIe s.' in
BSHAF, 1908, p. 261–312.

BIBLIOGRAPHICAL ABBREVIATIONS

AAF	*Archives de l'Art Français.*
Arch. Nat.	Archives Nationales, Paris.
Bellier de la Chavignerie	E. Bellier de la Chavignerie and L. Auvray, *Dictionnaire général des artistes de l'école française*, Paris, 1882–5, 2 vols.
Bibl. Nat. Est.	Paris, Bibliothèque Nationale, Cabinet des Estampes.
Bibl. Nat. Ms.	Paris, Bibliothèque Nationale, Cabinet des Manuscrits.
Blondel, *Arch. Fr.*	J.-F. Blondel, Reprint of *Architecture française*, ed. Guadet et Pascal, 4 vols., Paris, undated.
B.M.	*Bulletin Monumental.*
B. Mus. Fr.	*Bulletin des Musées de France.*
Boinet, *Eglises*	A. Boinet, *Les églises parisiennes*, Paris, 1958–64, 3 vols.
Brice, *Descr.*	Germain Brice, *Description nouvelle de ce qu'il y a de plus remarquable dans la ville de Paris*, Paris, 1684, 2 vols. in one; 1685, 1694.
	Description nouvelle de la ville de Paris . . ., Paris, 1698, 2 vols.; 1701, 1706.
	Description de la ville de Paris et de tout ce qu'elle contient de plus remarquable . . ., Paris, 1713, 3 vols.; 1717, 3 vols.; 1752, 4 vols.
	Nouvelle description de la ville de Paris, Paris, 1725, 4 vols.
BSHAF	*Bulletin de la Société de l'Histoire de l'Art Français.*
Comptes	J. Guiffrey, *Comptes des Bâtiments du Roi sous le règne de Louis XIV*, 5 vols., Paris, 1881–1901.
Congrès	*Congrès Archéologique.*
Corr. Dir. Acad. Fr. Rome	*Correspondance des directeurs de l'Académie de France à Rome avec les surintendants des Bâtiments*, publ. by A. de Montaiglon and J. Guiffrey, Paris, 1857–1908, 18 vols.
Courajod, *Lenoir*	L. Courajod, *Alexandre Lenoir, son journal et le Musée des Monuments français*, 3 vols., Paris, 1887.
Descr. Acad.	N. Guérin and A.-N. Dezallier d'Argenville, *Description de l'Académie royale de peinture et de sculpture*, 1715 and 1781, publ. by A. de Montaiglon, Paris, 1893.
Dezallier, *Descr. Acad.*	See *Descr. Acad.*
Dezallier, *Environs de P.*	A.-N. Dezallier d'Argenville, *Voyage pittoresque des environs de Paris . . .*, Paris, 1 vol., 1755, 1762, 1768, 1779.
Dezallier, *Paris*	A.-N. Dezallier d'Argenville, *Voyage pittoresque de Paris. . . .*, Paris, 1749, 1752, 1757, 1765, 1778, 1813.
Dezallier, *Vie*	A.-N. Dezallier d'Argenville, *Vie des fameux architectes et sculpteurs*, Paris, 1787, 2 vols.
Expilly, *Dict.*	Abbé J.-J. Expilly, *Dictionnaire historique et politique des Gaules et de la France*, Paris, 1762–1770, 6 vols.
Félibien des Avaux, *Invalides*	J.-F. Félibien des Avaux, *Description de la nouvelle église de l'hostel royal des Invalides*, Paris, 1702. Reference in the text is always to the complete copy in the Bibliothèque de la Ville de Paris, no. 4421.
Félibien des Avaux, *Versailles*	J.-F. Félibien des Avaux, *Description sommaire de Versailles ancienne et nouvelle*, Paris, 1703.
Fich. Laborde	Fichier Laborde de la Bibliothèque Nationale, Cabinet des Manuscrits, Paris.
Fich. Laborde, Doucet	Fichier Laborde du fonds Doucet, Bibliothèque de l'Institut d'Art et d'Archéologie, Paris.
Florent Le Comte	Florent Le Comte, *Cabinet des singularités d'architecture, peinture, sculpture et gravure . . .*, Paris, 1699–1700, 3 vols.; 2nd ed. 1702, 3 vols.
Fontaine, *Coll. Acad.*	A. Fontaine, *L'art dans l'ancienne France. Les collections de l'Académie royale de peinture et de sculpture*, Paris, 1910.
Fontenai	L.-A. de Bonafous, abbé de Fontenai, *Dictionnaire des artistes*, Paris, 1776.
Furcy-Raynaud,	M. Furcy-Raynaud, 'Inventaire des sculptures exécutées au XVIIIe siècle pour la Direction des Bâtiments du Roi', in *Archives de l'Art français*, nouvelle période, XIV, Paris, 1927.
GBA	*Gazette des Beaux-Arts.*
Granet	J.-J. Granet, *Description de l'église royale des Invalides*, Paris, 1736.
Guérin, *Descr. Acad.*	See *Descr. Acad.*
Guiffrey, *Liste des Pensionnaires*	J. Guiffrey, *Liste des pensionnaires de l'Académie de France à Rome donnant les noms de tous les artistes récompensés dans les concours des prix de Rome de 1663 à 1907*, Paris, 1908.
Guiffrey-Marcel, *Invent.*	J. Guiffrey, P. Marcel et G. Rouchés, *Inventaire général des dessins du Musée du Louvre et du Musée de Versailles, Ecole française*, 10 vols., 1907 ff.
Guiffrey, *St.-Luc*	J. Guiffrey, *La Communauté des maîtres peintres et sculpteurs dite Académie de Saint-Luc*, in *Archives de l'Art français*, IX, 1915.
Hébert	M. Hébert, *Dictionnaire pittoresque et historique, ou Description d'architecture, peinture, sculpture, gravure . . .*, Paris, 1676, 2 vols.
Herluison	Ch. Herluison, *Actes d'état-civil d'artistes français*, Orléans, 1873.
Hurtaut et Magny	MM. Hurtaut et Magny, *Dictionnaire historique de la ville de Paris et de ses environs*, Paris, 1779.

Jal   A. Jal, *Dictionnaire critique de biographie et d'histoire*, Paris, 1867.

Keller-D.   G. Keller-Dorian, *A. Coysevox. Catalogue raisonné de son oeuvre*, Paris, 1920.

Lami   Stanislas Lami, *Dictionnaire des sculpteurs de l'école française sous le règne de Louis XIV*, Paris, 1906.

Lapauze   H. Lapauze, *Histoire de l'Académie de France à Rome*, Paris, 1924, 2 vols. (1st vol. 1666–1801).

Lefèvre   A.-M. Lefèvre, *Description des curiosités des églises de Paris et des environs*, Paris, 1759.

Lenoir, *Mon. Fr.*   A. Lenoir, *Musée des Monuments français, ou Description historique et chronologique des statues . . . bas-reliefs et tombeaux des hommes et des femmes célèbres . . .* , Paris, an IX–1821, 8 vols.

Mariette, *ABC*   P.-J. Mariette, *Abecedario*, publ. 1853–62 by Ph. de Chennevières and A. de Montaiglon, in *Archives de l'Art français*, 6 vols.

Mariette, *Arch. Fr.*   P.-J. Mariette, *L'Architecture française*, reprint of original edition of 1727 by L. Hautecoeur, Paris, 1927–29.

Mém. inéd.   *Mémoires inédits sur la vie et les ouvrages des membres de l'Académie royale de peinture et de sculpture publiés d'après les manuscrits conservés à l'Ecole Impériale des Beaux-Arts*, by L. Dussieux, E. Soulié, Ph. de Chennevières, P. Mantz, A. de Montaiglon, 2 vols., Paris, 1854.

Mercure   1672, *Le Mercure Galant*

         1673–1716, *Le Nouveau Mercure Galant*

         1717–23, *Le Nouveau Mercure*

         1724–92, *Mercure de France*

         1793, *Mercure Français*

Millin, *Antiq. Nat.*   A.-L. Millin, *Antiquités Nationales ou Recueil des monumens pour servir à l'histoire générale et particulière de l'Empire français, tels que tombeaux, inscriptions, statues, vitraux, fresques etc. . . . tirés des abbayes, monastères, châteaux et autres lieux devenus domaines nationaux*, 5 vols., Paris, 1790–an VII.

Min. Centr. Arch. Nat.   Minutier Central des notaires parisiens, Arch. Nat., Paris.

NAAF   *Nouvelles Archives de l'Art Français.*

Pérau   Abbé G.-L. Pérau, *Description historique de l'hôtel royal des Invalides*, Paris, 1756.

Philipon, *Tuileries*   L. Philipon de La Madeleine, *Le Guide du Promeneur aux Tuileries*, Paris, an VI.

Piganiol, *Vers.-Marly*   J.-A. Piganiol de La Force, *Nouvelle description des châteaux et parcs de Versailles et de Marly . . .* , Paris, 1701, 1 vol.; 1707, 1 vol.; 1713, 2 vols.; 1717, 2 vols.; 1724, 2 vols.; 1730, 2 vols.; 1738, 1 vol. in 2 parts; 1751, 2 vols.; 1764, 2 vols.

Piganiol, *Descr.*   J.-A. Piganiol de La Force, *Description de Paris, de Versailles, de Marly, de Meudon, de Saint-Cloud, de Fontainebleau, et de toutes les autres belles maisons et châteaux des environs de Paris*, Paris, 1742, 8 vols. (7 vols. on Paris; 1 vol. on the environs); 1765, 10 vols.

P-V   A. de Montaiglon, *Procès-verbaux de l'Académie royale de Peinture et de Sculpture (1648–1792)*, publiés par la Société d'histoire de l'Art Français, d'après les registres originaux conservés à l'Ecole des Beaux-Arts, Paris, 1875–92, 10 vols.

RAAM   *Revue de l'Art Ancien et Moderne.*

Rambaud   M. Rambaud, *Documents du Minutier Central concernant l'histoire de l'art (1700–50)*, Paris, I, 1964; II, 1971.

Raunié   E. Raunié, 'Epitaphier du vieux Paris', in *Hist. générale de Paris*, Paris, 1890–1901, 3 vols.

Rich. Art. Fr., Mon. Civ.   *Invent. général des richesses d'art de la France*, Paris, *Monuments civils*. I, 1879; II, 1889; III, 1902; IV, 1913. Paris, Plon.

Rich. Art. Fr., Mon. Rel.   *Invent. général des richesses d'art de la France*, Paris, *Monuments religieux*. I, 1876; II, 1888; III, 1901. Paris, Plon.

RSBAD   *Réunion des Sociétés des Beaux-Arts des départements.*

Souchal, *Les Slodtz*   F. Souchal, *Les Slodtz, sculpteurs et décorateurs du Roi (1685–1764)*, Paris, 1968.

Souchal, 'Versailles'   F. Souchal, 'Les statues aux façades du château de Versailles' in *GBA*, 1972¹, p. 65–112.

Soulié, *Mus. Vers.*   E. Soulié, *Notice du Musée Impérial de Versailles*, Paris, 1859–61, 3 vols.

Tessin–Cronström, *Corresp.*   *Les Relations artistiques entre la France et la Suède (1693–1718)*. Extraits d'une correspondance entre l'architecte N. Tessin le Jeune et D. Cronström, publiés par R.-A. Weigert et C. Hernmarck, Stockholm, 1964.

T.-B.   U. Thieme und F. Becker, *Allgemeines Lexicon der bildenden Künstler von der Antike bis zur Gegenwart*, 1907 ff.

Thiéry, *Guide*   L.-V. Thiéry, *Guide des amateurs et des étrangers voyageurs à Paris*, Paris, 1786–87, 2 vols.

Thomassin, *Vers.*   S. Thomassin, *Recueil des statues, groupes, fontaines, termes, vases et autres magnifiques ornements du château et du parc de Versailles, gravés d'après les originaux par Simon Thomassin*, The Hague, 1723.

PHOTOGRAPHIC SOURCES

All photos not included in the following list were taken by THIERY PRAT, *Mareil-sur-Mauldre, France*

ALBERTINA, Vienna: N. Coustou 12[2]
ARCHIVES NATIONALES, Paris: Barois 9, 11, 18[2]; Blanchards 8; Buirette 5a; Chauveau 2[2]; Cornu 30[2]/31[2]; G. Coustou 35, 56; N. Coustou 20, 31–2, 45–6, 60[2]
ARCHIVES DU GRAND SEMINAIRE, Tarbes: Arcis 73
ARCHIVES PHOTOGRAPHIQUES, Arles: Dedieu biog.: portrait
ARCHIVES PHOTOGRAPHIQUES, Paris: Arcis 70–1; Barois 18[2]; P. Bertrand 14; Collignon 12; G. Coustou 7a, 36[1], 53, 68a, 69a, 77a, 83a; N. Coustou: 3, 70, 74; Coysevox: 43, 43a, 45, 49b, c, 74, 80b, 114[2]; Desjardins: 41a[1], b, c, 45c–g, m[4], 50, 52; Flamen 23; Fontelle 20
ASCHE S., Dresden: Coudray 6/7

BACHSTITZ GALLERY, The Hague: Coysevox 32
BARAKET, Jerusalem: G. Coustou 42
BASSET, Lyon: G. Coustou 40a; N. Coustou 64a; Coysevox 4b
BAYERISCHE STAATBIBLIOTHEK, Munich: Bourdy 5
BIBLIOTHEQUE NATIONALE, Paris: Arcis 28; Charpentier biog.: Crucifixion, Descente de croix; Chauveau 36a–d app.; Collignon 3[2]; Cotton 4[3], 5; G. Coustou 6, 50, 62, 65–9; Coysevox 41[3], 55[2], 96[2], 108; Drouilly 5; Flamen 13, 17; Frémin biog.: portrait
BULLOZ, Paris: G. Coustou 48, 54[1]; N. Coustou 67, 72; Coysevox 92; Desjardins 16; Frémin 7

CHARPEAUX, Arras: Frémin 31b
COURTAULD INSTITUTE OF ART, London: P. Bertrand 8; Coysevox 82b, 101; Dumont 11a

DESCOSSY, Montpellier: P. Bertrand 2a–d
DIDON, Lunéville: Dumont 21c, 23b
DEUTSCHE PHOTOTHEK, Dresden: Coudray 4b
DUPUY MUSEUM, Toulouse: Arcis 1/32 (engr)

ELLEBE, Rouen: G. Coustou 7b
ELY, Aix-en-Provence: Clérion 25

FORTT, London: Fontelle 19[1, 2]
FOURNIER, Moulins: N. Coustou 15–6
FRICK COLLECTION, New-York: Coysevox 80c

GIRAUDON, Paris: André 7; Barois 13; Blanchards 10[1]; Buirette 14; Carlier 3; Collignon 3[1], 5; Coudray 2a; G. Coustou 38, 39[1]; N. Coustou 4b, 40b, 60[1], 71; Coysevox 5b, 6a, b, 7b, 8a, b, 9[1], 12, 16–7, 23, 25a, 37a, 40, 41[1, 2], 42, 43b, 46–7, 51a–c, 55[1], 56, 58–9, 63, 73, 76–8, 82c, 85[1]b, 86, 89, 90, 91b, 93, 94b, 98, 99a, 102, 103a, 106a, 107, 114[1], 117–8; Desjardins: 30, 49, 51a
GODEFROY, Lyon: G. Coustou 68b
GUILBERT, Saint-Brice: Barois 7c, 10e, 14[1, 2], 17; P. Bertrand: 5, 6, 15, 20; Blanchards: 5c[3], 10[2]; Bourdy: 3; Buirette: 4, 15–8; Carlier: 1, 4, 5, 8b, 14–7; Cayot 7; Charpentier: biog, Gal. Girardon engr., 10[1, 2]; Chauveau 4b, 8; Clérion 14; Cornu 4, 20, 23; Cotton 4[1]; Coudray 11–5; G. Coustou: biogr., portrait, 5, 16–7, 36[2], 43, 45[1, 2], 47, 51, 54[2], 61, 76/7 engr.; N. Coustou: biogr., portrait, 7d, 21a, 25, 28/32, 34, 38, 57–8, 63, 69; Coysevox 13, 34, 49a, 54a–g, 60, 64, 72; Dedieu 20, 33, 41, 45[2], 49, 51–2; Desjardins 1, 14a, 15[3], 17, 21a–d, 37, 45, 51c, 56/7; Dossier 8[2]; Drouilly 20, 25; Dumont 26e, f; Flamen 25, 45, 55–6, 62; François 21; Frémin 8.

HEIMAT MUSEUM, BEZIRKS SAMMLUNG, Potsdam: Charpentier 1
HEIM GALLERY: P. Bertrand 7; Cayot 3c; Clérion 1; Collignon 1, 2; N. Coustou 44

JAN, Limoges: G. Coustou 58a

KUNGL. SLOTTET, Stockholm: Chauveau 10–3; 14a–b, 19, 20; G. Coustou 40b; N. Coustou 64b

LA MOUREYRE, Paris: Chauveau 16, 25 (*appendix*); G. Coustou 79; N. Coustou 45–6; Dedieu 1, 3–19, 21; Desjardins 28; Frémin 2a, b, 87[3], 190[1, 2], 192[1, 2], 195.

MACHELART, Cambrai: Drouilly 27
MARTIN, Orléans: N. Coustou 61b
METROPOLITAN MUSEUM, New-York: Coysevox 8c; Desjardins 47b
MUSÉES NATIONAUX, Réunion des (Documentation Photographique), Paris: Barois 7a; P. Bertrand 12; Buirette biogr: portrait, 6; Charpentier biogr: Mise au tombeau; Chauveau 2; G. Coustou 11–2, 21–2, 55, 82a, 83b; N. Coustou 14a, 49, 53[1], 54[1]; Coysevox 119; Defer 1; Desjardins biogr: portrait, 15[2]; Dumont 12; Flamen 32[1]; Frémin 4, 31a

NATIONAL GALLERY OF ART, Washington D.C.: Coudray 2b; Flamen 18
NATIONAL MUSEUM, Stockholm: Bertin 1a, b, 17, 21–5; D. Bertrand 4a–g; P. Bertrand: 12[3], 32[1]; Chauveau 7, 25; Clérion 6; Collignon 6[1]; Dedieu 45[3]; Flamen 51
NORDISKA MUSEET, Stockholm: Chauveau 15

O'SUGHRUE, Montpellier: Dumont 20

PAULMANN, Kunstbibliothek, Berlin: Bertin 5m, 12–6, 18–20, 33–6; Desjardins 41a[2]; Flamen 32[2]
PIQUE, Barcelona 4, Ed. Patrim. Nacional: Frémin 43/122 postcard

RIJKSMUSEUM, Amsterdam: Coysevox 9[2, 3]

SEELIG L., Munich. Desjardins 15[2], 44, 51b, 54b
SKULPTUREN SAMMLUNG, Dresden: Flamen 19b
SOUCHAL F., Paris: G. Coustou 69b
STAATLICHE KUNSTSAMMLUNGEN, Dresden: Coudray 4b; G. Coustou 81
STÄDELSCHES KUNSTINSTITUT, Frankfurt am Main: Coysevox 9[4]
STADTBIBLIOTHEK, Leipzig: Coudray 4a
STADTMUSEUM, Stockholm: Chauveau 17–8
STATENS MUSEUM FOR KUNST, Copenhagen: Collignon 15 (*appendix*); Desjardins 47b[1]

VIOLLET, Paris: Cornu 12a

WALLACE COLLECTION, London: P. Bertrand 31; Cayot 3a; Coysevox 5a, 71; G. Coustou 76b, 77b
WILDENSTEIN FOUNDATION: G. Coustou 7b[2] (*appendix*); Coysevox 7a, 94a, 95, 116; Frémin 36

YALE UNIVERSITY ART GALLERY, New-Haven: N. Coustou 21b
YAN, Toulouse: Arcis 42a–c, 48–51, 64b, 65b, 66b, 69b, 72, 89–93
YOUNG MEMORIAL MUSEUM, San Francisco: Coysevox 66b

INDEX

(References are to page numbers; works of sculpture are indicated in italics)

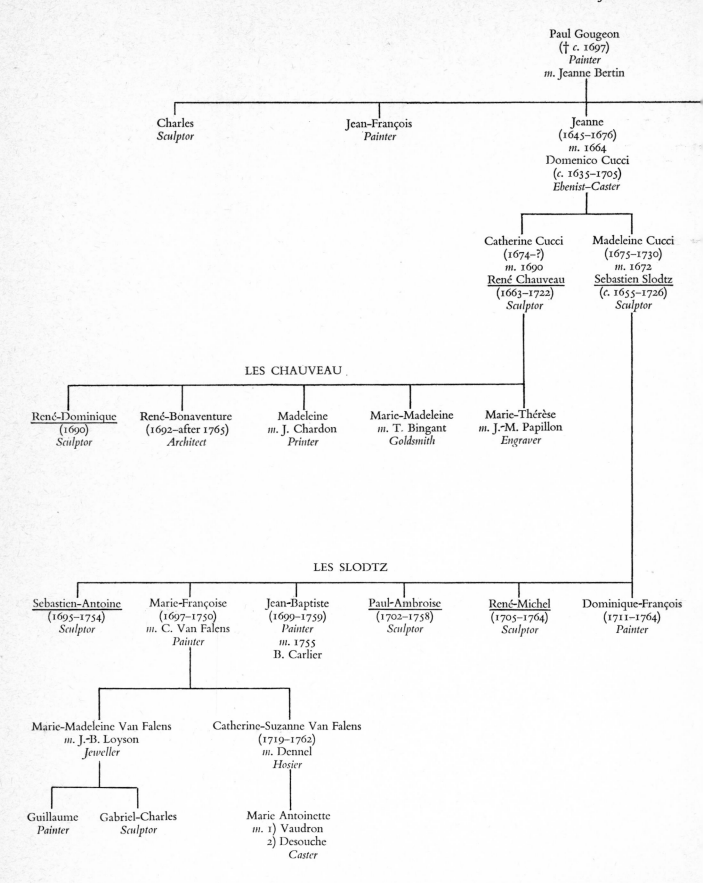

LES GOUJON

Paul Gougeon
(† c. 1697)
Painter
m. Jeanne Bertin

Charles
Sculptor

Jean-François
Painter

Jeanne
(1645–1676)
m. 1664
Domenico Cucci
(c. 1635–1705)
Ebenist–Caster

Catherine Cucci
(1674–?)
m. 1690
René Chauveau
(1663–1722)
Sculptor

Madeleine Cucci
(1675–1730)
m. 1672
Sebastien Slodtz
(c. 1655–1726)
Sculptor

LES CHAUVEAU

René-Dominique
(1690)
Sculptor

René-Bonaventure
(1692–after 1765)
Architect

Madeleine
m. J. Chardon
Printer

Marie-Madeleine
m. T. Bingant
Goldsmith

Marie-Thérèse
m. J.-M. Papillon
Engraver

LES SLODTZ

Sebastien-Antoine
(1695–1754)
Sculptor

Marie-Françoise
(1697–1750)
m. C. Van Falens
Painter

Jean-Baptiste
(1699–1759)
Painter
m. 1755
B. Carlier

Paul-Ambroise
(1702–1758)
Sculptor

René-Michel
(1705–1764)
Sculptor

Dominique-François
(1711–1764)
Painter

Marie-Madeleine Van Falens
m. J.-B. Loyson
Jeweller

Catherine-Suzanne Van Falens
(1719–1762)
m. Dennel
Hosier

Guillaume
Painter

Gabriel-Charles
Sculptor

Marie Antoinette
m. 1) Vaudron
2) Desouche
Caster